THE SHADOWS COME

PRAISE FOR

The Shadows Come

"In a sequel that surpasses the superlative *No Longer Alone*, we continue life's journey with Prentis and Avery, newlyweds trying to make a life on the harsh reality of the American Midwest after the turn of last century. War is raging, not only abroad, but in the hearts of neighbors who through their own insecurities and anger chip away at the sanctuary the young couple have created for themselves.

"Love, faith, courage, and action all set against a background of one of America's darker times come to life through the words of a gifted author. It's a rich story of seemingly small lives that end up mattering in the largest of ways."

~ **L. B. Johnson**, Best-Selling Author

"*The Shadows Come* continues Prentis and Avery's love story begun in *No Longer Alone*, stories that are based on her great grandparents. It is refreshing to see their love remain so passionate and appreciative despite their caring for a toddler, marriage breaking accusations, and the international trauma of WWI. This is a farm family that supported the war effort and grieved as world powers pulled everyone into darkness. Inman gives a clear picture into life during this time.

The Shadows Come is a captivating read about how the power of married love and Christian faith shine a light into the terror of a world war, the Spanish Flu, and personal loss. This is a well- researched family story that reminds the reader 'His eye is on the sparrow' and leaves us full of hope."

~ **Katie Andraski**, Author and Poet

"So many things to love about this book: Avery and PJ's love story, so many interesting facts about WWI, family and community helping each other, a young family learning to put their trust in God. I have read all of Melinda's fiction. This is by far my favorite. Definitely leaves me wanting more about this family. So well written. Such a beautiful story. I don't have enough superlatives to describe how I feel about this. Just read it! You won't be disappointed!"

~ **Michelle R. Schuck,** Literature & History Teacher

"Prentis and Avery face dark days. Family, community, and a close friend get sent off to a war, stretching their faith in God's sovereign will. They read every newspaper and pray fervently for both safety and a quick resolution. On a personal level, hopes are dashed, reputation is slandered, and they are fighting for joy. Their struggle reveals the power of their faith in the work of the Lord and His ability to carry them through loss, sacrifice, and danger.

"Striving daily to leave a legacy of faith, fighting to give others a voice, and honoring the ones they have lost, they are an inspiration of unwavering faith in the trenches and a steadfast, living hope firmly rooted in the gospel of Jesus Christ. You will walk away understanding what it was like to be a young couple with a little boy living on their little farm in Oklahoma, as well as what it means to trust in the Lord with all your heart even when the world around you is forever being changed."

~ **Kristin Lewis Robinson,** Life Coach and Author

MELINDA VIERGEVER INMAN

THE SHADOWS COME

The Shadows Come

By Melinda Viergever Inman

First Edition Copyright ©2019 by Melinda Viergever Inman
Cover Design by Rachel Rossano

ISBN: 9781706174325

Published by:

ShowKnowGrow
PUBLISHING

Show Know Grow Publishing
https://showknowgrowpublishing.com/
Houston, Texas

MELINDA VIERGEVER INMAN

SEQUEL TO NO LONGER ALONE
BASED ON A TRUE STORY

The

Shadows

Come

MELINDA VIERGEVER INMAN

ShowKnowGrow
PUBLISHING

Dedication

To Tim for the selfless love and support.

To my parents, my aunts, and my uncles: Jacqueline and L.D. Garrett, Elaine and Dan Viergever, Dottie and Roger Koeppen, P.J. and Linda Pinkerton: I am grateful for you and for all you contributed to make this story come alive.

Once again, to all the progeny,
to each and every one, including my own children and grandchildren.

To Tim and Janice Taussig, for the love, the encouragement, and the handmade sparrow.

To my generous Patreon supporters:
LeeAnn Marie Adams, Katie Andraski, Raymond Borrett, Michelle Broussard, Yvonne Cummins, Martha Draper, Christina Dronen, Laura Hartley, Shawn Hudson, Linda M. Johnson, Suzanne Jones, Rayni Lambert, Chip Mattis, Melissa McLaughlin, Alison Marie Plom, Christine Pohl, Diane Prieur, Kristin Robinson, Kim Schumm, Holly Spencer, Lisa Truesdell, Sherry Wasserstein, Peter Younghusband

THE SHADOWS COME

One

"THE WORLD MUST BE made safe for democracy."

Four days ago, April 2, 1917, President Wilson had announced his convictions to the world. Germany threatened to destroy Europe. Something must be done, and America's allies cried out for help and support. Today, all would learn the outcome. Avery guarded her expectations as she shielded her eyes and watched the road for Prentis to return with information from Wakita. Dry as powder, her throat constricted, and her heart pounded. Whatever news he brought, it would change everything, not only in their own little world, but also in the world at large.

Far in the distance, he raised a cloud of dust, pounding home at a pace that couldn't possibly coincide with a peaceful outcome. Man and horse charged up the drive, scattering dirt and gravel far and wide. Reining in Apollo, Prentis swung off the horse in one smooth motion, removing his Stetson and wiping his brow with his shirtsleeve. Already in motion, he strode toward her.

His steely blue eyes met hers, and she knew.

"Da Da!" Jack beat her to the greeting.

Avery glanced down at their baby on her hip, grinning so wide that all four of his teeth showed. More teeth bulged in his slobbery gums, soon to appear. With such a grin, even war couldn't snatch away Prentis's instant display of fatherly affection. Jack dove toward his father.

As he took the baby, she turned toward Prentis. His eyes met hers again. His jaw was set, and his lips compressed into a thin line. Everything about the man displayed determination.

"It's war, isn't it?" she said, her voice low.

"It is."

What they had feared for so long was now upon them. There was nothing more to be said.

They'd seen it coming.

A mere month ago, the country had learned that the Germans had attempted to ally with Mexico to attack America from the south. In return, should the alliance prove successful, Mexico would regain renewed sovereignty over Texas, New Mexico, and Arizona. German foreign secretary Arthur Zimmerman's telegram to the German ambassador in Mexico had urged him to offer that alliance to the Mexican government. The Brits had intercepted and decoded the message. That information had changed everything, bringing the war to American soil.

When added to President Wilson breaking ties with Germany because of their unrestricted submarine warfare, the sinking of American ships carrying goods to Europe, and all the multiple atrocities of the past nearly three years, it had only been a matter of time.

Four days ago, the president had stood before Congress requesting a declaration of war. That hadn't been a surprise. The Senate supported him. Now the House had too. The United States of America was finally at war.

Prentis grabbed Apollo by the halter and headed for the barn, cradling Jack against him.

Avery trailed behind, needing to gather strength. Turning her back on the world, she cast her eyes across their verdant wheat, swaying softly in the prairie breeze and barely beginning to ripen. Peace reigned on the farm, but outside its bounds and inside her heart, all was in turmoil.

What now, Lord?

Everything they believed would be tested. Could they trust God, even during war? The Lord had brought them through so much in hardship and in loss. But what if the worst came to pass?

***

Gnawing and teething on a leather rein, Jack sat inside the rectangular play area Prentis had recently created out of hay bales. One of the kittens had jumped in with the baby. Dust motes shimmered in the shaft of light beaming through the upstairs loft window, piercing the dark interior like a lightning bolt. Jack seemed fully occupied and content, chortling at the kitten's antics as it batted around the other dangling rein.

Avery turned her attention toward her husband. "Was there any other news?"

Prentis groomed the horse with focused intensity. He flicked his eyes up toward hers, his mind clearly on the ominous announcement. Apollo's saddle and blanket had been removed, and the horse glistened with sweat. The stallion's horsey scent filled the barn. Prentis glided the currycomb quickly and expertly, alternating with the brush. He didn't answer immediately.

"Only speculation," he said at last.

"What do you mean?"

"Everyone at the telegraph office had an opinion."

"What did they say?"

"We're in uncharted territory, Avery. Too many things to be settled."

"What was the general opinion then?" she said.

"Well, in spite of all that earlier bravado when the Lusitania was sunk, no one's keen on going to war. Most felt we'd been forced into it by the Kaiser. And, of course, Mexico. But nationwide, papers say only seventy-three thousand or so men have volunteered since the declaration."

He stood back to look at her. She nodded that she understood.

"Papers say the military stands at a little more than a hundred thousand volunteers," he continued. "That includes those new

13

enlistments. National Guard has about a hundred eighty thousand. Combined, that's only a fraction of what we'll need. Everyone's agreed. Then we've got Teddy Roosevelt determined to raise his own volunteers. That's all mixed up in it too. Probably affects recruitment."

"How will the government determine who goes?"

"That, my dear wife, is the question of the day. Clearly, few of us want to be involved."

Avery crossed her arms tight across her chest and chewed on her thumb.

This was where fear stalked her heart. In spite of the president's Food Will Win the War campaign and the need to keep farmers producing food for the entire world during this crisis, the government could do whatever it wanted. And it might want her husband.

"Avery," Prentis's voice crooned soft and tender. She looked up, fixing her eyes on his. "It's in God's hands. He'll take care of us no matter what. He always has."

"I know you're right," she said, her voice cracking.

"Mom, mom, mom, mom," Jack called, attempting to hook his little foot over the hay-bale barricade, so he could crawl out to her.

She scooped him up and looked back at Prentis. "He'll soon outgrow this. And then what will we do?" She chuckled softly, and he returned her smile.

"He'll be helping me out all over this place." Prentis laughed. "That's a fact."

"I'll take him inside and fix us some supper."

"You're a good wife to me. What would I do without you?"

"You'd be hungry." She gave him a saucy look and turned toward the house, balancing Jack on her hip. Behind them, she heard his soft laughter.

Even war couldn't dissipate Prentis's good humor.

***

Jack's first birthday on April 16 called for a family celebration. All of Avery's family gathered on Sunday the fifteenth after church—Floyd and Hattie, Jerry and Dorothy,

John and his wife Blanche with little Genevieve. Abe and Gene were now both in their teens, and Howard would be ten the following month. Avery's momma and daddy had packed their Model T with grandchildren and her youngest three brothers. Without the boys under Avery's eye on a daily basis, they all seemed to be growing up entirely too fast.

Of course, they'd also invited their pastor, Tom McKinney, who was their usual Sunday afternoon guest when he wasn't doing visitation. And, now that they lived near Gibbon, Prentis's brother Fred and his wife, Irene, were also in attendance.

The herd of small cousins chortled and squealed as they ran from room to room. Jack toddled behind trying to keep up, his infant delight beaming all over his face. The adults conversed loudly, uproarious laughter filling the house in spurts. With their entire home packed, it was definitely a livelier atmosphere than their little farmhouse typically enjoyed.

Nine days had passed since the declaration of war, but that seemed to be all the men wanted to discuss. Bits and pieces of politics floated in and out of the dinnertime conversation. After devouring the enormous roast Avery had prepared and watching Jack's attempt to blow out the candle on his cake, they all sang "Happy Birthday to You" wholeheartedly.

Then Prentis suggested the men join him on the shady front-porch steps to eat cake and discuss the wartime and political possibilities. Avery's momma picked up Jack and herded Howard and the rest of the children through the back door as Hattie and Dorothy carried the remaining cake out back. There, surrounded by Avery's blooming perennials, they would enjoy the peace of the garden and the tranquility of the grassy corner of lawn. The children could play in that space far removed from a world at war and any discussion of it.

Before joining them, Avery tarried near the doorway listening to the men. Blanche, her former student and now sister-in-law, stood right behind her.

Comments ricocheted from man to man.

"Russia may be out of it now, what with that revolution and the Czar abdicating."

"They've got their own problems, for sure."

"I'm more concerned with what we've got to muster here."

"No way we can avoid a draft, as I see it," Johnny threw in.

All the men shifted uncomfortably.

It occurred to Avery that, of course, Johnny was now of age, should a draft occur. She didn't like that one bit. Glancing at Blanche, it was obvious his wife didn't either. She met Avery's eyes and then walked out the back way with a heavy sigh.

"War College Division says we need a million men," Floyd said.

"Only got about a hundred thousand now," added Prentis.

"They expect one million to volunteer."

Everyone laughed at that statement.

"President wants to maintain a national army exclusively through the selective service."

"How will we muster that?"

"No idea."

Wearing grim expressions, all the men shook their heads.

"Then we've got to ship that million overseas."

"War College says we can't get 'em there until late next year, what with training and transportation."

"Next year!" Johnny said. "Don't see how that'll help much."

"Probably too little too late."

Here they all nodded.

"Bet it's already planned. President Wilson's been talking a draft since March."

"We'll see if he can pull it off."

"That new Committee on Public Information might have a tough time keeping us all in line."

Several chuckled at that, their countenances wry.

"Not many wantin' to get killed in Europe for a petty war started by the Kaiser."

They all nodded and groaned their agreement.

Avery didn't want to hear any more. Though she'd stationed herself in the shadows back from the doorway, Prentis had noticed her there. He had his eye on her. Pressing her lips together, she turned away to walk back through the house. But, behind her, the screen door screeched wide, its long spring protesting as it stretched. She twisted back to face him.

16

"Avery," Prentis's low voice caressed her name. Reaching for her hand, his fingers slid lightly down her arm. "God is still God, Sweetheart."

"Thank you for the reminder." She swallowed hard. "Yes, He is."

"Are you doin' okay in here?"

"I'll be fine. I simply don't want my brothers or my husband to be marched off to war. I'm going out back. I don't want to think about war as we celebrate Jack's birthday."

"Don't blame you." He pulled her closer. "That's why I herded all the boys outside. Give me a kiss, and I'll let you be on your way."

Softly his lips brushed against hers. Then he pulled back a few inches, his hand still gripping her wrist. She felt his gaze and lifted her eyes to his. He always seemed to notice when she needed reassurance. His love was a comfort.

"We're in this together," he said.

"Yes, we are. Our backs aren't against the wall yet."

He chuckled at her use of slang. "No, they're not. Enjoy the day. Forget the war. We'll keep it confined to the front porch. I promise."

She gave him another peck of a kiss, he released her wrist, and then he stepped back out into the world of men, casting one last glance at her as his hand slowed the screen door, lest it slam. In the kitchen she gathered a few glasses and the pitcher of fresh-squeezed lemonade and headed outside to be near the birthday boy.

When the back door swung wide, she heard Jack laughing hysterically as Howard played peekaboo with him. It was the baby's favorite game. His cousins Donald, Bernice, and Genevieve rolled around in the grass giggling at his reactions. Settling under the shade tree with Momma, her sisters-in-law, and the youngsters was like being an entire world away from the war discussed on the front porch, a world she prayed could remain unchanged and peaceful.

Her eyes fell upon the field nearest the barn. She studied all the mares with their new foals peacefully suckling or grazing beside them—five beautiful new horses. Why couldn't life remain that tranquil, transformed only by the changes in season and the natural cycle of life?

Then she recalled that the army had purchased their previous batch of yearlings only last month, and these would go next year. The hard-heartedness of mankind ruined everything that was beautiful.

***

In early May, Prentis stepped through the back door carrying a fat copy of the Wichita Eagle. Someone had brought the contraband Kansas newspaper down to Oklahoma, and he had scooped it up at the general store along with the other goods he'd purchased.

"You'll enjoy this paper, Avery." He sat her items on the counter. "Can't wait to hear your opinion."

Up to her elbows in soapy water washing the day's dishes, she lifted a wet finger to her lips. "Shh! I just got Jack down for his nap."

"Paper says The Committee on Public Information will have a news division and a pictorial office," he said, lowering his tone accordingly.

"A pictorial office?" She snorted, scattering soap bubbles.

"Precisely. Says they're hiring illustrators so they can use 'modern advertising techniques'."

"So, it's to be propaganda."

He chuckled. "Figured you'd see it that way."

"It should be business as usual for that office then. They've grown quite adept at making us discontent about our current possessions and desperate for the ones they're hawking."

"Yep." He smirked. "Now they're going to sell us the war."

"We'll have to hold on tight to our reservations."

"Yes, we will. The government's batting around ideas for military conscription, though no details have leaked out yet. Merely more speculation."

She looked up from the sink. "We learn so much more when you can get us a good paper."

"The Wakita Herald doesn't have the manpower or the resources to keep up with all this."

18

"No, they don't." She paused a moment. "So, there's not yet a particle of information about who they'll draft and how they'll do it?"

"Not yet. We'll know soon. I'm sure of that. Got to get a million men over there."

She nodded but kept her eyes on the washing, setting the final dishes to drain. Flicking her eyes toward where Jack slept, she wiped her hands on a dishtowel and jerked her chin toward the back door. Both went outside to sit on the back step.

"Was there any other news?" she asked, sighing as she settled on the stoop.

"Here's something that will interest you. Everyone was talking about it. Our neighbors up the road, the McKees, have people on their property interested in drilling for oil."

"What! There's oil here? I thought it was all near Tulsa."

"Geologists from the American Petroleum Company think we've got some."

"Well, I'll be."

"Yep. Automobile's changing more than just transportation. Got to have fuel. These companies are bound and determined to find it."

"Is that the only place they're drilling?"

"There're a few other places. Some north of town."

"How far down do they have to go?"

"'Bout four thousand feet. At least that's their estimation."

Her mouth dropped open, and Prentis could see in her eyes that her inner scientist was thinking her way down through the layers of Planet Earth.

"Some town meetings are coming up about it," he said. "A few people are investing in American Petroleum stock."

"Let's do that!" Her eyes sparkled. She delighted in every sign of progress.

"That's what I was thinking too. And, I think it's time we made a purchase."

Anticipating his next words, her eyes fixed on his.

"Watching you at Jack's party got me thinking. You were all lit up from having company. Occurred to me that you probably feel pretty isolated out here with a baby. Think it's high time we bought an automobile."

Avery threw both her arms around him and smiled up into his eyes.

"Are you sure?" she said. "Can we afford it?"

"So far this war has been profitable. Don't want to be avaricious. It's just a fact. Grain and beef prices have shot through the roof. We've got everything covered. There's also plenty of money in our savings. If the wheat is harvested securely, and we get a decent price—even though the government's all wrapped up in that now, I'd like to use your savings on a new automobile."

"I haven't thought about that savings account, since I gave it to you on our first anniversary."

"I have. Been pondering what you might need. We should spend the rest on you."

"You're positive?"

"I am. Just need to get the harvest in."

Avery leapt to her feet, spread wide her arms, and went dancing across the back corner of lawn before circling around, grabbing Prentis's hand, and pulling him into her dance. He waltzed her around the periphery. Pulling his face down, she gave him an exuberant kiss.

"If I'd known you'd respond like that, I would've suggested a Model T sooner."

She laughed joyfully. "You're such a good husband to me! I'll be able to go see my momma, maybe even shop in Medford."

"Henry Ford sure knew what he was doing when he made the Model T more affordable. We can swing it." Prentis paused. He didn't know if he wanted to deliver the next bit of news.

But she was too keen. She could always read him.

"What is it?" she said.

Taking her hand, he drew her back to the step and sat them both down. "Tom's thinking of volunteering."

"What! Why in the world would he do that?"

"He talked about it at Jack's party and again when I saw him today. He says if there's any time that a man needs a pastor, it's when he's at war."

20

Avery stared hard at him. He watched her eyes as her brain rifled through her inner theological files and then softened when she recognized the truth in Tom's assessment.

"He sees clearly," she said.

"I knew you'd think so."

"Still, I don't want him to go. He's your dearest friend and like a brother to me. But I know he's a man of God and follows where God leads him. This is something to pray about."

"It is. I waited to tell you. Had to get used to the idea myself."

"If he goes, we'll have decisions to make about where to go for church."

"We will." Prentis nodded. "The automobile might make that decision easier. There's one more thing I want to ask you."

"What is it?" She turned toward him, her eyebrows drawn together in concentration.

He paused longer for effect.

Raising her brows now, she gestured for him to continue.

"Charles Delivuk and George Strasbaugh have come to town. Do you want to go in for the wrestling match at The Opera House this Saturday? Ladies get in free."

Her mouth dropped open, and then she slapped her hand over it as a hoot escaped. Convulsing with laughter while attempting not to wake their baby, asleep right on the other side of the nearby window, her shoulders shook, and tears came to her eyes.

"The Opera House . . ." She erupted loudly this time. "For a wrestling match . . ."

"Has to be held somewhere. Don't know why it's not at the school."

"Imagine wrestling—" She fell off the step giggling. "At The Opera House!"

Inside the house, Jack cried. It was a wonder he hadn't awakened sooner.

"I knew you'd enjoy that." Prentis chuckled. "I'll go get him."

Grinning, he walked into the house.

During the winter, he had made some alterations. When Jack was older, he'd need his own bedroom. For now, Prentis had eked out space, building a wall almost all the way across one end of

21

their bedroom. Presently, that space formed a small alcove for Jack—still a part of their room, but with a wall separating. When the boy was a bit bigger, Prentis would finish the wall and install a door that opened into their living room. He stepped in to retrieve Jack from his crib.

As soon as Prentis appeared, the baby began to bounce up and down with delight where he stood perched at the rail, holding on tightly. Prentis scooped him up and planted a kiss on his cheek as Jack called, "Da. Da. Da. Da."

It was a joy to have a son. Prentis hoped and prayed he'd be left here at home to care for his family and to raise Jack. He was certain most men felt the same, but a large number of them would have to go. Only time remained to discover who that would be.

Two

AVERY SETTLED DOWN ON the front porch with her eyes fixed on the road. Prentis had gone to town to learn about the draft. The president had announced that its organization was complete. Now all the men would need to register and to comply. The newspapers would tell them what to do.

Rather than accompany him in the buggy, she had preferred that he ride alone into town. A lone horse was much faster. He'd be able to grab up a good newspaper and return quickly.

In the grass at her feet, Jack played with Sam. The dog seemed irritable today. Every time Jack tugged at his ear or plopped into the grass near him, the dog shifted away from the baby. This canine touchiness was new. It occurred to her that Sam was getting mighty old. By her calculations, he had to be at least fifteen, since he had been Prentis's boyhood dog.

On the horizon, she detected a smudge.

Shielding her eyes, she stood to get a better look. Prentis had left early, hoping that a paper of worth could be found. She felt certain The Wakita Herald would make a special run, but one never knew. She fixed her eyes on the smudge.

Jack shrieked, and Sam growled low and soft.

"Sam!" she spoke sharply. "Bad dog!"

Shame-faced, the dog peered up timidly. Sam hadn't adapted well to Jack's mobility, now that he toddled everywhere. However, growling at the baby would not be tolerated. Wearing a guilty expression, Sam lowered his head. She bent down, patting his head to reassure him that he was still loved, though a small person had taken his place of importance.

Looking up, she again cast her eyes toward the smudge. It was now assuredly a cloud of dust. Prentis was heading home. What had he discovered? Lifting Jack into her arms, she held him close, so she didn't have to keep her eye on the dog.

Jostling Jack on her hip, she studied her beloved man racing home. What would he tell her? Presently he swept into the drive, bringing the dirt cloud with him.

"Here it is, Avery." He leapt from the horse. "I grabbed the last copy of the Wichita Eagle."

Handing it to her, he took Jack.

"Have you read it?" she asked.

"I have." He grabbed the reins and headed toward the barn with both baby and horse in tow. "I'll take Jack to the barn so you can read it undisturbed. We'll be back soon."

Her eyes were already on the article and its instructions. Everything was spelled out. She couldn't help herself—of first importance were the exemptions. She simply had to read them before anything else. It was imperative. How were they organized?

Firstly, every man between twenty-one and thirty-one had to register on June 5, 1917, each in their county seat, if their county had less than thirty thousand residents. That was only eighteen days away. Much could happen between now and then. Surely the wheat would come ripe. That meant Prentis, her brothers, and all the men of Wakita would have to register right in the middle of harvest.

Those who were eligible and liable for immediate service made up the first category. This group of men was primarily unmarried registrants who had no dependents. But the group also included married registrants, if their spouses were independent and/or if they had one or more dependent children over sixteen with enough family income to withstand the draftee's absence.

Prentis was not in that category. None of her brothers of age fit there either. She heaved a huge sigh of relief. Tom McKinney did fit, though. She frowned.

The men who were temporarily deferred, but available for military service, were next. These were married registrants who had spouses and/or dependent children under age sixteen who had sufficient income for the family to survive the draftee's absence. Prentis and her brothers didn't fit there either. If they were drafted, none of their wives would have sufficient income.

The men in both of the first two groups would go to war first. So far, so good, at least from Avery's perspective. A tinge of guilt niggled her for having entirely selfish considerations. Many others were most assuredly unhappy that their husbands and sons would go first. She sighed.

Next her eyes scanned what she had hoped and prayed for all along—the farmers affected by the Food Will Win the War campaign. Those temporarily exempted, but available for the military, included local officials as well as single draft registrants who solely

25

provided for dependent parents and/or dependent siblings under age sixteen. Also exempted were registrants who were employed in agricultural labor or industrial enterprises essential to the war effort.

This third category was a relief, though the exemption was only temporary.

The fourth category was complete exemption for extreme hardship. Prentis and her brothers fit there perfectly. The category included all registrants with dependent spouses and/or dependent children or siblings who would have insufficient family income if the registrants were drafted.

The president had surely kept her brothers and her dear husband safely at home. When added to their deferral for also being farmers, their safety seemed to be a certainty.

She scanned the remaining last category of complete exemption and ineligibility. Tom need not go! Members of the clergy and theological students preparing for the ministry were exempt. A few other groups were mentioned, but no one she loved fit into those categories.

Tom had been spared. Why, oh why, did he want to volunteer?

She would let that go for now. This was the moment to thank God. Prentis wouldn't be taken, and her brothers would also be kept safe. They had a patriotic duty to cultivate food for the entire world, as well as to provide for their own families, who wouldn't be left destitute. Relief and praise washed through her. Joy filled her heart. She ran toward the barn.

Bursting through the door, she startled all the horses. All looked up from their placid chewing with ears alert, a few nickering. With arms wide, Prentis turned from grooming the horse. He swept her up, just as she burst into tears.

Softly, he crooned, "Dear sweet wife of mine. No need to worry. God took care of me."

"Yes, He did." She sobbed into his work shirt. "Thanks be to God!"

Then she gave way to her tears, letting them flow abundantly, pouring out all over Prentis's shoulder. Patting her back, he held her tightly as she vented all the emotion of the past two years.

Eventually, she calmed and sniffed into his shoulder. He handed her his folded handkerchief, and she blew her nose loudly. Out of the corner of her eye, she caught a glimpse of Jack. Standing in his little hay-bale corral, stock-still, he stared at her.

"I'm afraid I've scared the baby to death." She laughed, still sniffing.

Tilting his head to see Jack better, Prentis chuckled. "It would appear you have."

"Come here, baby boy," she said, turning to grab him up. "Momma's all right."

Studying her seriously with sober thoughtfulness, Jack held himself aloof, as if she might have lost her mind. His expression made them both laugh all the more.

"Not something he's used to seeing every day." Prentis laughed.

"No. That's not the typical behavior of his momma."

**

Just in time for lunch, a horse came cantering into their farmyard. Avery peeked out the window and discovered Tom stepping off his horse and already in a serious conversation with Prentis. She set another place at the table, glad that Jack was already sound asleep, so they'd be able to converse. Quietly, she shut the bedroom door.

Greeting them at the back door, she explained, "Tom, I'm so glad you're here. The table's set for you to join us.

27

We'll have to converse quietly, so we don't wake the baby. I want us to talk through it all without distraction. Can we do it?"

Both smiled and nodded. They clearly welcomed her input. Once the food was on the table and Tom had offered grace, they got right to it.

"Tom," Avery spoke softly, "I read the exemptions. You need not go. What will you do?"

"That's why I'm here. I'm praying and trying to ascertain what the Lord wants. Will the need for my services as a pastor be greater here or abroad?"

"We'd hate to lose you," Prentis said, "but I certainly see your point."

"Boys in foxholes would seem to be a field ripe for harvest," Avery added. "They'll need spiritual comfort and guidance. But can you go as a pastor? Is there a place?"

"That's what I'm investigating." Tom looked from one to the other. "I've written to Senator Robert Latham Owen to see if he can tell me anything. Until then, I'm praying and waiting."

"A good man," she said, turning toward Prentis. "A Cherokee and a staunch supporter of women's suffrage."

Nodding, he met her eye. She saw that he didn't want to lose his friend but was resigned, if Tom felt he should go to war. Now she looked again at Tom.

"We'll pray with you, Tom."

"Thank you both. Until I've decided, let's keep this in confidence."

"Of course," both responded simultaneously.

Silently, all of them dug into their lunch, considering the changes coming should Tom go away. Avery would miss him sorely. She hoped he wouldn't go.

Prentis polished off his potatoes and leaned back in his chair. "There's a practical farming consideration mixed up in all this."

Avery frowned, wondering what farming had to do with the draft.

"I think my wheat will come ripe right about the time we have to register."

"I was thinking the same when I looked at mine today," Tom said.

"Well, this is poor timing by the president." Avery fixed her eyes on one and then the other. "We have to harvest our wheat and simultaneously take an entire day off to register."

Both men chuckled.

"Avery, we appreciate your heart," Prentis said. "You're always on our side. But I doubt the general staff, or the War College, took the concerns of northern Oklahoma into consideration when planning the draft. They have to get men to war quickly. Hang the harvest."

Tom nodded. "We figured something like this would happen."

"You were already planning for it?" she said.

Prentis nodded. "Knocked around a few ideas at Jack's party."

"What did you decide?"

"If possible, the older men and the boys will carry on for that one day we're away."

Tom added, "Obviously, not as much will get accomplished that day."

"But, it won't set us back too much."

"That makes sense," she said.

"We'll definitely need prayer for that day," Tom said. "It will be chaotic, and no one likes their harvest delayed, what with the uncertainty of the weather. I imagine that day will be even more tense than it normally would be, since men will have been dragged away from their livelihood at the most important time of the year."

Avery nodded. "Praying is something I definitely can do."

"Your dad and I decided we would get your three younger brothers to help bring in the wheat," Prentis said.

"All of them?"

"Floyd and I seem to have our fields ripening at the same time, like in 1914. Looks like we'll be up first for harvest. Everyone else is behind. Fred, John, and Jerry will help Floyd out, along with Hattie's dad and her brother, Joe."

"But all the young men will have to leave to register."

"And leave they will," Prentis said. "Mr. Pitzer said he would organize the older neighboring men who can lend a hand. Alf Riley already rode over and pledged his help."

"Alf Riley!" Avery said, "That's a bold move."

"I think he's still trying to make up for all the trouble his wife has caused you."

Tom already knew the story about Mrs. Alfonse Riley, so Avery was glad she didn't have to explain. As the head of the Sunday School Department, Mrs. Riley had removed Avery from her teaching position for marrying a man who did not attend church, though he was a Christian. Mrs. Riley had also been the source of all kinds of gossip and unkind statements about Prentis, as he had been unaffiliated with a church at that time.

Mr. Riley, on the other hand, had exhibited kindness toward Prentis and Avery's family throughout the entire ordeal, evidence of his good opinion of Prentis's character. And here he was again, offering to help her brother, Floyd, and Floyd's brother-in-law, Joseph Pitzer. Mr. Riley's Christian behavior put some heart into Avery, helping her not to dwell on the recent gossip Mrs. Riley seemed to be spreading around the countryside.

This current slander struck Avery clean to the bone. She hadn't even told Prentis. It was too appalling and hurtful. Shoving aside the reminder, Avery focused again on the harvest discussion. Tom and Prentis had continued on without her.

"We'll get it done," Tom was saying, "with the good Lord's help."

"That's always the make of it."

A whimper, followed by a cry, from the bedroom removed Avery from the rest of the conversation. She stepped in to retrieve Jack, then nursed him in the rocker by his crib. He continued to nurse several times a day, though he was now one. She knew he would one day taper off. Having been the big sister in an extremely large family, she had watched her mother nurse many children and was quite comfortable breastfeeding, regardless of modern trends.

Even though there were all sorts of new scientific mothering methods being bandied about involving bottles and boiling and sterilization, she had decided to nurse Jack as long as he desired. For one thing, it was safe. And surely, if the good Lord had provided all mammalian mothers a natural way to feed their infants, why mess with what God had designed? This was one time she didn't trust tinkering with the system.

When she stepped out, Tom had departed, and Prentis was washing the dishes.

"Let me finish up," she said, "so you can play with Jack before heading back out."

"That's tempting." Hands still in the water, Prentis leaned down to kiss Jack on top of the head. "But I don't mind sparing you this task today." He continued washing.

Handing Jack his rattle, she balanced him on her hip. "So, what did you two decide?"

"Tom's already got men from church lined up to help."

"So, we get all the boys. Now that Gene's fifteen and Abe eighteen, it's like having two extra men. Howard can help me in here, watching out for Jack. I'll have plenty to keep a ten-year-old busy."

"That's what I figured."

"I guess we're all at God's mercy again, with the timing and the implementation."

"That's usually the case," he said, smiling at her.

Three

MONDAY, MAY 28, PRENTIS'S wheat tested ripe and ready for harvest. From the grain elevator, he galloped north toward Gibbon to get the boys. Once each had packed a few items into a knapsack, they mounted up. Howard and Gene rode two to a horse.

Before he took the sample, he had informed Avery of his plan. If he didn't reappear at home by noon, she was to take the buggy into town for supplies. She had rigged a harness for the small wooden seat in the wagon, so she could travel safely with Jack. The trip was half an hour or more into town with the buggy. Prentis reckoned they'd all arrive home about the same time.

***

In the general store, Avery carried Jack as she shopped, directing one of the young women employed there to haul this item or that up to the front, awaiting her purchase. Surprising her when she stepped around a

33

large display, Avery ran right into Joseph Pitzer. She hadn't seen Hattie's brother for quite some time.

"Why, Avery Pinkerton! Hardly expected to see you in the general store!"

"Hello, Joseph. I'm not often in town. It's good to see you."

From Avery's hip, Jack smiled widely at Joseph.

"My word, Avery! Other than his dark eyes, that baby's the spittin' image of Pink."

"He does take after his father. Now that his hair is lighter from the sun, it's even more obvious. One would think I had nothing to do with the matter."

The store was packed, but all conversation around them had quieted, as if everyone wanted to listen in. This was one time when having been friends since childhood was helpful. Joseph pierced Avery with that all-too-familiar look, cocking one eyebrow, and she understood his intentions entirely.

"I'm sure you've heard the gossip going about," Joseph said, raising his voice slightly.

"Why, yes, I have!" Her voice indicated her indignation as she also used more volume. "It's appalling. I can't believe anyone would spread such lies."

"Definitely couldn't have been started by a person of good reputation."

"Nor could it have been voiced by a Christian," Avery added.

Joseph's eyes twinkled at that. He shook his head. "Definitely not something a Christian would say or do, spreadin' lies of such a serious nature."

"I've been wondering about the legal recourse for slander."

"Now, that's worth considering."

Fussing and lunging for the floor, Jack draped himself over Avery's arm, anxious to get down. It was time to go.

"Well, Joseph," she said, "it was good to see you. I hope your harvest goes well. I've got to get back to the farm with these supplies. We're starting tomorrow."

"Best of luck," he said.

"Joseph Edward Pitzer, you know I don't believe in luck. There's not one iota of truth to it. I believe in the sovereignty of God."

"Oh, yes, pardon me." Chuckling, he tipped his hat. "Don't want to get you goin' about theology. Once the Bible thumpin' starts, there'll be no stopping you. Give my regards to Pink."

She laughed. "I will."

That was a good morning's work, Avery thought as they parted ways. Now they would see how effective the gossip mill in Wakita proved to be. Hopefully their conversation would put the entire mess of falsehoods to rest. She was glad Prentis hadn't heard the scandalous rumor. It was too appalling, almost sacrilegious in its implications.

***

The next day began before dawn. At the first singing of the birds, both Prentis and Avery slid quietly out of bed, dressed, and tiptoed out of the still bedroom to begin organizing. Little Jack continued his soft breathing in the crib, as well as the boys on their bedrolls on the front room floor. Avery stoked the cookstove fire, and Prentis stepped outside to ready the horses.

Soon all their neighbors would arrive, and harvest would begin. The draft registration was in one week, so they'd only get halfway through before losing their strongest manpower for at least part of one day—all the men between twenty-one and thirty-one. Everyone in the countryside seemed prepared to help out this year to make up for that lack.

In the kitchen, Avery began churning out pancakes, one buckwheat flapjack after another. Within a few minutes, disheveled boys appeared in the kitchen, peering over her shoulder.

"Get your blue jeans on over your union suits," she said. "Wash up and attend to your creature needs. Once you're all dressed and ready, you can start working on this pile of food."

Lickety-split, three hungry boys prepared for the day, and soon all stood in the kitchen with plates in hand, including Prentis. She divided up the pile, and they all settled at the table with their portions. She continued to bring in pancakes. After working through the entire mixing bowl of batter, they finally seemed to slow their consumption.

She heard Howard groan. "I don't think I can eat another bite."

Laughing, she called in from the stove, "That's a sign it's time to stop eating."

At some point, Jack had joined them. Prentis held him on his knee and fed the baby bits of pancake, one bite at a time. He appeared to like them as much as the others.

Prentis looked up at her. "Figured you didn't hear him wake up. Thank you for making our favorite breakfast this morning. What would I do without you?"

"You'd be hungry." She grinned. This was a common exchange between them. Prentis's lean and hungry time of bachelorhood wasn't so far in the past that her cooking had lulled him into husbandly complacency.

He smiled and winked at her. "Everything's ready outside. I'm going to play with Jack for a while, since I won't see much of him for the next two weeks. Will that give you some space to get the noon meal started in the cookstove?"

"Indeed, it will. Thank you!"

She'd made the first day's pies yesterday when she returned from town, and so now she placed the enormous pork shank in the hot oven and began scrubbing potatoes to add later.

"Howard, can you go out and gather the green beans?"

He responded that he could, and out he went.

Before long, Abe stuck his head in the front door. "Daddy's Model T's comin' up the road and a bunch of neighbors too. Looks like it's time."

Avery grabbed up Jack and stepped outside with Prentis. All the boys loped out to the drive, welcoming everyone as they pulled in with their buggies. She watched both her momma and her daddy disembarking from the Model T, and then she noticed a backseat passenger.

It was Mr. Riley himself. This was a surprise!

They all stepped over to the automobile to greet this group.

Prentis shook her father's hand and then turned to shake Mr. Riley's. "Alf, this is a pleasant surprise! Thank you for coming all the way down here to help."

"You're welcome, P.J. Your father-in-law and I are getting up in years, but we still have some work left in us."

"Thought we'd come down to see how you were organizing," her daddy said, jumping into the conversation. "We'll help wherever we can. This was Alf's idea, and a mighty good one."

All the gathered neighbors had heard this exchange. The men all nodded. On their faces Avery read confirmation of character, rejection of gossip and lies, and eagerness to support Prentis in his harvest. A great heaviness lifted from her heart.

Sam began barking up a storm as George Miller came driving in with the binder. His son followed with the thresher. The hive of activity grew even more frenzied now as the horses were all hitched together to the binder, one pair after another, so it could be driven through the field to harvest and bind the wheat in stalks. They had plenty of horsepower and perfect weather.

As usual, Prentis directed Mr. Miller to position the thresher on the north side of the barn. Once it was in place, he ran the thick twenty-foot long belt to connect the thresher's flywheel to the tractor's motor. When the grain was threshed from the wheat stalks, the stalks would shoot out to form an enormous pile of straw, plenty for Prentis's barn stalls this year.

Prentis had decided to haul the grain right into town. The president had urged farmers to get as much food to Europe as possible, therefore the threshed grain would not be shoveled into Prentis's granary, but would land in his wagon. One of the boys would drive each wagonload of threshed grain into town, one after another.

Daddy and Mr. Riley conversed with the other older farmers. Nodding, they all agreed with Prentis's decisions. Many of them had come out to advise and to offer their help and their wisdom. This was their way of assisting both the war effort and the young men who had to bear the brunt of it. Community support would help the young men carry this heavier load so suddenly thrust upon them.

Having not expected Momma, it was a great joy and relief to have her help for the first day at least. The two of them walked back inside, Momma holding baby Jack.

In the kitchen, Momma said, "I hear tell of a conversation you had in the general store."

"Oh, you did? That circulated quickly."

"Indeed, it did. A very timely and wise conversation in my opinion."

Howard piped in. "What did you talk about, Avery?"

Frowning, Momma caught Avery's eye before she responded.

"It was merely an everyday discussion, Howard, about harvest and life. I ran into Hattie's brother Joseph and hadn't seen him for a while."

"That's all?"

"Yes, I'm sorry to disappoint you, but that's all it was."

He stalked off to play with Jack. "Don't sound so wise to me."

Momma and Avery smiled. She hoped and prayed that conversation had ended all speculation, especially when added to Mr. Riley's appearance down here at their harvest and his offered help with Floyd's harvest on draft day. One kind man might accomplish more than all the rest of them put together, even more so than her conversation with Joseph Pitzer.

But a truth now dawned on Avery. If every single man here, there, and who knew where had heard this vicious rumor, how could Prentis himself be uninformed? Had he known all along but kept it from her, because he was aware that its insidious nature would devastate her? That would be just like him.

But the idea of asking him and bringing the lie out into the open hurt her dreadfully, attacking everything sacred in her life. This was a spiritual wound. Her heart had grown increasingly embittered toward Mrs. Alfonse Riley, the obvious source of the gossip.

***

On Thursday, May 31, the Medford Patriot-Star informed all the citizens of Grant County that draft registrations would occur on June 5 at the typical voting locations where men always cast their ballots. Wakita's young men need not travel fifteen miles down to Medford to register. All were to head to Wakita bright and early on Tuesday of next week. The newspaper informed them of the questions that would be asked and the proper way to answer. They were to study the paper to be prepared so the registration would move along with speed.

They worked hard all week. Prentis took in more than sixteen bushels an acre, a good return. When they stopped to rest on Sunday, Avery decided she would heed his advice and stay home to rest, rather than attending church. All was quiet that morning because her parents had taken the boys home last night. Every day had been a test. Could her body fight off her once regular migraines while working so hard and receiving so little sleep? So far, all had been well, but taking a day of rest seemed wise, especially since the Almighty Himself had ordained it.

In the cool of the morning, they awakened all wrapped up in one another. A rare occasion, Jack still slumbered in his own bed, even though the sun had risen.

"I've got my wife all to myself," Prentis whispered over her shoulder.

She rolled over to face him. "Yes, you do."

"With a baby in the house, a man's got to grab any intimacy with his wife that he can."

She laughed softly and pulled him closer. "That's fine by me."

When he wrapped her up in his arms and warmed her lips with his kisses, she melted into him, eager for this connection. A baby surely did make this pleasure rarer, and their exuberance in one another had to be enjoyed quietly, since the baby slept right around the corner. But it was such a relief to be held, cherished, and savored by him. She needed him right now, especially with all those lies floating around, invading her tranquility.

Afterward, she cradled his head upon her bare abdomen, running her fingers through his hair. Still, he held her tightly.

"I'd like to stay right here as long as I can," he said softly.

She whispered, "Until the infant tyrant whisks me away, you mean."

He chuckled. "Yes, until then."

Basking in his physical touch, she realized it had been a while since they'd lingered long in embrace. Holding, nursing, and caring for Jack provided her so much physical contact that she hadn't noticed. They used to spend so much time together in this bed.

"Surely," she whispered, "when he's older, we'll regain more space for intimacy."

"That's my hope and prayer," he said softly.

"I've missed you too."

He looked up at her. "That's good to hear."

"Do I not tell you enough?"

"You're a pretty wonderful wife, Avery. I have no complaints."

"Now that Jack's growing more predictable, certainly I can attempt to be even more wonderful. I fear I've neglected you."

"No need to fear. All new mothers are absorbed with their infants. The period merely lasts longer with humans than with farm animals, and that's a good thing."

"Yes, it is. My heart would break if the entire process of raising him only took one year."

"So would mine," he said. "I love being his father."

"You're a mighty good father."

They held one another silently for a long while, completely at peace, enjoying this rare morning. Avery was glad she'd heeded his words and stayed home today.

"I've also been trying to be a good husband." He kissed her abdomen, then he planted his chin on her belly and looked up at her. "I've been protecting you from something I heard."

Serious and alert now, she stared down at him.

"I didn't think you knew about it," he said. "But, I overheard a conversation this week—two men discussing your talk with Joe Pitzer in town. Then I knew you'd also heard the lies."

"Oh, Prentis, I didn't think you knew, so I said nothing. I was hoping and praying you hadn't heard. It's horrendous!"

"It's an awful accusation to make about another person. I'm grateful for Alf Riley's kindness and his presence here, because his wife has surely sullied your name and reputation."

Tears ran down Avery's cheeks. "I hope you know that contrary to those lies, I would never be unfaithful to you—not with Joseph Pitzer, nor with any other man on earth."

Prentis sat up and pulled her into his arms. Leaning back against the headboard, he cradled her, looking down into her eyes. "Of course, I know that. I never for one second believed the lies that woman has been spreading far and wide. I know you would never be unfaithful to me."

"I'm so relieved."

"I've known you all my life, Avery. I know your character. Anyone who's acquainted with you knows you would never do such a thing. Anyone who doesn't isn't worth worrying about."

"It's not so easy for me. My desire for the approval of others seems to always win out."

"You're human. We're all the same."

"What I don't understand is how she could concoct such a tale."

"I'm glad you brought that up," he said. "Your dad and I have pieced it together. Seems Jack being born three weeks early set it off. Someone calculated back to when he would have been conceived if that had been his true due date. Remember when I went up to see Fred with Tom after our first tornado?"

She nodded.

"Well, apparently Joe Pitzer happened to be down in our neighborhood that week—the week that would have produced Jack's birth on April 16."

"I had no idea," she said. "I was having so much fun with Howard while you were gone. Remember, he stayed with me all week?"

"Yes, I surely do. But even if you'd been here all alone, I never would think or believe such a thing about you, Sweetheart."

"Thank you."

"So," he said, "take all that information, and then remember that Jack had a head full of thick black hair when he was born."

"And with those tiny bits of conjecture, Mrs. Alfonse Riley decided to slander me?"

"It would appear so."

Avery was stunned. The fact that Joseph Pitzer had once been sweet on her had prompted that woman of evil intent to gather tiny bits together and manufacture the most heinous of lies Avery could imagine, untruths so weighty and crushing that she could barely think them— adultery, illegitimacy.

"You need to pray for me, Prentis, because I surely hate that woman."

With compassionate eyes he looked down at her. "I've never in all my life heard you say you hated anyone. That tells me exactly how difficult this is for you."

"I know I'm sinning to feel that way toward her. I'm to pray for my enemy and forgive those who offend me. Jesus and the apostles all say so. But my heart is not cooperating."

"I will surely pray for you, Sweetheart, and you pray for me. I feel pretty much the same."

"Bitterness is like poison, Prentis. We have to let this go, lest we be the worse for it.

Four

JUNE 5, 1917, THE INFAMOUS DAY of the draft registration, Avery awakened feeling Prentis's absence. She rested her palm flat on his side of the bed. Cold. Sliding away from Jack, who had awakened to nurse in the night—unusual for him—she stood, careful not to stir the bedclothes. The almost full moon had earlier sailed through the sky, leaving the early morning bereft of light. In the darkness, she almost ran smack into Prentis.

His large warm hands steadied her.

Together they stepped out into the main room, moving silently, so as not to waken all the boys sleeping on their floor. Out the front window, she detected the first brightening barely showing along the horizon. The sun would rise around 5:15 that morning.

Avery helped Prentis with his stiff collar. He already wore his suit pants and had his jacket draped over a nearby chair. The scent of pomade hung in the air.

Probably what had awakened her, for his movements were as quiet as a cat. The fragrance always reminded her of their wedding day, warming her with the memory.

"You'll be the most handsome man registering today," she whispered.

He snorted and continued the battle with his tie.

"Do you want me to fix you some breakfast?"

"No," he said quietly. "Want to get going. Let the boys sleep."

They slipped into the kitchen, and she groped about for what she needed. "Here's the tail end of a loaf of bread. You can nibble as you ride." She tucked it into his jacket pocket.

"Thank you. You always take such good care of me. Tried not to wake you."

"I didn't hear a sound."

"Hope to get this over with as quickly as I can."

"Thank God that you don't have to ride all the way down to Medford."

"Amen to that." He snorted again. "There are about twenty-one thousand residents of this county, and around five thousand of us will be registering today. Would have been a madhouse in Medford if we'd all had to meet in that one spot, especially during harvest."

"That's for certain."

On the back porch, Prentis slipped into his jacket, straightened his tie again, and then settled his Stetson. She kissed him warmly, and he surprised her when his lips caressed hers with passion. With his hand on the small of her back, he pressed her body tightly to his. Returning his kisses, she responded. Eventually he released her, touching his lips softly to her forehead.

"When a man's going to sign his life away, he likes to be reminded of what he's got at home awaiting his return."

45

Tightly, she squeezed him about the waist, but she could feel the tension in his body. Now that he was girded and mentally prepared, he was ready to go. She released him.

"Off you go," she whispered. "I'll see you afterward for the parade."

He kissed her forehead again and then slipped silently out the back door. She stood at the back-porch window but could see nothing outside. Shortly, Hector passed the window with Prentis in the saddle. Enough light showed now that she could detect the dun horse clearly. When they reached the road, she heard the horse take off with speed as the sun slid over the horizon.

Wide awake now, she opened her Bible. Romans 8 seemed a good chapter to read this morning before everyone arrived to continue harvest. It would remind her of the sovereignty of God, even over world war.

***

The sun beamed over the horizon as Prentis headed toward town. When he arrived, he discovered that everyone had acted upon the same impulse, arriving as early as possible. They were to begin at 7:00 a.m. The downtown teamed with young men anxious to get this task completed. Prentis wished a parade hadn't been planned so they could all simply get back to their wheat harvest. God only knew what tomorrow's weather might bring.

Many of the oldest men in town—veterans of the Civil War—were on site. Other than elected officials, the rest of the crowd were all young men registering. The other men appeared to have gone out to keep harvest going for the young men, lest any crops be lost to bad weather.

Both saloons had been transformed into restaurants for the day as no alcohol was to be sold. Their doors were thrown wide, displaying well-lit interiors serving more substantial fare. No alcohol was in sight. Men stood inside drinking coffee while eating what looked like pancakes and eggs. The livery, the general store, and the bank were also well-lit, though not open for business quite yet. Registration day looked to be profitable for the town's businesses.

Floyd Slaughter and Joseph Pitzer hailed him from the inside of one saloon. John Slaughter stood outside on the boardwalk with Tom McKinney. All were eating steaming plates of food with hot cups of coffee balanced precariously on the edges. Prentis tied Hector to the hitching rail, shoulder to shoulder with their horses. The downtown was packed. Overheated horseflesh and fresh manure provided fragrances that mingled with those given off by pancakes and coffee.

"Pink!" John Slaughter called. He stood at the other end of the hitching rail, cramming enormous bites of pancake into his mouth.

"John." Prentis nodded. "Never saw you stuff your food in quite so fast."

"Momma'd kill me if I went in there with Floyd, no matter whether they're serving hard drink today or not. Daddy might do worse. After that, Bernice would take a whack at me. They're already gonna be mad at me when this is over, so I decided to stay outside. Told the proprietor I'd eat as quick as I could, so he could have his plate back for the next customer."

"Sounds like a workable plan. Curious why they'd be mad at you though."

"Don't intend to take the exemption," John said before devouring half a pancake in one bite.

Prentis was taken aback. "You're willing to leave Bernice and your baby to go fight?"

"Yes, I am," he mumbled around the pancake. "Hope they draft me. Can't stand injustice."

47

Prentis knew that to be true. He recalled that in 1915, John had gotten into a fistfight over the poor treatment of native people and persons of African descent in the moving picture *Birth of a Nation* when it was featured at The Electric Theater. After the fight, John had almost ended up in jail but had paid a fine instead. Of course, he would want to go fight in Europe. Prentis decided to leave that topic alone.

"Didn't know you were registering down here, John."

"I'm not. Got up early to ride down to see you all before I head back to Gibbon to register. Jerry and Fred are holding me a place in line up there."

Prentis nodded and turned toward Tom. "Mornin', Tom."

"P.J." Tom handed him a steaming cup of coffee.

He nodded his thanks. "Registering for the draft doesn't give me much appetite. But I can always use coffee."

John now stood at the saloon door, calling for Floyd to come get his empty plate. He'd clearly taken the threat to his health seriously, and there was no way he'd step inside.

The sun blazed now at full strength casting long shadows toward the west, illuminating the teeming mob in sharp relief. Several hundred men milled about the barely two-block-long downtown, along with some of their wives and families who had accompanied them. Grant County officials scurried here and there, running back and forth from the school right north of the downtown. Already the day was heating up. They would swelter in their wool suits for a large part of the day. It looked to be unpleasant.

Floyd and Pitzer strutted out of the saloon, appearing fortified and ready for the registration. Pitzer's eyes were bloodshot, as if he'd done a little fortifying with alcohol the night before.

"Pink." He reached for Prentis's hand.

"Pitzer."

As they shook hands, a hush surrounded them, as though the crowd had drawn back a step, so all could observe this friendliness between the two.

"Saw that boy of yours last week." Pitzer threw his arm around Prentis's shoulder. "He's the spittin' image of you, other than he's got Avery's eyes."

"That's what everyone tells me. Avery and I are pretty proud of him."

"And you should be. Looks to be a good strong boy."

"That he is."

Pitzer then shook hands with John and Tom.

Floyd met Prentis's eye. Both nodded, well aware of the audience and the conveyed message. Their cool exteriors hid the deep burn of anger under the surface of their composed expressions. Avery's integrity had been called into question, Avery—Sunday School teacher, Bible school graduate, and the kindest and purest woman Prentis had ever known, a true woman of conscience— sullied by a mean-spirited gossip. It was all he could do to keep his visage stoic. Like Avery, he determined that he would not hate that woman.

"Good to see you, Pink," Floyd said.

"Likewise. No matter the occasion."

All of them lapsed into discussion of their individual harvests, what kind of yield they had gotten so far, and how the wheat was testing at the elevator. Periodically they laughed at something John or Pitzer said. Eventually, the volume of the surrounding men discussing their own harvests and the war returned to normal. The show was over. Nothing to see here.

The mayor now stepped into the bandstand, lifting a bullhorn.

"It's now seven a.m., so we're ready to begin. We're attempting to run this occasion with military precision.

Everyone can now head north toward the school. Line up, one behind another. Snake your line down the street as far as need be. When it's your turn, step up to one of the available registrars. Be sure to have your answers prepared, so you don't slow down the process. As soon as you're done, skedaddle on out of there."

Everyone chuckled at his final statement, so much for the military nature of the event.

John headed out on horseback as they headed north on foot. Prentis grabbed Hector's bridle and moved him to a hitching rail off the main street, one he knew had a deeper watering trough and a shady tree. There was no telling how long this would take.

It was impossible to count the men in the crowd. He hadn't heard how many their small town expected. Each municipality completed its own registration. Dotted all over Oklahoma, gatherings such as this occurred in every small village where men voted.

After arriving at the school, they waited in line for quite a while. Prentis found it increasingly difficult to be there rather than out harvesting his wheat. All the men seemed tense and agitated. Probably they entertained similar thoughts to his—they wanted to be hard at work in their fields, getting their wheat in. Time seemed to slow. Everyone shifted their weight from one boot to the other, back and forth, sighing with impatience. He seated his Stetson low on his brow, shielding his face from the sun. Ducking under the rim, the sense of privacy was a relief.

Finally, at long last, they could see inside the school doorway and up the stairs. Eventually, they stepped out of the sun and into the shady entryway. When they reached the top of the stairs, Prentis craned his neck to peer into the main hallway. Two women wearing large hats were each seated at a long table, their backs against the wall as the men stepped up to the tables to register.

Now that the goal was near, time seemed to have stopped.

Each applicant ahead of them took an unbearably long time.

Each registrar asked a seemingly never-ending list of questions.

All stood on weary feet as each awaited his turn.

Sweat trickled down their faces, running in under their stiff shirt collars, dampening their hair, and finding its way down their backs and under their leather belts. Would he have to wring out his wool suit when it was all over? Men tugged at stiff collars and fanned themselves with their hats. Like a thick fog, the odor of hardworking, sweaty, wool-covered men settled over the crowd in the stairwell.

Still, the process continued. And then, finally, at last, they stepped into the hall.

Now Prentis waited at the head of the line. His introverted nature agitated, he tilted his hat back, watching to see which registrar would be available next. The tight discomfort of having to interact with a person he didn't know well settled in his chest. Hopefully, it would be mere asking and answering of questions. A man at the farthest registration table straightened, wiped his brow, and stepped away. Prentis headed that direction.

Sitting at the table now available to take his registration, he found Mrs. Alfonse Riley looking up at him. Queasiness smote him in the stomach.

Lord God Almighty, You'll have to get me through this.

Up he stepped, removing his hat. Giving him a mere glance, she was all business.

"Please state your name," she said.

"Prentis J. Pinkerton."

She entered his information on the card. "One 's' or two?"

"One."

"What is your age?"

"Twenty-six." He watched her scribble that in. She also filled in Wakita, Oklahoma, on the following line of the card.

Without looking up, she asked, "Date of birth?"

"January 6, 1891."

She recorded the date. "Are you a natural-born citizen, a naturalized citizen, an alien, or have you declared your intention?"

"Natural-born citizen." As he spoke, she entered his words.

"Where were you were born, Mr. Pinkerton?"

"Kingman, Kansas. United States of America."

"What is your present trade, occupation, or office?"

"Farmer," he said.

"By whom are you employed?"

"I work for myself."

"Where is your place of employment?"

"My farm is three and a half miles west and one mile south of Wakita." As he spoke it, she wrote it.

"Have you a father, mother, wife, child under twelve, or a sister or a brother under twelve, solely dependent on you for support?" she asked. "Specify which."

With a growing sense of personal offense, he said nothing, but merely stood looking down at her. He wanted her to look at him. The seconds ticked by. His breathing came shallow and rapid. Eventually, she lifted a frowning expression of consternation at his delay.

Prentis looked her right in the eye. "I have a wife and one son, of whom I'm very proud. Our son is the joy of our lives. People tell me that he looks quite a bit like me."

A blush spread across her cheeks. Hastily, she looked back down and recorded the words "wife and child." Keeping her eyes on her work, she asked, "Are you married or single?"

"Happily married, and I thank God for it."

Her blush deepened as she penned "married" onto the card. "What is your race?"

"Caucasian."

Watching her write, he noticed that she misspelled the word. Clearly, he'd rattled her. She was a former schoolteacher. She knew how to spell. For some odd reason, he felt a twinge of sympathy for her dilemma. It had to be God at work, softening his heart.

"Do you have any previous military service?" she asked.

"No."

"Do you claim exemption from the draft?" she asked, keeping her eyes on the card. "If so, specify your grounds for exemption."

Her hands were shaking. More pity flooded in. God was good to work on him right then, as he stood looking down at perhaps his greatest foe, a woman motivated by who knew what—envy of Avery, broken experiences from her own past? Only God knew.

"My grounds for exemption are my wife and our child," he said. Dropping his voice, he bent low so only Mrs. Riley could hear him. "I forgive you for what you've done to them."

Mrs. Riley's head snapped up. Embarrassment and shame showing clearly on her face, she met his eyes for only a brief moment. Then quickly, she looked back down and recorded his exemption. Turning the card around, she shoved it across the table toward him.

"Take your card to the head registrar before you sign on the bottom line," she said tersely.

He stood up straight, looking down at the top of her hat. Obviously, she wasn't going to meet his eyes again. "Good day to you, Mrs. Riley. Thank you for your service to our country today." With that, he resettled his Stetson and wiped his sweaty palms on his suit pants.

53

His last stop before leaving was the registrar, Mr. H. J. Green. The man flipped the card over and asked him to describe himself on the back. Prentis wrote in his physical description.

"Now, Mr. Pinkerton," the head registrar said, "read that entire card. If all is accurate, sign your name on the line."

Prentis read, signed, and passed it back. Mr. Green added his signature, filling in the precinct, county, state, and date. Then he pulled a blank bluish-green certificate from his pile, filled it in, and handed it to Prentis, proving he'd been registered for the draft. An eagle was embossed at the top of the page.

"Keep that document in a safe place," Mr. Green said.

"I will, sir. Thank you for your service today."

"You're welcome, young man." Mr. Green smiled and nodded.

Prentis headed for the door. Carefully, he folded the document and tucked it into the pocket inside his suit jacket. He would place it safely in their document box when he arrived home.

Stepping outside, Prentis found his brother-in-law Floyd, Joe Pitzer, and Tom McKinney standing in a cluster awaiting him. All wore looks of concern.

"Well, that had to be awkward for her," Pitzer said.

"Appeared to be," Prentis said. "Wasn't business as usual for me either, but it's over now. Don't really want to talk about it. Wish we could go back to our farms and get to work."

They all patted him on the back. It was past noon, Prentis was hungry, and he wanted to go home. Instead, they would wait there until the afternoon parade. They walked the few blocks back to the main street. A throng filled the entire downtown. Everyone they passed shook their hands and praised their patriotism and bravery.

Prentis didn't feel particularly brave or patriotic. He felt wrung out and emotionally shaken. Then, he noticed Ulysses hitched to a wagon—his wagon. He looked up, and there sat Avery wearing a wide-brimmed hat with a big picnic basket wedged between her feet. Jack was harnessed into his little seat, smiling and reaching for him as he bounced up and down.

Relief whooshed through his chest, as if a heavy weight had been lifted.

An unexpected surprise, Mr. Riley sat in the wagon beside Avery. The man was covered in straw chaff, his face smudged and dirty. He stood up straight, lifted his hat—revealing his clean white skin above the hatband—and hailed Prentis, who raised a hand in greeting. Apparently, the older man had spent the morning helping at their farm. Rather than merely observing, he clearly had worked hard today.

Prentis's throat thickened. Inhaling deeply through his nostrils, he extinguished a sob and adjusted the tilt of his Stetson. A man couldn't cry in public. This kindness was unanticipated. He was glad he'd treated the man's wife as a Christian should, for on this trying and sultry day, he certainly could have had a completely opposite reaction.

Stepping toward the wagon, he offered Mr. Riley his hand. Wearing a kindhearted expression, the older man crawled down and gave him a firm handshake. The crowd surrounding them hushed, observing their interaction.

"I hitched a ride with your wife," Mr. Riley said, "so I could come in for the parade. We're all proud of you men for stepping up and signing the line to serve our country."

Prentis nodded. He hadn't been prepared for all of the praise and thanks. He was merely doing his duty and what the law required.

"My wife is working here today," Mr. Riley continued. "I'll go find her now."

"Thank you for your help, Mr. Riley. Means the world to me. Your wife is in the school."

"Thank you, son. Glad to help. Looks like you'll have a good crop this year."

Something nudged him from behind. He turned to find Avery with Jack on her hip, smiling as she handed him a large jug of water. Behind her, Tom now carried the picnic basket. Taking the jug in one hand, Prentis wrapped his other arm about her waist, drawing her close against his side. After taking a deep swig of water, he kissed her. He might live after all. So far, it had been a hard day, but now she was beside him.

"Let's go eat where I left Hector," Prentis said. "There's a good shade tree there."

They headed back the way he had come, a block over where a spindly elm tree stood. There they found his horse, surrounded by other horses whose riders also knew the spot. Floyd, Hattie, and Pitzer walked just ahead of them, heading toward the same tree.

Avery threw wide the blanket she had brought, and then she placed Jack right in the center. Tom set down the basket, and the three of them sat in a circle around the baby, keeping him corralled in the middle. The first pull from the basket went to Jack. Once he was happily eating, she brought forth fresh rolls, fried chicken, baked beans, and a strawberry-rhubarb pie.

Now Prentis knew he would indeed live through the day.

Five

THE RAT-TAT-TATTING OF A drum sounded, ricocheting and reverberating against the main-street buildings. *It was time!* Excitement welled up in Avery, a thrill that the community had come together to honor their men—men who had been shoved into a position that most of them didn't want, and yet they had stepped up with dignity and a healthy respect for duty.

Previously the news had swept through the crowd that every single man eligible for the draft, those who resided in Wakita proper or in Wakita township, had indeed registered. What would the statewide statistics be for today's registration? For Wakita, at least, there was an understanding of obedience to civil authority and a comprehension that even though their state was young, they were all in this together as citizens of the United States.

Stuffing their goods back into the basket, she prepared to leave their picnic site.

Grabbing up Jack, she turned toward Prentis. "Jack and I are going up to Main Street. I'm going to find a shady awning, if I can. Watch for us as you parade by. For now, can you two carry the basket and the jug, so we can set them in the wagon?"

"Of course, we can," Tom said.

They walked toward the wagon. "We're all so proud of you men for bravely stepping up," she said. "Of course, I've watched you do that your entire life, Prentis. You're an impressive man, my husband. And so are you, Tom."

She flashed them both a beaming smile.

Tom smiled widely, and Prentis glanced at her with loving eyes before dropping his head. As usual, praise made him uncomfortable. But honorable men shouldn't be taken for granted. Many men didn't hold duty of such supreme importance.

Once everything was stowed, she pulled Prentis's face down for a kiss.

"I see what you do," she whispered, "and I'm glad you're my husband. Other than the Savior Himself, you're God's greatest gift to me."

His eyes looked evenly into hers. "I feel exactly the same about you."

Now she kissed him, smack on the lips, right in public.

When he pulled back, he winked at her, and his smile spread wide.

"That'll give everyone something to talk about," he said quietly.

"Good!" Turning, she headed toward Main Street.

There wasn't much shade at this hour. She waved at Hattie, who had found an awning across the street. Avery settled for standing on the south side of the road, pressed up tightly against a building that cast a narrow shade covering half the boardwalk. When Prentis went by, she would hurry Jack forward to see his father.

Neighbors found their way toward her, once they'd seen her. Mary Beth Miller was among them. Avery had always liked Mary Beth, other than for one fleeting moment at the first dance she had attended with Prentis in Wakita. But now, Avery was happy to stand and chat with her. Over this past year, Mary Beth had begun coming over to visit on occasion, and their time together was always enjoyable. They sewed while discussing the week's sermon, the news, and the local goings on. Mary Beth acquainted Avery with Wakita life.

Now the measured cadence of many drums sounded from the direction of the school. The crowd pressed forward, all attempting to get a good look. Mary Beth cleared a path for Avery to bring Jack forward. Soon the drum corps passed right in front of them, leading the parade. Jack bounced up and down to their beat, clapping his hands and shrieking with excitement. It was almost more fun to watch him than the parade. Mary Beth met her eye as both of them chuckled at the baby's antics.

Next came all the school children in first through eighth grades. Mrs. Shaw, their teacher, led them as they sang a patriotic song. They did their best to march in straight lines, but it proved difficult with so much going on at once. Still, Avery was impressed. She knew how much work it would take to prepare those children to carry out their instructions. While they sang, a costumed Uncle Sam and Columbia walked alongside, interacting with the crowd.

Jack drew back when Uncle Same came near. The man's makeup was heavy, and he didn't look like any man Jack knew.

"Jack," Avery said, "that's Uncle Sam."

"Sam?"

"Yes, Uncle Sam."

"Nuncle Sam."

"Yes, that's right. What a big boy you are!"

Bouncing on her hip, he laughed and clapped in response as a lone drummer in Civil War apparel walked up the street, beating cadence. Behind him rows of Civil War soldiers in uniform passed solemnly and silently. That certainly reminded the crowd of the cost of war.

Some of the old men could still wear their uniforms properly; some had bulging buttons, but all were dignified. These men had seen atrocities. They knew what the young men who had registered might face if they were called to duty. The crowd grew quiet and somber as they passed, the remembrance of these facts sinking in and bringing to mind the solemnity of war.

They were followed by the Women of the Culture Club, the organization that brought in special speakers and booked performances for The Opera House. Everyone applauded politely, glad for the entertainment the women brought to the community.

Next came Judge Swibert from Enid. He had spoken at their earlier patriotic assembly when the *Lusitania* was sunk by the Germans. Behind him walked the men who had registered.

Like a thunderclap, the entire crowd roared with approval, the volume growing and swelling. Everyone applauded and cheered the bravery and patriotism of their young men.

Shouts rang out.

"There go our boys!"

"Brave men one and all!"

"Hurrah for the men of Wakita! Hurrah!"

All were dressed as Prentis, in their suits and ties with hats donned. They walked silently, all wearing solemn expressions. Row after row passed. Avery had meant to count the rows to tally how many had registered, but instead she found herself looking for Prentis.

Voices rang out as people glimpsed their men. Smiles appeared among the newly registered.

Spotting Floyd, Avery called his name. Somehow, he heard her over the racket. Both he and Joseph Pitzer beside him aimed big smiles their direction. Mary Beth and Avery waved enthusiastically. Lifting Jack, Avery pointed, hoping he could see. But they passed too quickly.

But here came Prentis, only three deep in his row.

Avery stepped into the street, aiming Jack the right direction. "There's Da Da!"

Prentis's face had been solemn, but now he broke into a wide smile.

Jack bounced up and down. "Da Da! Da Da!"

Probably able to read the baby's lips, Prentis grinned even wider, and then he was gone, marching on down the street. A few steps past them, he ducked his head, his bashful side kicking in again. That gesture was so endearing, her chest filled clear to the top with love, swelling with pride and satisfaction. Jack continued to reach toward him, calling his name.

Then he looked at Avery. "Da Da bye-bye."

"Yes, Jack! Da Da went bye-bye."

A sentence! Her teacher brain was ecstatic. He was ahead of his age. A two-word sentence! She lost all track of the parade and forgot to search for Tom as she studied Jack's face watching his father marching away. The boy could talk. Prentis would be delighted.

The loud horn of a long gleaming Buick caught her attention. Behind the men now came one automobile after another. My, how they shone in the sun! She hoped they could purchase their own modest Model T after the harvest. Only time would tell.

After the entire parade had passed, the crowd headed toward the school. There was to be entertainment, and the speaker would surely have something inspirational to say. At the school, all spread out, separating into family groups on the lawn.

Prentis found them and settled onto their blanket with Avery and Jack. Immediately, Jack climbed up onto him, embracing him tightly about the neck. Prentis gave him a smack of a kiss on the cheek, and then Jack nestled into his lap. Now he turned his attention to Avery.

They gazed into one another's eyes. She was so proud of him and the kind of man he was in his solid, stalwart core. His character showed in all of his actions, and she was glad to be his wife. His eyes were filled with love as he looked into hers. Each smiled softly at the other. Nothing need be said. She leaned against his shoulder.

Meeting the needs of the entire group, the sky grew overcast, lending much needed relief from the heat. Prentis had removed his jacket, now that his duty was done, but Avery continued to fan them all with the handheld folding fan she'd brought from home.

In front of the crowd, the school children now carried out a flag drill. It was quite impressive, given the short amount of time they'd been given to learn and practice. Everyone gave them hearty applause when they finished.

Next, the local orchestra rendered some lilting John Phillip Sousa numbers. These were always great fun. The tunes made Avery long to rise and parade through the city. Then one of the talented male quartets rose, rendering a patriotic number that had them all on their feet by the end. These musical numbers were both greeted with loud bursts of cheers and ringing applause.

Judge Swibert rose and soon had them all in stitches, especially when he poked fun at Herbert Hoover's attempted manipulations of wheat market pricing as the new "Food Administrator." As a farming community, they all appreciated these pokes at the pompous, newly appointed government official who thought he knew everything. Judge Swibert was always a humorous and entertaining speaker.

But he soon turned to the topic at hand, the bravery of the men who had registered that day and the war that destroyed the world's peace. He approached the pinnacle of his speech, moving them all with such fervor and heartfelt patriotism that Avery thought she might weep, but a disturbance behind them drew her attention.

She glanced over her shoulder and detected a dark sky coming up fast from the southwest. Groups of people were already packed up and heading toward the Methodist Church. Turning to Prentis, she gestured with her head.

After looking, he whispered his instructions. "You and Jack hurry to the Methodist Church. I'm going to stick this out with our horses."

She raised her eyebrows.

"I'll be fine. See the red tint in the sky. I think we're dealing with a dust devil, not a tornado. I may take the horses north about a mile to avoid it. Maybe west. I need to see what direction it's heading. A good gallop will get us out of the path quickly."

"If you're certain, we'll be off."

"I'm certain."

Avery rose with the baby, who had fallen asleep on his daddy's lap. She threw the blanket over the two of them, and he snuggled in against her neck, blissfully unaware of the proceedings. Prentis grabbed all their possessions, gave her a kiss, and headed west toward Hector, Ulysses, and the wagon. Tom followed. All around them people were performing the same storm avoidance tactics. The poor judge kept talking, seemingly unaware of his shrinking audience.

As Avery hurried toward the church, a furious gust of grit and cold air hit her full in the face, almost knocking her back a step. She leaned hard into the wind, hurrying her pace while covering Jack's head with the blanket.

Lifting her countenance, she was surprised to see Mr. Vance holding the door wide, helping the crowd to gain entrance and then directing them toward the basement steps. Clearly, the new reverend hadn't arrived yet from Chicago. His arrival had been discussed by those seated nearby.

"Welcome," he said. "Do you need help with your things?"

"No, thank you. Has the new reverend not arrived?"

"No, his mother is very sick, so Reverend Wallock remained to care for her. Just hurry on down there. You'll be safe underground."

"Thank you."

Down they went into the basement. She remembered doing the same when the patriotic assembly was held in 1915 after the sinking of the *Lusitania*. Floyd had signed a document saying he was willing to be drafted, should the nation go to war. Hattie had been expecting their second child, and Avery had wept alongside her to think of Floyd wanting to go fight.

In that instance, an actual tornado had been barreling down on Wakita. Today it looked like merely dust, and she stood alone hoping and praying that Prentis had gotten the animals to safety. Mary Beth Miller found her in the crowd, and the two of them huddled together praying.

The judge was the last man to make it down the stairs. "It seems you all manage to throw a tornado or dust storm of some sort at me every single time I come to speak." He laughed. "I may have to start rejecting invitations from the city of Wakita."

They all chuckled. A few men pounded him on the back.

Someone said, "We do the best we can for our speakers."

All laughed again as they waited it out.

64

After what seemed an eternity, one of the local men ran down to inform them that it was finally clear to leave the basement. Avery was vastly relieved to find Prentis outside with the wagon and Hector hitched behind, awaiting her appearance. Now Prentis pulled Avery close, kissing the top of her head.

"I'm glad you made it to safety, Sweetheart. The horses and I avoided most of it."

"I'm so glad!" She hugged him about the middle.

Prentis helped them into the wagon, then clicked his tongue to the horses.

"Let's go home," he said. "This has been a long and exhausting day. Don't think I want to see another soul, other than you and Jack, for many days on end."

"But the harvest continues tomorrow."

"Indeed, it does. Somehow, I'll pull myself together and carry on."

Six

AVERY WORK WITH A start—terrified. The entire house shook violently.

What's happening?

Lightning cracked, splitting the night, filling the room with shards of stark brightness. The flashes captured Prentis in mid-motion, freezing his movement from here to there, already on his feet shutting windows. The house shook again as thunder rattled the walls and glass panes. The storm appeared to be directly upon them.

From the other side of the wall, Jack screamed in terror.

Prentis hurtled around the corner and returned, carrying a frightened baby boy clutching tightly about his neck. Avery reached for Jack and put him to her breast. His eyes large with terror, he snuggled in against her, comforted by her milk and her warm embrace.

Again, an enormous thunderclap reverberated. *Boom!*

A crash sounded from the area of the baby's crib. Jack's eyes grew even wider, and Prentis rushed back into the alcove. When he returned, lightning revealed his shocked expression.

"Avery, the ceiling's collapsed!"

"What!"

"A heavy section of plaster broke loose and fell right into Jack's crib."

"If you hadn't brought him, he would have been in that bed!"

"Yes, he would." Prentis nodded.

"He would have been injured!"

"It would appear the good Lord has kept him safe and perhaps spared his life."

Avery burst into tears, prompting Jack to release her breast and join her. Both of them wailed. Prentis settled onto the bed and pulled them into his arms. The storm continued, but the longer they embraced, the fainter the thunder sounded and the slighter the vibrations of the house. Soon only the thrumming of heavy rain remained. Prentis reached to crack a window, and the soft scent of rain-washed earth enveloped the bedroom.

"When I built that partial wall, some of the plaster must have loosened."

"That has to be it," Avery said.

"It's all I can think might have caused that."

"Thanks be to God for sparing our baby! First his conception was a miracle, and now his life has been spared. God must have a special purpose for this boy."

"I agree."

Peace rushed through Avery, warm comfort in God's watchful care. Prentis pulled her near, holding both her and Jack close.

***

A bright ray of daylight shone in from the front-room window, striking Prentis full in the face. He awakened, still propped up with pillows against the headboard. Avery lay heavily upon his chest with her nightgown unlaced, all having fallen asleep clinging to one another after the storm. Jack had let loose her breast and now lay across her lap, his mouth slightly open and his little chest rising and falling with small toddler inhalations.

Prentis loved looking at them. Their morning fragrance wafted subtly on the slight breeze from the open window. Avery's long black hair tumbled about. Their skin appeared flawless and satiny smooth in the soft morning light. Their dusky tones blended subtly with their European ancestry, their darker hues evident in all their flesh. Jack was clearly his boy—hang whatever that woman said! But he was also clearly of non-European origin.

What might trouble a woman so deeply that she would take upon herself the role of gossip and busybody for an entire county? What had happened to her? Where had she become broken? And how had she ended up married to such a kind man as Alf Riley?

Perhaps he would never know the answer, but he had told her that he forgave her. And forgive her, he must. He knew the Bible well enough to know that. The English version of the Lord's Prayer taught him by his Catholic father popped into his mind.

He closed his eyes and silently prayed.

Our Father, Who art in heaven,
Hallowed be Thy Name.
Thy kingdom come; Thy will be done,
On earth as it is in heaven.
Give us this day our daily bread,
And forgive us our trespasses,

As we forgive those who trespass against us.
And lead us not into temptation,
But deliver us from evil. Amen.

There it was—forgive us as we forgive those who trespass against us. There was no way to dodge that, and the principle was also stated elsewhere in the Bible.

Father, help me to forgive. Let me be mindful of my own failings.

Feeling observed, his opened his eyes and found Avery gazing up at him from her recumbent position. Smiling softly, she watched him. He returned her smile.

"It would appear we survived the night," she mouthed, making nary a sound.

"Yes, we did," he whispered back. "And the Lord has granted us a few days alone."

"God is good." She smiled softly at him.

Jack appeared not the least affected by their whispers.

She gestured toward the door with her eyes.

He nodded, and both began the slow-motion ballet of vacating a bed while leaving a sleeping baby lying in it undisturbed. Over the past year, they had perfected the art with such gradual motion that nary a spring squeaked. The last movement of the dance involved Avery's patient extraction of the arm that supported Jack's upper back, which she accomplished with unhurried deliberation. Her last fingertip slid carefully out from under his head, and both froze, evaluating the impact of the removal of human touch.

Jack's breathing never altered, and his eyes remained closed. Oh, so gradually, they turned to tiptoe toward the bedroom door. As they reached the doorway, both stopped again, glancing back. This was usually the spot where he awakened. But Jack lay sprawled out on his back, still blissfully asleep as he now made nursing motions with his mouth.

They looked at one another and smiled. They had done it.

Both crept through the kitchen, down the back steps, and out the back-porch door. Prentis threw down upon the damp concrete a thick towel he'd grabbed as they tiptoed through. Together they sat on the steps, shoulder to shoulder in the cool summer morning, clad in only nightclothes and union suit. Their hillcrest sprouted thick cedar, Osage orange, scrub oak, and sumac that covered the cliff and the house's north side, shielding them from public view.

Sam trotted wagging from the front of the house, and both gave him a good pat and an ear scratch. It was too wet to harvest today. They would have to wait until the fields were dry again, lest all the wagons and machinery sink into the mud. Today God had granted a holiday.

"Now," Avery spoke softly, the open window being near, "tell me all about yesterday."

Prentis started at the beginning. Her scientific mind would want to know every particle of information, as she usually put it, so he detailed the entire day and the procedure. When he finished, she sat silently contemplating his words.

Eventually, she stirred and gazed warmly into his eyes. "Thank you for standing up for us with Mrs. Alfonse Riley. You're the best husband in the world and an exceptionally brave man."

"Only did what was right. A man protects his own."

"You always do what's right, and I'm keenly aware of that fact. Not all men do. You're a rare gift of a husband. Thank you for being yourself."

He leaned in, kissing her forehead. "It's easy when a man has an exceptional wife."

"Well, thank you, but you were already doing right before I came on the scene."

70

"I aim to please God. It doesn't always work out that I do."

"You seldom miss the mark."

He shifted uncomfortably. "You know that's not true, Avery."

"I've poured it on too thick again, haven't I?"

He snorted. "You have. My shy nature is all riled up."

"I'll change the subject." Leaning hard against his shoulder, she conveyed her empathy. "So, Johnny didn't take the exemption. I guess we shouldn't be surprised."

"That's what I thought, given the make of the man."

"We'll have to wait and see what God does, if He allows the lot to be drawn for Johnny. What about Tom?"

"Told me he's communicating with the army about the chaplaincy. He already heard back from Senator Owen."

"We knew he'd respond quickly," she said. "Senator Owen's done such good for the Cherokee and for the state. Hopefully, he'll help secure the vote for women in Oklahoma at least, and maybe eventually in the entire country."

"I'm certain that day will come, Avery."

She smiled at him. "We can hope and pray. What did the senator tell Tom?"

"He replied with full instructions and praise for Tom's decision as a Christian pastor. Tom got right to it—sent the Secretary of War his application, a photograph, and proof of his theological education. I want Tom to tell you. There's more. He'll come over after harvest."

"I'll be interested to know," she said. "He'll still be in harm's way, but I understand his motivation. I think he's right to do it."

Prentis turned and studied her face. There was a courageous set to her shoulders and her chin. As usual, she'd risen to the occasion.

"I have to agree," he said, "though we'll lose him here. Men under fire in trenches need spiritual support more than farmers peacefully growing the food to feed them."

She nodded. "But we'll sorely miss him."

"That we will."

That stark reality hit Prentis hard. It would require them to meld into a larger church in town, one that didn't have their young, progressive, and understanding pastor. All of Prentis's fears pertaining to church rose momentarily to the surface, souring in his throat and clutching at his chest—the family feuds of his extended family, the war of words, the battles that had pummeled him throughout his boyhood and into his youth, the judgment and hypocrisy of church members that niggled at his sense of justice and Christian love, particularly Mrs. Riley's actions. Glad he'd done his own biblical investigation before beginning to attend church with Avery, he quickly reviewed all the reasons believers assembled in church community.

He felt Avery's gaze upon him and turned toward her.

With understanding eyes, she studied his face, then caressed his cheek, rubbing her thumb across his morning stubble, as she was wont to do.

"As I've said before, you're a brave man."

"Don't feel particularly brave about going to a new church, but I'll do my best."

"You always do. I'll be by your side, no matter what."

"I know you will," he said. "But once more, this is between me and God."

"No matter how difficult the battle, He loves you still and remains unchanged."

"That's a reassuring thought."

"Da Da," Jack's soft voice sounded from the open window. His little eyes peered out at them, and his small fingertips grasped the window ledge.

"You're needed inside." Avery laughed. "I'll make us some breakfast."

Prentis smiled. "Jack and I are the best cared for men on the planet."

***

It took three days before their fields dried out. And then, several more days' work were required before harvest was completed. They had good yield, sixteen to eighteen bushels on the remaining acreage. The price was even higher at $2.50 per bushel, more than the new Food Administration had established for the following year and more than twice the amount Prentis had gotten in 1914 when he harvested his first crop on his own farm.

In spite of Mr. Hoover and the government's attempted interference in setting a "fair price," this year had proven profitable. Prentis maintained that because the Lever Act said nothing about the 1917 wheat harvest, all the fuss would amount to nothing, this year at least. The price was good, and since the president had urged farmers to sell at harvest, he was glad to oblige.

Two-thirds of their 160-acre quarter section remained in prairie grass for the livestock. A little less than one-third was planted in wheat with the rest in alfalfa. Prentis cheerfully pocketed $2,295. As usual, he set aside annual expenses in their savings account, reserving the rest for improvements and expansion. They had plenty to operate on for the coming year until the next harvest, and God willing, enough to get them through next year too, should wheat prices plummet now that the Food Administration tinkered with the market.

When he added the sale of the steers, they'd be fine. They could buy that Model T with Avery's savings. He couldn't wait to see the look on her face.

After selling the last load of wheat and depositing his money, he headed home with an empty wagon, bringing a bag of licorice for Avery, a surprise, and all the local news.

"This candy isn't much compared to what I've gotten you in the past."

"There isn't much to choose from in our small town."

"You're right, so I brought this instead."

From inside the parcel, he pulled out a Sears catalog.

Avery grabbed hold of it and squealed with delight. He'd never heard her do that, and he'd known her all his life. Watching her reaction, he laughed for joy, filled clear up with love for her. He lived to make her happy.

With the catalog balanced on her lap, they settled on the front porch, gazing at the goods inside. Jack toddled about on the grassy lawn below the porch steps. All was well.

"Oh," he said, "I almost forgot. We need to talk about that Model T."

She rewarded him with a wide smile.

***

Officials from the US Department of Agriculture later reported that 3.1 million acres had been planted in wheat that year in Oklahoma. They had set a record. The combined hard work of the farmers of Oklahoma would support the war effort.

Simultaneously, reports came in that nationwide 9,586,508 men between the ages of twenty-one and thirty-one had registered at their local draft boards. That gave the government a large pool from which to draw as they prepared the first wave of men for war. But Oklahoma papers reported that though all the men of Wakita had registered, other polling locations had different results. Officials estimated only slightly more than half of the state's men within the required age range had put their names on the line. The response to patriotism and duty had varied statewide.

When Prentis informed Avery, she stated, "We've only been a state for ten years. We're a mix of people. Some of us left behind oppressive governments in Europe. Some are Cherokee who no longer trust the government after they stole our land and drove us westward. Others came west because of inequities dished out by our government. Then there are people who needed a hand up because they couldn't get ahead, and finally there are other native people and tribes corralled on reservations after being crowded out of their land, that land having been promised for all time by the government. Now that same government wants us to fight and perhaps to die. I'm guessing folks are leery of the power the federal government wields when they call to war men whose families have suffered all of this."

"I'm guessing you're right about that."

Her assumption was proven correct when President Wilson's Committee on Public Information flooded the nation, and particularly their state, with encouragement to support the war effort. James Montgomery Flagg's Uncle Sam posters began to appear everywhere, mass-produced for maximum effect. First the parade, and now the posters. After one trip to town, Avery harangued Prentis about propaganda most of the trip home.

"It's not needed here. Wakita's men registered. Do they think the men of Oklahoma are stupid? Do they think our men can be persuaded by bright posters and at-a-boy statements?"

"Apparently, they do," he said.

Other states had established restrictions to assure their male populace registered. In Utah, law officers could demand to see a man's registration certificate at any time. No certificate meant an investigation of that individual. Some states printed the registrants in the local newspapers, using public shaming to motivate. Federally, passports weren't issued to men who couldn't provide the certificate to prove they had registered.

Oklahomans remained distrustful. They talked of it quietly with one another. Even the loyal citizens of Wakita had reservations. But Avery also predicted that when their first boys went, that would all change. They always backed their own.

Seven

THE FOLLOWING WEEK, TOM arrived for their annual farm improvement discussion. After the meal, Jack tottered about the house playing and tugging pots, pans, and books from their stowed locations. Meanwhile, the three adults remained at the table discussing their next moves. When they were done, Avery figured she'd simply return everything Jack had unseated.

"Explain to Avery all you told me about the chaplaincy," Prentis said. "I want her to hear it from you. She'll understand more about it than I did."

"All right." Tom looked hard at Prentis. "If you're sure you don't mind hearing it all again."

"Don't mind at all."

Nodding, Tom faced Avery but turned his eye occasionally toward Prentis as well. "There've been letters back and forth from the college about the need for chaplains. The chaplaincy is a long tradition, as far back as there's been war on this continent. The Chaplain Corps was established in 1775 by the Continental Congress."

"Yes," Avery said, "my Grandpa Slaughter has mentioned what a comfort the chaplains were to soldiers during the Civil War."

Tom agreed. "Having a pastor—which is what a chaplain truly is to a soldier—is as necessary when a soldier's at war as it is when he's safely at home. Probably more so."

"I believe you're right."

"In a combat environment, a chaplain acts as a continual reminder to the soldiers that God is with them. They're not abandoned merely because they're on the other side of the earth trying to do good and being shot at as a result. That alone is trauma enough. But they also need even more pastoral care due to the spiritual damage that accompanies war as well as—"

"By 'spiritual damage,'" Avery said, "I assume you're referring to the dreadful decision to kill another person, even if they're 'bearing the sword' for their own government."

Prentis jumped in. "That's Romans 13, right?"

Tom and Avery both signaled their agreement.

"You're right, Avery," Tom said. "The right to kill for matters of war and justice rests with the state, not the individual. That's why the government can direct the nation to go to war and can also draft the citizens. When the individual soldier picks up his gun to kill another human during war, he's acting on behalf of the government, not as an individual. Still, he's the one who has to pull the trigger, not Uncle Sam. And the pulling of that trigger in war causes a dreadful issue of conscience. That's why there's a category for 'conscientious objectors,' men who want to fulfill their duty in some other way, but morally can't see themselves pulling the trigger."

"Shooting someone would be next to impossible," Prentis said. Avery agreed.

"There's also the horrific nature of war," Tom continued. "We've all read the papers."

They nodded at this.

"We know about the barbaric conditions in No Man's Land. It's enough to cause torment to a man's soul, making him feel that God has abandoned him and mankind. Even to forget that mankind has been sinful since Adam. We can be creative and yet sinister creatures, able to concoct all sorts of agony to inflict on one another. Like crucifixion, for instance. That's why Jesus had to come down here, become one of us, and die a horrific death for us."

"Makes perfect sense to me," Prentis said. "Had to work through a minor version of feeling God had abandoned me when my dad died, and I was out there alone supporting the family."

"That's hardly minor," Avery said softly, placing her hand on his.

"Compared to war it is—barbed wire, corpses littering the battlefield, the constant stench of death, and knowing that any moment you might be rotting out there too."

"Well," she said quietly, "when you put it that way, I see what you mean."

Somberly, Prentis and Tom both nodded.

"Just trying to make a point," Prentis said.

"Your point is taken," she said.

"There's a type of moral injury that comes from that," Tom continued. "They're seeing these horrific sights, they're part of the killing, and they could die at any moment. A man needs a pastor helping to guard his soul as he wades through that quagmire."

"We understand and support your decision, Tom," Prentis said.

"Yes, we do," Avery added. "So, what happens now?"

79

"Well, I've applied. That comes first."

"Prentis informed me where you are in that process."

"D.L. Moody's own son Paul will be General John Pershing's personal chaplain."

"He's truly following in the footsteps of his father."

Tom nodded. "Not only Moody Bible College, but the Baptists as well have been leading out on this, pressing the need to better develop a chaplaincy. Right now, Chaplain Moody is headed over with the expeditionary forces under General Pershing's command. They've set sail from New York City and Hoboken, New Jersey. They may have already arrived. Moody will be organizing the US military chaplaincy. It will be its own branch, rather than under the British chaplaincy or the regular army, though he'll be consulting the British Army Chaplain General for advice. He'll organize as quickly as possible. I've asked to be part of the American Expeditionary Forces, so I can work with him. I'm enlisting as a chaplain. That's why on registration day I didn't take the ministerial exemption. I'll go soon."

Trying to absorb all of that information, they sat in silence. The loss of Tom weighed heavily on Avery, but when she looked at Prentis's face, she knew his loss was of tragic proportions.

Tom had seen the same. He gripped Prentis's shoulder. "You've been the best friend a man could ever have. I'll miss you."

"I feel the same about you," Prentis responded soberly, "even if you *are* a pastor."

Tom burst out laughing.

Before he began attending church, Prentis had frequently said that to Tom, who had been his steadfast friend even then. Avery recalled all the times Tom had helped Prentis on their farm, all while patiently waiting for him to discover what he would do about church. The entire time, Tom had never lectured, shamed, nor treated

Prentis as anything other than a brother and a fellow Christian whom he respected. Tom's pastoral behavior was far different than any other clergymen Prentis had ever encountered, an answer to Avery's many prayers.

"*Tsk.*" Sighing, Avery shook her head. "Men. Why do you turn such touching moments into a good laugh?"

"Can't help ourselves." Prentis tilted back in his chair to grin at her.

"It's a fact," Tom added.

Quietly, she sat, studying them both. Eventually they sobered under her disapproving gaze.

"You know, Tom," she said, returning to the topic at hand, "you've presented us with a terrible dilemma. Now we have to determine where we'll go to church. I don't know that we theologically agree on all points with any of the available choices."

"That rarely happens when choosing a church. Every church is comprised of sinners."

Prentis chuckled. "Amen to that."

"Well, we might as well hammer it out theologically anyway," she said.

At that moment a loud crash sounded from the kitchen. Jack shrieked. Avery jumped up. Hurrying around the counter, she encountered the biggest mess she'd ever seen Jack make. He had systematically emptied every one of the lower cupboards. One of his stacks of baking tins had fallen, the crash startling him. Both men stood behind her, laughing in the doorway.

"Avery, I'll reassemble the kitchen." Prentis picked up Jack. "You two step back in there with your Bible degrees and pick through the theology. I'd have to listen to all sorts of doctrine I can barely comprehend. Let me know your conclusions, and we can tackle farming after that."

"Are you sure?" she asked. "Your opinion is the most important one in my mind."

"Just give me the condensed version later."

"If you're absolutely certain—"
"I am."

***

Enlisting Jack's help, Prentis turned the cleanup process into a game. Together, the two of them put everything back. The baby laughed and clapped each time Prentis praised his efforts.

Prentis stoked the cookstove flame to get the water heated so the dishes could be washed. Before marriage, he'd maintained a fastidious bachelor's home. Cleaning was something he enjoyed far more than Avery did. It had always been this way, ever since they were youngsters.

As he worked, occasionally a word or phrase drifted in from the other room—*predestination, free will, human agency, Arminianism, Calvinism, soteriology.* He heard Martin Luther, John Calvin, Jacobus Arminius, Theodore Beza, and others mentioned, along with Garrett Biblical Institute. He was mighty glad to be in the kitchen, rather than at the table. Later, he'd join them to discuss farming.

***

The upshot of spending the day with Tom was that they now had two big decisions, not just one. They not only needed to choose a new church, but they also had to consider if they could manage Tom's farm while he was away, so he could return to it. Their additional contribution to the war effort would be to keep his farm producing, if his landlord approved. If so, Prentis would have two farms to sow with wheat in the fall, definitely a challenge, but worth it for his friend.

He would also oversee Tom's cows, breeding them with Rex next month, something he and Tom had carried out the previous year as well. Both were careful with their cows, stringent with cleanliness. Neither wanted disease to infect their herds nor cows to slink their calves. They pored over *Dr. Roberts' Practical Home Veterinarian,* discussing disinfectants and practicing his methods for inhibiting disease on their own farms. In short, Prentis trusted his friend. Tom's herd was the only farm, other than his own, where Rex's superior genetics had been spread abroad.

At this moment, Rex was out to pasture with Prentis's own cows, but he'd put the bull in with Tom's cows in July. Though he'd have double duty, Rex could easily get the job done, since the bull was now a little more than four years old.

In recompense for his time, Prentis would profit from the sale of any resulting steers from Tom's stock, but he would put Tom's brand on the heifers, keeping them for his friend's return. The sale of the steers would allow Prentis to purchase any extra feed he might need for the additional livestock, even though he had his own alfalfa and would probably enlarge that field in the fall. Before leaving, Tom would sell his previous year's steers and his horses and would bank the money. Therefore, Prentis wouldn't have any additional horses to feed.

If they were willing to manage his farm, Tom would put the matter before the church to see if the church body would help Prentis harvest his wheat next year. That would be one way the entire congregation could help their pastor keep his rented farm and return to it after the war.

As far as considerations about where to attend church when Tom left, they would have to reach a decision. Avery had told Prentis she needed to think for a few days, so she could consider how to deliver the information. And then, it was going to be entirely up to him, a far more difficult decision than the one about whether to help Tom. That was easy. Of course, they would.

Before that perplexing day of decision arrived, the early members of the First Expeditionary Division—men who had already enlisted before the draft—arrived in France on June 26, 1917. America was officially at war on the European continent, though these soldiers would not be immediately deployed. The rest of their force would continue to arrive behind them.

Everything rushed forward on a timeline determined by war. Every decision and action seemed completely outside the control of their human desires. Personal considerations and challenges didn't necessarily march to that drumbeat but were forced to adjust and to yield, their church decisions included. Even after Avery had detailed the theology, Prentis found this decision particularly challenging, maybe even more so with all the facts.

He needed more time, but the march to war didn't allow it. Tom would soon leave.

The following Sunday, after Prentis had informed Tom that they jointly approved of the discussed farming plan, Tom presented that plan to the church, receiving unanimous support for his brave decision. Though all would miss him sorely, everyone would pitch in to help Prentis with Tom's farm. This left the entire church facing similar decisions about church attendance.

Prentis couldn't decide what to do. Therefore, he focused on the practical considerations of getting Tom himself ready to go to war, a wrenching thought. On Monday, July 2, right in line with the farming plan, Tom showed up bright and early. They intended to move Rex down to Tom's pastures where his cows awaited the arrival of the bull.

After Avery had fortified them with breakfast, the two men headed toward the barn.

"Hector's a good horse, but I'm riding Ulysses today," Prentis said. "The bull's grown."

"That's why I rode my old cow pony. These two are wise old men."

"Hopefully, they can outwit any tricks Rex might throw at us."

Tom laughed. "They handled him just fine last year."

84

"That, they did."

Prentis saddled his horse and then grabbed his lariat off the nail on the barn wall. Ulysses was his tried and true, his favorite horse. Less temperamental than his stallion, Apollo, and more mature than Hector, Ulysses was usually his go-to horse. The mares produced his yearlings for sale. He used them for big jobs that required horseflesh hitched in tandem and also sometimes for pulling and plowing, but he relied on his two geldings for most of his farm work.

Leading Ulysses into the barnyard, he found Tom ready to go. Prentis bit his lower lip, letting loose the short quick whistle he used with Sam when they had cattle to move. Like a shot, Sam came barreling around from the front of the house, his tongue lolling in a doggish grin. Before mounting up, Prentis gave Sam a scratch behind the ears.

"Let's go, you good ol' dog. Let's see what you've still got in you."

Tom chuckled. "How old is Sam now?"

"At least fifteen. Maybe sixteen. Can't recall exactly which year I got him."

Both men guided their horses toward Rex's pen. The bull had been resting for less than two weeks, but Tom had fewer cows, and his cows were in season, so Rex needed to get back to work. Prentis would have preferred a longer rest for his bull, but Tom had to get out of town. This blasted war demanded it. A farmer had to adapt his farming plan to pressing circumstances.

On Ulysses, Prentis waited outside the pen, while Tom circled in on his horse, getting between Rex and the back fence. When Prentis gave a short whistle, Sam barked at Rex's heels, circling, harassing, and making a racket to get the bull moving. Languid in movement, not one to be hurried, Rex strolled casually out of the pen and toward Prentis, ignoring the dog's frenzied efforts, yet still in motion.

Tom rode in behind the bull, blocking his way back should he change his mind. Matching Rex's pace, Prentis turned Ulysses's head to the east, walking him toward the road. They promenaded past the front door where Avery stood with Jack on the porch, watching their procession of men, horses, bull, and dog.

Prentis smiled and raised his hat. The two smiled back at him. Jack spoke and reached toward him, but Prentis couldn't hear him over Sam's barking. So, he waved at his son.

They left the farmyard and headed west up the road. Prentis clicked his tongue, and Ulysses increased his pace to a trot. Sam barked non-stop, running back and forth behind Rex, prodding him into faster motion, while Tom's pace also pressed the bull forward at a nice even trot. When they arrived at the turn toward the south, Rex decided not to cooperate. He didn't follow Prentis around the corner but continued on westward.

Prentis wheeled Ulysses around, hurrying to head off Rex and turn him to the south. After repeated attempts at getting past Ulysses's stubborn blocking resistance and with Sam's barking presence every time the bull tried to move farther west, Rex finally turned back. Tom's cow pony blocked the way back toward the house, giving the bull only one option—southward. Yet, still Rex stood, as if considering his options.

Prentis tossed a lasso over Rex's head, and Ulysses stepped back, pulling the rope taut. The bull snorted an annoyed blast out his nostrils, tossing his head about.

"Giddy up, you bull," Prentis admonished. "Get!"

A sharp whistle from Prentis sent Sam back into action, making every destination but the one toward the south unwelcome. Rex resumed movement, nice and slow again, showing his resistance through his lack of speed.

With repeated effort, they eventually got him up to a trot once more. All was well for the next couple miles. Then they passed a neighbor's field with cows out to pasture. Rex veered toward the female of his species and into the ditch, running headlong into the barbed wire. In frustration, he stopped, snorting and stamping at this inconvenience blocking his way. They tried everything to get him going again. Nothing worked.

"We're close," Tom said. "What say I lasso one of my cows and bring her out?"

"Yep, do that. Better to entice him than to anger him."

"Never know what a bull might do."

"Even one you've known a long while," Prentis agreed. "He weighs at least eighteen hundred pounds, I reckon. Gotta respect that. Go get that cow."

Ulysses stepped back, tightening the lariat again.

"Sit!" Prentis called to Sam.

Horse, dog, and man all waited patiently, letting the bull cool down.

Eventually, Tom returned with a cow in tow.

Rex's nostrils flared. After getting a strong whiff of cow in standing heat, he headed toward greener pastures. Tom circled around, taking the cow with him back toward his farm, followed by the bull and Prentis riding Ulysses. The rest was smooth and easy. Sam trotted alongside in case he was needed. Tom swung wide the gate, and in went the cow followed by Rex, eager to do his job, the cow more than willing to cooperate.

"Cup of coffee before you head back?" Tom called.

"I'm always up for coffee, especially if it's nice and black."

"Only way to drink it."

As soon as they stepped inside, Prentis caught the slightly singed aroma of this morning's brew. He smiled. Clearly, Tom had left his breakfast coffee on the back of his warm cookstove. They grabbed cups and poured from

87

the stovetop percolator, then sat on Tom's back porch nursing the strong brew.

"It's nice and thick," Prentis said.

"Just the way you like it."

"It's got more staying power this way."

Chuckling, Tom nodded. "Indeed, it does."

Both took a long sip, savoring the invigorating fortification.

"When do you want to get your horses to market?" Prentis said.

"How 'bout next week? I'm getting all my personal papers in order and my theological library boxed up, in case it needs to be transported or shipped should I . . . well, you know . . . should I not return. Once that's in order, I'll be ready to sell my horses and the steers. You or my dad will have to sell what's left, if I don't make it back."

"We're counting on you coming home. But I don't think a man gets to make that call."

"No," Tom agreed. "As with so many things in life, we only *think* we're in control."

"Seems to me that life is mostly about learning that very lesson."

"I agree. The sooner we let go and trust God, the easier it is on us."

Prentis glanced at him. "Unfortunately, the letting go part seems to be a lifelong challenge."

"Yes. That's a lesson we take a lifetime to even begin to comprehend. And then, I've seen that final death struggle. We don't learn it truly until then."

Prentis's memory flashed back to his father's final moments as he gasped for breath, fighting and clawing to hold onto life while his heart betrayed him, failing and giving out far too soon. His father had not wanted to die. It had been a terrible struggle as they all stood round him weeping while Mother clutched his hand, tears flowing

88

down her cheeks. She begged him to stay, but he could not, no matter how tightly he tried to hold on. Finally, the fight went out of his eyes as the priest intoned the last rites. And then, his father had slipped away.

The mere memory of it felt as though it had torn a gaping hole right through his chest. Prentis had to glance down to verify that he was still whole. Surprisingly, he was.

"It's a mighty difficult lesson," he said softly.

"Indeed, it is."

***

On America's Independence Day—a day that had arrived due to the help of the French in the Revolutionary War—the United States 2nd Battalion, 16th Infantry, paraded through the streets of Paris. It seemed to put the heart back into the French people. Help had arrived! France had helped America, and now America was helping France. At Lafayette's tomb, Captain C. E. Stanton stepped forward to announce, "Lafayette, we are here!"

It was official. America was now engaged in the war.

Under the command of General John J. Pershing, the first group of fourteen thousand men of the American Expeditionary Forces prepared for whatever lie ahead. The Medford *Patriot-Star* informed the citizens of Grant County that Marines were being trained within earshot of the cannonade to accustom them to the sound of fighting. Having insisted that American soldiers be well-trained before heading for Europe, General Pershing had no intention of rushing that training, neither in America where the rest of his troops prepared, nor among his soldiers once they arrived in Europe. The general would not cave to pressure from the British to insert his men immediately into Allied fighting units.

Expressing the British opinion, Sir William Robertson stated that the sooner some Americans were killed, the sooner the entire country would take a real interest in the war. Unmoved, Pershing resisted. He would not yet allow American forces to fill gaps left in the French and British armies due to the horrific loss of life they'd already encountered. With President Wilson's backing, General Pershing withstood all pressure. American doughboys would be properly trained, and then, when ready, they would fight. This was the general's primary concern, not British sentiment.

Looking up from the paper, Avery informed Prentis that she loved General Pershing for his decision to stand up to Allied pressure. Prentis felt the same. The fact that Pershing kept his own men first reinforced the trust they all placed in the general.

Meanwhile, softening the blow, America extended vast amounts of financial credit to Britain, France, and Italy. And so, of course, Congress raised the income tax on all Americans so the war could be financed. When they heard about that decision after the fact, it provoked a rant from Avery.

"Well, this is business as usual," Avery said. "They're going to bleed us dry."

"Unfortunately," Prentis stated drily, "manufacturers don't give away tanks and guns. They're not free for the taking."

"This war should never have started in the first place. Then we wouldn't need those items."

"Nevertheless, we're stuck with it. This being the human race, we shouldn't be surprised."

"Nothing surprises me nowadays."

"I'm fairly certain we can trace this war all the way back to Cain and Abel."

Avery sighed. "And to their parents."

The government also introduced something called "liberty bonds" to finance the products and raw materials needed by the Allied governments. The propaganda heated up as the government encouraged the general populace to purchase the bonds. That prompted Avery to dissect the assumptions hidden behind each poster, song, and appeal to the populace.

Her attitude reminded Prentis of how quarrelsome and cantankerous she had been before they discovered she was pregnant with Jack. Some sort of emotional upheaval was at work. He wondered if another baby might be on the way, but he kept that thought to himself.

By mid-July General Pershing had made an announcement requesting one million men. Avery read the news item to Prentis and then stopped, the newspaper falling onto her lap as she stared off into the distance.

"A million men," she whispered.

"Millions have already been lost," he said. "That's why they need our help."

"Yes, but these are *our* million."

Somberly, they stared at one another, reflecting on that fact.

A mere nine days later, it was telegraphed that the general had upped his request to three million. The thought was astonishing. Three million American men would be needed to untangle the mess the Europeans had made because a Serbian zealot shot an archduke and his wife in cold blood. In three short years, the Europeans had destroyed an entire continent.

Avery read the paper, laid it down, and walked right out of the room. Prentis scooped up Jack, trailing after her out the back door.

"Don't follow me," she said quietly, her voice shaking. "I don't want to scare the baby."

Prentis stopped, stock still with Jack in his arms. With somber expressions, they watched her disappear across the back lawn, heading toward the creek. She circled round through the field and then vanished behind the trees. Later, Prentis heard the wail of her cry carried softly in broken pieces upon the breeze and over the bluff.

Jack continued to play with Sam, not noticing her cry.

But Prentis heard it, and he felt it to the core. This was too much to be borne for a war that had nothing to do with them and that didn't occur on their own soil.

**

After wiring in their list of names, all the polling sites sent their registration cards to the county seat. The district board situated in Medford was responsible not only for registering the men, but also for making all future decisions about whether or not each individual man would be called into duty.

Because these decisions were made locally, the draft board was able to consider which men needed to remain on their farms, whether they had taken the exemption or not. The board could evaluate specific family situations, such as death or illness in the family. They would handle all appeals and determine the physical fitness of the men who had registered. And then, they would call them into duty and place them on trains, sending them off to training centers.

With hoopla, glitzy society women in ball gowns, and military precision, the draft lottery began July 20, 1917, at 10:00 a.m. and ended in the wee hours of the morning the next day. In the Senate office building, capsules containing numbers were drawn from a great glass bowl, and the numbers chosen were recorded. This determined the order in which men would be called up from their various registration locations.

By the time the first lottery was complete, 1,374,000 men had been chosen, taken from the head of the liability list, every local district having supplied a fixed quota.

They deliberately chose twice the number needed. A list of the numbers selected was then mailed to each district.

Decisions had to be made by the local boards. After the boards had considered each man individually, applying exemptions and individual hardship situations, and sometimes granting exemptions when none had been taken, 687,000 men were selected nationwide for training and transport to Europe. Each man who had been chosen was informed.

On July 24, five hundred names were listed in the *Medford Patriot-Star* in the order in which they would be called into duty. Prentis brought in the mail and handed Avery the paper, pointing at the list. Her eyes moved to where he indicated, and then she read, commenting as she did. Prentis was safe, and so was John for now. She was relieved to find no Slaughters at all.

But Joe Pitzer was not safe. She read his name out loud and stopped, looking up at Prentis. He recalled Pitzer's night of drinking and the resultant bloodshot eyes on registration day. It was almost as if he had already known his life was in peril.

"Hattie and her mother will take that hard," Avery said.

"All of them will."

"All of *us* will."

A furrow formed between her eyes as she focused inwardly. Frowning, she sighed and then moved on down the paper. Prentis watched her eyes. He knew what she was looking at now and braced himself. Featured on that same page was a large advertisement for a seven-reel film about an item of interest to Avery—*Prohibition*, featuring a "heartrending story caused by whiskey."

Since the president's establishment of the Food Administration, restrictions on the use of wheat and other grains for the production of whiskey were being discussed under the guidelines of the Lever Act. Both he and Tom had heard increasing talk about this topic.

Avery looked up at him. "I hope and pray Oklahoma simply outlaws hard drink altogether."

"I know how harmful alcohol has been in your family, Avery." He pinned her with his eyes. "But I doubt that will ever happen."

"The damage to families is simply too much when added to this war."

"Regardless of what you and I think, too many people rely on their alcohol. Especially during a time of war."

He detected an argument coming his direction, but then she veered away—he saw it clear as day on her face. She shrugged and returned to the news, avoiding an exchange of words, a response he found unusual. She usually pressed her point.

A week later, on Monday, July 31, the *Medford Patriot-Star* spelled out the details for the first two hundred fifty men called. Pitzer was again among them. Claims for exemption could be made until Tuesday night, August 7, and all had to be in writing. After that, the paper stated, it was too late. The examinations for fitness were scheduled, with all the names listed for their specific days on Monday, Tuesday, and Wednesday of the following week.

Of the first one hundred called, only forty were moved forward for military service—Pitzer still among them. More names were drawn and listed, so they could obtain their quota. By August 7, they were still drawing, listing, examining, and rejecting. The first list of men rejected was posted, with no reasons listed. In all, Grant County was to process and send 572 men for this first draft, close to 10 percent of their young men of draft age. By the next week, the men had been chosen, notified, and publicized. It looked like Pitzer might be their first friend to go.

At that point, a rebellion erupted in Seminole County and surrounding counties in the center of Oklahoma. A group seized control of many local offices and buildings and organized an uprising. They intended to travel to Washington D.C. and force the federal government to end their war policy. Of course, local authorities quickly quelled what was named the Green Corn Rebellion. Once again, Prentis and Avery were aware that the patriotism found in their own county obviously didn't exist all over the state.

In the middle of all of that movement of young men, the US Food Administration finally decided to set a price for the year's wheat at $2.20 a bushel. When Prentis read that in the paper, he grinned. He had been right to sell before the government settled their price. He knew some farmers who had made even more money than he had. They'd all cleared quite a profit, and yet it might not occur next year, since the price was now set. He read further down that the Lever Act had actually banned the production of "distilled spirits" from any produce that was used for food. Avery would be pleased. But, how would the government's decision play out?

A few days later, a letter arrived from Prentis's cousin, Charles Pinkerton, informing them that their process in Kingman County, Kansas, was complete, and that he had been selected. The same week, Tom received his official notification that he could enter the army as a chaplain.

In just a few weeks, everything in their simple rural world had changed. The war rolled over them, enfolding them into the inevitable movement toward a great darkness looming on the horizon. That threat had driven some of their fellow Oklahoma residents to violence and insurrection. Good men were being whisked away— Prentis's cousin, his pastor and dearest friend, and his former romantic rival for Avery's affection, but now his friend.

No longer did they have control over their own destinies or vocations. It was out of their hands, yet another test of their trust in a sovereign and good God. Prentis was familiar with this test, but the test was difficult and unwieldy each and every time.

Eight

THE CLINESMITH MOTOR COMPANY had a 1913 Model T—the same model Avery's father had chosen the year Prentis started their courtship. One of the wealthier citizens of Wakita, Mr. C.E. Wetmore, had traded it in for a shiny new Buick. That trade gave Prentis and Avery the opportunity to buy an automobile that was only four years old at a lower price than they would have paid new. By the time Prentis was done negotiating, they had paid a mere $175. Bargaining for automobiles, it turned out, required the same strategies as purchasing livestock, a task at which he excelled. That left a small amount still in Avery's schoolteacher savings.

Prentis stepped to the front of their new automobile and awaited her cue, peering through the glass windshield as she completed the driver's tasks inside the auto. When she was ready, she nodded, and he pulled out the choke ring. Then he looked at her, and their eyes met.

"Avery, do you have the control lever all the way to the top?" he called.

Her father had ingrained that habit in all of them, lest anyone helping the driver end up with a broken arm should that step be neglected.

"Yes, I do," she said, nodding.

Holding the choke ring, he turned the starting crank twice, then stopped at the top. He then let go of the choke ring and turned the crank two more times.

"Ready, Avery." Prentis made eye contact again.

She made her adjustment inside, then looking at him, nodded again. Prentis pulled up the starting crank one more time, and the engine fired.

***

As Avery moved the power switch from battery to magneto, Prentis stepped back around to the passenger door to join her. Turning the mixture control the tiniest bit counterclockwise, she adjusted the fuel mix, easing off on the fuel. Now she pressed her boot hard on the brake.

Leaning toward Prentis, she gave him a quick kiss. He grinned as he met her eyes.

Then she adjusted the spark and the gas as she slowly eased off her brake foot and released the handbrake. Off they went, smooth as could be. Her year of driving her parents' Model T was still with her. They headed south out of Wakita and toward home. Avery laughed exuberantly as a few stray hairs whipped about her face in the breeze. Prentis smiled back at her, clearly delighted to see her so happy.

Avery had secured her hat with not one, but two hatpins stuck firmly through her coiffed hairdo. Battening everything down firmly, she had chosen a broad ribbon to tie securely under her chin. Everything was secure, and she couldn't quit smiling. The war was briefly set aside as they bounced along the rutted road homeward in their new Model T.

Long ago, when they were courting, her daddy had taught Prentis how to start the automobile. Now, as they rounded the corner by the cemetery and headed west, Avery explained all the particulars of how to drive the Model T. Prentis held Jack, watching her every move.

Getting lost in her thoughts, Avery planned a kind of harness to keep the baby in one place. Her mind was occupied with its design and with the newfound freedom the car would provide.

"Haven't seen you smile like this for too long, Avery."

She glanced over at him. "Really? But I've been so happy."

"I've noticed a change. You haven't been able to do much gallivanting since we got married. Not near as much as you did when you were a teacher."

"Well, that's probably true." She shot him a quick hard look. "But I've been perfectly content these nearly three years we've been married. I smile quite a bit, at least I thought I did."

"You do. But you're showing a spark I haven't seen for a while. Reminds me of when you went to church for the first time down here. You came bouncing home, practically bursting with joy as you told me they needed a Sunday School teacher."

"You're right, now that I think of it. How do you know me so well?"

"You've been the object of serious contemplation for most of my life."

His declaration brought such lovely warmth to her insides, she couldn't resist grinning. "I was incandescently happy on our wedding day and when Jack was born."

"Yes, you were. But your love, womanhood, and motherhood were all wrapped up in those smiles. You were transformed. This smile is different."

"What's so different about it?"

"Fun."

"What about after the tornado, when you chased me down all covered in mud?"

Now he grinned. "One of the best days of my life."

"You have to agree, I smiled then."

"Oh, yes," he said. "You certainly did."

They gazed at one another, remembering that time of new marriage before Jack arrived.

"I'd kiss you right now," he said, "but you've got to drive this car. That's one reason I still maintain the buggy is a better form of transportation. A man can kiss the woman he loves and drive a buggy simultaneously."

She laughed out loud.

He joined her. "We've proven that time and time again. But you're right. That muddy night there was plenty to smile about for sheer enjoyment. We had to get this Model T, so you would have that type of pleasure more often."

"You're the best husband in the world."

"Thank you. But I doubt it."

They now coasted up their drive and toward the barn. Avery glanced over to discover that Jack had fallen asleep. They'd lost track of time, and it was his nap time. She caught Prentis's eye and raised her eyebrow, tilting her head toward the baby.

He peeked down at him. Then he beamed at her.

"Do you think it's humanly possible to get this baby into his bed without waking him?" He spoke soft and low.

She glanced at him, and he looked back with a twinkle in his eye.

"We can always try," she whispered.

"Wouldn't mind stealing a few kisses from you in the middle of the day."

***

At first light, Avery stood on the front porch wrapped in a light shawl. A thick morning mist hung low behind the barn where fog rose from the creek bottom, giving an ethereal appearance to the field beyond. Shimmering in great glistening drops, dew lay heavy on the grass and the vibrant multi-colored zinnias blooming 'round the front porch. The recent moisture made for a wet and glorious morning, the promise of a humid late August day.

Along the edges of the drive, Tom's steers and horses tugged at nibbles of grass and drank from the stock tank. It was sale day up in Anthony on that Tuesday, August 21, an unusual time to be selling. However, Tom wouldn't be the only young farmer getting rid of livestock before heading to war. Others would know the young men were forced to sell, therefore, the bidding would likely be low. Still, they hoped Tom's stock merited good prices.

Both men saddled up, ready to head out.

Prentis leaned down from Ulysses, giving Avery a kiss, his lips warm. Hector stood beside him, led by halter. They would leave both geldings at the Wakita livery—their ride home at the end of the day. Tom sat on his favorite horse, taking one last ride.

"Be good while we're gone." Prentis winked at her, straightening from their kiss.

"I'll do my best." She laughed. "I usually get into all sorts of trouble, you know."

Both men chuckled, for that was the exact opposite of the truth.

Shielding her eyes from the piercing rays of morning sunlight low on the horizon, Avery peered up at Tom.

"I hope your offers are good, Tom. I'll be praying as you say goodbye to your horses."

"It's going to be a tough day," he said. "Have to admit it."

"Difficult day for us too," Prentis added. "Hate to see you go, but know you have to."

Somber now, both men reseated their hats, adjusting the rims to ride low as they drove Tom's cattle eastward, right into the sunrise. Prentis whistled for Sam. With two cow ponies and a cow dog working them toward the road, the livestock cooperated. Sam's incessant barking propelled them forward, moving in synchronized harmony. Ten steers and four horses now ambled along, gradually picking up the pace.

Clutching at her breaking heart, Avery watched their progress. Imagining how Prentis and Tom must be feeling, she begged God to help them today. Once they'd disappeared over the rise, she headed toward the barn to milk Artemis in the cool quiet of the morning.

With her head pressed against the milk cow's warm flank and her hands engaged in stripping its udder, Avery let her mind wander. The fresh milk's odor nauseated her today. Recently, this had crept up on her, coming and going. That seemed odd.

Wondering if the men had gotten to town yet prompted another stab of heartache. How would they function without Tom? She really had no idea. His loss and so many jolting changes brought tears to her eyes.

She'd been weepier than usual and felt a bit crampy. Her women's times hadn't returned since Jack's birth. Maybe her body was gearing up again. That might explain her recent emotions. It seemed she was always either crying or irritated. She attempted to hide her emotional turmoil under a pleasant expression, but recently, Prentis's eye had been fixed on her, watching her with concern. She wasn't succeeding at her ruse.

Slapping Artemis on the flank, Avery stood, signaling that she was done. The cow swung its head back to look

102

at her, placidly chewing a mouthful of hay. Avery chuckled.

"Thank you," she told the cow. "Now off you go."

Avery threw wide the stall gate for Artemis to head to pasture. She lifted the pail and trudged toward the house, her opposite arm held wide for balance. On the back porch, she covered the pail with cheesecloth.

Prentis was such a fastidious farmer that pasteurization wasn't a concern on their farm. They had only one milk cow, and their livestock never had tuberculosis, typhoid, or any other ailments, as had occurred a few years back in the big cities on the east coast. Many people had taken ill in those cities, so the milk there now had to be pasteurized. On their farm, however, whatever Artemis produced, they used fresh, preserved, or sold to the general store.

Pausing a moment at the bottom of the kitchen stairs, Avery listened. Had Jack awakened? Softly from his alcove bedroom, infant babble sounded. He was talking to himself. She smiled.

Carefully, she stepped down into the cellar with the full milk pail, heading for the northeast corner. It was always coolest back in that area. She settled the pail there to give the cream time to separate. Once the cream had risen, she'd skim it off to make butter. Then she'd dump the skimmed milk into the gleaming silver can for Prentis to transport to town to be made into cheese. He'd also take along their butter to sell, since they had plenty in the icebox.

The cheese and the butter sales were her contribution to their farming industry. She peeked at yesterday's milk in the can and lifted the cloth to examine her cheese. All looked well. Time to get Jack. He would help her gather the eggs.

"Jack," she called. "Momma's coming."

In reply, the crib squeaked with his excited bouncing. She smiled. The baby brightened an otherwise melancholy day of loss and uncertainty.

***

Prentis spent the rest of August reading the conscription news, watching Avery can tomatoes, and disking the soil to prepare for wheat planting next month. The weather had grown hot as Hades, causing work to be difficult. Scorching winds from the south had blown in, removing the earlier traces of plentiful rain and making every task even more trying. Gritty dirt blew down their necks and striped their sweaty skin with filth embedded in every single body crease. Prentis often spied dust whirlwinds in the distance, shimmering on the horizon.

Additionally, looming over them was the departure of so many men for the war, a dust storm of its own kind, dirtying them all, leaving everyone undone. Every week they scanned the paper to see who had made it through the investigative process and when the first batch of men would leave. The men had gone through exemption appeals—not even newlyweds were exempt—and thorough examinations. And now, it was time for them to depart.

***

On August 26, Tom stood before the congregation—his final Sunday. Until that moment, Prentis had resisted acknowledging that Tom would actually leave them. Oh, he knew it logically and rationally—they'd sold Tom's livestock, but it wasn't real until now, his final day in church. The opening songs had been sung, the Apostles' Creed repeated, and now they all awaited his last sermon until he returned. Gripping the pulpit, Tom scanned the room, as if feasting his eyes on their familiar faces.

Finally, his eyes stopped and rested upon their small family, smiling back at them.

Jack had dropped off to sleep and now slumped, warm and relaxed upon Prentis's shoulder. Avery's slender hand slid into his. Clearly, she felt as he did. They both needed fortification as they listened to their pastor and friend for the last time. They would pray for his safe return. As Avery laced her fingers through his, Prentis squeezed her hand, leaning his shoulder against hers.

"It's a true blessing to have served this body of believers," Tom began. "You have all exemplified true Christian community. We're not perfect, but we have been a body of people who love one another, not simply in words, but with our actions. When there is a need, this congregation steps up and meets it. When help is required, we all pick up our tools and get to work. The character and integrity of this congregation has been one of unity, mission, and true love, one to the other. I will miss my fellowship with you all acutely.

"But, our nation is now at war. Our boys are bearing the brunt. Young men from our community are heading off to fight. Men at war need a pastor, a source of encouragement in difficult situations, a light that gives hope in times of great darkness. For that reason, and because of God's call to help with that need, I now find myself leaving this dear fellowship and heading off to war. In going, I feel as though I'm furthering the mission of this church body. As all of you have done, I will be helping in the best way I know how.

"I'm to travel directly to France, where I will join Chaplain Paul Moody as he organizes a military chaplaincy in Europe under the authority of General John J. Pershing, a general who has exhibited determination to care for the physical and the spiritual needs of the men under his charge. Because of his policies, our men are

105

now training in France, and they will continue to train until they're ready to fight.

"There I will receive the rudimentary basic training required to keep myself safe in a theater of war. But I don't go to war to be kept safe. I go to war to serve. I intend to stay as close to the front as I'm able, in the trenches with the men, helping them as thoroughly as I can in the difficult circumstances of the Western Front. My concern will not be for my safety but for the welfare of the congregation of men under my care there. Our boys will be my greatest commitment and responsibility. I will serve Christ with all my heart in this.

"How I hope to come back to you when this war is over! Prentis and Avery Pinkerton have helped a great deal to make it possible for me to return to my home after the war. That is my plan, unless God deems otherwise. I'm grateful to you all for the assistance you've promised with next year's harvest and with any other situation Prentis comes across as he administers my affairs, and I'm grateful to the Pinkertons, as they've lightened my load while I've been preparing my goods and papers for my departure."

Avery seemed not to breathe as Tom said this. Prentis squeezed her hand again, and she cast him a quick glance before fixing her eyes again on Tom.

"There's talk of a chaplaincy school soon to be organized, at the soonest in early to mid-1918. But I'm needed now. On Tuesday, I'll head out for Fort Jay on Governor's Island in New York. I'll be commissioned there before boarding a ship with our regular army troops being transported to France. I'll work alongside Chaplain Paul Moody in his endeavor.

"Having attended Moody Bible Institute in Chicago and completed ministry at Pacific Garden Mission, I feel the Lord has prepared me for this ministry to men in life's hardest places. I lost my wife and child during my ministry there, yet another experience God has allowed to prepare me to serve our young men in one of the hardest places of all. War wasn't what any of us sought. We didn't want this situation, as none of us ever do want the trials that God allows to cross our paths, casting shadows across the sunshine. But, nevertheless, I know from my own experience, that our Savior is with us and He is dear, especially in the dark places when the shadows come. Now that you know my heart and my plans, let's turn to our text for the day."

Prentis couldn't focus on the text as he pondered the words of his best friend. He was proud of the man, honored to have called Tom his pastor. He looked forward to his return and planned to pray every single day for his safety and his homecoming.

THE SHADOWS COME

Nine

PRENTIS AND AVERY HAD both collapsed into their chairs in the living room, too tired from the week's labor, the events at church, and a final bit of work they'd helped Tom complete. It was difficult to function. But, food for a mid-afternoon meal was cooking, and all was ready for Prentis's cousin, coming down to tell them goodbye before he headed off to basic training.

Outside, Sam's barking was followed by the sounds of a horse clopping into their farmyard.

"P.J.," a voice hailed them from the yard. "Call off Sam!"

Their guest had arrived. Both rose and stepped outside. One word from Prentis and Sam sat quietly as instructed.

Avery had known Charles all her life, since her family had also moved here from Kingman. Their lives intersected occasionally, and, of course, he had been at their wedding reception.

108

Charles was tall like Prentis, but of medium build. His thatch of thick black hair didn't cooperate, even with pomade, and Prentis had a similar thatch in dark brown. Charles was also a farmer. In fact, he now rented the family farm where Prentis had grown up near Cleveland, Kansas, taking it over since Fred had decided he didn't want to spend his life farming.

Avery had prepared two roasted chickens, garden vegetables, and a peach pie for supper. She figured Charles would be as capable of putting away a huge quantity of food as Prentis had been when he was a bachelor. Charles walked in and grinned as he inhaled the aroma. Her suspicions were confirmed. The man was hungry.

"Well, praise Jesus, Joseph, and Mary!" Charles said. "Avery, the smell of that food is just like heaven. Should have convinced some woman to marry me by now, then I would've had delicious food to eat and a wartime exemption. Wouldn't be headin' off to Camp Funston and then to the other side of the world to fight a war I know nothin' about."

"Life doesn't seem fair at times, does it?" she responded.

"Nope. But then, maybe I'm better off. Not everyone's as lucky as P.J. It could've turned out for me like it did for poor Alf Riley."

"Alf Riley?" Avery said. "You know Alf Riley?"

"Why sure," Charles said. "I've known of him my whole life. The old timers say that back in the days before the Land Run, he lived east of Kingman, halfway to Wichita at Garden Plain. Just a spot on a dusty road back then, not many people livin' there. Don't know if it even had a name then—wasn't incorporated as a town until about fifteen years ago."

Avery glanced at Prentis to see if he knew that. He raised his eyebrows, then shrugged.

"Let's sit down and eat," Avery said, "and you can tell us all about it."

"Sounds perfect to me." Grinning, Charles stepped toward the table. "I'm starved."

She chuckled. "Prentis always was too when he was a bachelor."

Bustling around, Avery brought in all the food she'd prepared, serving each as much as their plates could hold, then giving smaller portions to herself and Jack. Since the table was small, she set the serving dishes on their living room's now cold potbellied stove so she could retrieve them as needed. Once all were settled, Prentis said grace, and the men tucked into their food.

"Carry on, Charles," Prentis said. "We're well acquainted with Alf and his wife."

"Well, let's see." Charles got a faraway look. "Where to start? Hmm. All of this is from my dad. When he was my age, Alf was a successful businessman in Wichita—"

"Alf Riley?" Avery said.

"Yes, indeed. He was a different man then."

"I'll say," Prentis added.

"His business kept him busy," Charles continued. "He was an important man. It was a long time ago, so I'm not sure what kind of business he owned. But it had many locations, and he was Mr. Alfonse Riley then. He traveled from one place to the next, and Garden Plain was right in the middle. As a result of all those responsibilities and the fact that he kept his home in Garden Plain, rather than in Wichita or Kingman, he'd gotten out of the habit of goin' to church. The man had been raised in a good Christian family, but church simply became less important to him. He was always runnin' back and forth from Wichita to Kingman and around the area, and he let churchgoing get crowded out. It was at that time that Miss Eliza Brown moved to Kingman."

"Miss Eliza Brown?" Prentis said.

"That's Mrs. Riley's given name."

Prentis glanced at Avery, from his expression, as intrigued as she.

Charles continued, "Well, Miss Eliza Brown had a college education and was hired to be a schoolteacher. Mr. Riley was a patron of her school—he donated for school projects, and they became acquainted. Seems she set her cap on him. Her pursuit was pretty obvious to all."

"But," Avery interrupted, "he didn't attend church."

"No, he did not," Charles said. "But he was a church member, so his lack of attendance didn't seem to bother her. Long story short, she snagged him. They traveled back east somewhere for a big society wedding. Soon after their fancy honeymoon, they came back to Garden Plain, and Alf Riley lost all his money. His business went under. Seems he'd been involved in speculation. Somehow, he'd gotten in way over his head. Don't really know the particulars—not a businessman myself. But I do know that selling all their goods and livin' in reduced circumstances didn't agree with Eliza Riley, and she like to nagged poor Alf to death, even in public.

"You'd have thought that woulda turned him mean. He was used to bein' in charge. But instead, all that had happened to him—including that woman's nagging—humbled him in a good way. Whereas, Eliza . . . Well, it wasn't the same story. All over the county she talked, sayin' 'I should've known God wouldn't bless him. He wasn't attending church. It was a sign. I shouldn't have married him. I married the wrong man.' That sort of ugly thing. She seemed to think she was a cut above him. I've always felt real sorry for Alf after all he's had to live through with that woman. All of us do. He was and still is a good man."

"As I was growing up in Gibbon," Avery said, "he was one of the kindest men I knew."

Prentis nodded his agreement.

"When the land opened up down here," Charles continued, "they made the Land Run, so they could start over again. That's how they ended up livin' near your family, Avery, rather than stayin' in Kansas. Whenever a manipulative girl hoodwinked any of us Pinkerton boys, my dad would always tell us to watch out or we'd end up like poor Alf Riley. He still says it. That's probably the only reason I remember the story."

"Now that you tell it," Prentis said, "I remember your dad saying that when I was up to your place. I never knew what he meant."

"Well, now you do. Definitely teaches a man to take care when approaching the female of the species. It's a sad tale."

"A cautionary tale, more like," Avery said. "Thank you, Charles, for sharing those events. It gives us quite a bit to think about."

Talk between the two men turned to Pinkerton family matters—what this cousin and that uncle were up to now, how business at the livery stable fared since the surge of the automobile, and how the home farm near Cleveland was producing.

Jack had taken to Charles and crawled right up onto his lap. Charles played with Jack and seemed to find him delightful. He would be a wonderful father one day, whenever he found that good woman. Avery hoped he would and prayed this war wouldn't rob him of his life.

Knowing that Charles and Prentis would enjoy one another's company, she had earlier suggested that Prentis show him around the farm, so they could talk comfortably. Not long after the pie had been consumed, they headed out to the barn. Quite a bit of time passed before they reappeared, and Avery stepped outside to join them.

Prentis shook Charles's hand. "We'll be praying for you while you're under fire."

"That means a lot to me. Don't forget to say the rosary."

"I'm not a Catholic anymore, Charles, but I will surely pray."

"That's right. I always forget. Appreciate your prayers. I'm sure I'll need them too." Charles turned toward her. "Thank you for the delicious meal, Avery. I'll have that good food to think on while I'm stuck in a foxhole somewhere."

With a troubled heart and stinging eyes, she gave him a hug, holding back her tears.

Prentis draped his arm about her waist, and the two of them stood side by side with Jack on Avery's opposite hip. Charles swung up onto his horse, then he tipped his hat and off he rode, heading north. Fred's place was his next farewell visit. He'd have a long ride spread over two days as he stopped to see friends along the way. Then, to war he'd go. Silently, Avery prayed.

Lord God, please bring Charles back safely. I hope and pray, dear Jesus, that he'll one day be blessed with a good woman to ease his labors. Please let him come home in one piece.

Prentis lifted Jack out of her arms. "That certainly gives us a lot to think about."

"I'll say. When a person hears the stories of hardship others have gone through, it softens everything, doesn't it?"

"That it does. I've got even more respect for Alf Riley after hearing his history."

"As do I. Trial seems to have produced character in him, making him a far better and humble man. That's evidence of Christ in him, even though he wasn't attending church. Growing up in my home church, I've seen Mr. Riley consistently and quietly perform one act of kindness after another. He's done it behind the scenes. I only know about his goodness toward others by hearing my father and mother talk about it, Daddy being a deacon."

Prentis nodded. "Whereas, Mrs. Riley . . ."

"That *is* concerning, isn't it? Could be she truly is a goat among the sheep, not that anyone can assume such a thing."

"No one knows a person's heart but God Himself."

"That's true. But if we even suspect Mrs. Riley may not truly be a believer, then we need to treat her with all the more kindness. We need to show her Christ-like love."

"I don't feel that temptation to hate her anymore."

"Neither do I," Avery said.

***

The following afternoon, Sam's wild barking in front of the house informed everyone within earshot that they had more company. Avery strained to see out the window. There sat Joseph Pitzer on his horse. That was a surprise! Sam kept up his barking, heralding the arrival. She hoped Jack could continue sleeping through all the racket.

"Pink!" Joseph shouted. "Call off your hound!"

"Sam!" Prentis yelled from the barn.

The dog sat, as he'd been trained.

As Avery stepped out the front door, Prentis strode toward Joseph, who swung down off his horse and hitched it at the rail. After patting Sam on the head as he passed, Prentis gave Joseph a hearty two-handed handshake.

"Pitzer! Glad to see you."

"Headin' off to war." He turned to give Avery a smile as she joined them. "Wanted to give you both my regards before I leave."

"Do you have time for a piece of pie?" she asked.

"You know me, Avery Veretta Slaughter Pinkerton. I always have time for pie."

114

She laughed softly. "You're exactly like my husband when it comes to pie."

"Never could resist it." Joseph chuckled along with her.

"The baby's asleep," Prentis said. "How 'bout we sit out here on the front porch? We've got some shade here." He looked toward Avery.

"Oh, yes! Let's do that. If Jack's still asleep after all that barking and shouting, it would be better if we stayed out here."

Avery bustled back into the house, stopping first outside the bedroom door to listen for any sounds of movement or waking. She heard none, but she still stood there, waiting, feeling as if God had something to say to her. She needed to calm her emotions. For some reason, she felt overly emotional about Joseph's departure. Heaviness pressed at her breastbone, a deep sorrow.

Lord, please help that man. Keep Joseph safe.

This goodbye to her childhood friend—a friend who had loved her without her knowledge until Prentis began courting her—overwhelmed her. She'd been so emotional lately that she chalked up these emotions to whatever had been making her so cranky. She tidied it up that way, but still, she felt as though she were saying goodbye to Joseph for the last time.

Bustling into the kitchen, she pressed the sadness down, cut extra-large pieces, plated them, and headed back. Prentis swung wide the screen door as she approached. She looked into his patient and understanding eyes. Knowing she'd have her hands full, he'd been watching for her, probably also observing her long wait outside the bedroom door.

"Peach pie!" Joseph beamed at her. "My favorite!"

"It's Prentis's too," she said. "I'd forgotten you liked it. I'm glad I have it on hand."

As they ate their dessert, they batted around the war news. Newspapers now estimated the death toll at around seven million, an absurd number of fatalities. After General Pershing's announcement of the need for three million soldiers, even more men would be called into duty. Joseph was full of new information.

"They're building military training camps as fast as they can."

"Are they building all over the country?" she asked.

"The National Guard camps are mostly in the southeast. For regular army, they're building camps across the Midwest and along the eastern coast. They'll train millions."

"Hear tell those areas most closely duplicate the European terrain," Prentis added.

"That's what I hear too," Joseph said. "They're slappin' them training centers up fast. I'm off to Camp Funston in Kansas. I'll be whipped into shape by Major General Leonard Wood."

"My cousin Charles is bound for there too," Prentis said.

"If I run across a Pinkerton, I'll know he's related to you then. With such an outlandish name, I doubt I'll meet many."

"Unlike Pitzer, which is as common as Smith."

The two men laughed.

"They're gonna drill us and instill military discipline in us." Joseph paused to laugh again. "Probably be good for me. They'll even train us how to handle that poison gas. Come hell or high water, they'll do whatever it takes to get us ready. Then off we'll go to France."

"I hate to think of a friend going into battle, Joseph," Avery said. "We'll pray for you."

"For once, I'm not gonna tease you about that, Avery. You pray for me all you want. God knows I'll need it." Joseph jumped to his feet, both of them rising with him.

"I've lost track of the time. I'm expected at the Millers for supper. Need to say goodbye to Mary Beth."

"Mary Beth?" Avery smiled widely. "What have you been up to, Joseph?"

"That's one thing I love about you, Avery." Joseph laughed heartily. "Of course, you haven't heard all the gossip about Mary Beth and me. You may be the subject of gossip—thanks largely to Mrs. Alfonse Riley—but you're never the source of it. You avoid it completely. You've never even *heard* the gossip. You're a good woman."

"She certainly is!" Prentis gave her a big smile, hugging her tight against his side.

"All those lies about us will disappear." Joseph fixed his eyes on hers. "Don't you worry about it, Avery. The truth will win out. I've been after Mary Beth for a while. That's what brought me near this farm so long ago. Mrs. Riley knew I was down here, but she didn't know I was trying to court Mary Beth. Tonight, I'm hoping I can persuade her to wait for me. Want to marry her when I get back from this war. Hell, I wish I could marry her before I leave!"

Ignoring his expletive, Avery smiled. "We certainly hope you're successful, Joseph."

"I hope you can pull it off," Prentis added. "Winning a good woman sets a man up for life."

"That's a fact," Joseph said. "Just look at you!"

All shook hands heartily, and then Joseph swung up into the saddle. He wheeled around to head out, then tipped his hat toward her and smiled at them both. "I'll see you two when this war is over. I'm not planning on making the supreme sacrifice. Take care of one another."

"We will," she called. "God bless you, Joseph."

"I hope so!" He laughed. "I'll need it."

Grinning, he rode out of the barnyard.

"We'll never see him again," Avery whispered.

"Sweetheart, you don't know that."

"For some reason, I feel I do. I have no idea why I'm so emotional lately."

"Might we be expecting another baby?"

Her hand flew to her mouth. "Oh, goodness! I hadn't even considered that. It may be. I guess we'll have to wait and see."

After gathering up the plates, she headed inside, needing to be alone.

God, help me with everything in front of us. I don't know what it is, but I'm already feeling the grief of it. It could just be my wild emotions. Or is it a baby? Lord, help me.

Ten

THE LAST FAREWELL WAS the most difficult. Sliding open the barn door, Prentis waved Tom in as he arrived on Hector. In the tranquil stillness, Tom loaded his saddlebag and his leather travel bag into the Model T. Silently, Prentis led Hector into the stall, removed Tom's saddle and blanket, then set about grooming with brush and currycomb. His heart was too full for words.

Tom left his blanket thrown over the rail where Prentis had placed it, but he hung his saddle on the barn wall peg beside Prentis's. Then he leaned over the rail.

Prentis glanced up. "That saddle will be waiting right there for you when you get back."

"That'll be a good day."

"It surely will."

Turning back to grooming, Prentis focused on the horse. Both men were silent.

As Prentis finished up, Tom broke the stillness. "It's difficult to leave the two of you in the middle of this crisis with Mrs. Riley."

"That woman has made quite a mess." Prentis looked up at Tom. "She surely has."

"You've shown her amazing forbearance. As your pastor, I have to say I'm proud of how you've handled this."

"As your friend, I'm reminding you that you can't see my heart."

"That's true."

"Choosing to forgive is easier if you feel forgiving," Prentis said.

"It surely is. And feeling forgiving is a mite easier when the offense is smaller."

"Yes, it is. There's some newly discovered history that's helping with that though."

"Oh, yeah?" Tom said.

"We learned some facts about the Rileys' early years together."

After repeating all he'd learned from his cousin Charles, Prentis led Hector to the outside pen and the water trough. Deep in thought, Tom followed, head down as he considered.

After several minutes of silence, he spoke, "That's a heap to unravel."

Prentis nodded. "It surely is."

"Makes me wonder if she objected to you because you reminded her of Alf. Maybe she thought she owed Avery the benefit of her knowledge, hoping to spare her."

"Could be." Prentis nodded. "That's occurred to me."

"Her view was that her own choice had been bad. That being the case, her intentions may have been good during your courtship. But the carrying out of those intentions wasn't completed with Christian charity."

"Which taints the entire thing."

"It does," Tom said.

Both men stood silently as Hector drank from the trough. Ulysses ambled over to join in.

"Then, there's the fact that her choice wasn't indeed bad," Tom said. "I don't think it's occurred to Mrs. Riley that she ended up catching a husband of superior quality. If it *had* occurred to her, when you were courting Avery, she would've considered more than merely your church attendance. She would have considered your character and your profession of faith. If she had, she would've seen that you would make Avery a good husband. I don't think she knows that Alf is a good man, a kind man, a strong Christian. He shows it through his actions, not his words. In fact, he's a man of few words. He reminds me of you."

Prentis snorted. "He's a better man than I am. Couldn't live with a woman like that."

"You might surprise yourself if Avery turns into such a woman one day."

They looked at one another, laughing at the mere idea.

"I don't see that happening," Prentis said.

Tom grinned widely, slapping him on the back. "You never know."

"Something to look forward to."

Both chuckled.

"I appreciate your humor today, Tom, for this day is one of life's hardest."

"Feel the same."

"I know you're not concerned about your own safety, but for all of us, I hope you'll keep your head down." Prentis pinned him with his gaze. "We want you to come back. You'll be sorely missed. You're been a wonderful pastor and the best friend I've ever had."

"Thank you." Tom met his eyes evenly. "I have to say that about you too. I'll do my best to get back here in one piece."

"And we'll be grateful, should you accomplish that. We'll pray for you every day."

"I know I can count on your prayers, and I'll keep you all in mine."

Avery approached with Jack in one arm and a picnic basket in the other, but she paused silently to study the two of them before heading inside the barn.

"Are you two ready to go?" she asked quietly.

"Well, no. Don't think I'll ever be ready to do this, but we've got to get Tom off to Fort Jay." Prentis sighed. "Don't like this one bit."

Tom patted him on the back as they stepped outside the corral to follow Avery.

When they entered the barn, she was fastening Jack into the backseat of the car. Then she moved to the front of the Model T to perform the passenger duties. Prentis climbed in to drive. Once they'd gotten the automobile running, she settled into the back with the baby.

"I did my best to let you two say your goodbyes," she said, "and I imagine Jack will be happy for this short trip. We don't want your last memory to be a shouted conversation over the melodious sounds of a screaming baby."

"A screaming baby hasn't bothered me yet," Tom said.

"Well, that's true, now that you mention it. I've never seen you flustered by crying babies."

"It was part of my pastoral training." Tom wore a straight face. "Even taught us how to preach nice and loud, so we could be heard over screaming infants."

Prentis guffawed, laughter bursting from him as he turned onto the country road. "Is torture generally part of pastoral training?"

"Of course. Else how would they prepare us for the ministry?"

Laughter erupted from all. Prentis glanced back at the baby. With a serious expression, Jack looked back and forth to each one, not understanding the joke.

"I didn't have to complete that part of the course," Avery added, "having done my degree by correspondence. It would have come in quite handy."

Exchanging glances, the three of them smiled widely.

Jack chortled a fake baby laugh, joining in, since laughter was in order. That tickled them all, causing even more mirth. Tom twisted around and smiled at the baby.

"I'll definitely miss you, little man."

"Man." Jack nodded.

That brought even more smiles and gaiety.

Avery opened the basket and passed out sandwiches and peaches from their tree. Altogether, the ride to town was lighthearted, probably the best way to send off a friend on a potentially deadly mission. Once they'd purchased Tom's ticket, they stood close to one another, huddled together, ignoring the few people nearby who were also boarding. Their group stood still on the platform, even after the "All aboard!"

Then all shook themselves, realizing that, unbelievably, the moment had arrived. Hugs were exchanged and pats on the back. Before they knew it, they were waving goodbye, and Tom was gone. The train grew smaller in the distance, and then Prentis looked into Avery's eyes.

Tears ran down her cheeks. Swallowing hard, he fought to keep from responding in kind. Instead, he held her tightly, Jack sandwiched between. They all clung to one another, standing there for a great while. Eventually, they turned and headed home in silence, trying to figure out how they would carry on without Tom.

***

Prentis finished up the last amount of work securing Jack's seat to the Model T's floorboard. Thinking over these last days of getting everyone off to war weighed heavily. It didn't feel as if much time had passed before Avery reappeared carrying Jack and her small leather bag.

Prentis lifted Jack from her arms. "Did you sleep, son?"

Jack nodded. "Sleep."

"Good boy! Now you're off on a trip with Momma."

"Mom-mom go bye-bye?"

"Yes, son, and you too."

Prentis glanced up at Avery, catching her smile.

The small seat was now fastened to the floor behind the driver's seat, right in the middle of the automobile. Prentis strapped Jack in, kissed him on top of the head, and shut the door. Avery crooked her elbow, leaning against the driver's side window, studying his face.

"That seat is bolted to the frame," he said. "It's not going anywhere. The harness you made works well. You're all set."

"Are you entirely certain you don't mind us staying the night?"

"We bought this Model T so you could visit your family, among other things. Hattie will want you, now that her brother's gone off to war, and your family will be thrilled to see you. On top of all that, this visit will cheer you up."

"I do need cheering. Thank you for noticing. But I don't want to leave you so soon after we've said goodbye to Tom. I'll miss you. We've never slept apart since we married."

"It's only one night," he said. "I'll be fine, though I'll miss you too."

"I've fixed all you'll need for meals."

"You already showed me. It's all in the icebox."

124

"I don't know if I can drive away from you," she said.

He chuckled. "I know you can—you're a strong woman."

Waiting, she kept her eyes on his.

"I'll only be disking. Got to get my fields and Tom's ready so I can sow the wheat."

Still she sat. Her eyes penetrated, prodding into his thoughts.

"All right," he said, "as usual your mere look can pry out a confession. I need to be alone. Have to hash out Tom's departure and talk to God about it."

"Ah," she cooed softly. "I wondered why you were hurrying me off so soon."

He smiled. "I was trying not to rush you."

"You could have simply told me that you needed time alone."

"I guess I could've, but I didn't want you to be concerned or feel insulted. I've already told you everything, but there's an argument I need to have with God about it."

She cupped his cheek, stroking his midweek stubble. "You know He always wins."

"I know He does. Still, I've always talked to Him straight. It's not honest to keep my feelings to myself. I need to lay out my case before our Father in heaven and aim my whys and wherefores at Him. Alone, behind horses and a plow, is the best place to do that."

"Well, I've never tried that method, but I'll take your word for it."

"After the field, the silent house will make my time with God even more effective."

"I understand," she said. "Now that I see your need, I'll gladly head north. The time with my family will do me good. I need to talk to my mother."

"Go!" Jack called from the backseat.

Prentis chuckled. "The boss has spoken."

Leaning in, he tousled Jack's hair. His kiss was returned by a wet baby kiss. Laughing softly, he stroked Jack's cheek with his thumb.

"I'll miss you both. Have a good time. Now, let's get this automobile started."

Prentis stepped to the front of the car and waited for her cue. Once they'd completed the entire start sequence, he stepped back around by her door as she eased off on the fuel. Her boot now pressed hard on the brake. She leaned toward him, and they exchanged a quick kiss.

Then off they went.

A sense of pride swelled in Prentis's chest. He didn't know any other women who had tackled driving an automobile. Avery was quite a woman—strong, adventurous, and courageous. Standing in the barnyard, he waved until they disappeared in the distance, in case she might look back in the mirror. It would touch her heart to see him waving as they departed.

Heaving a sigh, Prentis walked toward the barn.

"All right, Lord, let's have it out, You and me."

When Prentis stepped inside the barn, all the horses looked up at him. Before harnessing, he pressed his forehead against the face of each one. Seeming to be attuned to his state of mind, each horse leaned into him, nickering softly. Peering into their stalls, he saw that all had eaten the mix of alfalfa and grass hay he had tossed into their feed boxes earlier. They'd also had plenty to drink.

One at a time, he led out the chosen four, harnessing each to the disk plow. To spread the work out more evenly, he used four, since there would be twice the usual amount of plowing. They would disk about three or four acres today, rather than the usual five to eight, since it was now early afternoon. Both he and Tom had about fifty to fifty-five acres in wheat, so he'd work here for a couple weeks before traveling over to Tom's for the same task.

126

There, he'd switch the team around. After the plowing would come the spring tooth to smooth out the land, preparing a soft bed of soil for the seed wheat he would sow at the fall equinox.

It was plenty hot, and the work was dusty, so he stepped over to the yard pump and splashed out some water from deep in the earth, filling both of his grandpas' Civil War canteens and then strapping them on. Today, at least, he'd be drinking dusty water, since Avery wouldn't be there to bring him fresh.

Ulysses nickered back at him, the sound rumbling deep, and all the horses tossed their heads and twitched their ears toward him. He hadn't spoken to them, he realized, all the while he'd been hitching. Stepping around, he caressed their muzzles as he spoke softly to each one.

"All right, you've guessed it. I'm not myself today."

Ulysses pressed his head against Prentis's, giving it a shake as their foreheads met, seeming to indicate his solidarity with his master. Hector nickered low in his chest, tossing his head. The mares whinnied softly, leaning into him.

Prentis chuckled. "It's almost like you all can read my mind."

Stepping back to the disk plow, he clicked his tongue, and off they went.

Out in the field, the disks broke up the soil one final time. But Prentis's mind was elsewhere. He mulled over the situation. Why had God seen fit to allow this conflagration on the other side of the world to get completely out of hand? The war now robbed the American prairie of young men who'd never traveled far from home all their lives—men solidly anchored within their families and communities—tight family bonds torn asunder.

Family, friends, pastor—what did they have to do with a fight in Europe?

They'd be shot at now and put in all sorts of danger on ships at sea, peaceful men who wanted nothing more than to marry, settle down, farm the land, and enjoy a simple and quiet life. Nothing about their lives would ever be the same after their war experience—Prentis had read the papers. He'd heard of shellshock and the diseases rampant in the trenches.

Theologically, he knew that evil men made evil decisions. But God promised to work all of this together for their good, because they were His children and He loved them. In His sovereignty, God had allowed these things into their lives for a good reason. Prentis knew this.

But for now, he wished God had left well enough alone. They'd had a good thing going. They'd been comfortable. For the first time in his life, he'd been taught by a humble and godly pastor within a body of believers who loved one another. He had joined a church.

But all of that goodness had only lasted a brief nineteen months. His friendship with Tom had extended a year beyond that, beginning while Prentis was still searching and trying to comprehend if church attendance was a necessity in a believer's life, and, if so, why.

Change was always difficult. It reminded him of when he'd gone up to Kingman to help with the calving when he and Avery were engaged. Upon arriving he'd discovered that everything in his life had altered. His mother was engaged, she was selling the farm, and he had to act quickly to purchase this farm before he'd been ready. Loading up all his childhood possessions and overturning all he'd been familiar with had been disorienting.

Uncomfortable with his thoughts, he shrugged his shoulders against the strap attached to the plow and took a deep breath. His chest tightened, and his cheeks felt as if all the blood had gone right out of them. His stomach

128

dropped, and an overwhelming sense of despair hit him hard.

Father in heaven, I don't understand this. Why?

The horses kept walking, the dirt kept rolling over, and Prentis kept plowing.

No lightning bolt blasted from heaven. No still small voice spoke. No booming pronouncement sounded forth. But Prentis knew God watched him, and somehow, he felt as if God were near. At least that hadn't changed. No matter Prentis's discomfort and confusion, no matter if all had changed in his life yet again, he knew the truth. God was always with him, even when He didn't explain Himself and even when events drastically altered Prentis's life.

Prentis didn't care for this particular trajectory, but he knew that God wouldn't have allowed this if He didn't intend to orchestrate it for their good. He always did.

That being the case, could he quit focusing on what they'd had and what could have been? Could he now focus on living by faith today, no matter how he felt about it?

"Father, I'll try," he whispered. "Not my will, but Thine be done."

Eleven

BY THE TIME AVERY arrived at her parents' farm outside of Gibbon, Jack had spent more time in the automobile than he liked. The trip had taken about forty minutes, because Avery discovered she no longer desired to speed, especially with the roads still bumpy and ridged with dried mud carved by hooves and tires after the latest rainfall. Driving fast seemed to have been vanquished by motherhood. Safety, not speed, was the more important requirement.

While there was plenty to see from her perspective, Jack's seat on the floor prevented him from seeing much of anything, except the inside of the Model T. Therefore, he had cried the entire second half of the trip. Her head now pounded. A migraine threatened.

Going up the driveway, her chest filled with a sense of overwhelm, sorrow, relief at having arrived, and pain from her throbbing head. They glided around the barnyard and came to a stop by the kitchen door.

Everyone appeared at the doorway and from around the farmyard, and when her momma opened the automobile door, Avery burst into tears.

Momma grabbed her up, patting her on the back. "There, there, sweetheart, it will be all right. Everything is in hand."

Avery heard the boys whisk Jack out of the seat. Then they carried him off to the barnyard to see what Grandpa was doing.

"I'm sorry to arrive in such bad shape, Momma," she sobbed, "but my head is throbbing, and my heart is broken in two."

"You go on up to your room. Lie down, and I'll bring up the aspirin."

Avery trudged up the steps and glanced around the space. Her momma now used Avery's old bedroom as a sewing room. Everything appeared to be stowed safely away for their visit. Momma had already opened the windows.

Plucking out the two hatpins and untying the wide ribbon that held it all securely, Avery removed her hat, set it on the dresser, and unpinned her braid. Next, she loosened her boot bindings and slipped off her boots. Now that she was comfortable, she lay back with a sigh, unbuttoning her top buttons and sinking into the softness. Throwing her arm across her eyes, she shut out the afternoon light and attempted to release all her tension.

Momma tiptoed in to give her the aspirin. Together they decided that a nap might be the best medicine. They'd talk later. Relieved of all responsibilities, Avery let go her sorrows, had a good cry, and then allowed herself the luxury of sleeping in midday. Before she knew it, the soft creak of someone settling onto the bed brought her back to wakefulness. She opened her eyes. There was Momma again, seated at the foot of the bed.

131

"Thought you might not want to sleep too long," Momma said, "lest you end up prowling around in the night with your days and nights turned around."

Avery stretched and yawned widely. "I needed that rest, Momma. I'm feeling better. Thank you for that and for waking me. Where's Jack?"

"He's outside with your brothers. Before the boys come in, let's have our talk."

"There's a pile of troubles. We said goodbye to Charles Pinkerton, Joseph Pitzer, and Tom McKinney in the last two days."

"Oh, my!"

"We had some good conversations with them all and learned so much information that I hardly know how to process it. It was difficult to see them go, especially Tom, who's so dear to us. On top of that, something strange is happening with my body."

"Let's start with that."

Avery nodded.

"Don't need any boys listening in to female talk," Momma said, "and they're all outside now. So, tell me. What's happening?"

"I feel like I did when I was first expecting Jack, the same sort of emotional agitation. But I'm also crampy and nauseated. Prentis wonders if we might be having another baby."

"Have your monthly times returned yet, since you had the baby?"

"No, they haven't started."

"Well, if you're expecting, it will show." Her momma smiled. "You'll know soon enough."

"That's what we decided."

"Another baby would be such a blessing!"

"Yes! We'd be so happy."

"A true cause for rejoicing." Momma beamed at her.

"The next item . . . We learned some information about Mr. and Mrs. Riley."

The two eyed one another silently. The unexpressed struggle of two Christian women needing to discuss a topic without engaging in gossip restrained their words.

At last, Avery determined how to proceed. "Do you know the Riley's entire story, Momma?"

"Indeed, I do, since before they married. We knew them then."

"All this while, you've known?"

"Yes, that's why your father and the other deacons have shown such patience toward Eliza. And, it's also one of the reasons Alf has been one of your father's closest friends. A man who's been through crushing trial often needs another such man to lean on."

Avery hadn't considered that. Yes, both Daddy and Mr. Riley had been through horrific, devastating, and reputation-destroying hardships.

"Momma, do you believe Mrs. Riley's a true Christian?"

"Only the good Lord knows."

"Well, you're right about that. But their story certainly gave us a different perspective, and it's making it possible to forgive her. On registration day, Prentis told her he forgave her. She was the one who registered him for the draft."

"I'm so glad, dear. Prentis is a good man. He's been grievously injured by her attack on your character. Even though I know what happened to the Rileys, it's still been difficult not to take up an offense on behalf of you and your family. However, I'm certain we can trust your reputation and your good name into God's hands."

"Yes, that's what we're attempting to do."

"How did she accept Prentis's forgiveness?"

"She didn't."

"Ah," Momma said. "That's too bad. We must continue to pray."

"Yes, we must." Avery paused, considering how to ask the next question. "Are you aware that Joseph Pitzer was courting someone and has been for some time? He told us before he left."

"Yes. Mary Beth Miller."

Avery exhaled a blast in frustration. "It seems I'm in the dark about everything."

"Well, sweetheart, you no longer live up here or attend the same church, and both of those matters required discretion. So, it wasn't something I could write about. If you'd been here, you *might* have known about Mary Beth, but Joseph kept his courting private. You may recall that one of his courtship attempts was met with a shove off the porch and a slammed door."

"Of course I do, poor boy." Avery considered the night she shoved Joseph off the porch when he tried to kiss her. "Well, somehow Mrs. Riley learned that he was down near our house about the time Jack was conceived, but she had no knowledge that he was courting Mary Beth."

"Yes, that's true. But we couldn't announce Joseph's romantic intentions to the wider world, just to make clear what he'd been doing down there. There would have been no reason to do so before this gossip. Nothing had happened. Eliza Riley's assumptions weren't known then."

"I understand. For quite some time, none of us were aware of what Mrs. Riley thought or said. Everyone was innocently going about their own business without explanation, because none was required. Unfortunately, that resulted in Joseph, Jack, *and* me all being sullied."

"Nothing can sully you when you're innocent, dear girl. It will not stick. With Alf's behavior at harvest . . ." Momma held up one finger as she ticked off her list. "Prentis's treatment of Eliza on the day he registered for

134

the draft, your public conversation with Joseph at the general store, everything generally acknowledged about your character, and everyone's familiarity with the source, I'm certain this lie will disappear. She's a troubled woman, and everyone is acquainted with the character of all involved. We must be patient and trust the Lord."

Avery sighed. "Why does spiritual and personal growth have to be so difficult?"

Momma smoothed back Avery's hair and drew her close to kiss her forehead. "Such is human nature. We only learn our lessons when they're administered in difficult ways."

"That's so true, Momma."

"You're probably learning the truth of that as a momma, now that Jack is on the move."

A loud cry echoed through the house. "Mom-mom!"

Avery jumped up. "There's our boy. Let's go get him."

"It's me carrying him in," responded Hattie's voice.

"Hattie's here!" Thrilled, Avery threw her arms about her Momma. "You surprised me."

***

After supper and Hattie's departure that evening, Momma played hymns on the piano. Howard stretched out on the floor beside her, moaning that he had stuffed himself with too much peach pie, it being in abundant supply now that the tree limbs creaked and groaned with the burden of the ripe and delectable fruit. Jack danced and ran through the room, jumping or climbing over Howard with each pass. Each time Jack couldn't clear the hurdle, Howard huffed out his overstuffed agony as Jack plopped onto him.

Amused by both boys, yet deeply saddened by all the departures, including Hattie's, Avery considered the words of each hymn Momma played. Obviously sensing her mood, Gene tugged Avery toward the piano. They joined Momma, all of them harmonizing together in soprano, alto, and tenor. Singing hymns to her mother's piano playing lifted her spirits. She smiled at Gene.

Then Momma pulled out a piece of music and turned toward Avery.

"Sweetheart, here's a new composition you might enjoy. It's by George M. Cohan. The song is called *Over There*, and it's got such a catchy tune."

After Momma had played it through several times with Gene singing along, Avery knew the chorus by heart. Holding Jack, she sang while dancing him around the room.

> *Over there, over there*
> *Send the word, send the word over there*
> *That the Yanks are coming*
> *The Yanks are coming*
> *The drums rum-tumming everywhere*
> *So prepare, say a prayer*
> *Send the word, send the word to beware*
> *We'll be over, we're coming over*
> *And we won't come back till it's over*
> *Over there*

It was propaganda, but that made it powerful. The snappy tune and the rhyming words caught hold of the listener. A sense of cynical resignation and pessimism swept over Avery. There was no resisting it. She might as well surrender. War fever would sweep the nation. They were doomed. This war was going to be fought with everything they had. The entire nation would get behind the effort, including Oklahoma. Their boys were all going over there.

Passing Jack to Gene, Avery stepped out onto the front porch and had another good cry.

Lord, I feel like I'm losing my mind. There has to be another baby on the way.

However, as she considered each of the good men who had departed, she comprehended that it was much more than merely a possible pregnancy. They'd been struck to their core. *Their* boys were going. The British general had been right. When their own boys began to die, the United States of America would rise up in vengeance terrifying to behold.

Twelve

EVEN THOUGH SHE'D ONLY been away for a day, Prentis was relieved to have Avery home again. When she arrived right before dark, he had pulled her out of the Model T and swept her off her feet and into his arms. Even though her stay had been brief, she hadn't liked sleeping alone either, even if it was for only one night. She said she'd missed his physical presence and his steadying strength. He had missed hers, too, especially with Tom newly departed.

Simply having her near made him a stronger man.

They now lingered over breakfast, both of them enjoying several cups of coffee as Jack tottered around examining the cracks and crevices, pulling out newly discovered lint and dead bugs, mashing whatever he found, and cramming his toys under bookshelves and furniture. Typical toddler behavior. He was out to discover the world, piece by piece.

Now that he was on the move, they put the house back together before going to bed each evening. Yesterday, there had been no mess, since the two had left so early. But Prentis had missed his son, even for the one night, never mind the clutter and general messiness.

"When we arrived home, I told you all about my visit," Avery said, peering at him over her cup's rim. "Now, tell me about your conversation with God, if I can be privy to the details."

Prentis tilted back in his chair, trying to sort out what he was ready to share. Then he rocked forward and took a long swig of coffee.

"Still in the thick of it," he said. "Don't think I can talk yet."

Avery caressed his hand. "I'll pray for you. I know it's a heavy load. I feel it too."

"It is, and I'm teetering under it."

"On the outside, you look quite strong."

"Well, at least one thing's in order then." He snorted, pushed back from the table, and downed the last dregs of his coffee. "Need to get to work. I'm riding over to Tom's first to check on everything, just to make sure all is in good order."

"We'll see you at lunchtime then."

He pulled her in close, tight against his chest. When battling internally, her nearness strengthened him. After holding her a long while, he felt Jack grasp his leg. Prentis looked down. The baby had joined their embrace. Prentis scooped him up and included him in their family hug.

"You're the best baby in the world, Jack, and your momma's the best wife ever."

"Mama best wife."

"Yes, your momma." Prentis laughed. "She's a good one."

"One!" Jack held up one finger.

"That's how old you are now. You're one." Prentis smiled at Avery. "Look at him, counting now and communicating better every day."

"He's a smart boy."

Prentis planted a kiss on each of their faces and then headed out. When he rode by on Ulysses, they were on the front porch, waving. As he smiled and lifted his hat, he thanked God for his family and the comfort of having them near.

***

When Prentis rode into Tom's barnyard, the absence of his friend hit him hard. Normally, Tom would've stepped out of the house or the barn, ready to greet him with a cup of stiff black coffee before they got to work on one project or the other. Instead, silence pervaded the place. The blinds were drawn. There was no scent of the cookstove. The horses weren't in the paddock.

Prentis headed toward the windmill's water tank, stepping off Ulysses to hitch his horse to the rail there. Immediately the gelding lowered its head to drink. It was going to be another scorcher. This felt like the hottest day they'd had yet. Yesterday, the disking had been miserable and dustier than usual, and today would be a repeat, once he got back to his farm.

He stood for a while making a headcount and then watching the cows in the distance. The water tank was full, and they all looked well. Soon they'd know if Rex had done his job.

All was in good shape, so he walked around the house checking all the doors and windows. Then he circled the barn, which was largely empty, locking it up tight again. The quiet stillness made his chest ache with loneliness. Tom was truly gone. This empty farmstead testified.

The push had been relentless. Time had marched onward. From declaration of war to everyone leaving to be trained to fight had been a mere four-and-a-half months. He'd had his emotional brakes on the entire time, as he really had about this entire war since its beginning. But, of course, nothing stopped the grinding wheel of time.

Father God, how can I get by without such a good pastor and friend?

He left that question hanging, knowing God would make it clear eventually. When Prentis's father had died, he had felt this same agony of loneliness, this same shove of relentless out-of-control change overtaking his whole life. Things were not as they were meant to be. Fifteen-year-olds weren't supposed to bury dead fathers nor be left to support the family. Dear friends weren't supposed to be parted by a war that had nothing to do with them.

He yearned for the coming time of no more death and no more parting. He yearned for all made right in the world and everything as it should be. With a sigh, he acknowledged that the day would come soon enough. He had to leave it in God's hands. God alone knew what needed to occur to get them all to that day. Prentis let go, at least for the time being.

Lord, help me to trust You.

***

Sunday, September 2, a beaming shaft of bright light shone into Prentis's eyes. The dreaded day had arrived. Inwardly he groaned, his stomach churning. He didn't think he could do this. Starting anew at a strange church felt impossible. How could he go from sitting under Tom's teaching in his familiar church to an unknown entity preaching from a Wakita pulpit?

Avery had detailed the theological arguments pro and con for each of the available Christian churches—there were three choices. None of them fit squarely with the foundation Tom and Moody Bible Institute had laid.

There were disagreements here and there. "Disputable matters," Avery called them—similar to what they'd had to sort through when planning their wedding with Protestants on one side and Catholics on the other.

But all three Wakita churches preached the Gospel, and all held to a view of Jesus as the Son of God, sent by the Father to redeem mankind. He was crucified, dead, and buried, and on the third day He rose from the dead, as the Apostles' Creed spelled out. All a person had to do was repent and place their trust in Him. God Himself had done all the work.

These were the essentials. All held them. Now to decide which church to attend.

Trying not to wake Avery, Prentis slowly rolled onto his back and stared at the ceiling.

Father God, I don't have a clue what to do. Hiding out here seems the best option.

He didn't want to make this change or this decision. Life felt out of his control, though in reality it never had been under his governance in the first place. More yielding. That seemed to be the essential lesson of life—more yielding to God of things that could not be controlled.

Beside him, Avery inhaled sharply, as if she'd been surprised or hurt in her sleep.

Quickly, she rolled out of bed and crawled toward her dresser, pulling wide the bottom drawer and digging frantically, tossing everything out that was in her way. Grabbing a handful of cloth, she now slid out the chamber pot and settled onto it, glancing over at his side of the bed. Her eyes widened to see him wide awake, alert, and watching her. Her middle convulsed with a silent giggle that doubled her over, and she covered her smile.

Lifting her hand, she mouthed, "I didn't know you were awake."

142

He rolled over to her side and onto his elbow, whispering back, "What's all the fuss about?"

Inspecting the chamber pot, she swallowed hard.

"My first woman's time since I got pregnant with Jack over two years ago."

"So, there's no baby on the way."

"No." Her eyes glistened. "That's a disappointment. I thought for sure."

"So did I. You had all the signs."

"The Lord is certainly teaching us big lessons, isn't He?" She sighed. "The course of our lives is in His hands. We're not in control."

"I was thinking the same thing. Seems more so lately, though it's always the case."

Studying the chamber pot, she frowned. "Do you mind if we skip church today? Something's not right."

"Don't mind at all. Didn't think I could attend church this morning without Tom anyway."

"I wondered if you might feel that way."

"His farm was so quiet, his absence fresh. Not yet ready to look at a pulpit that doesn't have him in it."

"I understand," she whispered. "Let's rest here at home."

Leaning across the gap between bed and chamber pot, he cupped the back of her head and pulled her face toward his for a kiss. "You're a good woman. Thank you for being yourself. You're kind and gracious all the time."

She returned his kiss. "I try."

"Like I frequently tell you—you succeed."

Jack's voice sounded from the other side of the wall, "Da Da!"

"I'll get the little man and feed him something while you attend to your female situation."

"Thank you, Prentis."

Scooping Jack up and kissing him soundly, Prentis stepped out, shutting the door behind him. This turn of events was unexpected and disappointing, but it did provide more time to adjust to Tom's pastoral absence. He settled Jack into his highchair and handed him a piece of bread.

Eventually, Avery stepped out. Her face was drawn.

"Prentis, can you look at that chamber pot?"

"Is something wrong?"

"I think I've had a miscarriage. I may have lost a baby."

The bottom fell out. He felt as if he'd been hit in the stomach. All he could do was rise and hold wide his arms. She stumbled into his embrace. All the pent-up tears about everything that had happened during the last several months came pouring out. And now, a lost baby.

Neither had any words. All they possessed were sobs of grief.

After holding her a long while, both of them reassured Jack, and then Prentis stepped into their bedroom. He'd seen it enough times to recognize it. Farmers had to evaluate this sort of situation all the time. She had miscarried. There was the evidence. Prentis couldn't merely dump the chamber pot into the outhouse. It didn't seem right. There lie the premature remains of their baby. His heart ached as he gazed down at the little one who might have lived and brought joy to their home. Gathering up the pot, he stepped into the living room.

"I have to bury our—" A sob cut off his last word. He swallowed hard.

Her face fell, and the tears started again. Jack's little face grew somber.

"We'll come with you," she whispered. "God, help us."

Avery picked up Jack, and the two of them followed Prentis out the back door.

Back by the trees, he dug a deep hole, two feet down. Shovel by shovel, he confronted this new reality, his heart breaking even more with each thrust of the spade.

Weeping softly, Avery stood beside him. Then, gently, he emptied the tiny form and other contents into the fresh earth.

Using his bare hands, he cupped the soil, softly sifting the red earth into the hole, all the while wondering about this little life that they would never know this side of heaven. Smoothing the mound, he patted it down.

Death triumphant.

Dust of the earth, from dust to dust.

Jack squatted down beside him, imprinting his little handprints into the dirt. Avery's hands joined theirs, gently caressing the mound, a final goodbye in their gestures. They gathered rocks and covered the small mound completely, so nothing could dig there.

It was all they could do.

Once complete, they stood silently. Jack, seeming to sense their solemnity, stood quietly with them. Tears still coursed down Avery's cheeks.

Finally, Prentis found his voice. "The Lord gives, and the Lord taketh away. Blessed be the name of the Lord. We give this baby back to You and look forward to seeing her with You in heaven one day."

"Lord," Avery whispered, "we give You our daughter. How I wanted a Margaret."

Moaning, Prentis drew her near. "It sure does hurt, but we give her to You."

Prentis lifted up Jack and wrapped his arms around the two of them. The Lord had taken someone precious. The image of a little girl who looked like Avery danced across his mind's eye. It was too much. For a long while they stood together, overwhelmed by their grief.

***

Week after week passed, and Avery continued to bleed. They lived their days as each came, one at a time, trying not to focus on what might have been. They didn't travel into town for church. At the fall equinox, Prentis sowed the wheat on the two farms, having just completed the disking of both. The Bolsheviks rebelled in Russia. The war in Europe raged on.

A letter arrived from Tom stating all was well, and his training was nearly complete. Pastor-like, he asked if they'd chosen a church. They hadn't answered his question when they responded to his first letter. He had enough to worry about, but he'd ascertained from their silence that they hadn't decided. Knowing him, another letter would arrive with encouragement about their church decision. Even while training for war, he still pastored his flock at home.

The American Expeditionary Force had a minor participation at the front, their first foray into battle. And by October 11, the *Medford Star-Patriot* ran its first batch of letters from the boys gone off to war. In the wider world, big things were happening.

Alongside Prentis, Avery read the papers. They noticed. They discussed.

Meanwhile, in the recesses of their hearts and minds, they strove to understand their own small corner of the world. Avery grew increasingly pale. When she dressed in the morning, she pinched her cheeks to add some color. She laundered her menstrual cloths repeatedly, hanging them in the bright sun to bleach them. She even sewed more from leftover baby flannel.

In mid-October, at her mother's urging by mail, they drove into town so Avery's health could be evaluated. The new young physician had been called up to go to Europe. They needed field doctors desperately. So, the older family practitioner had stepped back in to care for the citizens of Wakita. He had overseen Avery's pregnancy when she was expecting Jack, and he checked her over thoroughly. Keeping her eyes on his face, she awaited his response.

His forehead creased. Next he sighed. "It was a miracle when you conceived that first baby," he said, "and now there's been another miracle. But, sadly, this baby couldn't hold on."

"I've had continuing problems since we lost this baby." Her voice cracked, so she stopped speaking.

"I'd like to do a more thorough exam to see if you've expelled everything," he said.

Teary-eyed now, she nodded.

He powered up a machine and gave her a whiff of nitrous oxide from a facemask, and then he proceeded. It was uncomfortable, but the gas made her feel as though she didn't care. She felt a pinch and a brief stabbing pain, and that was all. When he was finished, he handed her a paper sanitary towel. She took a deep breath, attempting to clear her head.

"You'll need to put that on," he said. "Just fasten it to your belt as you do with your regular cloths. Keep your menstrual cloths clean and bleached—also your belt, apron, suspender, or menstrual garments, whichever you use. Get some of that newfangled bottled bleach to add to your wash water. They've started carrying it at the general store. But, be careful with it."

"I hear it's dangerous," Avery said.

"It is. Keep it away from the baby. It's poisonous. Try not to get it undiluted on your skin. If you do, wash immediately until you feel the slippery feeling of the bleach no more. Bleach will take the color right out of any cloth it touches, so handle it with care."

She nodded.

"We must avoid infection. The bleach is a disinfectant. It will destroy any germs or bacteria that might be on your menstrual cloths."

He looked hard at her. She nodded again, assuring him that she had heard.

147

"Your bleeding will be a bit heavier now," he continued. "You hadn't miscarried all the tissue. Now I've taken care of that. You should stop bleeding within the next few weeks. Remember how long it took after you had your first baby?"

Avery nodded. "Will I be able to have more children?"

"You and I both know that's in God's hands. I have no idea how you had the first one!"

"Thank you, Doctor."

"Come back in about six weeks, and I'll check you again."

When she stepped out, Prentis looked up at her, anxiety written all over his face. Jack was undisturbed, playing with his wooden cars on the floor. Prentis paid the bill, picked up Jack, and then took her elbow to escort her out. She explained everything to him. He looked relieved.

"I'm glad the doctor could do something," he said. "I hope this resolves the issue."

"I do too."

"Can we have more children?"

"He said it remains as it was before. Nothing's changed. It was a miracle the first time. It will be a miracle if it happens again."

"If the good Lord wants us to have another, He'll bring that about."

"Yes, He will."

With all her might, Avery put her hope right there.

Lord, I believe. Help me in my unbelief.

***

Before leaving town, Prentis ran across the street to the general store to buy the bleach and to see if they had any newspapers left from the morning delivery. He was able to gather up one. Folding it tight, he grabbed the bleach and a few other items they needed, paid, and then returned to Avery and Jack in the auto.

The *chicka-chicka-chicka-chicka* of the idling engine was the first sound he heard as he stepped out. The second was Jack calling, "Da Da!"

Prentis had reworked the seat's attachment to the Model T's frame, thus enabling Jack to peer out the bottom of the windows. Prentis smiled as he detected the two dark eyes and the headful of blond baby curls. Seeing his father's smile, Jack bounced up and down.

Prentis handed Avery the newspaper. "Look at this, Sweetheart. All I could do was skim the headline." Then he turned to smile at Jack. "That's my boy!"

Jack grinned.

The rest of the way home Avery read loudly, so he could hear over the engine. The paper speculated that the American Expeditionary Force might play a small part in some upcoming military action. They looked at one another.

"Tom isn't even there yet," Avery said.

"You're right, but he will be soon enough. And if I know Tom, he'll be right up at the front in those trenches where he can do the most good."

"And we'll be so proud of him for doing so. We wouldn't think as highly of him as we do if he weren't that kind of man."

Prentis glanced over at her. "That's a fact. Still, I hope he keeps his head down."

"I'm sure he'll take every precaution."

There was a pause while Avery perused the tightly spaced lines of newsprint.

"Oh, my!" she said. "Listen to this. The Bolsheviks have put Lenin in charge of a communist government." She read him the entire article. "The British are battling in France. I never can pronounce the French locations, so you'll simply have to take my word for it. Seems they have to take and retake the same locations." She looked hard at him. "What an incredible waste of human life."

With that she wadded the paper, clutching it on her lap as she turned to stare out the window. What they wouldn't do to have back that one little life, and yet here the war raged onward, robbing so many people of precious lives they also did not want to lose.

And for what purpose?

They traveled the rest of the way home in silence. There wasn't much else to say. This war cost them all too much in every possible way.

Thirteen

THE AMERICAN RED CROSS burgeoned as the first boys went off to training and on to Europe and war. Though Clara Barton had watched the Swiss in action when she traveled in Europe during the Civil War, she hadn't formed the Red Cross until 1881. The organization founded to "prevent and alleviate human suffering in the face of emergencies by mobilizing the power of volunteers and the generosity of donors" came into its own when America entered this war.

Early in the war, the Red Cross had sent a mercy ship filled with supplies to aid the efforts in Europe. As the war progressed, Tom, Prentis, and Avery had kept an eye on the workings of the organization through reports in the newspapers. In May, President Wilson had appointed the War Council for the American Red Cross. They could now raise funds and more effectively arrange shipments and medical personnel to cross the ocean to Europe. They were to organize the response of the American people to the atrocious conditions.

Now that America had entered the fray, local Red Cross chapters sprang up in every town. In Wakita, Red Cross Captain Grant Harris, along with Lieutenants Mr. L.P. Scott, Mrs. Trask, Mrs. C.E. Wetmore, Mrs. Harrington, and Mrs. Harris, organized the first fund drive. Volunteers were needed to collect money for supplies to be shipped over to Europe, and women were needed to knit socks. Avery read of these efforts in the *Wakita Herald*.

Though she continued to be indisposed, she could still knit. Therefore, when Mary Beth Miller rode her horse over on a chilly late October day, bearing multiple skeins of thick gray wool spilling out of her satchel, Avery was thrilled, not only to have company, but also to *do* something. It was better to serve than merely to wring her hands and pray pretty much non-stop. Once they were seated by a low fire in the living room, both of them settled into the large overstuffed chairs. With Jack duly asleep for his nap, the pleasure of conversation began.

Mary Beth and Avery regarded one another over their enormous teacups, their eyes twinkling. It had been a long while since they'd seen one another. Both reseated their cups on the hand-painted china saucers Avery had brought from home, and then they smiled widely.

"I'm so glad you rode over here, Mary Beth," Avery began. "I've been longing for female companionship."

"We've missed you at church."

"I've been indisposed since that first Sunday after Tom left."

Mary Beth's eyebrows shot up and her face grew sympathetic. "I'm so sorry—such a long time to feel unwell. Is there anything I can do?"

"There really isn't much to be done, other than waiting to see what happens. We've been to the doctor, and his prescription is rest."

Mary Beth nodded, and both of them sipped their tea.

"Which church have you decided to attend?" Avery asked.

Mary Beth sighed. "After Pastor Tom, you know what a challenge that is."

"Indeed, we do. We seem to be stalled in our decision making."

"Oh, I can understand that, particularly as close as you two are with the pastor."

Another sip allowed time for contemplating which way to turn the conversation.

"Yes, it's been quite difficult," Avery said. "Has your family decided?"

Her eyes met Mary Beth's. It was the Christian woman impasse again—how to discuss a local issue without gossiping or disparaging any of the involved parties.

"We've decided on the Methodist Episcopal Church. They needed a piano player for worship, and you know how well my mother plays."

"That does sound like a good fit." Avery sipped.

Mary Beth joined her, both eyeing one another over the teacup rims.

"They have an organ, too, do they not?"

"Oh, yes!" Mary Beth stated enthusiastically. "Mrs. Williams does a fine job on that organ, and the reverend plays as well."

"So, the Reverend Anthony Mark Wallock has finally arrived."

"This past week was his first in the pulpit. Have either of you met him?"

"No, we haven't had the opportunity."

"He's gracious as well as highly educated."

153

"Tom told us he graduated from the University of Chicago," Avery said, "and received a graduate degree from the Methodist school, the Garrett Biblical Institute."

Mary Beth nodded in agreement.

Avery passed Mary Beth the plate of cookies. They munched several bites of oatmeal-raisin. Avery had been surprised to find any cookies left in the kitchen when Mary Beth arrived. She had made them on Sunday, and Prentis usually gobbled down the entire batch when she baked. That thought made her smile.

"So, Mary Beth." Keeping her own expression neutral, Avery looked evenly into her guest's eyes. "Let's get to the heart of the matter. Can the reverend preach?"

"He can." Mary Beth wisely took another sip before continuing. "However, I'm sorry to say that he comes nowhere near Pastor Tom in the pulpit."

"I don't think we can find that in any of the available churches—the Baptist, the Congregational, nor the Methodist." Nodding, both sipped. "But did he preach the Gospel?"

"Yes, he did. He's a fanciful man with flowery language—he spoke at least one phrase in Latin. Worship, pageantry, and praise are his strengths, I think. But, yes, he did indeed preach the Gospel."

"Everyone brings different gifts with which to serve the Lord," Avery stated as Mary Beth hid behind her cup to sip.

"That's what my father said on the way home from our first visit."

"Your father is a wise man, one of Tom's elders. Is there a place for him to serve?"

"Oh, yes, he's already volunteered," Mary Beth said. "They have a need for several adult Sunday School teachers, and he'll also serve on the board if asked."

Both munched their cookies, and Avery poured out more tea, which they sweetened and stirred with languid spoons.

"It's a different structure than Pastor Tom had in place." Mary Beth brushed some crumbs off her skirt and onto her saucer.

"That it is. The Methodist Church has local boards, not elders. The Methodists have been significant to my family. Some of my Cherokee forebears were saved under the preaching of John and Charles Wesley's associate Francis Asbury in Virginia. They baptized whites, people of African descent, and native peoples alike right into their churches. They, at least, had the proper Biblical understanding that in the eyes of God, race shouldn't separate us. We're all one human family. Ephesians is quite clear. Believers shouldn't segregate. The Methodists have long been affiliated with the United Brethren and the African Methodist Episcopal Church. There's a rich tradition."

Avery met Mary Beth's eyes evenly, waiting to see what she detected there. Now Mary Beth would know that not only Joseph Pitzer was Cherokee, but that Avery was as well and that she had determined sentiments on racial equality and intermarriage within the church.

Mary Beth didn't miss a beat. "That's something Pastor Tom mentioned also when he talked to our family. Part of living in Oklahoma as a Christian has always included the melding of all races and tribes. We work for unity here."

Mary Beth had passed Avery's test. Before speaking, Avery stirred her still quite hot tea. "We discussed that with Tom as well. We're gradually growing resigned to the fact that nothing can duplicate what we had in our small country church. But, can we hear good Bible teaching and serve with other Christians of good heart?"

Mary Beth met her eyes evenly. "I believe we can. We could probably do so at any of the three churches."

"I agree. I've left the decision up to Prentis. Having familiar faces in a church would make it more inviting to him, I think. May I inform him of your family's decision?"

"You absolutely may," Mary Beth said. "And, while we're handling sensitive topics, I may as well throw everything out into the open, especially since so much has been in the news about women and the right to vote—"

"Oh, please, Mary Beth, I do hope you're going to tell me that you're a suffragette."

"Yes, I am. I was hoping the same about you."

"Indeed, I am."

Both women laughed together, smiling as they relaxed even more. This was a controversial topic in Oklahoma, as it was almost everywhere in the country, and one never knew who was for or against. They clearly agreed on a variety of controversial subjects.

"It's so nice to know we can speak freely on that topic," Avery said.

Nodding, Mary Beth set aside her saucer. "Indeed, as well as many others."

"One such topic is Joseph Pitzer. Before he left, he informed us that he was pursuing you."

"He let me know when he arrived for supper that night. I'm glad you know."

"His absence must be extremely difficult for you. If you'd like to talk about it, I'm glad to listen. I've known him since childhood."

Mary Beth's eyes glistened. "I would love to be able to talk about Joseph. I know you're discreet. Thank you." She dabbed at the corner of her eye. "Now that the sensitive topics have been handled, let me show you what brings me here today. I've brought you strong gray wool." She reached farther down into her bag. "As well as oatmeal and the military olive green."

Mary Beth showed her all the colors and then handed her the entire bag from inside her satchel. Avery probed into the woolen softness, testing the fibers between her fingertips. This dense wool would keep the feet of their men warm. She inhaled the oily scent of the wool, and she smiled. Mary Beth pulled out a pattern and handed it to her. It was for a knit hood.

"There's a need for socks more than anything, and with winter approaching, these hoods." Mary Beth passed her an already knitted specimen.

Avery studied the hood carefully. Then she took a sip from her nearby tea and grabbed her knitting needles from her sewing box beside her chair.

"How about we get this show on the road? Let's start now."

"That's what I was hoping you'd say." Mary Beth smiled widely at her.

Obviously, she had passed Mary Beth's tests as well. They enjoyed a solid hour of knitting, chatting about the war, dissecting the politics of women's suffrage, discussing details from Joseph's last letter to Mary Beth, and considering more perspectives on church choice. When Avery heard Jack stir and Prentis step into the back porch simultaneously, she realized the afternoon was long gone. They began gathering their items and tidying up.

"Will you come again soon?" Avery said to Mary Beth. "It was a joy to spend the afternoon with you."

"I will. Shall we set a specific day?"

"Wednesdays at naptime are fine, exactly like we did today. Will that work?"

"That sounds wonderful." Mary Beth put on her wrap and headed toward the front door, dipping her head when Prentis entered the room. "Hello, P.J."

"Mary Beth." He nodded. "How's your family? I've missed seeing them each week."

"They're doing well." She smiled at both. "Avery can catch you up. It's wonderful to see you two. Hope to see more of you in the future, though." Her eyes twinkled at Avery.

And then, out she went.

Slowly, Prentis turned toward Avery and studied her, wearing an expression of appraisal.

"I don't know how we're going to do it," he said, "but we're going to church this coming Sunday. You've been holed up here suffering too long without the company and encouragement of other believers. You need to go to church."

Gently, she smiled at him. "You could determine that with just a glance."

"You're beaming. You need companionship."

"My insightful husband, I believe I do. You also wear the same lonely and discouraged expression, by the way."

"I've become aware of that."

***

The last Sunday morning in October found Avery lightly rouging her cheeks so she didn't appear wan and sickly. Hoping she could get through the next few hours, she was also girded and swathed in everything possible for feminine protection—undergarment apron, ladies' belt, and far more cloths than normal. Today she even wore her voluminous woolen burgundy skirt that swished fuller than her normal silhouette. She squashed down her anxiety about possible accidents. Church was essential. She needed to be there.

They rode toward town, bundled warmly, for there was a cool bite in the air.

"You're anxious." Prentis glanced over. "What's got you upset?"

"Well, Tom isn't in the pulpit."

"That's well established. But that's not why you're anxious."

"It's my condition," she said. "There could be all sorts of possible embarrassing dilemmas."

"But, you've attended to that. Did this bother you when you taught school?"

"Oh, no," she said, "it didn't."

"Then why—"

"As a teacher, I never had to sit down. That's why I wore my burgundy skirt."

Obvious confusion showing on his face, Prentis glanced at her. With furrowed brow, he looked back at the road, clearly mystified by her statement. Just as she inhaled to explain, an expression of comprehension spread across his face, and he beat her to it.

"Ah!" he said. "I see. Are you prepared adequately?"

"I am."

"Then try to enjoy yourself and focus on the service."

"I will. You poor man, having to learn information you probably wish you never knew."

"I'm a farmer, remember." He chuckled. "I understand the mechanics of the matter. You're my wife. Everything about you concerns me. I need to be informed about your body, especially now, when you're not well." He fixed his eyes briefly on hers. "We can leave at any time. Just give me the sign, we'll head for the door, and I'll whisk you away."

She heaved a sigh of relief. "With that knowledge fortifying me, I think I can do this."

He smiled over at her, and she thought she might be able. He was right. She needed it.

They entered Wakita and chugged up outside the large white church building one block off Main Street. Pulling her timepiece from her skirt pocket, Avery saw that it had taken less than ten minutes. The new automobile really did change everything.

Prentis disembarked and hurried around to help her. Then he unfastened Jack and hoisted him into his arms. Together, they stepped toward the church. Familiar faces as well as unfamiliar greeted them. Jack fussed and reached for her, seeming to be overwhelmed. Prentis chuckled and passed him to Avery.

"He's shy like his father," she whispered to him.

He looked into her eyes, giving her a smile.

Mary Beth scurried over as her family also entered, compassion flitting across her face as she scanned Avery's apparel and furrowed brow.

Prentis gave George Miller a hearty handshake as Mrs. Miller hurried inside.

Mary Beth leaned near. "I'm so glad you could come this morning."

"I hope it goes well."

She whispered, "I'll have my eyes open."

"I've covered all the bases," Avery said, "but thank you. That helps me relax some. I'm a bundle of nerves."

They smiled at one another, and in went their little family, whisked into a new church world that wasn't familiar or comfortable. After leaving the foyer entryway, which was all they'd experienced of the church in the past, they stepped into the sanctuary.

Being inquisitive, Avery knew that in 1896, shortly after the Land Run, a building had been erected just south of town on the location currently occupied by the cemetery. The Methodists had bought that building a couple years later and moved it into town. It remained until 1902 when this new building was built on the vacant lot that had been used for parking on the corner. Once complete, the old building was transported up to Gibbon to serve as a hardware store—one Avery was familiar with, having grown up there. A parsonage was constructed where the old building had previously sat.

Wood was scarce and costly in Oklahoma. It wasn't unusual to reuse buildings in new locations.

The sanctuary was large and airy with a high arching ceiling and rows of lofty frosted windows along each side. No stained glass in the front, but a large cross drew her eyes upward to its position near the peak. Below that, sat a blue built-in baptismal tank. The floors were burnished hardwood, and they matched the pews. The aisles teemed with people greeting one another and pausing to chat. Sunday School seemed to have been recently released, and children ran in and out among the adults with mommas in hot pursuit.

Striding up and down the central aisle wearing a black suit similar to Prentis's, a man who could only be the Reverend Wallock, shook hands and engaged in quiet conversation with each group. He appeared to be about Prentis's age, and he wore no vestment. Quickly, he was upon them where they had stopped toward the back.

"Welcome! I'm Mark Wallock." The man's gray eyes were piercing.

The two men shook hands.

"P.J. Pinkerton," her husband stated. Placing his hand lightly on Avery's back, Prentis turned back toward the reverend. "And this is my wife, Avery."

The friendly face of the reverend bent near, and Jack leaned right out of her arms toward Prentis, who snatched him up before he fell headlong onto the floor.

"Whoa, son!" Prentis exclaimed.

"Reminds me of how we're to trust the Lord," Reverend Mark Wallock said, chuckling softly. "Simply falling into His arms like children, knowing He'll catch us."

Prentis studied him. "You're absolutely right, Mark."

The Reverend Anthony Mark Wallock now turned toward Avery.

Shaking her hand firmly, he said, "I've heard about your theological education, Mrs. Pinkerton. Welcome to the Methodist Episcopal Church. We're always in need of Sunday School teachers."

Avery returned his smile. "Thank you, Reverend. First, we need to see if we fit."

"Of course." He laughed. "Your patriotic pastor's reputation precedes him. He's left some big shoes to fill for all the pastors here in town."

"I wouldn't say his motivation was patriotism, but rather, having a pastor's heart, he was concerned about the boys who went to war. He's a good man. But I've heard you are too—" At this the reverend held up his hand to object, but Avery hurried on. "You remained back with your mother during her illness. Did she accompany you here? I hope she's well."

Reverend Wallock swallowed hard. "I'm sorry to say, but my mother passed away in Evanston right before I came here to fill my assignment."

Avery immediately regretted her blunder. Her first public outing in months, and she had put her foot, nay, her entire boot right into her mouth. Every comeback response was knocked right out of her mind by his tragic and unanticipated answer.

But Prentis stepped closer. Jack clutched tighter, his little face matching the somber adult expressions all around him.

"I'm sorry to hear it, Mark," Prentis said. "Losing a parent is a tragic loss. Don't know if we ever truly recover."

Reverend Wallock's eyes glistened. "I agree. You've lost a parent, too, haven't you? I've now lost both. I hope to never forget the sound of their voices."

The two men studied one another with warm and friendly eyes.

"I'll pray for you," Prentis said. "Lost my father over ten years ago. Still miss him."

"Thank you, P.J. I'll pray for you as well."

The piano struck up with Mrs. Miller's enthusiastic introduction to "Amazing Grace." Reverend Wallock shook Prentis's hand again and then hurried up the aisle. From the pulpit, the reverend led them in worship, belting out each verse with a well-trained voice as he flourished his hand, carving paths of melodious harmony through the air while keeping the tempo. Tom he was not, though Tom could sing with the best. Avery knew she had to try not to judge one man by the other in every interaction. People differed in their gifts and their responses to God's love.

The sermon was topical, rather than systematic. The Gospel was proclaimed, Jesus's role as the Prince of Peace—even during a time of war—was emphasized, and encouragement was given. The reverend's parting benediction stood them all on their feet.

"The Lord bless thee and keep thee. The Lord make His face shine upon thee and be gracious unto thee. The Lord lift up His countenance upon thee and give thee peace, both now and forevermore. Amen."

Fourteen

MIDWEEK, THE SOUND OF a Model T chugging into their barnyard drew Avery toward the window. As the automobile drove up the lane, she detected Mr. Hampton at the wheel and Reverend Wallock in the passenger seat. Avery put on the water to boil and then glanced about the living room, noting the disarray caused by a curious toddler. She set about tidying as best she could.

Soon, she heard men's voices near the house. Prentis had obviously intersected them.

"Avery!" he hailed loudly from the back door.

Hurrying through the kitchen, she found Jack crying and Prentis wearing a concerned expression. Jack's arms were covered with scratches, and a few bled. The baby dove for her.

Avery scooped him up. "What's happened?"

"I'm not certain. He was around the corner of the stall. I heard Sam growl at something, and then Jack cried out. I stepped around, and this is how I found him."

Avery investigated his wounds. None were too serious. Maybe he'd had a run-in with the rooster. "Were the chickens about?"

"May have been. I was focused on Ulysses's hoof. It's not looking good."

Behind Prentis stood the two men from town. Having arrived exactly as all of this took place, they waited somberly and patiently, concern showing on their faces. Prentis noted Avery's glance over his shoulder, and he turned.

"So sorry," he said. "Not very hospitable. Welcome."

Both of the men chuckled.

"We're sorry to intrude unannounced," Reverend Wallock said. "There are no phone lines out here yet, and the only recourse we had was to simply arrive and hope for the best. Mr. Hampton is completing his Red Cross Fund Drive, as he's the captain for these parts of rural Wakita, and I'm making a ministerial call. I don't have my transportation figured out yet, so I had to rely on him. Please, excuse us."

Prentis stood silent, as did Avery, absorbing all of this information.

"Well," Prentis said at last, gesturing for them to enter. "Come on in."

With Avery leading the way with the sobbing baby, they all trekked through the back porch, up the steps, through the messy kitchen containing a sink full of dirty dishes, and then into the cluttered living room. Inwardly, Avery sighed, her housewifely pride taking a beating.

"I'm going to leave the reverend for his visit," Mr. Hampton stated, "and go on around this part of the county to do my part for the Red Cross drive."

They both stood staring at him, trying to discern what he meant.

"Oh!" Prentis said. "Let me get my donation right now."

"No, P.J." Mr. Hampton held up his hand. "We're not expecting you boys who've registered to donate at all. Merely being ready to go is enough."

"Well, at this point, I'm doing nothing for the war effort but growing food and waiting. I'd like to donate, if you'll take my money."

"Of course, I'll take your money, if you feel you must give." Mr. Hampton smiled as Prentis disappeared.

Over Jack's cries, Avery heard Prentis digging through his sock drawer where he kept cash on hand. Their money might be low. He hadn't restocked for quite a while. She wanted to scurry around and tidy, but now that the men were in the house, she couldn't. So, she smiled politely, attempting to appear gracious. Thankfully, Jack was settling down.

Prentis returned. "All I've got is three dollars on hand."

Mr. Hampton took it and inserted it into a large bank envelope with Red Cross officially emblazoned on the side. "For a young family, that's a generous amount—enough to cover at least a week's groceries. Can you spare it? Are you certain?"

"I'm certain. I'd like to give more, but I've got no more cash here in the house. We want to take care of our men who've gone to war."

"That's what we're attempting to do," Mr. Hampton said.

"I'll look you up later to make a second donation."

"Thank you, young man, though you're already doing your part." Mr. Hampton shook Prentis's hand and turned to go, looking at the reverend. "I'll return for you after I've covered the area."

"That will be fine," the reverend replied. "Thank you."

Avery followed Mr. Hampton to the back door and then returned to wash Jack's little arms. She heard Prentis talking with the reverend in the living room. Little snippets of their conversation drifted in. But the baby appeared to want to nurse. He'd been gradually weaning himself, but when he needed comfort or when he wanted to drift off to sleep, he still seemed to need her. Giving Prentis the eye as she stepped into their bedroom, she hoped he understood the message that she needed a few minutes alone with Jack. Rocking quietly in their bedroom, she tried to relax.

Lord, forgive me for my vanity. I didn't want the reverend to see my house like this.

***

When Avery passed through to their bedroom, Prentis noted her meaningful look. When he heard the rocking chair, he knew that Jack had needed the comfort that only a mother could provide. Now was the time to get to work.

Turning to the reverend, he said, "How are you with a dishtowel, Mark?"

"I'm a professional." Mark Wallock smiled widely.

"Good! Then let's help out my wife and get this kitchen tidied."

Washing dishes and doing laundry were some of the earliest tasks Prentis had completed with Tom when they were new friends. Washing dishes with a man told you a lot about him. Within minutes, Prentis had the wash pan full of hot soapy water, and they had their system worked out. He washed the dishes in the suds and then rinsed them in the pan of clear water, and Mark manned the dishtowel. He was proficient.

"I did quite a few dishes while my mother was ailing," Mark said. "It seemed to allow her to rest easier if I kept the house clean, especially the kitchen. I'm sorry we intruded unannounced. I know how a woman hates to have guests arrive to find the house in disarray."

"Couldn't be helped. This is rural Oklahoma."

"That's certainly true." Mark smiled.

"While we work," Prentis said, "why don't you tell me about your home and family. Must've been hard to leave right after your mother passed."

"It certainly was. My father did well in Chicago, and he made sure we were comfortable. I grew up in a large home, three stories including an attic and a broad front porch."

"What about the rest of your family?" Prentis asked.

"Where should I start?"

"The beginning."

"I was born in Schildberg, in the Moravian region of Austria. My parents emigrated here when I was two. All of my extended family is there, right in the middle of the war."

"I didn't know that." Prentis looked at him. "Did you grow up speaking German at home?"

"Ja, wir haben nur zu Hause Deutsch gesprochen."

Prentis chuckled. "I'm guessing that means you did."

"Yes." Mark laughed with him. "We only spoke German at home, though my parents spoke good English. They said German was the language of home. When I started school, I knew English from going to church, from times when people came to visit, and from being out in public. Since I've lived here most of my life and I had good voice training, I don't have an accent."

"I bet this war was hard on your parents."

"I believe it killed my father. Every time he talked about the assassination of the Archduke Ferdinand and his wife Sophie, he became apoplectic. He urged me to return to Austria to fight for the land of my birth, alongside my cousins, but I'm an American through and through. He never understood my position. He died of a heart attack about a year after the war began."

Prentis paused his washing to look at the reverend. "That's hard. What about your cousins?"

Mark Wallock nodded. "War is grievous. I'm sure their lives have been destroyed by this conflict. After moving here, our family didn't remain close. I've only seen them once since, but I pray for them every day."

"The loss of your father isn't that long ago."

"No, I lost my parents one right after the other."

"Life can be downright intolerable sometimes," Prentis said.

"It can. Thankfully, the consolations of the Savior are rich and abundant."

"Yes, they are. I felt the same when I lost my father."

"You mentioned it was over a decade ago. How old were you?" the reverend asked.

"Fifteen."

"I'm sorry to hear that. It's a hard loss to deal with as a young man."

"Yes, it was."

Both washed silently as they gathered their thoughts.

"I didn't take the ministerial exemption on my draft card." Mark glanced at him. "If my father had lived, that fact alone would probably have killed him. Thankfully, he'd already gone ahead to be with the Lord."

"Do you want to go to war?"

"I would gladly go to the battlefield for the same reasons as your Pastor McKinney, and if I'm drafted, I will apply to be a chaplain. But, I felt it imperative to make a clear statement to my colleagues and friends. Within the cities, tensions are high toward German-speaking immigrants. By not asking for that exemption, I'm openly and officially identifying as an American. I have no loyalty to Austria, though my parents remained loyal until they died. I'm an American."

The dishes had been finished, and they now faced one another in the kitchen.

"That makes sense to me," Prentis said. "Not only does it give you an opportunity to serve your country if called, but it also makes clear that you're on the side of the Allies."

Somberly, Mark pressed his lips together. "That was my intent."

"The rest is in God's hands then, whether we're called or not."

"Yes, we're all in the same predicament."

"What predicament is that?" Avery's voice caused them both to turn.

Jack had been comforted, and Avery looked composed but pale. Prentis didn't know if it was the angle of the sun through the front windows, or the slight shadow in their north-facing kitchen. The sinews in her neck were more prominent. Under her eyes, her skin was purpled. She didn't look well. It had only been two weeks since she'd seen the doctor, but she showed no sign of improvement. The worsening had come on gradually. He was now greatly concerned.

"War, Mrs. Pinkerton," Mark said. "We're all awaiting the casting of the lot, so to speak, to determine who will go and who will remain."

"Ah, yes. Did you take the ministerial exemption?"

"No, I did not. I was explaining my position to your husband."

Avery now looked behind them at the kitchen counter and then at each one individually. She smiled. Prentis glanced over at Mark. The reverend wore one of her aprons to protect his suit pants, while he himself had a dishtowel thrown over his shoulder.

"Thank you both for what you've done in this kitchen," Avery said. "Reverend, Prentis probably didn't tell you that he's far better at cleaning than I am. Now I can make us some coffee, and we can all sit down to talk, if you have time."

"I'm afraid you're stuck with me until Mr. Hampton returns."

"It's our pleasure," she said. "Do you intend to wash the dishes each time you come?"

Prentis saw the twinkle in her eye, but the reverend didn't know her well yet.

"A drop-in guest has to ingratiate himself in any way he can," Mark said.

She studied the reverend's face and he hers, and simultaneously they burst into laughter.

"I'll make the coffee," Avery said, smiling widely, "and you two take Jack and sit down."

***

When Avery entered the living room with the coffee and a plate of cookies from her most recent batch, she found the reverend on the floor with Jack constructing roadways for his little handmade cars to travel upon. The roads were comprised of books from Prentis's bookcase.

Prentis removed each book and handed it across to the reverend, who helped Jack place the next section where he wanted it to go. The baby then drove the wooden car across that next part. They had a roadway that ran from the bookcase on the south side of the house to the small table under the north window. Jack could now drive all the way across the living room.

All looked up at her.

Jack beamed wide. "Mom-mom, cars driving."

Prentis and Reverend Wallock both wore boyish grins of delight.

Joy bubbled up inside Avery, washing through her and bringing with it a sense of wellbeing and delight in this small domestic tableau. She hadn't felt this way for a while. Maybe they would live through these current troubles. Maybe it would be all right for Tom to be so far away. Maybe they had found a new church home with this kind man at the helm.

God and church had always been at the center of her life, and now God had sent a new pastor. A sense of relief engulfed her. In spite of her failing health, the baby they had lost, and all their missing loved ones, she no longer felt as if the middle had fallen out of their lives.

They spent the rest of the morning drinking coffee, playing with Jack, learning more about the reverend, and becoming acquainted. The reverend asked if she wanted to teach a Sunday School class, and she informed him that she'd have to defer that privilege until she was in better health. He didn't pry. Avery appreciated that.

As they all conversed, she smiled at Prentis often. When Mr. Hampton returned, their little family, including Jack, stood on the porch smiling and waving goodbye to both men.

"I'm glad he came," Prentis said.

"You know, Tom would have done those very same things—dishes, playing with Jack."

"Yes, he would have, and he did. He would've dressed less formally, but he would have done the same things."

"That's what I was thinking." Avery smiled. "I wonder if the Reverend Anthony Mark Wallock owns a pair of blue jeans."

Prentis laughed. "I'm guessing no. He's a city boy."

"Mock bye-bye," Jack said.

Both parents smiled at him.

"Yes," Prentis said, "Mark went bye-bye."

"But he'll be back," Avery said.

Avery smiled widely, turned, and walked inside. Yes, they might live after all.

***

When Mary Beth arrived on Wednesday as planned, they knit socks with intensity. Both expert knitters, they could converse without missing a beat. Avery informed Mary Beth of the reverend's visit, and Mary Beth divulged details from Joseph Pitzer's last letter. He wrote that the very men who had gone to Camp Funston to be trained were now building the training camp.

"Joe says they have their own coffee roasting house," Mary Beth said.

"Can you imagine the delightful aroma?"

"That's what I thought."

The scent of coffee beans filled Avery's mind. "How delicious that would be!"

"Joe's work crew is currently erecting a theater."

Avery stopped knitting and looked at her. "In the camp?"

"Yes, he says Camp Funston is like a small city. The nearest town is miles away—Junction City, Kansas. At the camp, they've built schools, workshops for constructing all they need, libraries, their own infirmaries, general stores, and even social centers for recreation when they're off duty. Some of the construction workers are newly arrived from China."

"China!" Avery said. "Imagine that! I hadn't pictured any of this. To train millions of men for war, small cities would need to be built to house everyone. That makes sense."

"It's somewhat mindboggling, isn't it?"

"That it is."

"Now, listen to this part." Mary Beth dug through her satchel. "You have to hear how Joe describes it."

Avery smiled, happy that her childhood friend had found a woman who adored him.

"Let me see if I can find the place." Mary Beth skimmed the back of a tightly written page. "Here it is. And I quote. 'Now, I didn't think I was spoiled when I arrived. I'm a hardworking man, grew up simple, a farmer who typically puts in at least a twelve-hour day. But I'd never shared a bedroom with a hundred and forty-nine men—'"

"One hundred fifty men sleeping in one room!"

"That's what I thought."

"Please, keep reading," Avery said. "I'm sorry for interrupting."

Mary Beth found her place again. "He writes, 'With so many fellas all in one spot, they have to keep us occupied from sunup to sundown. They even bring in opera singers and movies for us to enjoy after work. They want us to fall into bed tired. An infantry has a hundred and fifty men, so the entire infantry sleeps in one large room, row after row of beds. Imagine a bunch of stinking men, filthy socks, out in the sun all day. That's life at Camp Funston. Knowing one another well is part of making us into a fighting unit. There we are snoring and making all sorts of noises in our sleep. Didn't really want to know that many other fellas this well, but I sure do now. Before we nod off, one fella will say something on one side of the room, and someone will answer from the other side. Everyone ends up laughing, or fighting, depending on what's said. It's like sharing a room with over a hundred brothers! Then a foreign officer will check in on us and shout out, "You chaps bloody well better pipe down! You think this is jolly good fun, but you won't think so at five a.m. revelry or when you're staring down the barrel of a gun." That sobers us up right quick. We all settle down after that, I tell you.'"

Avery smiled. "He writes like he talks. I'd love to hear him tell that in person."

"I agree." Mary Beth wore a wistful expression. "I'll be glad when he returns."

Reaching across the small table between them, Avery squeezed her hand.

174

A slow tear ran down Mary Beth's cheek. "I wish I'd just married him, but instead I made him wait."

"He's grown, personally and in your heart, hasn't he?"

"Yes, he certainly has."

"You could tell him that by mail, you know."

"Yes." Mary Beth sniffed. "I guess I could. You don't think it would be too forward?"

"The man has already begged you to marry him. How many times?"

"At least three, maybe more."

"Then I think he'd be delighted to hear that from you."

"I'll tell him then. It simply didn't seem prudent to marry before he left." She paused, blushing. "What if there was a baby, and Joe gone to war? How would I have managed?"

"I understand," Avery said softly. "Tell him. Learning you wished you'd married him would be good for him to know before he heads over to Europe."

"I do think I'll write back and say just that."

They knit silently for a long while, lost in thought, each musing over different memories of Joseph Pitzer and how this war had changed his life and theirs.

Fifteen

PRENTIS RETURNED HOME FROM a trip to the McKee farm. The construction of the oil well derrick had begun, and it looked to be a colossal structure. Operation was to begin November 15, so they would need to build fast. Coming through the back door, he shrugged out of his heavy coat, catching Avery in the kitchen preparing their lunch.

"Sweetheart, the size of that derrick!"

"Did they get it started?"

"They did. It's enormous! When it's complete, I think we'll be able to see it from here."

Jack straddled her hip. As Prentis stepped into the kitchen, he reached for the baby.

"Now that will be something!" she said.

"The rig builders are hard at work—pulleys, horses, engines, all sorts of machinery. They're constructing what's called a 'standard California derrick.' It'll rise to seventy-four feet. Once it's up and ready to go, they'll begin drilling."

She looked up from her food preparation. "How did they know where to dig?"

"The geologists surveyed. Mr. J.W. Lewis of Hager, Bates, & Lewis in Tulsa did the work. They've been right in past surveys—the Garber well, in particular. At least, that's what all the men who had come out told me, Mr. Trask and Mr. Clinesmith among them."

"I'll take your word for it." Avery smiled at him.

Jack squirmed, and Prentis set him down. The baby toddled to the kitchen doorway to play with his cars and trucks.

"The company leased a lot of land," Prentis continued. "Sixteen thousand acres all around this part of Oklahoma, last I heard. They're poring over the countryside trying to find the best locations for petroleum. People are hoping they strike it big."

"Well, since we're invested, I'd like that too. But even if they don't, it's all in God's hands. He put the oil down there."

"Yes, He did. There was also talk about the first American casualties in Europe." Avery's face fell, and Prentis realized too late that he shouldn't have aimed their conversation in that direction. "There was a rumor that a boy from Medford had died, but one of the men at the McKee's said the information was incorrect. The boy was a relative of that Medford family, not an immediate member."

"Someone's son, nevertheless."

"That's for certain. A son, just like our son, and a grievous loss to them."

Both stared at one another, their eyes locking.

A long silent pause filled the room, followed by a sinking sensation in his gut. How had it become normal everyday conversation to consider whether a county resident's son had been shot and killed in a faraway place? They lived in a new world.

Scrambling, he turned the topic away from war.

"Are you feeling better? You look good."

"A little, yes, though nothing's changed. It's merely that the sun is shining right in the south-facing windows, now that it's lower on the horizon, and the scrub oak is a lovely color on this northern ridge." She nodded toward the kitchen window. "It's difficult to feel glum when surrounded by such beauty, even when I don't feel well, our country is at war, someone's son just died in that war, and people we love are gone to fight in it."

"It *is* beautiful out that window." He fixed his eyes on the scrub oak visible through the glass panes. "That's why my dad put the window right there."

Both grew silent. Avery mashed the potatoes.

Prentis sighed. "I'm sorry I brought up that poor boy who died, especially now."

"The fact is, people are dying." She kept her eyes on the potatoes.

"Yes, not only over there, but in our own house. Our own baby died. I went to the McKee's to watch the construction, because I wanted to escape having to think about it. Should have left the local talk out of it, but I brought it all back with me."

Sympathetic, she met his eyes. "I love you, Prentis. We're both hurting, we're at war, and we lost a baby. We can't avoid it. Yet still, today, in spite of the pain, the beauty of God's creation soothes my heart. That's what I'm focusing on. We have to rejoice in what God has given right in front of us. Otherwise our losses will consume us heart and soul."

"You're right." He kissed her on the forehead. "A good reminder."

They heard a crash in the living room and hurried toward the doorway.

178

Attempting to climb up the bookcase, Jack had brought an entire row of books crashing down upon him. Both rushed in, lest he pull the entire bookcase over on himself.

"As you were saying," Prentis said, "rejoice in what God has given right in front of us."

"Lord, keep our boy safe." She said softly. "I think we've arrived at the training phase. For his own good, we have to tell him he can't do this."

Wearing a solemn expression, Prentis squatted down beside Jack.

"No, son. You can't get these out without Dad or Momma helping you."

"Get 'em out!" Jack said.

"No, we're not getting them out. Let's put them back."

"Out!"

"Back in they go." As he said that, Prentis replaced the books. "Come help Dad."

Quickly, Prentis slid book after book onto the shelf. When he was down to the last few books, Jack picked up one and handed it to him and then another.

"You're helping! What a big boy!"

"Help," Jack agreed.

"We'll play with them later. Right now, Momma has food for us."

"Eat?"

"Yes, let's go eat." Prentis scooped him up.

As usual, Avery had prepared them a delicious spread for their midday meal. One large bowl held the pile of mashed potatoes. Right in the center, a pat of butter melted into rivulets of flavor. There was ham and squash. Prentis knew she'd also baked an apple pie after breakfast.

"Avery, you take such good care of us. It puts heart in a man to sit down to a large and generous meal on a chilly fall day. Thank you."

179

"Tank 'oo, Mom-mom."

She smiled at little Jack, sitting there in his highchair pushed up to the table.

"You're both welcome."

Avery gazed into Prentis's eyes, and they exchanged looks of joy and gratitude. No matter their losses, no matter what came next, what God had given was a joy to their hearts and the delight of their lives. They would focus on the blessings.

***

Now the war news began to arrive thick and fast, for American troops had engaged. Those first troops were men who had already been in the army before America declared war and joined the Allies. They had the most experience, and they went bravely into battle. There were only fourteen thousand of them, merely the beginning of America's involvement. Nevertheless, the news was sobering. They wondered when Charles, Tom, Joseph, and the others would see battle and what would become of them.

A letter arrived from Tom. The first they'd had in a while. Training and deployment had kept him busy. They cherished his words sent all the way from Europe.

October 1917

Dearest friends,

Here we are now in France. I'm not even certain what day it is here or over there. If you'd ever told this Kansas boy that he'd be in France one day with D. L. Moody's son, off to war, I would have told you that you were crazy. Maybe we're all crazy.

I don't have long to write. Sea travel didn't agree with me. Spent most of the trip hanging over the rail emptying my stomach into the Atlantic. Then landed here. Don't understand a word of French, and it was disorienting to disembark. I couldn't even walk straight.

We've got a lot of work to do embedding chaplains into fighting units, so we can be true pastors in the men's time of need. We'll go wherever they go – combat, trenches, hospitals, recognizance. Imagine what their mommas would want for their boys. That's what we'll be doing with all our hearts, serving Jesus by helping these men.

How I miss you two! Your letter caught up with me. I'm glad you started attending the MEC and that Mark Wallock came to visit. You need the Christian fellowship and the teaching – we all do, even pastors. I'm glad you've made him part of your family, as I am. I pray for you every day, and I miss all of my church desperately.

Keep me in your prayers. I'll write again soon. God bless you!

  Affectionately,

Tom

***

Throughout the end of October and into November, war news hit them with force, like an iron mallet. Each stroke of the war hammer beat with a reverberating clang, driving home the absolute necessity of the commitment of their friends and family to the fight.

American forces were desperately needed. That was clear.

The Italians lost more than three hundred thousand men in one fight when the Germans and Austrians attacked at Caporetto. Reeling back in complete chaos and total disarray, the Italian army retreated, able to muster no defense before the military might of the Germanic horde.

Nikolai Lenin and the Bolsheviks seized St. Petersburg and effectively eliminated the Allied Russians from the fight by promising land, peace, and bread. The entire Eastern Front would now collapse, sending all the German soldiers to the Western Front.

In the messy bog of Flanders, the British Army received a devastating loss of nearly a quarter of a million troops after striving for four months to capture Passchendaele, to no avail. The British troops were unable to muster any type of offense.

By springtime, it was feared that with the full force of all the German troops now in the west, they might push all the way through Europe. Then all of that effort would be for naught. Americans needed to begin fighting. Leaders in the Allied countries begged for American soldiers to step into the fight, striking back at the Germans with their vast numbers.

Would General Pershing decide they were ready?

**

Prentis had hung a swing from the biggest tree on their property. It was north of the house, one of the comforting trees right outside Avery's kitchen window. When she worked in the kitchen, she watched the foliage change from season to season. In this season of loss, looking out that window at the foliage strengthened her, reminding her of God's beauty and grace.

Today it was chilly, and the wind snapped and sighed, hinting at the coming cold season. Nevertheless, Avery felt she needed to escape to that swing. The tree still maintained a few leaves, the stragglers, those holding on tightly with all their might, loathe for winter to come and snatch away the final vestiges of summer.

Since Jack was sleeping soundly, Avery quietly exited through the back door, making sure it closed soft and easy, so as not to wake the baby. Listening outside the bedroom window for any sound of disturbance, she stood by the door for a few minutes. Obviously, he still slept.

Then she slipped around the corner.

Pulling her wrap tight, she wound the shawl over her head and about her arms, and then she twined her arms around the ropes that held the swing. A soft giggle escaped. She probably looked like an Eastern European peasant woman. In the papers, she had seen pictures. No one would recognize her. She smiled.

God knew it was she. He always did. She had slipped out here to be alone with Him. Of course, she was always with Him, but rarely ever alone. Alone, she needed to be. Tomorrow was her follow-up appointment with the doctor. Nothing had changed.

She settled herself into the swing, making sure all of her feminine undergarments were positioned as they should be, and then she lifted her feet. Back and forth faintly, and then at increasing heights, she pointed her toes first forward and then backward. The wisps of hair that had loosened from her braid whipped about her face. The mid-November breeze stung sharp upon her cheeks. Her eyes watered from it. Or was it the overflow of tears? She couldn't tell.

The middle of her ached. Great loss was coming. She didn't know how she knew, but she did. This wasn't like her first fear that Prentis would be marched off to war. As newlyweds and before Jack had been born, that idea had tormented her. No. This was a settled certainty.

She wasn't afraid. She simply knew it was coming. She felt as if God was preparing her for enormous sadness.

But she also felt fortified by Him, as if His Holy Spirit wrapped her round about like this shawl, penetrating and warming her heart as well.

The loss would be wide, and it would be deep. The loss would be personal. That's all she knew. Simply that it would be, and that God was with her.

Tears left tracks along her cheeks as she swung, waiting, listening, hoping to be told exactly what was coming, so she could brace herself. But, rarely did that ever happen on this earth.

Rather, the lesson was to trust God in it, whatever it was and whenever it came. So, trust she would, and He would hold her. She knew He would. Still, she wept, for she would never be the same. She knew this too. Refining involved pounding and smashing the malleable clay, God the Potter and she the clay. She would be reshaped. What would she be? Only time would tell.

On the backswing, Prentis surprised her, catching her in mid-flight as she hung in space before the forward motion. His arms were strong, and he held her close, nuzzling his face against hers, squeezing her tightly to his chest.

"Do you have any idea how much I love you?" he whispered over her shoulder.

"No matter what?" she whispered back.

"No matter what."

And then she wept all the more. She couldn't tell him why, and she didn't know if he would understand. But the kindness in his eyes and the gentleness of his touch stated clearly that he understood, that he loved her, and that he would be there beside her as they suffered the coming losses together.

All would be well with their souls.

***

On the way to Avery's doctor appointment, they left Jack at his Grandma and Grandpa Slaughter's house. Her momma and daddy had comforting words for her and for Prentis as they prepared to learn what might be wrong with Avery's body. Everyone was filled with apprehension. But, having parents like hers—people who had gone through a lifetime of trouble—was a great blessing when facing her own trial.

As they climbed into the Model T, Momma stood beside her door with some final words.

"Whatever happens, daughter, God is with you, and He loves you dearly. Nothing ever changes that."

Avery nodded. "Thank you, Momma. It's good to be reminded."

Chiming in from Prentis's side of the car, her daddy had similar words. "In His own time and in His own way, the good Lord will work this together for good in your life—whatever it is. He's done it time and time again in our lives, and He always comes through."

Nodding, they soaked in these reminders.

Then off they went. Avery couldn't take her eyes off Jack as they pulled away. They hadn't ever left him before, and his face appeared astonished, stunned almost to see them driving away. His eyes were large, and as they reached the end of the drive, his little arms reached toward them. His small mouth shaped itself into a round O. Avery knew he was howling for them to return. *Poor baby!* They would be back soon enough.

Prentis squeezed her hand for just a moment, before grabbing the steering wheel again.

"He'll be fine," he said, glancing at her.

She nodded. The ride was silent. Too much was at stake for chitchat, and they both knew something wasn't right. They'd hashed and rehashed, and they knew the promises of God.

Flocks of birds rose into the air before their oncoming car, sparrows mostly, all of them chirping together in chorus. Their car drove over a spot where wheat had spilled onto the road while being transported. The birds all swooped upward and then immediately back downward behind their automobile. Avery turned to watch the cascade of birds, all of them landing again, eating, and rejoicing over God's bountiful provision on a late November day.

Instantly, the lyrics to a new song they had sung recently came to mind, and she had to sing it. It seemed the only logical response on a cold fall day when going to a doctor's appointment to learn bad news.

> *Why should I feel discouraged,*
> *Why should the shadows come,*
> *Why should my heart be lonely,*
> *and long for heav'n and home,*
> *When Jesus is my portion?*
> *My constant Friend is He:*
> *His eye is on the sparrow,*
> *and I know He watches me;*
> *His eye is on the sparrow,*
> *and I know He watches me.*
> *I sing because I'm happy,*
> *I sing because I'm free,*
> *For His eye is on the sparrow,*
> *and I know He watches me.*

Prentis joined her, and they sang it through again. Neither could remember the rest of the verses, having only recently learned the song, but that one verse sufficed. It was more than enough. They had reached town.

When the nurse called Avery back, she asked if Prentis could come. The nurse said she would ask the

186

doctor. It wasn't usually done. She returned quickly and said he had agreed. Then the nurse urged them to follow her back to the examining room.

They sat silently in the room. Avery's hands clutched tightly together in her lap. Prentis reached over to slide his large warm hand in between hers, and she squeezed it tightly. His eyes were gentle and communicated more than any words. He was with her in this.

Now loud steps pounded purposefully down the hall toward them. Briefly, they flicked their eyes toward one another. Then the doctor burst in.

"Well, it's good to see the two of you!" The doctor smiled, reaching to shake Prentis's hand as he stood. "I hope you've got good news for me today. How are you feeling, Avery?"

As he looked into her face, his expression changed. He took in her entire countenance.

"I wish I could say the opposite," she said, "but I feel worse. Nothing has changed."

Now the doctor's face grew quite serious. "I'm sorry to hear that. I wondered if that womb of yours might cause problems at some point. Let me complete a physical exam and see if that gives us more information. Leave your cloths secured with your belt. I'll need to examine them as well. That will help me to ascertain what might be going on."

Avery nodded and rose to step behind the curtained screen in the corner. In the privacy of the changing area, she removed her skirt and wrapped the provided sheet around her waist, protecting her modesty. Timorously, she now stepped around to the table. The doctor had brought forward a bright light to shine on his work area. Prentis took her hand and helped her onto the table. Then he sat beside her head with his hand resting on her shoulder.

A small screen at her waist kept them from seeing what the doctor was doing and helped Avery feel somewhat shielded from the stark and humiliating nature of the procedure. Grabbing hold of her hand, Prentis whispered into her ear that he loved her. And then the doctor got to work. The examination was quite painful. He applied pressure to her lower abdomen, mashing on this and on that, and painful sensations arose that she had never before experienced.

Occasionally, he muttered in Latin, "*Placenta accreta?*" and then, "*Placenta increta?*" and then after more mashing, "Perhaps *placenta percreta*? I never thought I'd see this again."

Then he peered over the screen at them. "P.J., do you want to see this? You're a farmer, so you'll know what you're looking at."

"I'll stay put." Prentis fixed his sympathetic eyes on hers. "I think I'm more useful to my wife on this end of the table."

Avery gripped his hand even tighter, glad he hadn't gone down to investigate.

The doctor now stepped over to the sink to wash his hands. "Avery, you can sit up." He scrubbed and dried and then he sat down somberly, lost in thought.

"Give it to us straight," Prentis said.

"All right. Straight it is. Avery, I'm sorry to say this, but your uterus has to come out."

She had no idea what she'd expected him to say. Medicine? More time? Maybe surgery to repair something or the other? This wasn't what she'd expected. Instantly, tears overflowed, running down her cheeks. She covered her mouth with the hand Prentis didn't grip.

Prentis took all of this in, and though his face appeared as mournful as hers, he swallowed hard and spoke. "Is that the only option? Is there no other treatment?"

"No, I'm afraid this is all we can do. It's rare, but I've seen this before. The mother died."

Prentis gripped her hand even more tightly. "Is my wife going to die?"

That possibility hit her in the pit of the stomach. *Was she? Would Jack lose his momma?*

"I certainly hope not," the doctor said. "We need to schedule the surgery immediately."

The doctor stood, gathered up his papers, and headed toward the door. Apparently, that was all he intended to say. A sense of hopelessness washed through Avery.

Prentis stood. "Can you *please* tell us what's happened?" His voice cracked.

The doctor stopped and turned around, taking in both their faces. It was clear by his flabbergasted expression that patients didn't typically ask for explanations. He appeared puzzled, but then sympathy eased its way onto his face. He stepped back toward them.

"I'll try to explain this in layman's terms." He paused, gripping his chin for a moment. "I think that lost pregnancy resulted in a small part of the placenta growing into the uterine wall—the wall of the womb. It may have even grown through the uterine wall and out into her body cavity, maybe adhering to something. I'm uncertain, but it feels like it may have. It would be unusual for how far along she may have been, but it's a possibility. Either way, right now the parts of placenta still in her body are in danger of causing infection. That could take her life or injure her other organs. Her womb wasn't built for pregnancy." Now he took his eyes off Prentis and aimed them at her. "Young woman, I have no idea how you had that baby. It had to have been the good Lord. But now, it's the end of the line for your uterus."

His eyes were compassionate.

Avery had no words. Helplessly, she looked toward Prentis.

"When and where do we have this surgery, Doctor?" he said.

"I'm sending you up to Anthony. There's a surgeon at the hospital there, Dr. Galloway. I'll write him the details in a report, and I'll make your appointment. I want him to get you in as soon as possible. He probably won't need to see you until the day of surgery. There's no mistaking what's going on. Simply go up for surgery on the assigned day. For now, I suggest you go home and rest. I'll write to tell you when the surgery is scheduled, or I'll find a way to get the news to you if the surgeon wants to operate immediately."

Avery still couldn't speak. Unhindered, tears ran slowly down her cheeks.

The doctor patted her on the shoulder and shook Prentis's hand. "I'll leave you to talk it out. There's no other appointment behind you right now. Take your time. Leave when you're ready. God bless you both."

Out he went. Prentis engulfed her in his arms, holding her tightly as she pressed her head to his chest and wailed out her grief. No more babies. No more possibility of babies. No Margaret, ever. And her womanhood stripped right out of her body.

How could she bear it?

Sixteen

THE COLD WAS NOW upon them. Prentis kept both the cookstove and the pot-bellied stove in the living room blazing away. Snow arrived the day before Thanksgiving. They hadn't intended to travel anyway, since Avery had to rest, but the snow and the mud that would follow could potentially destroy any plans Prentis had made. Her surgery was next week on Monday, December 3, and the weather would determine if they drove up to Anthony or took the train.

She had moved through the past week like a phantom. Silently, often in the darkness of night, she crept around the house, completely lost to him and to Jack.

For the first time in their lifelong friendship, he was the one urging her to speak, rather than the other way around. Pulled in upon herself, even her posture had changed. Typically, her shoulders were thrown back and her stance confident. She was used to commanding a roomful of children or an adult Sunday School class. First the problem in her womb had drawn her inward, and now it was as if she had collapsed upon herself, her entire body protecting the inner wound. C-shaped, she curled around her womb. It seemed intuitive.

They had missed church, and now they would spend Thanksgiving Day at home. Prentis had begged her parents to come. It disrupted the holiday for the entire family, but Hattie and the other wives banded together and insisted they could spare Minnie in the kitchen. Since he'd tried to keep those plans secret, Avery was unaware that her momma was due to arrive any moment, if the roads allowed. Her parents would bring a small meal to eat with them, and then they would take Jack home, if the snow didn't melt and the roads stayed passable. So far, the weather held.

As the war had ground them down, its unrelenting march sweeping them into patterns entirely unfamiliar and foreign, so now her surgery swept them all along. All of 1917 had felt wholly outside their control as forces beyond themselves had moved them to places they did not want to go. Often those events had taken him back to 1906, the year his father had died.

Life had felt the same then. That also had been a silent time, alone in his work, alone in the barn, alone in the fields, alone in his room. Surrounded by people coming and going, aunts and uncles, his poor mother, his siblings. But each suffered alone, all surrounded by family, yet unable to articulate what they felt in their loss. Stoic and intent on continuing to do their work and to somehow live through their loss, they had pressed on.

And now, here he was, Avery beside him, both of them attending to Jack and their home duties, but neither knowing what to say or how to say it.

"I love you," seemed the only thing either could articulate, other than the mundane.

He hoped and prayed she found her voice soon, for he had surely lost his.

Prentis heard the Model T outside. They had arrived—the road had cooperated.

Avery stirred in her chair, looking up from her knitting with an annoyed expression as she readjusted her posture. Not knowing who might have arrived, her brow furrowed, and her eyes darted toward the bedroom door, her usual escape tactic. Stowing her gray woolen knitting project, she began moving yarn off her lap.

"I think you'll want to stay," he said. "There's no reason for you to get up."

She frowned at him.

"It's your momma and daddy."

The silent tears flowed again, running down her cheeks. She stared into his eyes, and all the love and passion he held for her pressed hard into his chest. It hurt him to see her suffer. Wordlessly, she held out her hand to him, and he grasped it, smoothing the back with his thumb.

"I asked them to come," he said. "I knew they would comfort you."

Mutely, she nodded.

"I love you. Nothing changes that. Ever."

The tears flowed even more freely. She nodded again.

Jack stepped over to her, his little face serious. "Wuv 'oo, Mom-mom."

She pressed her lips together, the corners turning upward as she reached out to caress his head, running her fingers through his baby curls.

"I love you both so much," she whispered.

"We know it," Prentis said. "I'm going out to help your dad bring in the food."

There was a knock at the back door and then the creak of it opening.

Avery's momma called, "We're coming on in. Momma's here, darlin'."

Avery's eyes fixed on his, expressing her gratitude and appreciation. "Prentis, you take such good care of me." Then the tears erupted again.

He kissed her forehead and headed toward the back door, passing Minnie as she came in and thanking her. He headed out to help Abe bring in the crates of food. As he stepped into the back porch, he heard soothing sounds from her momma and more crying from Avery.

Prentis stopped, spun around to scoop up Jack, stuffed him into an extra coat, and took him outside. Might as well give the two women some time alone.

Once the food was inside and all the hot dishes were tucked into the low oven to warm again, Prentis took his father-in-law out to the barn to check on the horses. With Jack in tow, they looked in on all the livestock, discussed the pregnant cows and mares, and talked about Tom's farm. They had time, so they saddled up and rode over to look in on Tom's house and animals.

Jack rode in front of Prentis, bouncing along, tucked inside a fleece-lined greatcoat. His little head peeked out of the top, his eyes wide. He chattered away in baby talk, and Prentis understood bits and pieces here and there, responding as was appropriate. Basically, Jack kept up a running commentary on everything he could see from his perch on the horse.

It was always hard to ride into Tom's barnyard and see his silent house. The cows were all huddled up close to the barn. Prentis broke the thin film of ice on top of the water tank, being careful of the slippery track of frozen water from the runoff. Both he and Abe thought the cows looked good. They tossed some feed into the trough. So far, the cattle were wintering well.

Prentis always checked the house, lest squatters had made themselves at home. It was so cold inside that his breath came out in a puff of frozen condensation. All was well inside and out. He would be glad when his friend returned and his possessions filled their rightful spots, rather than sitting boxed around the room, awaiting shipment, should anything happen to him.

Having ascertained that everything was at it should be, they mounted up again. Jack reached for his grandfather, so Prentis lifted him up to ride between Abe's arms on the trip home. This gave him the vantage of watching Jack from afar, observing his delight and his banter with his grandfather. Though he couldn't hear what his son said, Jack's little mouth was constantly in motion, and his grandfather nodded and commented.

Prentis's heart filled with love for the two of them. He couldn't help but whisper a prayer.

"Thank you, Lord, for what You've given, no matter what You've taken away."

***

That evening, Prentis lay facing Avery on their bed. Everyone was gone now, Jack packed up for a couple weeks with his grandparents and uncles. The parting had been hard, and Avery had wept profusely, even though she knew he would be doted on.

Now they stared at one another. Prentis smoothed back her hair.

"Feel like I've lost you again," he said.

She creased her forehead. "What do you mean?"

"You're in a faraway place. You're not here. Where have you gone?"

"I've gone nowhere. I've been right here."

"No, you haven't. Your body's been present and accounted for, but not yourself."

She didn't answer immediately. He watched her eyes as she dug through her inner musings.

"I've been in a dark place," she whispered. "The shadows came."

"Care to tell me about it?"

"I don't want to drag you into my dark thoughts and the hopelessness I've been feeling."

"We're one flesh, remember? You've already dragged me in. But you're not talking about it, so I'm stumbling around in the darkness."

"What do you mean?"

"This war and all these troubles remind me of when my father died. I've been back in 1906, feeling all of fifteen, watching you from afar and wondering where you've gone. Back then, all of us went through the motions. None of us knew how to say what we were feeling, and so we each suffered alone, even though we were side by side. I want us to talk. I'm in this with you."

"I'll try." She swallowed hard. "I keep begging God, 'Please, don't let this happen. Please, *please*, don't let this happen.' And yet—" She paused, fighting back tears. "And yet, it's still happening. I'm afraid."

"Of the procedure?"

"Well, yes, that's part of it. But I trust the doctors. They've had so much schooling, and it's been explained. I understand why it has to happen."

"Then what are you afraid of?"

Rolling away from him, she turned her back. "I can't look at you and say it."

"Why ever not?"

"I'm afraid of what I'll see in your face."

His eyes smarted, and his throat thickened. Silently, he crawled over her and out of the bed to sit on the floor facing her. Several times, she blinked in the dusky light, and then she closed her eyes. Tears ran from under her closed eyelids.

"You don't ever—" His voice cracked. He swallowed hard. He tried again. "You don't *ever* have to be afraid of my reaction about anything. I love you with all my heart. I've loved you for as long as I can remember. I'll love you until the day I die. Why would you be afraid of *me*?"

His question hung in the air between them.

Her face screwed into a tormented expression of agony. Still her eyes remained closed.

She spoke softly, "I'm afraid—" Deep sobs erupted from within her. He gripped her shoulder, soothing the tight band of muscle with his thumb.

Then she whispered, "I'm afraid you won't love me anymore."

"That's impossible!"

Still her eyes didn't open. "They're taking my womanhood out of me. I won't be the same."

"You'll still be you. I'll always love you."

"No," she said, the finality of death in her voice. "You won't."

Prentis was flabbergasted. Unsure how to proceed, he sat staring at her.

Then he recalled something. "Do you remember that time before Jack was on the way when you didn't think you'd ever get pregnant? You'd helped me with the calving, and then your woman's time had come, and once more you weren't pregnant." Her eyelids opened slightly. "I held you in my arms on this bed, and I told you that I didn't care if we ever had children. My love for you stands alone. It's not dependent on your ability to reproduce. I've always felt this way."

"But . . ." she said, stopping once more to cry.

"There aren't any buts about it."

She held up one finger. "Oh, yes, there are."

"What then?"

"We won't ever be able to be intimate again."

"That's not true," he said, stunned by her statement. "Why do you say that?"

"Momma told me that when a woman gets old and begins to have problems with her womb, they have to do this same surgery, and it makes her unable to be intimate with her husband."

This information knocked him back a notch. Could this be true? He had no idea. This was not a topic that anyone discussed in polite company. This had never crossed his mind. He understood female anatomy. He didn't know why any other of her woman parts would have to be removed along with her uterus itself. There was no scientific reason to do it.

He felt her looking at him. He met her eyes.

"I was right, wasn't I?" she said.

"No. I was merely thinking of the anatomy behind your statement. I don't agree."

"But, what if we can never be intimate again?"

"Do you recall that I fell in love with you without ever having been intimate with you? And do you also remember that I haven't had intercourse with you since sometime in August or maybe September? Can't even remember how long it's been since you lost this baby and your body was injured. In that time, have I ever acted as if I didn't love you?"

"Well, no—"

"That's unfair to a man to assume such a thing. I'm committed to you for the rest of my life. Of course, I want us to be intimate again. But nothing would ever make me stop loving you."

She looked at him hard, studying his face. "I've always trusted you."

"And with good reason. I've always loved you."

"You've never harmed me in my entire life."

"That sounds like a good batting average to me." He chuckled softly, caressing her cheek.

"Crawl up here and hug me, and I'll tell you the rest."

He heaved a sigh of relief, saddened that she'd been in this dark place without telling him. Once he was on the bed, he pulled a quilt over both of them and cradled her from behind, both curved together into one.

"I feel unattractive," she said, "as though I'll cease being a woman."

"Oh, you'll be every bit a woman. You're gorgeous inside and out. That won't change. I never said these months of not being intimate have been easy." He laughed softly.

She reached over her shoulder and stroked his stubble. "I suppose it's somewhat like the time before we married. No one thought I could cook or clean, because I held a paying job and Momma did most of the work at home. They acted as if, somehow, I wasn't a real woman. That wasn't true of me though."

"No, it wasn't. You're a real woman, believe me. I married you because you're you, not because you can clean a house or cook a meal. No matter how you feel about it, you'll continue to be beautiful after this surgery—a real woman. No doubt in my mind. And when we're old and wrinkled and gray, I'll still think you're the most beautiful woman on God's frozen earth."

"All right," she said. "I've decided to believe you."

"No matter what happens," he whispered into her ear, "we'll deal with it."

***

When Dr. Galloway introduced himself, Prentis was relieved. The doctor appeared to be around forty, young enough to be up on the latest surgical techniques, but old enough to be careful and reliable. Since the surgery was not for cancer or prolapsed uterus, but for retained placental parts, he informed them that he would probably only take her uterus. Everything else would remain, since Avery was in her twenties. Of course, he had to wait to see

199

what he found during surgery. He made no promises. His surgical plan could always change.

Dr. Galloway told them he would use both ether and a spinal injection, for recent research had determined that this produced the best outcome. He also performed surgery in Wichita, so he had collaborated with others on this procedure. Everything he said left Prentis reassured and reduced the tightness with which Avery clutched his hand.

The mortality rate for the surgery was between 11 percent and 16 percent, Dr. Galloway informed them. Prentis didn't like that one bit. But, as always, it boiled down to leaving Avery in God's hands. It seemed that was always the case in every trial. Could they let it go and trust God completely? Prentis looked at Avery. She appeared brave today, strong. She had been singing hymns.

"In two or three hours, I'll step out here when I'm done," the surgeon said. "We take this surgery slow and easy, so as to leave undisturbed everything that will remain."

"Thank you," Prentis said. "I'm entrusting the most precious part of me into your hands."

Dr. Galloway shook his hand. Prentis kissed Avery softly on the forehead. He told her that he loved her with all his heart, and then she was gone, whisked out the door and rolled down the hallway toward the surgical theater. He watched her until she was out of sight.

Then Prentis collapsed into a chair, his head in his hands, begging God to get his wife through this, and if He saw fit, to allow them to be intimate one day when this was all over. But he had to yield that to God, and he did repeatedly, laying it down like a sacrifice, committing his own manhood and Avery's womanhood into the hands of the One who had created them both. What the good Lord would do with those prayers remained to be seen.

200

He heard a soft noise and looked up to see a nurse kindly studying him.

"I'll take you to the waiting room now," she said.

"Oh, thank you."

Then out he went to sit and meditate in silence as he waited. It was the longest wait of his life. He stared at the floor and prayed, begging God over and over again for the same things. It was all his mind could do, and it was all he wanted in the whole world.

About two hours later, he looked up to see Mark Wallock stroll in with the Slaughters and Jack. This was a surprise. He was glad to see them, for he was completely at the end of himself by now. Two hours meant the surgery might be complete or it might mean they had encountered some sort of complication. Having them nearby to talk relieved his acute anxiety, but at the same time, it felt sacrilegious to turn from his repetitive prayer to chat about mundane things like the weather and the price of beef cattle on the open market.

It comforted him, though, to have Jack sitting on his lap, talking about his time with his grandparents and his "nuncles." Prentis listened absentmindedly, his thoughts still in the operating theater sending those constant repetitive prayers up to the Almighty. The hand on the hospital clock now marked nearly three hours. His anxiety left him feeling stretched to the breaking point.

At last, a nurse stepped into the room. "Mr. Pinkerton, you can come with me."

Everyone rose.

"You'll all have to wait," she said. "Dr. Galloway wants to speak to Mr. Pinkerton alone."

Prentis's stomach dropped. Alone.

What kind of news did the doctor intend to deliver? Somehow, he put one foot in front of the other, following the nurse through the doors and into the sterile environment of the hospital. At last they entered a small room where she instructed him to wait for the surgeon to appear momentarily.

More silent waiting. More prayer. There was nothing else he could do.

Finally, Dr. Galloway stepped in. Prentis looked up quickly, scanning his expression, detecting nothing. He rose, and the two men shook hands.

"I'm happy to say that your wife came through the procedure just fine," the surgeon began.

"That's a relief." Prentis started breathing again.

"She still needs to get through the recovery, which is just as dangerous as the surgery itself. I was hoping I could somehow save her uterus. I didn't tell you beforehand, so as not to give you any false hope. You're young, and I know you probably want a family. I did all I could. Unfortunately, I did have to take her uterus, but only her uterus. After assessing the organ, I have to inform you that there was no way she could have ever carried a child to term. Her uterus was positioned oddly in her pelvis and malformed, almost underdeveloped, as if she hadn't gone through puberty. I'm sorry, but you won't be able to father a child with your wife."

"We already have a son."

"Did you adopt a little boy?"

"No, she gave birth to him on April 16, 1916."

The doctor wore a look of incredulity. "That's not possible."

"He's just arrived with Avery's parents. They're in the waiting room, if you'd like to see him."

"Indeed, I would." They both stood and began the walk back. Dr. Galloway kept talking. "There's no way that young woman could have borne a child with that uterus. No way at all. Can your doctor in Wakita verify this?"

"He can. He tended to her all during her pregnancy. Did all the examinations."

202

"Did he deliver?"

"No, that was my privilege. Her labor was quick, and the doctor didn't get there until a few hours later. But he was her doctor all during her pregnancy."

Now they stepped through the door. Everyone looked up.

"Avery's doing fine," the surgeon said to all. "The surgery went very well. I just had to see this boy."

"Da Da!" Jack called, running across the room.

Prentis swung him up in the air and then turned him about to face Dr. Galloway. The man looked back and forth between Prentis and Jack.

"I've witnessed a miracle," the doctor said. "That boy is clearly your child, and he has your wife's dark skin and eyes. Is it really the truth that your wife gave birth to him?"

"Indeed, she did."

The doctor addressed the others. "Did all of you see her when she was expecting?"

Her parents nodded that they had.

"Well, I'll be! Wonders never cease." Dr. Galloway turned toward Jack and smiled. "Little man, you are a miracle."

"Merckle," Jack said somberly.

All of them laughed together.

The surgeon turned to reenter the hospital corridor. "Come with me, Mr. Pinkerton. I need to tell you what I predict for your wife's recovery. I'll let you take a peek at her."

Their regular doctor in Wakita had said all the same things. Jack shouldn't be here. He was a miracle. God must have a purpose for him, and surely, if God could do that, He could determine when Avery's womb was done working. It wasn't God's plan for them to have more than one son, and one son was a cup overflowing with blessing.

Prentis thought he might live.

Seventeen

THE TWO WEEKS OF Avery's hospital stay were chaotic and entirely outside the norm of their quiet lives. The Millers and the Herns helped with their livestock and Tom's, and Sam guarded the farm. Prentis usually slept in a chair in Avery's room. After the hospital staff discovered he was sleeping wrapped in blankets in his automobile parked outside, they had invited him inside.

Because the weather remained dry but cold, he drove down to the farm daily to check on everything and to reassure his livestock that all was well. He fed Sam and praised him for being such a good guard dog. Stopping first at the Slaughter's farm, he informed them of Avery's progress and picked up Jack and one of the boys to help him complete any tasks that needed doing. Then he returned them to Gibbon. Afterward, he headed back up to Anthony, spending the night in the chair again, watching Avery recover.

He grabbed food wherever he could find it, usually something from their house or the Slaughters' kitchen, and then back he'd go. He didn't want to leave Avery's side unless necessary. Eventually, the nurses figured that out, and one or the other packed him a big meal with a few snacks in a brown paper bag each day. Their kindness touched his heart.

As Avery slept, he sat and watched her, thanking God that she was alive and healthy, that the doctor had performed her surgery in such a way that allowed renewed marital intimacy, and that she was no longer in peril, wasting away before his very eyes, drop by bloody drop. The moment she had first awakened from anesthesia had created one of the happiest memories of his life. His wife would live! He cherished that memory every day.

The advantage of being tall and having long arms had allowed him to lean over her hospital bed gripping the raised bars on either side. Waiting for her to awaken, he had stood there indefinitely, right above her, looking down upon her as he studied her features. She was so beautiful in repose. At last her eyes had blinked open. This time they didn't quickly close once more but remained open. She focused on his face.

Recognizing him, a slow smile had spread, one he hadn't seen in what felt like ages.

"You," she had whispered. "I was longing for you."

Returning her smile, he said he'd been longing for her as well, and then he had informed her of all the surgical details. Looking downright angelic, she had then closed her eyes and praised God for granting her more days on this earth and marital intimacy once more. Nothing would prevent their oneness. When she opened her eyes, she had told him that she loved him. He returned her affirmation, and then she had nodded back to sleep.

But marital intimacy was far in the future—the doctor had said a full six weeks of recovery were necessary after she returned home, on top of these two weeks in the hospital. Two full months were required for internal healing.

Now that Prentis knew what was coming, the anticipation would make it more difficult to put aside his desires, but he would. He had waited for her before, and he would now wait for her again. He praised God every day for his unrequited passion, because it was ignited by the knowledge of what the future now held, a certainty in a world of uncertainty.

Gazing at her as she slept, he thanked God.

While she dozed, he read the Kansas newspapers of his youth. They were all available in the hospital, and the nurses always brought them back for him. The war hadn't been put on hold while they dealt with their personal crisis, and dear friends had only been raised up to the Lord with bare mentions in the preceding weeks. So, while he watched over her in the quiet hospital room, he caught up on both his reading and his praying. He had plenty of time to converse with God silently, both in her room and while driving back and forth. Reading took care of the rest. Having learned his lesson, he didn't tell her any of the war news. She would know soon enough.

To deal with their own internal crisis, the Russians had bowed out of the war as expected, signing an armistice with Germany and ceding large swathes of Eastern Europe to the Germans. Leon Trotsky had been the new Bolshevik government's representative when the armistice was signed. A few days afterward, there were rumors that French officials had engaged in treason and that their prime minister wanted to negotiate with Germany now that the Central Power's eastern troops would move to fight them on the Western Front. The result was that Georges Clemenceau was now named the new prime minister. Calls for more American involvement increased.

Air raids, scarcity of supplies, weariness of battle, and the anticipation of American involvement had decreased all of the Allied offense across the front, though most of the American Expeditionary Forces had now arrived in Europe.

Their forces had trickled over, first the soldiers already trained, and now the soldiers who had been trained more recently. Tom, they already knew, was there now in France. Once they had arrived, all of the soldiers had even more training to complete, but still, in spite of Europe's pleas, General Pershing wouldn't let them go into battle until they were truly ready.

The recently trained men landed in Liverpool, England, and in St. Nazaire, France. Once landed, they were allowed to rest and recover from the trip there, as Tom had also needed. Many had lost weight from seasickness, the boys predominantly being landlocked American Midwesterners. The last unit was due to arrive right before Christmas, the newspaper surmised. Most information wasn't published for the sake of security, so for all they knew, the troops had already made it over and might even now be fighting.

America had issued another declaration of war on December 7, this one against Austria-Hungary, the land of Reverend Wallock's birth, for they had allied with the Germans, bringing the German-speaking world together as one fighting unit.

The British had also captured Jerusalem from the Turks. A world war was messy and complicated, with many of the parties not giving a hoot about the Archduke Ferdinand's assassination, but rather joining the fray for their own political purposes. Attempts to seize this country, to commit genocide against that race, or to capture this or that capital had been commonplace since the beginning.

Prentis was relieved to be living in Oklahoma, far removed. He didn't have to make the decisions their leaders, his cousin, and his friends would soon be making in this general mess. As he looked up from the newspaper at his sleeping wife, recovering her bloom and growing healthier every day, he thanked God for his many blessings.

***

It was Christmas Day, and Avery was finally at home, sleeping in her own bed and bothered by no nurses. Though theirs would be a quiet celebration, still she was overwhelmed by a sense of gratitude and joy that she was home at last. It was such a relief, even though Tom was not with them and she was still mending, having only returned eight days ago.

The months of illness after her miscarriage and the following surgery had impacted her body drastically. Would she ever regain her former vigor? Today they would feast at home, merely the three of them, not at the Slaughter family home. Quiet and recovery were necessary.

Prentis had started a low fire in both the pot-bellied stove and the cookstove. Then he had taken Jack along to fetch their Christmas dinner from her momma's kitchen. Momma had written that Avery wasn't to lift a finger, but to send Prentis. He would return with the feast. Resting in her chair with her feet on the hassock, Avery inhaled the festive scent of the fresh popcorn-festooned cedar tree in the corner. Opened to 2 Corinthians, an epistle filled with comfort in suffering, her Bible lay on her lap. She'd read verses sixteen though eighteen in chapter four several times.

Though our outward man perish, yet the inward man is renewed day by day. For our light affliction, which is but for a moment, worketh for us a far more exceeding and eternal weight of glory; while we look not at the things which are seen, but at the things which are not seen: for the things which are seen are temporal; but the things which are not seen are eternal.

During difficult times, this was a favorite passage, but she couldn't wrap her mind around any of it today. She couldn't seem to focus with any depth. All she could do was to simply *be*. Spreading wide her hand, she laid her palm flat on the softly worn pages of her Bible. Though she couldn't absorb God's words today, she caressed His Word, feeling His nearness.

Her energetic intellectual curiosity for investigating the Greek text and delving into cross-references and historical context was lacking completely. But still, she was at peace merely being, knowing that God was with her and that He understood her situation even better than she did. Resting in God was a new experience. Passionate about research, she usually focused on striving to work out her salvation and to utilize the gifts God had given her.

However, at rest now, she pondered the beauty of the Savior, who had allowed Himself to be broken for her, redeeming her from her own brokenness as a result. On this Christmas morning unlike any other, He seemed glorious to her. She imagined Him in infant form, wrapped in swaddling cloths and lying within a manger. So meek. So humble . . .

A noise caused her to startle. Without realizing it, she had drifted off to sleep. Scooting up in her chair and closing her Bible, she puzzled over what noise had sounded forth. Now she heard the back door open and the tumultuous tramp of little feet. Jack came running in.

"Mom-mom!" he called. "Gramma make foods!"

Grinning, Prentis hurried in behind him. "Did you hear the horn? Jack wanted me to sound it as we pulled in."

"Oh, that must be what woke me." She laughed softly. "Yes, I heard it. Were you both warm on your trip?"

"Yep," Jack said. "Lotsa blankets."

He crawled up on her lap, seeming to have transformed into a big boy during her illness and recovery, though he was still not yet two years of age. He spoke in sentences, wore little boots, and smelled of the outdoors, the aroma of Christmas food, and his daddy's shaving soap—one of her favorite fragrances.

"You should see all the food!" Prentis said. "Let me haul in the rest. I was only able to carry the turkey this trip. I'll tuck it into the oven before I go back out."

"Come kiss me first," she said.

That broadened his grin. "A man's always ready to accept an invitation like that from his wife."

Rather than planting his lips softly on her forehead, he gave her a thorough kiss right on the lips. Jack giggled. Avery smiled widely as Prentis straightened and stepped back. Their eyes met, both promising more to come. That was still at least six weeks away and required the doctor's go-ahead, but she recognized the look in his eyes. He needed her, and she needed him.

Wearing a wide smile, he turned to retrieve the food, whistling as he went out the door.

The tune was one that had encouraged them both throughout the fall and now into the winter. She considered one of the verses, which she now knew by heart.

'Let not your heart be troubled,'
His tender word I hear,
And resting on His goodness,

210

I lose my doubts and fears;
Though by the path He leadeth,
but one step I may see;
His eye is on the sparrow,
and I know He watches me;
His eye is on the sparrow,
and I know He watches me.
I sing because I'm happy,
I sing because I'm free,
For His eye is on the sparrow,
and I know He watches me.

A sense of happiness and contentment filled and expanded within her. It was as though loving and gentle hands had lifted an oppressive burden that she had carried for a long while. She felt as light-hearted as a girl. Everything had changed, but Jesus was the Master Shepherd. He led them up a new path, out into a new pasture. Tentatively they stood at the edge of this meadow, ready to wade into the tall grasses. His eye was upon them.

Surely, everything would be well again.

***

The New Year arrived, finding them snowed in yet cozy by the stove. Jack played with his blocks and his handmade wooden cars, preparing roads and driving throughout the living room, making soft vibrations in his mouth and throat to produce automobile sounds—this was a new age, producing new types of child play. On that day, for the first time in months, Prentis saw Avery reach for the newspaper. That mere gesture told him she was on the mend.

He buried his face in his steaming coffee cup, hiding his smile. He had to be particularly gentle with her, and she might not welcome his comments or teasing about emerging from her hibernation to read, but it was hard to keep from grinning.

"I saw that," she said, not even lifting her eyes from the newsprint.

Of course, she had. "I can't hide a thing from you, can I?"

Still, she kept her eyes on the page. "I could feel your grin, clear over here."

Now he let go with the laughter. "It's good to see you reentering the world."

"I need to find out what's happened. I'm woefully behind."

"Lucky for you, the papers have summaries of the war news."

"So-called 'luck' has nothing to do with—"

"I know—it's the sovereignty of God. It's only an expression, Avery." He paused a moment reflecting on early marriage. "All right, I'm going to get this off my chest. Are we starting all over again with arguments about word choices and citations?"

Now she looked up at him, her expression incredulous. "You're absolutely right. I feel as I did then, when I was usually out with people, teaching school, interacting at church, yet week after week, we couldn't go anywhere due to the weather."

Now his grin widened. "You've got your gumption back. We're on the downhill slope."

"I believe we are." She returned his smile.

"The doctor told me to guard you carefully during your recovery. Let's not rush this."

"Yes, we'll follow doctor's orders. Only four more weeks to go."

"More like five or more, and then you have to see the doctor first."

"All right," she said. "I see you're going to be a stickler."

"The fact that you've got some fight in you makes me a mighty happy man."

"I never thought I'd hear a man say that."

"When we were first married, I'd go outside to tend the animals, glad that you were inside waiting for me, even if I'd stepped out in the middle of an argument. Even fighting with you made me happy."

"I can't say we've ever 'fought,'" she said.

"Here we go again—word choices. Let me rephrase. Even 'arguing' with you made me happy. Is that better?"

"Yes, sir. Thank you."

He grinned at her. "Glad to oblige."

She raised her newspaper again. "I need to bone up on this war."

"You're even using slang again!" He laughed out loud. "This is a good day, Avery. Can't even begin to explain how happy I feel right now."

Then he spread wide his own newspaper, and the two of them sat side by side while Jack played. By their warm stove in their comfortable chairs with feet sharing the same hassock, they read contentedly, commenting on news items that captured their interest. He did his best to fill the gaps omitted by the newspapers' yearly summaries, so he could bring her up to speed.

Snuggling his wool-covered feet next to hers made him happier than he'd been in a long while. These small blessings of domestic tranquility had been at risk, but now it looked as if they might make it.

Eighteen

ON TUESDAY, JANUARY 8, 1918, IN response to parlays between Russia and the Central Powers at Brest-Litovsk, President Wilson delivered an important speech to Congress detailing his Fourteen Points plan "for every peace-loving nation." Avery pored over this significant article carefully, folding the paper in half for ease of reading.

The spokesmen of the Central Powers desired to discuss the possibility of peace. So, the president spelled out the terms necessary for an open and free discussion among leaders of goodwill throughout the world, if this peace was to exist. One stipulation was that all lands illegally taken in wartime had to be returned to the rightful country from which they had been seized. The German generals, of course, weren't enthusiastic about this idea.

If the Central Powers refused to be reasonable, President Wilson reaffirmed that American troops were determined to engage in battle and bring the war to a just end. A solid wall of three million American troops, fresh and willing to fight, would soon sweep across France. These terms would then be obligatory. After this speech, their enemies certainly knew the terms necessary for peace once American troops joined the Allies to fight together to prevail.

As to lasting peace, though they were calling this "the war to end all wars," Avery doubted that would happen until the Prince of Peace Himself established a new heaven and a new earth. But she gave the president credit for having enough foresight and hope to attempt to negotiate that peace now, before their own troops had even engaged the battle as a whole. If he prevailed, perhaps the war would end immediately. What a blessing that would be!

Earning a law degree and then following that up by studying history, political science, and German, President Wilson had received one of the first PhDs in Political Science ever awarded at Johns Hopkins University. He had later gone on to become the president of Princeton University. With those credentials, the fact that he would present such well-considered proposals to Congress was almost a guarantee. Understanding academia, she could picture the president up at all hours considering and drafting what he hoped would bring world peace.

Men of his stature tended to think that with enough education and reason applied to any situation, mankind could overcome and achieve utopian bliss. However, on the ground among actual humanity, their grand schemes rarely came to peaceful fruition.

The Bolshevik Revolution in Russia, founded upon Karl Marx's ideals, seemed to be another such attempt to make all even and fair for everyone. However, there had been a lot of bloodshed for a scheme that promised peace and equality. Avery was skeptical.

After listening patiently to her arguments as she read the speech and commented, Prentis looked up from the harness he was mending near the woodstove.

"We can at least hope and pray the proposals will bring peace. Can't we, Avery?"

"Well, yes. But I don't think the terms will work. History has proven that repeatedly."

"That's true. But it's the president's job to try to solve this problem and bring this war to an end, hopefully before our loved ones have to fight. He has to be an optimist, especially since the war's still deadlocked on the Western Front. Otherwise he'd merely throw up his hands and tell us there's nothing we can do. We can at least be open to his ideas, can't we?"

"I think it's a waste of time. No one will listen."

"Really, Sweetheart, you've lost your sense of hope. We either need to get you out of this house, or you need some company."

Stunned, she laid aside the paper and looked at him.

"You're absolutely correct. I think it's time to have Mary Beth over for tea, even if I merely sit in this chair for her entire visit."

"An excellent idea!" Laying aside the harness and the saddle soap, he rose. "I can ride over to the Millers and let Mary Beth know you'd welcome a visit next week. Won't take me but a few minutes. I'm guessing Apollo would be glad to have a run."

"Do you mind?"

"Not at all. I live to please you and to take care of your needs. The roads are frozen hard, and it's a good time to run that stallion. When should she come?"

"Our usual day would be fine."

"Wednesday, right? During Jack's nap?"

She nodded. With that, out he went.

Silently she sat, trying to remember the last time she'd had fellowship with another Christian woman or

216

interaction with anyone outside her family. It had been three weeks since she'd left the hospital, and a while before that since she'd seen Mary Beth—maybe that last time she'd been in church. She couldn't even recall.

The longer she considered it, the more the anticipation rose within her. *Happiness. Contentment. Joy.* That was it. Each small step of this healing process had been unexpected and gradual, but once she'd acknowledged that things were indeed changing for the better, she'd been able to recognize the gladness she felt about each new step toward wellness.

There were no longer any reservations, no holding back lest she be crushed with disappointment over her faltering health. She was truly improving. She would be having company. A small giggle escaped her, and a wide smile spread.

Thank You, Jesus! You're putting me back together again!

***

On Wednesday, Mary Beth Miller came bustling in out of the cold, removing her wraps and her warm scarf. The mere sight of her filled Avery with contentment.

After letting her in and taking her wraps, Prentis offered to stable her horse.

"Why, thank you, Prentis," she said.

Smiling, he nodded and then shifted his eyes toward Avery. "You two, enjoy your time. The army will be here soon to purchase our foals. Got to get them ready. I'll be halter training in the corral."

"Enjoy yourself," she said. "I know you love our horses."

"Indeed, I do."

Out he went. Avery detected the hasty escape of a shy man in his expression, which she found endearing. Smiling widely, she turned toward Mary Beth, glad to have a couple of hours to talk with a dear friend. She poured the tea and passed the cookies as they settled in.

"Avery, you're looking very well!"

"Why, thank you."

"The color's back in your cheeks. You're on the mend!"

"I do believe I am, Mary Beth. It's been six weeks now since my surgery."

"We've all prayed for you so fervently. We still do."

"Thank you. I'm more energetic, enough to be cantankerous at least." She laughed softly, thinking fondly of her husband outside. "It was Prentis who recognized that I needed company and conversation."

Mary Beth laughed. "He's a good husband, isn't he?"

"He's the best. If every woman had such a kind, thoughtful, and observant spouse, the world would certainly be a happier place."

Mary Beth blushed a tiny bit and dropped her eyes. "Speaking of husbands, I took your advice. I wrote to Joe and told him that I wished I'd married him before he left."

"And what did he say to that?"

"He wrote back such a joyous letter filled with all sorts of declarations of love. I treasure it and read it every morning and every night. Sometimes in between."

"That's wonderful! You've given the boy some hope."

"Thank you for advising me. I'd hate for him to go into war without knowing how I truly feel about him."

"He has something wonderful to anticipate. That will get him through the hardship."

"I hope and pray for his safe return."

"We all do. We promised him we'd pray, and we have been."

They smiled at one another.

Along with her yarn and the current work in progress, Avery pulled forward an enormous pile of wool socks and hoods. "I may have been sick, but I kept my hands busy. These are all for the Red Cross."

"Well, it's a good thing I brought a large satchel! A shipment is going out tomorrow, since we're deep into winter now. Our boys in Europe will certainly be glad to see these!"

"It's a lot more personal now, isn't it? Now that *our* boys are over there and more will soon follow, it changes everything."

"Yes, it does. Now, all our hearts are wrapped around the outcome of this war."

***

After Mary Beth left that afternoon, Prentis came inside to find Avery collapsed in her chair without much left in her. Telling her to stay put, he fried some eggs for their supper, toasted some bread left from their breakfast, and took care of Jack.

Still, even though her face sagged with fatigue, she couldn't seem to quit smiling or talking. She filled him in on all the news far and wide, and he felt great satisfaction.

"Prentis, you were right about me needing company."

"Seeing you all lit up confirms that," he said. "But, you need to get stronger, I think, before we take you out in public."

"I agree."

"How about some walks around the farm? Or maybe some time on your swing? I know it's January. But we've been having some warm days, and you have some sturdy boots."

He'd often said that when she was expecting Jack. She laughed. "That's a wonderful idea! It will do Jack some good, too, to have me with him outside. You've taken such good care of him, Prentis! I've been down so long that I almost forgot there's a wider world out there."

"Come out and see those yearlings before they're sold. A finer group of colts and fillies I've never seen. I'm getting them halter- and blanket-accustomed and training them to respond to the most basic commands. They're already well-mannered horses. I think we'll get top dollar again."

"We usually do," she said. "You're a renowned horseman and rancher."

He gave her a wide grin. "That's why I don't put Apollo out to stud, as you well know. No use scattering his good seed far and wide to reduce the demand for our yearlings."

"What about the calving?"

"Our cows will start around mid-February. It will be a longer season with Tom's cows after, but that's how I planned it when I put Rex to pasture."

"That's only a little more than a month away. Tom isn't here, and I doubt I'll be much help, between Jack and my recovery. What will you do?"

"Men from church have volunteered. Thinking of asking Howard, Gene, or Abe to help too. What do you think?"

"I can keep them up with their schoolwork while they're down here, if their teacher will send me her notes. Or they can simply catch up. Rural schools always work around farming and ranching needs."

"That's true," he said. "I'll take it up with your parents then. See what they think. Need to talk to your dad about selling our steers and buying some more heifers."

The rest of the evening was spent in pleasant conversation and play with Jack. Once they'd tucked him in, they sat by the fireside. Prentis read aloud to Avery, something he enjoyed doing regularly. Her comments grew further and further apart. He glanced up. She'd dozed off, slid down into her chair, and her knitting had fallen into her lap. She was worn out. Marking his place and putting Dickens aside, he stood to pick her up.

Gazing down at her, the warmth of overwhelming satisfaction filled his chest. Not only would she live, but she would also thrive. Today she had felt well enough to ask about the farm and to have a friend spend a couple of hours in their home. There were no longer dark circles under her eyes, and the bones at the base of her neck didn't protrude due to gauntness. Her health was blooming again, right before his eyes. Though they wouldn't see the doctor for several weeks, he knew they had passed the worst. He would get to keep his wife.

Thank You, God, for Your mercy. You're a good Father to me!

Stooping down, he scooped her up. She roused. Between the two of them, they got her into her flannel nightgown. While she cared for her creature needs, he banked the stoves for the night. Then, he tucked her in, blew out the lantern, and crawled in, drawing her close.

He couldn't remember the last time he'd felt this content. Inhaling the fragrance of her hair, he pulled her into the curve of his body, and she snuggled her head in under his chin, sighed with satisfaction, and dropped right off again.

In the darkness, he smiled.

***

Beginning the next morning, Avery bundled herself and Jack into hats, scarves, boots, and heavy coats for a walk around the barnyard. They started slow and easy, taking in only the chicken coop. That morning, she gathered the eggs and fed the chickens. Once that had been accomplished, she was done for the day. Back in they went.

The next day, she completed the same task but broadened her duties, adding a stroll to peek at Apollo in his pen. Jack squealed with excitement, unused to being outside with her in the winter sunshine and heading toward the farmyard. He loved seeing the animals in their pens.

For every day after that, one after another, she added one small increment of physical exertion, a short walk, or a small task, taking Jack with her, holding his hand as he toddled along in his boots. After being mostly bedridden for many weeks, she was surprised by how taxing each activity proved to be. She used to complete them all with no thought.

Every day she grew increasingly aware of how much Prentis had been doing the entire time she'd been sick. Not only had he kept up the farm, but he had cared for Jack every day, taking their boy with him as he worked. He had kept them alive and warm in a tidy house. Occasionally, neighbors brought by a meal, sometimes twice a week. That had certainly helped. But the rest had been all him—all of the chores that she usually completed, all the cleaning and laundry. Each day as it dawned on her more fully, she couldn't help but thank him.

Of course, he always responded humbly. Yet, she would persist.

"Did what I could, Sweetheart," he would say. "Wanted to keep you from worrying about anything but getting well. You would do the same for me, if I were sick. I sure didn't do anything with the high quality you have for running this household, though."

"That's not how I see it from here," she would say as she looked around at the immaculate kitchen and tidy house. "I think you do all of this far better than I."

"No! Not at all," he would say. "I know what it's like to batch. I'm not much of a cook or a homemaker. You're far above and beyond me."

"Well, regardless, I feel such love and appreciation, seeing how much you've done and realizing that I never

222

had to worry about anything. You, by far, have to be one of the world's best husbands."

Modestly, he would duck his head, clearly embarrassed by her high praise.

"I poured it on too thick again, didn't I?" she would ask.

"You did. I'm just an ordinary man."

"You're far from ordinary, Prentis. But I'll leave off with just a thank you."

"You're welcome."

With that, he would head out to the barn to recover. She was so grateful for all that he'd done that she tended to pour on too much praise in one dose. That outcome was frequent.

***

After two weeks of careful and thoughtful addition of daily activities, Avery found herself doing at least half of her regular duties, though most couldn't be completed in their entirety. For instance, she could clear the table and get the dishes into the hot water. But, at first, that was where her energy ended. As the days passed, she completed more of each task. Prentis still picked up what she was unable to accomplish in every category, except knitting, but the fact that she was now engaged in her usual wifely duties gave her a sense of satisfaction.

She smiled more. She felt better every day.

They stayed close to home. They didn't attempt a visit to church yet. On Sundays, Prentis read aloud from the Bible, they talked about the passage, and they sang a hymn or two.

Moving at her own pace transformed winter into a time of healing and refreshment. The sun shone brightly, and it was cold, but not wet. Being outside in January was a blessing from God. And the ability to complete a bit more work or exertion every day made her feel strong and well and herself again. She thanked the Lord that she was getting back on her feet.

Nineteen

THE SUN WAS FAR from rising on Monday, but already Prentis was up on horseback alongside Avery's father, heading out with a herd of cattle. They hoped to return late tonight, perhaps tomorrow if they ran into any trouble. They would go all the way to Wichita, taking the train from Medford on the Atchison, Topeka, and Santa Fe railway line.

The shortages caused by the war had created a rise in prices, and Prentis wanted to stay ahead of government regulations, so this was a good time to sell. Today they removed ten bovine members of the animal kingdom from his farm before the calving, helping Prentis manage his grassland and alfalfa for the coming season. They expected to get the best prices in Wichita.

Avery stood on the porch watching them prepare, her features darkened. The living room lantern light shone behind her, so Prentis couldn't make out her face. Nevertheless, he smiled at her, knowing she could see him just fine. It didn't feel right to go so far away from her.

Gene and Howard stood below her on the porch steps. Out in the barn, he'd shown them what needed done, and last week he'd herded over Tom's cows and laid in extra feed. At sixteen and eleven, the boys would be able to take care of everything. Wrapped snug in her formerly controversial Oriental coat, Avery tousled the boys' hair and then waved at Prentis.

Last night she'd told him how happy she was that he could get the steers to market. It needed doing. He'd been housewife and nursemaid for long enough, she had said. Of course, he didn't feel that way. He'd been glad to take care of her. While he was gone, he had no idea how he'd keep from worrying about her.

He lifted his hat in farewell. It was difficult to leave her after all she'd gone through. But he knew all would be well. The boys were with her. Her father had helped him do everything possible around the farm, and they would be back quickly. Still he hesitated, taking a good long look at her standing there blooming with health. Thanks be to God for that.

With a slight tilt of her head, she waved him onward. Clearly, she had detected his hesitation. Watching her as long as possible, he reseated his hat and then wheeled Ulysses around and into action, following her dad and the steers out of the barnyard and hustling the stragglers into action. It was difficult to ride away.

"Sam!" he called out to his dog. "Go home. Stay."

The dog whined but obeyed. Avery needed Sam to keep an eye on their homestead.

Though home tugged at him, they made good time down to Medford, keeping the cattle moving at a brisk pace, an easy task between the two of them. The sky was growing light along the horizon when they drove the herd into the cattle yard near the railroad station. The horses headed right for the water trough, and Prentis swung down from Ulysses, slung his reins over the post, and strode inside to pay for passage.

The AT&SF stationmaster stepped out with him, and they all headed back toward the stock car to load the cattle. Ulysses and Hector would be stabled at the nearby livery until they returned, but for now, they were needed to get the cattle herded up the chute and on board. There was the usual resistance, bawling, and stubbornness, but the two geldings made rapid work of the troublemakers. Now all headed up the cattle chute and on their way.

"Train arrives in thirty minutes," the stationmaster said. "How long you stayin' in Wichita?"

"Hope to be back tonight on the last train," Prentis said.

"You should beat the snow easy then."

"Snow on the way, you say?"

"It's a few days out. Not expected here until end of the week. But the agents out west telegraph that we've got a doozy headed our way."

At this news, Prentis met Abe's eyes.

"Good to know," Prentis told the man. "We'll finish our business and get right back."

"Should work."

"That's our hope."

The stationmaster nodded, spat a stream of black tobacco juice into the soft dirt, and headed back into the station. Silently, Prentis and Avery's dad turned their horses toward the livery.

"What do you think?" Halfway there, Prentis broke the silence. "Should we go?"

"We're here. Your livestock's loaded. The news from out west gives us several days. Looks like we oughta make it back."

"I'm uneasy. Been so worried about her, I think it's softened me up."

"You're a husband." Abe Slaughter chuckled. "You're supposed to be soft on your wife."

Prentis laughed. "They do work their way down deep into our hearts, don't they?"

"Yes, they do."

Both men grinned, happy to be contented husbands.

After paying the board and getting both horses unsaddled, groomed, and fed, they grabbed some coffee at the small restaurant nearby and drank it down while consuming large plates of scrambled eggs and sausage. The thundering roar and rumble of the inbound train told them it was time to go. As they left, Prentis bought a newspaper at the counter.

When they neared the platform, the stationmaster stepped outside, heading toward the rails. Bursts of steam and the ear-splitting, body-shaking reverberations of the coal-powered engine accompanied each movement of the train forward and then slowly backward to couple with the cattle car on the side rail. Soon the agent appeared again from behind the station.

"All aboard!" He could barely be heard.

They climbed onto the train, found plenty of empty seats, and chose one under an already lit oil lamp. Soon the train lurched several times and then inched away from the station, about half full of riders. As they glided back onto the main line, their pace quickened. Prentis opened wide *The Daily Oklahoman* and reached up to adjust the lamp, hoping to catch up on the war news.

Next thing he knew, they were slowing for their first stop at Caldwell. He'd fallen asleep and had slid down until his shoulder was pinned into the seat corner with his face pressed against the window. The people standing on the Caldwell platform must have gotten a chuckle out of that. With his coat's sleeve, he wiped the smudge off the window.

Abe snored beside him, his chin resting on his chest.

Prentis straightened, collecting the newspaper from where it had fallen on top of his boots. Now that he was awake, he got to work on the paper. There was enough light that he could read, though the oil lamp still burned, and it did help. With about two hours left to kill, he decided he'd read from front to back. It kept him occupied all the way there. Abe didn't awaken until they pulled into Wichita, not even for the stops at Wellington, South Haven, and Derby.

When they exited on the east side, they were assaulted by the familiar odor of frightened livestock, manure, a packed feedlot, and the nearby meatpacking plant. The two men exchanged glances, both of them smiling. Prentis hadn't been there since he'd started farming in Oklahoma, since he usually made all of his sales in Anthony now. But as a young man, he'd always brought their cattle to the Wichita Live Stock Exchange on 702 E. 21st Street, first with his dad and then with Fred and his cousins. The fond memory of his father flooded his heart and mind.

The familiar scene was a welcome sight. The building was the Stock Exchange's fifth one, erected in 1909 after several previous fires had wiped them out and relocations had moved them. There it sat, right in the middle of the smelliest part of town, populated by animals for slaughter and plants for packing and rendering. Flying an enormous American flag, the three-story masonry building with its white colonnade across the front was like a beacon of his boyhood, the most beautiful livestock exchange he'd ever seen. Built when he was a child, it still remained.

They got right to work. With the assistance of the Wichita Live Stock Exchange cowhands, they got their livestock unloaded and corralled for sale. The auction would begin soon.

The auctioneer toured around, examining each lot and conversing with the owners, together determining fair prices for the market and informing the auctioneer of what they hoped to make. Meanwhile, professional cattle buyers circulated, trying to eavesdrop on these conversations in order to finagle the lowest prices possible. Prentis and Abe kept their voices low as they spoke to the auctioneer, stopping in mid-sentence once or twice until a nosy cattle buyer meandered away.

Prentis's livestock were of top quality. Rex's seed and his proven cows produced sturdy Hereford stock. They all looked to be at least market weight—a thousand to twelve hundred pounds. The livestock exchange scales would confirm. He sold mostly steers, but he'd also brought a couple of heifers and a cow. He couldn't keep them all, since he also had fourteen horses, one milk cow, and her calf. His grassland allowed for a maximum of forty head of livestock, though the alfalfa helped. Each year, selling his colts and fillies, his steers, and any cows who hadn't produced well improved his cash flow. When coupled with his wheat harvest, they brought in the money.

After their discussion with the auctioneer, Prentis and Abe sat a few rows back as the crowd gathered. Meat was needed as American boys were gathered from the far corners of the country to be trained in centralized locations, and then those troops on the other side of the ocean needed to be fed as well. In addition, all of Europe needed food. Prentis hoped for top dollar.

The familiar music of the auctioneer's patter as he cajoled, shamed, and tickled the gathered cattle buyers into giving up their money soothed Prentis's nerves. He knew the rules, and he typically won. It wasn't like wartime news, and it certainly wasn't like nearly losing his wife. This was simple. The rules were based on weight, quality, and need, easy to quantify.

Lot after lot of beef on the hoof was sold, one pen after another, until finally the auctioneer arrived at Prentis's lot of ten head. Listening to the seesaw rhythm of the man's voice and watching the bidders, Prentis shot up a prayer. A bidding war broke out when they finished with the cow and heifers and moved on to the steers. They were solid like Rex, walking slabs of beef. After much wrangling, they went to a well-dressed man with an enormous white Stetson.

The heifers and the cow had gone for $8.70 per hundredweight, and the steers for $9.20. At his first auction, after establishing his Oklahoma farm in 1914, his steers had gone for only $6.90 per hundredweight. That had been a good price then, but now the world needed his beef.

At the end of the day, he came away with a tidy sum of $1000.

"What say we grab us a steak at the Live Stock Exchange Restaurant?" he asked Abe.

"Always up for steak."

"That's what I thought. We can eat and then head home."

***

The inside of the Wichita Live Stock Exchange was something to behold, like walking into another world— white marble, dark wood, and glass. The building held fifteen livestock commission firms, the stockyard company officer, the branch officers of the packing houses, The Wichita Terminal Railway Company itself, and a national bank. Prentis remembered walking over the tile floor in the entryway when he entered with his father, who had business at that bank. The floor contained a four-foot wide mosaic of a bull's head right in the middle.

Across the street stood the old exchange building with its attached Stockyards Hotel. The buildings had been moved there when the Union Stock Yard Company had decided to build the current immaculate exchange building. Abe and Prentis crossed the street now and headed toward the restaurant inside, famous for the best steaks in Wichita. They were not disappointed. Neither could remember ever having a better thick cut of beef. But, when they stepped outside to return to the terminal, they were hit by a cold, sharp breeze blowing hard from the west.

The two men exchanged glances. It certainly felt as if they weren't going to miss that snowstorm after all. Only time would tell. Hoping for the best, they boarded the train.

The tracks headed straight south from Wichita, stopping at Derby and Wellington before turning westward at South Haven. As they rolled southward from Wichita, all they could detect in the fading afternoon light were thick storm clouds to the west and a lot of wind.

So far, so good. No snow.

But when the tracks turned west, they soon detected flecks of snow here and there close to their window. The farther west they travelled toward Medford, the thicker it fell. Accumulated snow now showed on the dark earth, growing in depth with each mile westward.

In Medford, they stepped out to a white world caught in a blizzard, the wind bitterly cold. They couldn't take the horses out in this. It wasn't safe. The stationmaster brought out a pile of woolen blankets and welcomed them to stay the night by the hot stove, since they couldn't travel.

Before Prentis could even speak his worries out loud, Abe reminded him that the boys knew how to care for livestock in a storm and that Avery would be fine. Prentis knew he was correct. They were both weary to the bone after the early start and the long day, and he would simply have to trust God with Avery and his life's work. He stretched out on one of the station benches with several thick wool blankets wrapped around him, gave it all to God, and fell asleep.

***

Peering out into the darkness, Avery lifted the curtain once again. It was obvious. They weren't going to make it home. The snowstorm had been a complete surprise. She doubted they'd be able to come in the morning either. She told herself not to worry. Neither her father nor Prentis would attempt anything foolish, and they wouldn't force the horses to travel in this, knowing the injury that would result.

Resolved, she turned toward the boys peering over her shoulders into the night.

"They're not coming," she said. "You're stuck here with a big sister who can't do all the work I once could. So now, you two are the men. Prentis told you what to do, and Daddy taught you well. So, bundle up, and head on out there to take care of the livestock for the night."

"We're one step ahead of you, Sis," Gene replied, eye to eye now with her at sixteen.

Realizing they were already wearing their coats, Avery laughed. Each wore wool socks and gloves, ready to get their boots on in the back porch. Howard grinned at her.

"We can take care of this farm," he said. "We're men."

"Men," Jack said.

Avery had to smile. "Yes, I can see that. Daddy taught you well. I'll make up a batch of cookies while you're out there. Do you want to take this little man with you?"

All three nodded.

"You must be careful, since Jack will be along."

"We will be," Gene said. "We're experienced nuncles."

He picked up Jack and began bundling him into the woolen coat they had gotten him for Christmas. Howard went to fetch his boots to slip on over his tiny wool socks. And before she knew it, out they went. Pulling out all the ingredients, she got to work making oatmeal cookies.

If all went well, they'd be able to take care of everything. Meanwhile, she'd pray that her daddy and Prentis were entirely safe and warm, wherever they were.

***

Prentis and Abe awakened the next morning to a world of white and a stiff western wind. Snow drifts were deep, and everything was covered in ice. Apparently, during their train ride yesterday morning, a warm front had pushed through, spitting rain on everything. Behind it came the blast of freezing wind straight off the Rockies, blowing across the prairie. Everything that had previously been wet was now encased in ice. Branches creaked under the weight. Everything was impassable. They were stranded in Medford.

First, they trudged through snow to the livery to check on the horses. Both nickered when they came in, Ulysses snorting blasts from his nostrils in greeting. Prentis stepped toward him.

"How are you, boys?" Prentis cooed, caressing their muzzles and placing his forehead against first one and then the other. "We've come back for you."

Tossing their heads about, deep neighs rumbled within the horses' chests, interspersed with snorts, expressing their affection. They looked well cared for, as Prentis had expected. The barn was warm from the heat of the animals' bodies. He retrieved some oats and added them to their feed trough, and then he crawled into the stall of first one and then the other, giving each a gentle rubdown across their backs and shoulders. Both snorted their pleasure. He was satisfied. All seemed well at the livery.

So, the two men headed toward the sidetrack café for coffee and eggs. A train was due down from Wichita today, and that was the only highlight they had to look forward to until everything thawed. Prentis didn't know if he could take it, even though there was a checkerboard and one old book. Waiting there with nothing useful to accomplish and his farm and wife needing him couldn't be borne. They were a mere fifteen miles from home.

"I may walk home." He looked at Abe as they finished their second cups of coffee.

"Let's see what the day brings."

The waitress filled their cups again. She was clearly eavesdropping. "Word is there's no thaw anywhere this storm hit," she said. "Nothin' but cold and ice."

"Where did you hear that?" Prentis said.

"Some folks who came through earlier, tryin' to make the train."

"I still say waiting's a good idea," Abe said. "Don't want to freeze out there."

Prentis turned toward the waitress. "Is your general store open?"

"Sure is," the woman replied.

Prentis looked hard at Abe. "I hear what you're saying. It's good advice. I'm willing to wait today, but I've got to make a plan. I trust the boys. Know they'll do a good job. But—"

"You're worried about my daughter."

"Yes, sir, I am."

"Your woodpile is stacked high," Abe said. "Your provisions are adequate. The animals had all been brought in from pasture and are corralled near the barn. All is well."

"If she hadn't just come through so much, I probably wouldn't feel like a caged beast stuck here. But, as it is, I don't think I can wait if we're still stuck here in the morning."

"If that's your plan, I'll stay with the horses and bring them out once the roads are dry."

Prentis looked up at his father-in-law, grateful for this man's patience and understanding. During many trials, he'd been a rock and support. Having come through so many hard times, the man was patient and understood God's sovereign control. Even though Prentis saw the caution in Abe's eyes, he still knew the older man had his back no matter what he decided.

"Thank you," Prentis said. "That means the world to me. I'm walking to the general store to buy more wool socks and whatever else I can find that will keep me warm."

"I'll stay here at the café. Plenty of coffee and all the news."

"Then we've got a plan."

***

The morning was frigid. Trying to warm the house, Avery fed wood into the fires in both the cookstove and the pot-bellied stove in the living room. The boys had headed out again to tend to the animals. When Howard came bursting back in carrying Jack, they startled her. He set Jack right beside her and turned to rush back outside.

Avery grabbed his shoulder. "What's happening out there?"

"One of those cows is getting ready to calf."

She let him go, and out he dashed.

This posed a dilemma. Practically since they could walk, her brothers had been taught how to take care of cattle. They'd all been out there with Daddy, listening to him and being instructed in what to do and how to do it. They were now eleven and sixteen. Gene was older than Prentis had been when he took over the family farm. They could handle it. In fact, she'd seen them in action with Prentis when they pulled a calf. Without a word, they knew exactly what to do. It had been like watching a choreographed dance as they'd all maneuvered around to get that calf born.

The big sister in her wanted to check in on them, but that would mean taking Jack out, and there was no telling what they might encounter. She didn't want to scare him. Prentis would teach him, but it seemed a bit young to start when he wasn't yet two.

Prentis would have at least one surprise when he returned home, whenever that was. At least one of his calves would already be delivered. Had the weather cooperated, he would have been present. But the weather showed no break. The wind still blew, and the ice was thick.

That morning, the boys had needed to break up the ice on the stock tank. When the tank got low, the windmill still kicked into gear to bring up the water. Nothing had frozen there, so all was fine. But her fruit trees' branches were hanging low and creaking heavily in the wind.

Since the boys were occupied with the cattle, Avery decided to gather the eggs. Usually, there weren't many in the winter. As the days grew longer, however, production sometimes began early, and she always enjoyed checking on her hens. She would tend to her chores and let her brothers do so, too, treating them like men, because they soon would be.

The chicken coop was warm and well insulated. Prentis kept it lined with bales of hay in the winter. However, glimmers of morning light shone through the boards here and there, and tiny dustings of snow had blown in around the door. When she walked in holding Jack's hand, the chickens all clucked contentedly.

"Good morning, girls."

"Girls," Jack repeated in his small voice.

The hens clucked in response and shuffled around, most rising from their repose.

Avery let Jack toss out the chicken scratch, and the birds strutted about pecking at it and clucking contentedly. She emptied the tin water pan, and then poured in some fresh water from the bucket she'd brought from the house. Jack peeked into the roosts that were low—she couldn't lift him yet. They found two eggs from the dozen hens. Jack picked them up gently and handed them to her.

"Good job, little man! We can use these to make breakfast."

"Eat," he said.

"Yes, let's go fix some food. I have a feeling all the boys on this farm will be hungry soon."

***

Nothing changed all day Tuesday. Prentis had waited it out, but tomorrow morning, he would walk home. That night, the train disgorged another group who had been in Wichita. More Wakitans exited the train, joining them in the station—A.C. Mead, Mr. and Mrs. Earl Mead, Miss Wilma Mead, Vester Carder, and Oliver Hott.

It was good to see familiar faces, especially Oliver, who was on a furlough from the army. Prentis told the other young men of his plan to head home tomorrow, and they decided to join him. First thing in the morning, they'd purchase more woolen undergarments for the new arrivals, Prentis having purchased his yesterday. And then, they'd all walk home together.

Most of them had friends and family in Medford, so they headed out to lodge at the homes of their acquaintances and family. But A.C. and Oliver remained at the station so they could get an early start. There were plenty of wool blankets, and the stove kept them all nice and warm.

***

As the sun cleared the horizon, Prentis eyed the vast white expanse heading northwest out of Medford. He shoved the two sandwiches he had purchased at the café into his overcoat pocket and strapped the newly purchased canteen across his shoulder. A.C. Mead and Oliver Hott did the same, also carrying flasks. All wore as much wool as they could layer on. They were prepared for anything they could imagine happening along the way.

After much thought and discussion with the older men who remained in Medford, they had decided to follow the railroad line from Medford to Wakita. There was better drainage and elevation on the tracks, thus allowing the sunlight to melt and hopefully clear the snow there. The railroad tracks would give them the straightest line, and it would be impossible for them to lose their sense of direction should another snowstorm blow through. For Prentis, it meant that he could stay the night in Wakita if the trip took them longer than expected.

They hoped to make it to Wakita in four hours.

"Are we ready, men?" Prentis said, his voice muffled by the wool scarf.

Both nodded, and they all stepped out from the railway station.

"This should be interesting," A.C. said. "I don't typically travel on foot."

"I've been whipped into army shape," Oliver said. "Seems like a normal day to me."

All three laughed at that, and A.C. asked Oliver to tell them about his experience at the base where he'd been training before deployment. Oliver regaled them with stories of long waits, longer hikes, target practice, and gas-mask training. Before his battalion shipped out, he had gotten a brief furlough to come see his sick mother. But then, he would be shipped off to war.

239

A.C. and Prentis both offered their condolences over the state of affairs.

The wind was stiff. It hadn't taken long for their woolen scarves to grow rigid with ice from their frozen exhalations as they laughed and spoke. At that point, conversation ceased, and each man focused on keeping a steady but fast pace.

Oliver Hott carried a handgun, should they encounter any need for it. But, so far, they had only seen one small herd of deer that seemed to have found a pile of spilled grain. Keeping their eyes on their destination, they moved forward in single file, walking up the center of the tracks.

Then A.C. motioned toward the northeast. Coming toward them rapidly, a large pack of coyotes trotted into view. He turned back to look at the other two. Oliver pulled out his pistol.

"Don't know what to expect," Prentis said. "That's a large pack."

"They usually keep their distance," A.C. said.

Prentis nodded. "Let's all keep an eye on them. Their numbers might make them bold."

Oliver loaded his weapon as he walked.

They kept up their pace and continued onward, estimating where their path would intersect that of the coyotes. Prentis counted twenty in the pack. It was hard to determine, since the animals were on the move. Soon, the coyotes stopped in front of them, standing stock still facing them down. The three men all stopped, keeping their eyes on the pack.

Slowly, Oliver aimed his pistol and fired, taking one down. When the bark of the gun sounded, all of the coyotes jumped, shying away from their fallen comrade, turning as one, and heading off toward the east.

"We'll rotate. Whoever brings up the rear after me," Prentis said, "keep an eye out lest they circle around and come up behind us."

From his place in the rear, Prentis kept his eyes constantly moving. Aiming northwest, they continued walking between the two rails. By the time they'd passed the coyote's carcass, hawks had already arrived. Occasionally, Prentis turned to look in all directions behind, but he saw no coyotes.

Eventually, A.C. fell to the back, Oliver moved up to break the crusty snow, and Prentis took the middle. Overcast weather continued, so they couldn't really trace the sun's arc. It was impossible to tell what time of day it was. They continued walking fast and with purpose.

"A lone coyote behind us," A.C. said.

Prentis and Oliver turned to look. Then all scanned to find the others. None were in sight.

"Let's all be alert," Prentis said. "Glad you have your gun, Oliver."

"A.C., let me know if he comes closer," Oliver said. "I'll turn and shoot."

Prentis readjusted his scarf, turning it 'round, so a less frozen section rubbed against his face. His cheeks felt raw from the chafing. Silently, they moved forward, walking as quickly as they could and remaining alert. So far, they hadn't relocated the animals. Other than the lone coyote behind them, maybe the pack had moved on, though, it didn't seem logical for one to remain.

A.C. pulled out his stopwatch. "Another hour in. Let's shift."

They changed position again and kept up the pace, each scanning as they stepped carefully along the railroad ties. Oliver brought up the rear now, Prentis the front.

Finally, he spied them. Pointing off to the west, Prentis directed the eyes of the other men. The pack had circled all the way around them from behind. All turned to check on the lone coyote still trotting along behind them, gradually drawing closer. They picked up their pace.

The crack of Oliver's gun caught Prentis by surprise. A.C. jumped. Both men glanced behind to the see the red stain on the snow.

"I thought he'd gotten close enough," Oliver said.

The animals were behaving aggressively. It was winter's end, the pickings were slim, and they were clearly hungry. Their pups must have been recently born, creating offspring to feed.

The men kept walking as Oliver reloaded, replacing the bullets he'd spent so far. Prentis noticed that the pack now trailed them, trotting single file and moving at their speed on an identical line of travel. Their predatory behavior was unnerving and rare. He'd never experienced anything like this before. Usually, he faced coyotes with a gun in his hand while riding a horse.

An impasse seemed to have been reached. The pack came no closer. The men walked along at the same pace. The pack stayed at a similar tempo. This continued for a long stretch. Prentis reckoned they'd been walking a few hours.

"What's the time, A.C.?" Prentis said.

"We're three hours in."

"Good," he and Oliver stated simultaneously.

Everyone remained alert. It wasn't long before A.C. pointed to the east. Part of the pack had split off, half on their left and now the other half on the right. It seemed as if they still maintained their distance, but up ahead Prentis spied that the tracks went through a deep ditch.

The railroad cut was largely packed with snow that had blown in great high drifts at the entrance. That cut would allow the coyotes to come in closer, enabling them to jump down upon them from either side. They had to determine if they were going to try to walk through the cut, since it was snow packed. This required caution. Over his shoulder, Prentis voiced his concerns.

Almost immediately after, Oliver fired a shot.

242

"They're closing in," he said. "Don't want to go through that cut with them any closer."

"Makes sense," Prentis said.

"Look!" A.C. said, pointing east.

The pack on the eastern side took off like a shot straight north. In the distance, the men detected the small herd of deer they'd noticed earlier. Obviously, the wind had shifted, and the pack had caught the scent. The coyotes on the western side now followed suit. As they neared the unsuspecting deer, they separated again and closed in from all sides. In the melee that followed, the coyotes seemed to bring down at least two does, but the rest escaped.

"Well, that's a relief," Oliver breathed. "But I'm still keeping my gun out."

"I'm all for that," A.C. said. "Could have been us."

"Look ahead." Prentis pointed. Trails of smoke drifted upward from Wakita's chimneys. "Looks like we could be there in less than an hour. We'll make it in time for lunch."

"It will be good to warm up," Oliver added.

"Yes, it will."

Relief washed through Prentis. He'd sit a while at the general store, eat his lunch, and bask in the heat of the stove. Once he was warmed clear through and his socks were good and hot, he'd walk the four-and-a-half miles home. He should be able to get there in an hour and a half. Hopefully, he'd make it before sunset. How he longed for home! What had been a one-day trip had turned into an entirely different venture.

***

In the fading light, Avery stepped out onto the front porch, shaking out the tablecloth. She had fed the boys an early supper of pinto beans, ham hocks, and cornbread, and they had gotten cornbread crumbs everywhere. That was the one drawback of serving the dish.

From far in the distance, she heard a shout.

Peering into the growing twilight, she attempted to see who had called. A dark figure appeared to be at least a quarter mile down the road. Someone was out on foot! That was a surprise. Stepping back into the house, she put on her coat.

"Gene, you keep an eye on things, and all of you boys clean up the rest."

"Clean!" Jack said, clearly excited. He loved putting his hands in dishwater.

"What's up, Sis?" Howard asked.

"There's someone coming up the road, and he or she hailed me. I'm not sure who it is, but they might need help."

"I'll come, so you've got a man with you," eleven-year-old Howard said.

Inwardly, Avery smiled. "I'd love to have the protection of a man. You come along, Howard. Bundle up. Gene, do you think that you and Jack can take care of this kitchen?"

"Yep, Mom-mom," Jack answered for them both.

Grinning, Gene shrugged. So, Avery and Howard walked out into the dusky twilight. Behind the house as the sunlight faded away, the sky flamed orange and red and rich-hued shades of lovely, like a kiss from God. The stunning beauty distracted her from whoever was out there. When she finally turned, she looked hard. That was Prentis's hat. It was he!

Avery hurried up the drive, followed by Howard. They met Prentis on the road, and she threw wide her arms. Howard grinned from ear to ear as Prentis tousled his hair.

"You're home," she said. "And you walked! From whence did you come?"

244

"Medford," he said through the stiff wool scarf covering his face. "About froze to death. It was a long day, five-and-a-half hours of walking."

"Where's my daddy?"

"Coming as soon as it's safe to bring the horses. I couldn't bear being away. Wanted to make sure you were all right and not overdoing it. Had to get home to you, so I took out on foot."

"Well, I'm sure glad to see you!"

"And I you." He pulled her close, eyeing her face over his scarf. "Are you well?"

"Yes, I am." She walked alongside him, stepping up the slope of their own drive.

"Howard." Prentis turned toward her brother. "Did your sister follow the doctor's orders and not overdo it?"

"Yep. She sure did." Howard grinned at her. "We saw to it. Other than one of your cows deciding to calf early, everything went as expected."

"Prentis, let's get you home and warm you up." Avery jumped in, hoping to veer him away from talk of calving. "I want to hear everything once you're thawed—the sale, the trip, the snow, and how you came to be walking home."

"That sounds like heaven," he said. "Have I got a story to tell you!"

Twenty

ON FRIDAY, FEBRUARY 4, TWO full months after the surgery, their small family climbed into the Model T. Now they would learn how Avery had healed and if all their careful effort had paid off. Prentis felt the weight of the long ordeal lifting. He hoped all was well.

They were to drop Jack off in Gibbon for a short visit with his grandparents before heading to Avery's appointment. Hopeful that they might have some time alone, they had written her parents in advance, asking if they would keep Jack until Sunday. They could meet then at the church in Wakita.

When they arrived, Jack spied the house and got excited. Both of Avery's parents came outside to greet them and to exclaim over Jack as they gathered him and his leather suitcase. His little nose was red, though he had been well bundled. Having stayed with his grandparents so much recently, he waved goodbye happily without any tears.

246

As they pulled away, Prentis glanced over at Avery.

She turned toward him. "Look how much he's grown up! Last time we left him, he cried."

"Remember, he spent two weeks with them when you were in the hospital. I drove down here every day from Anthony. Took him and one of the boys to the house to do chores. Then I brought them back and came up to the hospital again. Jack got used to staying here. He knows we'll return. Feels secure. Hasn't cried about it for a while. I told you then, but you were sleeping most of the time. Wasn't sure if you'd remember anything I said."

"I was mostly in oblivion while in that hospital."

"You were on pain medication. It pretty much knocked you out."

"Jack obviously adjusted, didn't he?"

"He did." Prentis gathered great fatherly contentment from that fact. "Our boy is growing up strong and independent."

Avery sniffed. "Our baby isn't a baby anymore, and there aren't any coming after him. I missed so much!"

Baffled, Prentis turned toward her. This was mystifying. Why did these changes in Jack distress her?

"That's a good thing, Sweetheart. We want him to grow up strong. Wasn't your fault. You lost a baby and had a serious surgery. You were healing."

"You're right." She sniffled. "I'm sorry for getting emotional."

Keeping his eyes on the road, he reached to caress her cheek. She leaned into his hand.

"No need to apologize. Don't be hard on yourself. You've come through a terrible ordeal."

"You're right," she said. "I'll simply have to accept it. God has been so good to us."

"Yes, He has. Every single day, I thank Him for all He's given, no matter what He's taken away. That you're alive and well is a gift. A few weeks ago, I knew I'd get to

247

keep you. That's the only reason I went to Wichita. Knew you were going to make it, but still, I couldn't stay away. Had to walk back to make sure you were all right."

She turned toward him. "I can't even begin to imagine this from your perspective."

"It was a hard time. Glad it's past us now." He glanced over again, taking in her expression. "Can't wait to hear what the doctor says."

"You're such a good husband. You've taken such good care of me."

He laughed. "I love you. Couldn't help myself."

With twinkling eyes, she smiled at him and then turned, looking out the window.

"I feel as if I missed an entire chunk of my life," she said. "Since early fall, life has been a blur of pain, fear, and struggles of faith. I missed an entire season, it seems. Look at all the hoarfrost!"

The countryside was still covered in snow from the big storm. The roads had frozen hard, and the early sunlight sparkled and danced, bouncing off icy fences, frost-covered dried weeds, ice-encased trees, and seemingly millions of frozen water crystals embedded in the roadway. Glints of refracted sunlight blazed forth, gleaming and twinkling in all directions. It was nearly blinding as the blanket of white slowly transformed from blue light to yellow, the higher the winter sun rose in the sky. The scene was truly breathtaking. God's handiwork.

"It's so beautiful today!" She faced the window, clearly captivated by the scene.

"God's gift to you, Sweetheart. This is one of the prettiest mornings I've ever seen."

Turning toward him now, she beamed. "God's gift. I'll take it!"

***

The two sat side by side in the packed doctor's office. Sick mommas, babies, and children crammed into the room, typical for February. Several babies wailed loudly. This time alone with Prentis was precious, even if it had been hard to leave Jack. Avery sighed, wanting to get this over with, so they could go back home as soon as possible. The inner door opened, and the nurse eyed the stuffed room, spied them on the other side, and gestured to them with her head.

"Mrs. Pinkerton, you're the first patient of the morning."

Calm on the exterior, but rattled on the inside, Avery tried to rise. But, overcome with emotion, she remained paralyzed in her seat. They would learn so much today. What would they discover? What all had been lost? The possibilities overwhelmed her.

Prentis stood and lifted her gently by the elbow, helping her to her feet.

"Come on, Sweetheart," he whispered. "I'll help you."

"Stay with me," she whispered back.

"If you're certain." He stared deeply into her eyes, clearly waiting entirely upon her.

"I'm certain. You could probably nurse me in a hospital as much as you've seen. Now, if only I could get my legs and my feet to cooperate."

"I'll race you back there," he whispered, eyes twinkling mischievously.

"I'll win," she returned softly, finally able to move.

Now he laughed out loud, then smiled up at the nurse, as if to reassure her that they were on their way. The nurse returned his smile and fixed her eyes on them fondly.

Avery felt supported. This final checkup was the culmination of a team effort. A large group of people had kept her alive and functioning. Once they were past the door, they walked down the short corridor to the far end. There they entered the examination room.

"I feel as if we're awaiting the executioner," she whispered.

"No." Prentis leaned in to kiss her forehead. "This will be good news. We've followed all their instructions. We've been careful. You're on the mend. Don't be afraid."

"Yes, you're right. The Lord is with us."

Steady, measured footfalls pounded down the hallway toward them. Both stared at the door. In burst the doctor.

"Good morning," he said, shaking both their hands.

Then all sat. He asked them to relay how the recovery had gone so far. After they had filled him in on everything since Avery had left the hospital, the doctor looked pleased.

"Since it appears you're a part of the medical team, P.J., you're welcome to stay, if Avery wants you back here. The surgeon wrote and asked me to confirm that Avery's health history was true, and that Jack is indeed your natural-born son. He's still astonished, as am I, that she could carry a pregnancy to term. He also told me that he had entrusted you with quite a bit of responsibility, knowing you would keep all his instructions. Your meticulous care as a rancher and your delivery of your own son convinced him."

Prentis shrugged modestly. Avery watched him duck his head, his natural shyness coloring his cheekbones. Then both men turned toward her, awaiting her decision.

"Please, let Prentis sit here by my head, holding my hand like last time, while you do the examination. I must admit I'm frightened of the pain this exam might cause."

"Would you like a whiff of nitrous oxide?"

"Yes, I think I would."

The doctor flipped on the machine and washed his hands as Avery stepped behind the screen to remove some garments and to adjust others. Wrapped carefully in an examining room sheet, she stepped out and crawled up onto the table. Prentis sat beside her, facing her head, his eyes on hers, and his back turned toward the doctor. As she breathed deeply of the nitrous and then lay back to endure the exam, Prentis kept his eyes fixed on hers.

"Look at me," he said. "I'm right here with you."

Avery stared into his blue eyes looking back with so much love and compassion that her heart about burst. She squeezed his hand hard. The doctor was trying his best to be gentle, and the nitrous had taken away the fear and tension, so while the exam was uncomfortable, it wasn't excruciating. As the nitrous took effect, she felt entirely relaxed.

Of course, the doctor had to be thorough. Major surgery had been performed on a delicate and private part of her body. And so, thorough, he was. Finished at last, he stepped over to the sink and washed his hands, a thoughtful expression on his face.

"This time, I won't make you press me for information, young man." He glanced at Prentis. "I'll give you both my assessment."

Barely breathing, they awaited his words.

"Dr. Galloway has done the best job I've ever seen on this type of surgery. There's no reason for me to give you any kind of restriction. Everything is healed nicely. You may resume marital relations. There should be no problem whatsoever. You'll quickly forget that you've had any surgery done at all. Obviously, you won't be having menses any longer, but he's left you in very good shape, young woman."

Looking at one another, both heaved sighs of relief.

Then Avery turned toward the doctor. She felt Prentis's kind eyes upon her.

"Thank you from the bottom of my heart," she said quietly, her voice quivering. "That's all I can muster, given the personal nature of this surgery and the possible negative outcomes that we've been spared."

"I understand," he said. "You're welcome. I'll pass on your thanks to Dr. Galloway. Now off I go to attend to my next patient."

And with that, he vanished out the door, shutting it behind him. Astonished they stared at one another.

"God has surely taken good care of us today, Avery. That's better news than I ever hoped or dreamed."

"Yes, indeed," she said. "Praise God."

"Amen to that."

Prentis stood and wriggled back into his great coat.

"I'll go and pay the nurse while you dress. Then when you come out, I'll whisk you away and out of sight. We'll return to the privacy of our own home."

"Such an examination requires time to recover. I'll be greatly relieved to get home."

***

Prentis had paid when Avery stepped into the waiting room, her scarf wrapped around her face, as if her exit was intended to be incognito. After this personal invasion, she clearly craved privacy and a quick escape. He opened the door wide, so she could barge out of one doorway and immediately through another. Hurrying past her, he caught up. She performed the passenger duties, and they got their Model T running as fast as possible.

Rather than driving through the crowded downtown, he headed south through the few blocks of streets lined with houses. On the far southward side of Wakita, he turned west, taking a less public route before heading south again. Even over the motor, he heard her exhale her relief as they left the confines of Wakita and the public's gaze. He reached over to squeeze her mittened hand. Soon they made the familiar turn at the cemetery and aimed homeward.

"We're safe now," he said over the engine. "Nothing but home before us."

She collapsed upon the seat back. All her energy visibly dissipated, as if it had taken everything within her to endure what she had just experienced. And he knew it had.

"How about you take a morning nap when we return?" he said. "I'll go check on our livestock. Need to look at the cows. Expect more calving any day now."

She nodded her response. Within a few minutes they had arrived. He dropped her at the back door and drove toward the barn, leaving her to get herself settled and rested. He'd be in soon enough. He was glad they had a couple of days alone.

Of course, it took him longer than expected. One of his cows delivered, and he had to attend to the new calf, rubbing it down with the thick towels he kept for that task, making sure it was dry enough in the bitter cold, and watching to see if its mother responded as she should. As soon as the calf was tugging at her teats, she lowed contentedly. The other cows showed no signs of labor, so he could step back inside the house for now.

The aroma of ham baking greeted him at the back door. After hanging up his outerwear and removing his dirty boots, he washed thoroughly and then walked into the kitchen. A peek into the cookstove confirmed what his nose had already detected.

The house was absolutely silent, a rarity in a family with a small child. The bedroom door was slightly ajar, so he peeked in. Wrapped up in several quilts, she slept, her face tranquil. It occurred to him then that her face had mostly appeared anguished, even in slumber, during this entire trial. Now she appeared relieved and secure. He smiled and thanked God for it.

Not wanting to wake her, he settled in his chair, feet up on the hassock. He had apparently nodded off, for when he awakened, sunlight from their western bedroom window shone like a bolt onto the well-worn floorboards, dust motes floating about in the brightness. Their bedroom door was now open, and Avery sat snuggled into her chair, wrapped in quilts, quietly watching him sleep and appearing quite tranquil still.

When he looked into her face, she smiled.

"Come over here," he said softly, scooting up into the chair.

She gathered herself and all her wrappings, stepped over, and lowered herself into his lap. As the quilts settled, her bare shoulder slid into view. That was unexpected. It made his heart skip a beat, and he pulled her in close against him.

"I've got you all to myself," he said, "after not having you for so long. Can't even remember when. It's been like trudging through a desert that never ends. The woman I love has been lost in a red Oklahoma dust storm, like an elusive mirage I can never reach. Don't even know how many times I've had that dream. I can never get to you."

"Well, now you can." Soft and tender, she pressed her lips to his.

He returned her kiss, and then she pulled back.

"You never told me you had a recurring nightmare."

"Didn't want to trouble you. I did say that it was awfully difficult to wait for you."

"Yes, you did."

"It was more agonizing this time, because I knew what I was missing."

Cupping his face in both of her hands, she kissed him long and deep. He had finally found her. Yes, he had. Grabbing her up, he rose, stepped over the hassock, and carried her into their bed. In nothing flat, he stripped and slid under the quilts with her.

"How long can that ham stay in the oven?" he asked.

"Another hour or so."

254

"Good. We'll take our time."

And they did.

***

Wrapped in all their quilts and in one another, they lay quietly, each considering what had transpired. Softly, Prentis kissed the top of Avery's head, murmuring that he loved her. She nestled closer, nuzzling his neck with her cheek. Avery had mixed emotions. There was much to sort out.

"It's difficult to accept that our intimacy cannot and will not ever result in a child," she said. "I feel less womanly."

He snorted. "Believe me. You're ever bit as womanly."

"Thank you for that. I guess I'll simply have to accept it."

He lifted his head slightly, peering into her face. "You're gorgeous. Most beautiful woman I've ever known. You're still the same woman."

She considered that for a moment before responding. "In my mind, motherhood is a more important beauty, and now I can't produce children."

"Well, let's see. Got several things to say about that. You *are* a mother, and a good one. So, you already bear that beauty within you. It's always apparent. But, that aside, remember when you couldn't get pregnant, when you hadn't yet borne a child?"

"Yes."

"Well, you were beautiful then. Womanly. Always have been. I was completely satisfied with you. Feel the same now."

She gazed into his eyes. They looked back at her evenly and sincerely.

Then Prentis shoved himself upward. Bundling her in the quilts, he pulled her into his lap, snug against his body. She nuzzled his chest, then looked up into his piercing blue eyes.

"Wasn't even thinking about lost fertility today." He paused, looking hard at her. "My greatest concern was whether I might hurt you."

"No, you didn't. It was merely like starting all over again."

Keeping his eyes on hers, he nodded. Each pondered the newness of the situation.

"My love for you has no strings attached," he said. "I have no requirements. Want you to be exactly who you are. It's always been that way. It's why I waited for you for so long. You're an incredible woman. A lifetime of loving you, seven years of waiting, and then trying to win your heart were all worth it. I'm proud and honored to call you my wife, just exactly as you are. Please, believe that."

"I'm trying. This is my own internal struggle."

"Then I pray you'll work through it."

She nodded, pushed away, and sat on the bed. "I'm hungry. Let's go get that ham and all of those potatoes out of the oven. By the way, we're eating that all weekend."

"Sounds perfect to me. Your mother tucked in a pie when we dropped off Jack. I found it in a wooden crate sitting on the floorboards in the back."

She grinned. "Then we have everything we need."

"Indeed, we do!" He smiled widely. "It's peach."

***

The following day Prentis stayed abed late with Avery, exactly as they had the first year they were married. He had made sure of the animals' care the night before. No cows had shown any signs of labor then. As the soft light filtered into the room, he awakened, lying still as he grew conscious of the day and its circumstances. Then he smiled, for he could remain with her. They lay spooned together, the fragrance of her hair and her body assailing his senses.

Thank You, Father, for this woman. Thank You for all You've given, no matter what You've taken away, for sparing her life, her health, and our intimacy. You're so kind to us!

Shifting slightly in position, she burrowed even more securely against him, arching her back into his midsection as she moved nearer. Bliss and tranquility filled his chest. He buried his face in the crook of her neck and relaxed into her body, taking the extra rest provided that morning.

Later, he awakened to find her smiling at him.

"I was watching you sleep," she said. "I never have that privilege. You're always out of bed long before I rise nowadays."

Yawning widely, he stretched. "Woke early and thanked God for you. Then I allowed myself the luxury of more sleep. What a pleasure this is!"

She pulled him toward her, and they found satisfaction in one another's arms.

Afterward, Avery smiled into his eyes. "I'm going to exert myself even further by making you buckwheat pancakes. It may be all I'm able to do this morning, but I aim to make you happy in every possible way."

With that, she grabbed up her wrapper from the bedside chair, stuffed her feet into her woolen house socks, and shuffled to the kitchen. Lacing his fingers behind his head, he grinned, watching her go. It was a good morning!

"Need any help in there?" he called.

"Nope. You stay right there until I call you. Enjoy having the morning off."

He closed his eyes and thanked God for his wife and for marriage, recalling that God had said it was "very good" after he had created Eve and given her to Adam. He had to agree.

The scent of coffee and pancakes awakened him again. He had snoozed. That was unexpected. He must have been more fatigued than he had taken time to notice. Normally, once he was awake, he rolled out of bed and got busy. The past months had been exhausting, more so than he had recognized. These days off were probably a necessity. Thank God for it.

Soon she called him in. He leapt up, stepped into his warmest long union suit, layered on wool socks, and pulled on his blue jeans. Leaving the bedroom, he wriggled into his thickest flannel shirt. The house was warming. Clearly, Avery had stoked both the stoves.

"Don't you overtax yourself," he called into the kitchen.

"I won't," she returned. "I'm monitoring how I feel."

He stepped into the kitchen.

Keeping her weight evenly distributed between her two feet, she worked the cookstove. Glancing over her shoulder, she smiled. A pile of flapjacks stood tall on a plate over the spot where the heat radiated from the oven. The final few pancakes bubbled on the grill, and the coffee was ready for pouring. Without moving her feet, she filled his coffee cup and handed it to him. Then she deftly flipped the pancakes.

"See," she said, "I'm being careful. I'm not scurrying about. I'm conserving my energy. Can you set the table?"

He finished his first sip of coffee. "I sure can."

By the time he got everything ready, she had transported the warm plate of pancakes, the butter, and the maple syrup onto the table. They both sat down and grasped hands.

"Father God," he said, "thank You for all Your abundant mercies this morning. My wife is healing. I've held her in my arms again. And she makes the best

258

pancakes in the world. In Jesus's name, amen." He opened his eyes to find her grinning at him.

"I'm so glad you're my husband."

"Why's that?"

"I love that you pray exactly like you talk."

He shrugged. "How else would a man pray?"

She merely shook her head and laughed. Then she began loading his plate. Once most of the pancakes were in one big pile on his plate, with a few remaining for her, she passed him the butter, followed by the syrup. The two of them dug in.

He couldn't talk when he ate her buckwheat pancakes. He had to concentrate on his eating, wanting to savor every bite. She knew that, but she still liked to converse over meals.

"I think I'll gather the eggs and feed the chickens, and then I'll sit down to read my Bible. The house is so quiet, it will be nice to have some uninterrupted time in God's Word."

He nodded.

"Then I might take a nap, or not. I'm not sure. I'll see how I feel. I definitely want to try to catch up on the war news in the papers. But, before any of that, if you're planning on riding over to Tom's, I'd love to go along. I haven't seen his place in so long, and this would be a perfect opportunity."

"Yep," he was able to get out between bites. "Let's do that."

Back in he went for the next enormous bite. She talked some more about this and that, but he got distracted from her words by the realization that she was speaking again. During most of her illness and recovery, she'd been practically speechless. He loved the cadence of her voice—always had. He swallowed his last enormous bite.

"I've missed your voice," he said.

"I quit—" Looking stunned, she stopped in midsentence, staring at him.

Awaiting the rest, he nodded.

"I quit talking, didn't I?"

"You did," he said. "Came on slowly, rather than sudden. I realized it before your surgery. But, I was struck speechless too. Could barely communicate myself. Didn't even know how to tell you. Reminded me of the year my father died. None of us could find our words."

"I hadn't realized it."

"Seems we're both verbal again," he said. "So, why did *you* stop?"

Focusing on her face, he sat still. His gaze didn't waver. For a moment, she seemed to turn inward. Then, she met his eyes.

"I had no energy for speech, and all of my turmoil was unsettled and internal. I was grappling with God, and I had no words for it yet. I probably appeared to be quite stoic."

"Yes," he said, "you did. That's what happened to me too. When Mary Beth began to visit again, I noticed you were talking more than you had been. But just now, I was listening to your voice. Realized how much I enjoy simply hearing you talk. Then it dawned on me that you were communicating like yourself again. You're well."

They stared at one another.

He shoved back from the table and grabbed her up, pulling her right into his lap. "Avery, I'm grieved that you suffered so much that you were unable to speak."

His chest tightened, and his throat ached. Tears waited right below the surface, but he didn't care. Swallowing hard, he kept his eyes on hers.

"God was working on me," she said, "even in all of that. I'm still pondering what I've learned and what God wants me to take away from this experience."

"Take your time. Talk it out with me, if you want. I've missed hearing your thoughts."

She kissed him softly. "You're such a kind and loving husband."

He snorted. "I try." After pulling out his handkerchief, he blew his nose, wiped his eyes, and cleared his throat. "Didn't expect that."

"You love me. That one little teardrop is evidence."

He chuckled. "I hope you've got more evidence than that or we're in trouble."

Together they rose and did up the dishes. He went out to saddle the horses and told her to rest with her feet up until he came in to get her. Once he was outside, he worked slowly, checking on all the expectant livestock, giving her time to doze off if her body needed the rest.

When he came in later, he found her sleeping in her chair, so he quietly pulled out his Bible and did a bit of reading, waiting for her. He set his heart and mind on listening to her for the rest of the weekend, in fact for the rest of her life. He would never tire of hearing her speak.

Her voice was the most beautiful sound in the world.

***

On Sunday, they walked up the steps to the Wakita Methodist Episcopal Church. Prentis smiled at Avery when they heard Jack call out, then saw him come running toward them.

"Mom-mom! Da Da!"

"There's our boy!" Avery smiled widely and stooped to lift him into her arms.

But, Prentis intercepted him, grabbing him up first, so Avery didn't lift. Immediately he turned Jack toward her, balancing him between them. Jack's little arms grabbed round their necks. Avery's eyes twinkled. By then her parents had caught up. They laughed with delight to see the small family reunion.

"Thank you for taking him this weekend." Prentis shook her dad's hand and nodded toward her mother.

"We were glad to have him," Minnie Slaughter said. "He'll probably nap this afternoon. I think the boys wore him out. "

Howard, Gene, and Abe smiled at that statement, having followed behind.

A crowd gathered round them, welcoming Avery back, telling her they had missed her. The cold weather pressed all of them inside, funneling them into the building, a crowd of happy churchgoers.

But then, Mr. and Mrs. Alfonse Riley pulled up in their buggy. Prentis caught sight of them, and so did Avery's father, who turned to meet Prentis's eyes.

"Well, I'll be," he said quietly, for Prentis alone. "Look who all's here."

Abraham Slaughter lifted his hand to acknowledge Alf, who gave him a nod. The man wore a resigned expression. There had to be a story behind that.

Quickly, Prentis turned away, catching up with Avery, taking her by the elbow, and gently nudging her farther into the building. Absorbed in chatting with her mother and showering Jack with kisses, she walked alongside him. Clearly, she hadn't seen the Rileys. Inside, Reverend Wallock greeted them all warmly, encouraging everyone inside and out of the cold.

Up the center aisle, Prentis continued to guide Avery as person after person greeted her. He moved closer to the pulpit than usual, hoping to eliminate the possibility of the Rileys sitting in front of them. Maybe Avery wouldn't have to be troubled by them at all.

But then Mary Beth Miller called Avery's name.

Prentis winced as she turned around to greet her friend just as Mary Beth hurried past the Rileys. Prentis watched her father step into the aisle, blocking her view of the Rileys coming in behind him, but Prentis also noticed a brief hesitation in Avery's forward motion. Then she stepped into Mary Beth's hug. The two women chatted in the aisle. He heard Mary Beth mention Joe Pitzer and a recent letter. At the sound of his name, Prentis observed Mrs. Riley jerk her head that direction, her eyes keenly watching the two young women.

Awful busybody. Prentis sighed. *Lord, help me to forgive that woman.*

Avery said something softly to Mary Beth. Prentis couldn't hear her words, since she was turned away from him. However, not only he, but everyone nearby heard Mary Beth's reply.

Laughing joyfully, she exclaimed, "Joe and I are now officially engaged."

"Thanks be to God," Avery said, turning toward Prentis to include him before facing Mary Beth again. "You made the poor boy pursue you for three years. It's about time!"

Mary Beth held out her hand with an engagement ring on it. Immediately, from everywhere in the building, a throng of young women made a beeline, swarming up the aisle, everyone rejoicing with her.

"How did he get the ring to you?" Avery asked.

"His sister Hattie brought it down." Mary Beth glowed. "It's a family ring."

The girls all twittered with delight and excitement, all admiring the ring.

At that moment, Mark Wallock walked by, heading for the pulpit. The reverend stopped and congratulated Mary Beth, spoke quietly to her, smiled, and then headed toward the front. Once he was behind the pulpit, everyone took their seats. Avery bestowed one last hasty hug on Mary Beth before sitting down by Prentis.

"Why are we so near the front?" she whispered as she entered the pew.

Glancing at her, he shrugged. Then he fixed his eyes straight ahead, wondering how this messy situation was going to play out. But the drama wasn't over. The reverend smiled in the direction of Mary Beth's and the Miller family's usual seats.

"Welcome, everyone, on this cold February morning," the reverend began. "I have permission from Mary Beth Miller to let you all know that she and Joseph Pitzer are now officially engaged to be married. Given all the excitement in the center aisle, I knew we'd be unable to settle down and turn our attention toward our Savior without satisfying everyone's curiosity." The congregation chuckled. He was correct. "Let's congratulate Mary Beth with a round of applause. I'm told this young man pursued her for more than three years, and now he's off to war. He'll have one extremely important reason to keep his head down and bring himself safely home once he's finished his service. Keep them in your prayers."

Applause rang out, along with spoken congratulations from those seated near Mary Beth and the Miller family. Beaming, her mother applauded from the piano at the front.

Prentis felt as if they'd left their quiet home and walked into a tornado. How would these shared facts impact Mrs. Riley? Hopefully, Avery had the energy to endure all of the commotion. He'd do his best to get her out of there without running into the Rileys.

Jack now wriggled to get down. "Big boy," he said.

He stood between them as they rose for the first hymn and then repeated The Apostles Creed. Smiling, Avery stroked Jack's hair. What was she thinking? Perhaps she hadn't seen Mrs. Riley. Maybe when she turned back, her father had blocked the view of the Rileys well enough and Avery had focused on Mary Beth, missing Mrs. Riley completely.

The sermon was a good one. It was comforting to be back in church, worshiping the Savior, singing hymns, and hearing encouragement from the Bible. It made Prentis feel as if he'd been away from home, but now had returned. By the end of Mark Wallock's exhortation, Jack had fallen asleep between them. He slouched slightly toward Avery, asleep against her arm. As predicted, his uncles had worn him out. Prentis smiled at the thought.

As church ended, Mark paused at their pew and took Avery's hand before heading toward the back of the sanctuary and the front door to shake hands with everyone.

"In case you're exhausted and need to slip out the side door," he said, "I'm stopping here so you know how glad I am to see you feeling better, Avery. We're all happy to have your family back." His eyes took in Prentis and Jack, who had roused. And then he walked on.

"That's an excellent idea," Prentis whispered. "Let's head out the back door and get you home. I think you've had enough excitement to last you for days."

"I think you're right" she said. "I feel my energy draining right out of me. Do you mind?"

"You're asking a shy man if he minds avoiding a crowded church entryway?"

"Well," she chuckled softly, "when you put it that way, never mind."

She caressed his cheek, and he helped her into her warm Oriental coat. Prentis quietly told her father their plan. He gave an affirming expression and nod. Avery hugged her mother and grabbed Jack's suitcase, which Prentis transferred to his possession. Then out they went.

He secured Jack, and they were off in no time. Prentis headed due south through town, avoiding everyone, including the Rileys, who would head north toward Gibbon and Avery's hometown community. Soon they turned at the cemetery corner and headed west toward home.

"What a delightful morning," Avery said, peacefully. "Church was so encouraging, even if Mrs. Alfonse Riley was there."

Eyebrows raised, he stared over at her. "Your father and I went through all sorts of contortions to keep you from seeing her! And here you knew all along."

She kept her eyes fixed straight ahead. "I've entrusted my reputation into God's hands. He can surely handle that better than I. If I can trust Him with my very life and my womanhood, I think I can trust Him with Mrs. Alfonse Riley. That's one lesson learned during my recovery."

Prentis grinned at her. "Thanks be to God, Avery! I believe I'll join you in that perspective. You're absolutely right."

Eyes back on the road, he continued smiling. Then he glanced her direction. Her lips were compressed. Was she upset or struggling to keep a straight face? At last she turned toward him, laughing out loud.

"It *was* fun to observe you and Daddy working so hard."

She laughed heartily, and he had to join her. He was certain their efforts had been highly entertaining.

Twenty-one

WHEN PRENTIS CAME INTO the house to clean up, Avery was working in the kitchen. The door was open, because the weather had now turned unseasonably warm. The snow was melting, but it hadn't turned everything to mush quite yet. From the kitchen sink, she looked down into the back porch where he was pumping water to wash. Their eyes met.

"Avery, I was right," he said, scrubbing and splashing. "Tom's first cow birthed a healthy bull calf, right on time. I'm going to drive up to get the boys. Good thing it's a Saturday."

"When you mentioned that cow's behavior, I wondered if today might be the day. Be sure to have the boys bring all their schoolbooks and extra bedrolls. We don't have enough bedding."

He beamed up at her. "Will do. I want to come up there, grab you up, and kiss you. But my boots are muddy, and another cow is showing all the signs. Guess you'll just have to come down here, be kissed, and help me start the Model T."

Of course, all this ruckus had awakened Jack from his nap, but it was time for him to get up anyway.

"Jack's awake, Prentis," she called. "Let me grab him. Then I'll give you that kiss, and we'll come with you."

Prentis nodded and headed back outside.

Hurriedly, Avery lifted Jack from his bed, changed his diaper, and put on his coat. It occurred to her that lifting him was now a matter of course. She was well and herself again in every way. Smiling internally, she hurried out through the kitchen.

"We're going with Daddy in the Model T," she told Jack.

"Go with Da Da."

"Yes, that's right," she said. "We're going to get your uncles."

"Nuncles! Go!"

Smiling, Avery grabbed her light coat, slipped it on, readied Jack, and the two of them headed out of the house. Prentis waved to her from the barn.

"Got to stay here, Avery," he called. "Things are getting complicated. This cow's delivered fast in the past. Do you mind going up alone?"

"I'm not alone. I've got Jack."

As Prentis opened wide the door, she ducked inside the barn, carrying Jack. The cow was moaning piteously. Jack tensed, holding tightly onto her at the sound.

"It's okay, little man. Daddy will take care of the cow. Let's tuck you into your seat."

As she secured Jack, Prentis hurried over to help her get the Model T started. Into the driver's seat she went, and they moved through all the steps together. The motor fired, and immediately she began backing out.

"What about that kiss?" Prentis raised both hands, begging the question.

Laughing, Avery blew him a kiss as she turned to head up the drive.

"That's far inferior to the real thing," he called.

"I'll kiss you later," she shouted back.

Then she took off, rolling up the window. In the rearview mirror, she saw him grinning at her and waving as they pulled out. She laughed softly. How she loved that man!

"Bye, Da Da!" Jack called.

But they were long gone.

***

A couple of hours later, driving a now thoroughly mud-splattered automobile, Avery pulled back in with all the boys. She had avoided all the holes filled with water, and they hadn't gotten stuck anywhere. She felt pretty proud of herself and wanted to tell Prentis, but he was nowhere to be seen. That meant he was extremely busy. She looked over at Abe in the passenger seat.

"Abe, hop on out and get into the barn. It might be an emergency."

Out he hopped before the automobile had even stopped completely. She parked outside this time and glanced over her shoulder at the others.

"You two carry all of your goods inside, including Abe's, before going to the barn. Put it all by the dining room table."

Gene and Howard got busy. Avery untethered Jack and carried him inside. As they went in, her brothers came bursting back out at a run, headed toward the barn.

"Bye, sis," Howard called back, grinning at her over his shoulder.

Avery waved.

"Nuncles bye-bye," Jack informed her, looking up at her somberly.

"They're merely in the barn. They'll come back inside later."

"Come later."

"Yes, let's go inside and make order of the chaos we find there."

Jack studied her face with a puzzled expression, and then he turned toward the task. The aroma of the pinto bean stew met them when they walked in the door. That was good. She peeked in and heard it simmering in the cast iron pot. All was well. It would be ready for supper. Jack remained on her hip, her partner in dinner preparation.

Next, Avery stepped into the living room. She found everything thrown down hastily, as she had expected. Putting Jack on his feet, she dragged the drop-leaf table smack dab into the middle of the long room. Jack attempted to carry one table corner. After rearranging the furniture, she laid all the bedrolls neatly beside one another in a row under the northern window where the table had previously stood.

"Thank you for helping, Jack."

"Helping."

"Your uncles will sleep here. You must not touch their things."

Somberly, he met her eyes and nodded.

Next, she lifted the leaves of the table and pulled in every chair or stool they had, finally using the hassock as a seat, so at least everyone could sit down.

"Now that we're all arranged, let's go out to the barn and see what's happening."

The painful moans of the laboring cow greeted them as they walked into the barn. Avery stepped back out, opened the door of the Model T, and set Jack inside.

"Stay right here while I get Howard to play with you," she said.

Jack nodded.

Avery returned to the barn. There was Prentis, up to his armpit in cow. Abe held the poor cow's head, and Gene prepared some sort of traction tackle to give them more leverage, once they attached it to the presenting part of the calf. The look on Prentis's face was one of intense concentration. He grimaced as he tried to work the calf into a good position. That cow had never had trouble before. Avery could see plainly that Prentis was mystified and worried. She looked toward Howard and gestured with a nod that she wanted him.

"Whatcha need, sis?"

"Jack's in the Model T. Would you please take him into the house or into the backyard and play with him? He's too little to be in here. It frightens him."

"But, sis. All the fun's in here."

"I know. Nevertheless, you're needed outside."

Howard sighed, nodded, and out he went.

All the boys had long ago adjusted to the fact that on the Pinkerton farm at least, Avery, though a woman, was part of this process. At home, no one had spoken of such things in front of the women. She was glad the boys had adjusted and were more forward thinking.

Avery stepped over beside Prentis. There, the odor of birthing cow and Dr. Roberts' Disinfectall assaulted her. Each season, the smells of animal husbandry during calving took her aback. Once she'd adjusted, all would be well, per the norm.

"What's going on in there?" she said.

"Looks to be a large calf. See her size."

Avery agreed. "The cow's enormous. The calf definitely appears to be large."

"But what I'm feeling with my hand is not a large calf. And I'm feeling too many legs. We seem to have twins in there, rather than one large calf. Unless we have a deformed calf or conjoined calves."

"Can you feel both heads?"

"I cannot." He glanced briefly at her. "Everything's all tangled up together. No clear presenting part of one without pulling the whole mass of calf down."

At that moment, the cow moaned piteously and with great feeling. A contraction clearly had seized her. The two of them watched to see if it was effective. Nothing.

"Is there anything I can do?" she asked.

"Run inside and get me Dr. Roberts' guide. Might need you to read something out loud."

She turned to head for the door.

"Avery, on second thought, check the index before you bring it out. Don't recall much about calving in it. If that's the case, just leave it."

She hurried in, found it to be as he had said, kissed Jack, tousled Howard's hair, and hurried back out.

"There wasn't much on calving and certainly nothing about this."

"Well," he said, "guess we're on our own. This is the life, huh, boys?"

Smirking, Gene and Abe both snorted.

Then Abe knelt down next to the cow's head. "What say we try to pull the one out that you've got ahold of and see what follows?"

"I was just thinking that." Prentis scrunched his eyes shut as he pressed in more deeply, reaching, trying to grab what he needed. "Let me bring down that one foot. Got it!"

Once grasped, he leaned back with all his might, applying traction. Ever so slowly, he tugged until two little hooves came into view. With his eyes still on those feet, he held out his hand toward Gene, who passed him the rope.

Once the feet were secured, without a word, Gene took Abe's place by the cow's head. Abe—the older and stronger of the two—stepped over to help Prentis pull. They performed as if in a dance, one stepping aside as the other stepped in, all keeping their eyes on the task. Her brothers merely functioned as Daddy had taught them, but it always amazed her. They knew exactly what to do and when. That was why Prentis had trusted them when he went to Wichita.

Prentis and Abe both strained against the rope, attempting to move the calf down. Avery realized she was holding her breath. She inhaled.

Slowly, the calf emerged. It appeared to be fine. Prentis scooped it up and began rubbing some life into it with the coarse blanket he used for that purpose. At last he succeeded. The calf sputtered, bawled, and sputtered again. Avery watched all the tension leak out of her husband and brothers. Prentis glanced up at her and smiled.

"Not attached to the other," he said. "I was certain they were conjoined."

"Oh, my!" she said. "I don't want to know what would have happened were that the case."

He winked at her. "Then I won't tell you."

The boys chuckled. Clearly, they knew.

Prentis got the new calf up on its feet and to the cow's udder. As he did, they all kept their eyes on the business end of the cow until finally, eventually, the other calf slid into view and landed in the straw. With a clean blanket, Prentis now worked on that one.

It took longer. All of them stood silently, watching, hoping, praying. At last the calf sputtered. Everyone smiled. Soon two calves nursed on their mother.

"I'll go inside and get supper ready," Avery said. "You've had a tough day."

"Thank you." Prentis looked up from the calf. "You always take such good care of me. You boys need to look for a woman exactly like your big sister. When you find her, marry her quick! Don't let her get away."

The boys laughed.

"Our sister is the best," Gene declared.

"She is," Prentis said, his eyes on hers.

Smiling, Avery walked back toward the house, her heart warmed.

They'd be tired and hungry when they came in. Only a few cows of their own stock still awaited calving. Now Tom's first cow had produced twin calves. With Tom's cattle, they had twenty-five cows delivering that spring. Gradually, year by year, their herd grew larger as they kept their heifers for breeding and sold their steers. Last fall, Prentis had doubled the size of their alfalfa field for feed and had worked hard to keep all of their concerns afloat. Cash was always coming in from one thing or another, whether the crops or the livestock. He worked hard and took good care of them.

***

The second half of February had been consumed with calving. They had the boys with them for the rest of the month and well into March. Every moment they weren't working with Prentis or tossing a baseball back and forth between them while waiting on a cow, Avery had the boys bent over their books in the living room, keeping up with their schoolwork. She enjoyed their company, and it was wonderful to spend extra time with them. She missed her brothers.

When the calving was completed in March, the foaling began. Howard stayed to help with Jack, and Avery drove the older boys home. They had higher-level schoolwork and needed to catch up. With Jack under Howard's watchful eye, she and Prentis could easily handle the five mares. Their foaling proved as successful as the calving.

Twenty-six healthy calves and five new foals nursed alongside their mothers as the grass greened, the robins sang, the perennials burst forth from the earth, the lettuce and spinach unfurled from the dark garden soil, and the new springtime buds appeared. As soon as the calves were able, Prentis would separate out Tom's cattle and drive them back over to his place.

The foals were superb. The army representative eyed them when he purchased the yearlings, happy to see that he'd have five more yearlings from the Pinkerton's farm next year. The foals Apollo had sired with Persephone, Calypso, Penelope, Daisy, and Mabel were exactly what the army wanted. Prentis followed his farming plan.

To keep everything rolling along and profit coming in, he was already scouting around for some young maiden mares. Daisy and Mabel were growing quite old. Perhaps, by summertime, he would find the quality of horseflesh he sought. He even had Fred keeping an eye out for good livestock up in Gibbon and Kingman when he traveled up to visit his wife's family.

They barely had time to read the papers throughout the calving and foaling, but between the two, they had noted that Russia, now a socialist country, had exited the war. In early March, Soviet Russia had signed a peace treaty with the Central Powers—Germany, Austria-Hungary, and Turkey. The Russians had too much turmoil at home to be able to support a war effort.

"That's the good part about living through a war on the other side of the ocean," Avery said.

"Good?" Prentis replied. "You can find a speck of good in it?"

"Yes. It's on the other side of the ocean."

He nodded. "We can ignore it while we attend to our lives."

"Yes, but we got behind in our praying, since our hours were irregular."

He grabbed her hand, sat down, and bowed his head in prayer, starting with Charles and Tom and working his way down the list. She joined him.

Twenty-two

PRENTIS DROVE HOWARD HOME. He'd enjoyed having Avery's brothers around. They were his family. Howard talked his ear off most of the way, but now that they neared home, the boy grew quiet. Silent, he stared out the far window.

Without turning, Howard spoke at last. "I'll miss my sister an awful lot."

"I know you will. It's a hard thing when people grow up."

Howard glanced over at him. "Yes, it is. I'm almost eleven. Old enough to know that now."

"Yes, you are. Now that she's well again, the Model T will allow us to visit more."

"That's true."

"And then, we expect you to come and help us with harvest. If you're available, that is."

A half-smile crept slowly onto Howard's face. "I'm available. Glad to help."

Prentis kept his face serious, as if conducting business, but smiled inwardly at the boy's manlike phrases. "We're always happy to have you, Howard."

When they chugged into the barnyard at the Slaughter's home, both of Avery's parents stepped out of the house to welcome them. That was unusual. Abraham greeted him before taking Howard to the barn. As they walked away, Minnie watched until they had entered, and then she stepped nearer as if sharing a confidence. Prentis was mystified.

"Floyd was just over here, Prentis. They got a letter from Joseph. There's an awful illness up in Camp Funston. It's been raging through the camp since the first part of the month. It started when a large group of Chinese contract workers arrived with the flu. Most of them were sick."

"The flu is nothing to mess with."

"No, it isn't. There have been a few fatalities."

"That's odd. Healthy young men don't typically die from the flu."

"You're right. Floyd said Joseph wrote that he felt fine. That boy is strong as an ox. He never gets sick. But I know your cousin is there, and I wanted you and Avery to know so you can pray. I didn't want to worry Howard." She glanced toward the barn. The boy was still inside.

"I'll pass that on to Avery. My cousin Charles was often sick as a child. We'll pray. Thank you for lending us the boys. We surely were glad to have them. Had a good season."

"I'm so glad, Prentis. Doesn't surprise me a bit. Can I get you a cup of coffee?"

"No, thank you." He climbed back into the idling automobile. "I'm anxious to get back. Thanks for the offer though."

"Give our regards and affection to Avery." Minnie turned to go up the back steps.

"Will do." He waved as he drove away.

Fatalities among young adults with the flu seemed like an aberration. They must be working those boys too hard. Minnie had lost so many children to illness that Prentis wondered if she was overly concerned. Still, it wouldn't hurt to pray. He didn't want to worry Avery with it, but he had promised to tell her, so he had better do so.

When he drove into their barnyard, Avery came running out with Jack in her arms. Her eyes were wide, and her lips pressed into a thin line. Jack had clearly been crying, and his arms were bandaged. Braking, Prentis turned off the motor, leapt out, and hurried toward them.

"Prentis, he's been hurt. I'm not quite sure what happened."

Prentis grabbed Jack and peered under the bandaging. Long seeping cuts ran along his lower arms and another on his cheek. These wounds were more serious than the earlier injuries.

"Was it that rooster? If so, I think we need to have some chicken soup tonight."

"We were out in the yard. The chickens were all running about. I was cleaning out the coop and was bent over my work. I heard a ruckus, and Sam growled. I turned quickly to see what was going on. Jack screamed, and that rooster took off running. But I didn't see the attack."

"That's enough information for me," Prentis said.

Protective anger welled up inside. He'd had enough of these injuries that grew worse and worse. It looked clear cut. That rooster had gotten too aggressive. It was the end of his days.

"Take Jack inside," Prentis said. "I'm getting my hatchet. Boil the water."

Quickly, Prentis grabbed the rooster. Tucking it under his arm, he kept a tight grip on all its fighting parts. On the other side of the barn, he made short work of the problem and then plucked as many feathers as he could before returning the nearly denuded rooster to Avery.

"I'll let you finish up here," he said. "Taking Jack with me for the chores."

***

Having that problem solved was a relief! Leaving Napoleon, former chicken dictator of the barnyard, lying on the back porch, Avery mixed up the dough for noodles, rolled it out thin, and expertly sliced it into strips, spreading them apart on the floured countertop to dry.

Every time she worked on her countertop, she remembered the first time she'd seen the ingenious way Prentis had designed her kitchen. Shortly after they were engaged, he had brought her to see what would become her new home. All throughout the winter, he had built the cupboards, sizing everything specifically to her height. Kitchen work, therefore, always inspired gratitude and love.

As soon as the large pot of water boiled, Avery dunked the bird and removed the remaining pinfeathers, plucking it good and clean. Then she cut it up, saving the breasts in the icebox for tomorrow before adding the other parts to her soup pot. She added chopped onion and carrots, along with some parsley from the newly growing garden. Soon the savory aroma of chicken soup filled the house.

When Prentis tasted his first bite, he looked up at her. "We should've butchered that rooster a long time ago. You make the best soup in the world, Avery."

***

On Friday, March 29, Prentis was working in the barn when the sound of a Model T pulling up outside surprised him. He exited the building and saw Avery stepping out the back door of their farmhouse. Across the barnyard, they looked at one another, mystified to see Floyd's automobile.

Floyd, Hattie, and the Reverend Mark Wallock exited. Hattie's face was red. She had obviously been crying. Floyd and Mark both looked grim. Prentis hurried toward the new arrivals, afraid to discover what news they brought. Avery also ran. Prentis shook Floyd's hand and Mark's. Avery hugged Hattie.

"What's happened?" Avery said. "Please tell us!"

All stood in silence, their faces working with emotion.

Prentis glanced at Avery, who met his eyes, deep concern creasing her forehead.

"We need you to come with us." Hattie's voice quivered. "We have to tell Mary Beth that my brother Joseph has died. The telegram came today. They're shipping his body home by rail."

At that moment, Prentis realized he'd completely forgotten about the flu at Camp Funston. As Avery's hands flew to her face and all the color blanched out, he felt stricken. How could this have slipped his mind? Then he remembered—that blasted rooster. Now his poor wife had been blindsided by this horrific news. He pulled her into his arms.

"Avery, I forgot to tell you what was going on at Camp Funston—a deadly flu. I'm so sorry. I hope you can forgive me."

"You didn't know?" Floyd asked her.

Speechless still, Avery shook her head.

Prentis looked down at her. "I promised your mother I'd tell you, and then that rooster . . ."

Wordlessly, Avery nodded.

Hattie, Floyd, and Mark looked at one another, confused.

"When I returned, the rooster had attacked the baby," Prentis said.

All clear now, they nodded, concern on their faces.

280

"Jack's fine. The rooster provided us with several good meals."

That settled, they all turned again toward Avery.

"Poor Joseph." She wept. "Poor Mary Beth. They weren't able to marry. I'm so sorry, Hattie. You've lost your dear brother, like a brother to me too."

Prentis held her tighter, feeling awful for forgetting the news her mother had entrusted to him. Having been shocked, it took Avery awhile to regain composure.

"He never gets sick," she said. "He's the healthiest person I've ever known."

They all nodded in agreement.

"Why now? They only recently got engaged. Why would God allow this?"

Equally mystified, they all shook their heads and sighed, commiserating over the horror of it. Hattie reached for Avery, and the two embraced tightly, both weeping.

"Life isn't always fair," Floyd said.

"It's only the grace of God that gets us through these things we don't understand," Mark said quietly.

Lifting her eyes to his, Avery nodded. "Jesus, help us," she whispered.

"The Lord gives," Mark said, "and the Lord taketh away. Blessed be the name of the Lord."

They muttered their amens. Prentis handed Avery his handkerchief, and she blew her nose.

"Jack's asleep," she told him.

"I'll stay here with him, so you can go."

Sighing her resignation, she wiped her hands on her apron, glancing down at her workday apparel. She wasn't dressed for making a call—Prentis recognized the female expression.

"You look fine," he said softly.

She shook her head. "Let me tidy up a bit. This is too important to show up dressed like I've been cleaning the house."

Nodding his agreement, he smiled kindly when she met his eyes. Then she turned and headed inside. They all discussed the details quietly, but his mind was still focused on his poor wife. Within mere minutes, she reappeared in a church dress with her hair pinned up, all of those gleaming black locks neatly captured. Her black boots shined below her ankle-length skirt, as if newly polished. She secured her bonnet, tying the ribbon under her chin.

"I'm ready," she said. "Let's go."

Reaching over, she squeezed his hand and met his eyes. She had forgiven him for forgetting. He squeezed back, stroking the back of her hand with his thumb.

"Jack's still asleep," she said. "I was quiet."

They all climbed into Floyd's Model T, Prentis performed the passenger duties, and they chugged back out of his barnyard. He stood for a long while pondering the tragedy that had befallen them, praying for Joseph's family and also for Charles. How many more similar pieces of news would they receive before it was all over? The march to war had brought a difficult year. Prentis stood in the yard, praying for Mary Beth and the horror she would now face.

***

When Prentis asked, Avery couldn't even speak of it. It was outside her powers of description to capture such raw emotion, heartache, and remorse. She would never forget the sound of Mary Beth's wail as she sank to the ground, wrapped her arms about herself, and rocked back and forth crying out her questions. Why, oh why, hadn't she simply married Joseph before he left? She repeated that over and over, berating herself for her stupidity.

Then she might have a baby, a part of him, something that had seemed impossible to deal with before he left, but which had become increasingly significant as she realized she loved him. Why had she made the terrible mistake of putting him off?

Mary Beth wept, interrogating herself and refusing to be comforted. Nothing could be done. It was too late. He was gone.

Avery felt bruised internally, remembering her own fear before she bore Jack and the nightmares she had about the army marching Prentis off and leaving her alone. What she had merely dreamt, Mary Beth now experienced in real life and worse. How would she ever recover? There were no words to explain that to Prentis. Avery ached.

The following day, she awakened with a brain-piercing migraine. The throbbing intensity paralyzed her. This was the first migraine since she became pregnant with Jack years ago. She had hoped that those intense bouts of pain were behind her. But no, apparently there were other triggers. Death, tragedy, and emotion that could not be contained would do it.

She spent the day in bed with Jack and Prentis tiptoeing in bringing tea, cold washcloths, and aspirin. Not wanting to miss the Easter sunrise service or the funeral service for Joseph, she prayed for a quick recovery, but Saturday found Avery still flattened.

Jack helped Prentis bring in some crackers with her tea. Opening her eyes a bare crack, she found Jack's face and reached her finger to softly caress his check.

"Momma's sick, Jack," she whispered.

"Mom-mom sick."

"Yes." She couldn't move her head even to nod. "Pray for Momma." She couldn't speak any louder, and both of them leaned in closer, Prentis kneeling with Jack balanced on his lap.

Jack bowed his little head. "Jedus, Mom-mom sick."

Prentis flicked his eyes toward hers and smiled. She detected him through the crack between her lids. Hoping he would see it, she tried to raise the corners of her mouth to signal a smile. When he caressed her cheek softly and kissed midair right above her forehead, she knew he had.

"Let's go outside now and let Momma rest," he said.

"Rest, Mom-mom," Jack whispered.

Avery raised her hand slightly. It was best to merely pass out when the intensity of the pain was this overpowering. Blackness obliterated the pain. She drifted off to oblivion again.

When Avery next awakened, it was dark. Outside their bedroom window, the joyful singing of birds in their first waking sounded forth from the trees on the bluff. It was early on Easter morning. Without opening her eyes, Avery took stock of her head.

The bruise of a migraine lingered, but the intensity was gone. She reached for a cracker and the aspirin on the bedside table. After dissolving the cracker on her tongue, she slid two aspirin into her mouth as preemptive pain relief. Then she rolled over, her back against Prentis, thanked Jesus for His death and resurrection, and drifted off to sleep once more.

The aroma of breakfast woke Avery. Prentis carried a plate and cup into the bedroom while Jack carried a napkin. She smiled at them and slid up in the bed, resting her back against the headboard.

"That's an encouraging sight," Prentis said quietly. "Thanks be to God—you'll live."

"Yes, I appear to have made it through."

"We've missed the sunrise service, but we're right on track for the regular Sunday service. Would you like to attend?"

"Oh, yes! I was praying I wouldn't miss the Easter service."

Jack climbed up, and she pulled him into her lap. He wrapped his toddler arms about her neck and kissed her soundly.

"Mom-mom all better?"

"Yes, I am, Jack."

***

As they headed toward church, they found buggy after buggy lined up at the hitching posts along both streets to which the church was anchored. A corner lot gave more spaces for parking. Prentis pulled Ulysses in on the east side, securing him and giving him a good pat before coming around to help Avery down.

Already, the horse tore at the fresh green grass along the road, nibbling a treat. There was a bit of shade from the elm trees down at this end of the block. Being newly recovered from a migraine, a buggy ride had seemed like the way to go on this beautiful day.

When they entered the church, they were greeted by Mark Wallock. Ebullient and welcoming, the man practically glowed. Beaming at them, he shook their hands enthusiastically and patted Jack. Avery had periodically seen that sort of inspiring passion in a pastor. It was as if he had just discovered his life calling. Tom had displayed the same enthusiasm and gleam in his eye when talking about going to serve with the troops in Europe. Had her childhood pastor felt that way when he first began to serve their church in Gibbon?

"We're sorry we had to miss your first sunrise service, Mark," Prentis said.

"It was glorious!" Mark smiled widely. "Having a regular Easter sunrise service is something I've always aspired to as a pastor. It's such a powerful way to experience firsthand the emotions the disciples would have felt when Christ arose on that first Easter morning."

"What gave you the idea?"

285

"My parents spoke often of the passion play in Oberammergau. It's had such a powerful effect on the promotion of the Gospel. People travel from far and wide to attend, coming from all over Europe to see the performance. I've heard that wealthy Americans even travel over. I think the impact of that presentation must have planted the seed in my mind."

"We're hoping to attend your sunrise service next year," Avery said. "This week, I was struck down with one of my headaches. Prentis and Jack attended to me."

"I hope you're feeling better today."

"I am."

Easter bonnets and smiling faces pressed in upon them, crowding them forward, so they stepped into the church, making way as everyone squeezed through the entryway and into the building. All exchanged Easter greetings. The hymns were triumphant and resounding, everyone singing in exultant voice with full hearts.

From the pulpit, Mark expounded on the miracle of the resurrection over the power of death. Mentioning Joseph Pitzer, the reverend reminded them that Christ's resurrection promised justification for sinners in the eyes of God. He chose Romans 5 as his text, one of Avery's favorite passages. Tom had been teaching through this section of Scripture when she had first begun to attend his church. With both hands gripping the pulpit, Reverend Wallock looked down upon them, reciting Romans 5:8–11.

"But God commendeth his own love toward us, in that, while we were yet sinners, Christ died for us. Much more then, being now justified by his blood, shall we be saved from the wrath of God through him. For if, while we were enemies, we were reconciled to God through the death of his Son, much more, being reconciled, shall we be saved by his life; and not only so, but we also rejoice in

God through our Lord Jesus Christ, through whom we have now received the reconciliation."

Momentarily, Avery was distracted. That wasn't the translation she had memorized. Of course, Reverend Wallock, being a young Chicago-educated theologian would use the new American Standard Version. Quickly she pulled her mind back to the reverend's wrap up.

"The death and resurrection of Christ allow the world to be reconciled to God. Christ Jesus did the work, so that we may be saved. And He continues to impact the world as our Prince of Peace, even in this time of war with loved ones dead, more sacrifices to come, and the entire world bearing arms. We thank Jesus today for what He has done, and we pray, Lord Jesus, come quickly and bring the peace that only You can accomplish."

Affirmations and amens sounded around her as the reverend bowed his head to continue his prayer. She was grateful they had come. In light of their recent losses, she had needed to be reminded of God's peace and loving care. Tomorrow was Joseph Pitzer's funeral.

Twenty-three

THE DAY BEGAN WITH rain. It seemed fitting. They took the Model T and left early, lest they encounter any problems with muddy roads. The little Gibbon church Avery had attended as a girl began to fill up early, and she was glad they had arrived when they did. After hugging everyone in the Pitzer family, as well as Mary Beth and her family, who were seated with them, she and Prentis found a seat.

Jack's little face was sober today. He seemed to absorb the emotions of the room. At the front, the sealed coffin sat inviolable, death triumphant.

Avery's childhood pastor knew Joseph well, and as he sermonized, he also eulogized. Humorous stories were sprinkled throughout, all of them smiling and nodding as they recalled the quick wit of the young man and friend now lost to them. And then the pastor detailed Joseph's three-year pursuit of the woman he had hoped to make his wife. Everyone quieted their laughter, for here were facts most hadn't realized. Details previously unknown were shared—the length of his pursuit, the discretion he had used, the seriousness of his spiritual growth.

It dawned on Avery that this information had been provided by the Pitzer family intentionally, hoping to put to rest all malicious gossip that had tarnished the innocent. Now Joseph could rest in peace. Emotion pressed hard against her breastbone, welling up and coursing slowly down her cheeks. Prentis squeezed her hand. She gripped back, holding him fast.

The room had grown absolutely still during that account, which transitioned into Joseph's call into service and his unexpected death at Camp Funston.

After singing a hymn together, all rose to head for the burial. Avery stood, turned to gather her wrap on the pew, and caught the eye of Mrs. Alfonse Riley farther back in the room. The woman appeared stricken to the core. Quickly, Mrs. Riley averted her eyes, but Avery knew the expression of utter conviction when she saw it. Maybe some good would come of this. She wouldn't depend on it. She would merely trust God and let Him deal with Mrs. Riley.

Turning her attention back to the business at hand, she embraced Mary Beth, who had held it together throughout the service, but who now broke down. Avery held her tight. All the family stood with her, shielding her from view as they allowed the room to clear, so she might gain some privacy while regaining composure.

As she listened to Mary Beth's lament, Avery was overwhelmed with the senselessness of it, the heartbreaking unfairness inherent in losing a strong healthy young man to the flu—of all things—rather than to the heroic combat that had been his goal. That, they would have expected. This, they had not. She didn't understand God's ways, but she knew He was sovereign and good and that He had a purpose, though she surely did not comprehend what He was about.

After the burial, the ride home was quiet. Jack fell asleep, and the two of them rode, side by side yet speechless, both overcome with grief.

"I don't think I could have made it through the day without those final words the pastor shared at the graveside," Avery said as they neared home. "1 Corinthians 15:54-57 is powerful."

Prentis glanced over. "I was thinking the same."

"It makes me long for Christ's return, when we're all made new. 'So when this corruptible shall have put on incorruption, and this mortal shall have put on immortality, *then* shall be brought to pass the saying that is written, Death is swallowed up in victory. O death, where is thy sting? O grave, where is thy victory? The sting of death is sin; and the strength of sin is the law. *But* thanks be to God, which giveth us the victory through our Lord Jesus Christ.'"

"That will be a good day, for death surely does have a sting now."

"Indeed, it does."

"Will Mary Beth be all right?"

She glanced at him and their eyes locked. "I certainly hope so. She's a strong woman, and she loves Jesus. He'll have to get her through it."

Prentis nodded, returning his eyes to the road.

Right before he pulled into their drive, he glanced over at her again. "Did you happen to see Mrs. Riley after the service?"

"I did. I hope and pray God uses the pastor's words for good."

Nodding, Prentis compressed his lips. Nothing more needed to be said.

***

April kept them busy with all the usual springtime activities. The week after Joseph's funeral, they planted more vegetables in their garden and transplanted the seeds Avery had started inside. The wheat was greening up, and the alfalfa looked strong and hardy as it came in. The mares and their foals, along with the cows and their calves, dotted the landscape in pairs, evidence of the fruitful productivity of the calving and the foaling season.

Gradually, the days drew warmer, and the sun arced higher in the sky, beaming down upon them. Fluffy white clouds floated across the brilliant blue bowl of prairie sky, bringing a sense of relief that the winter was indeed past and would not be seen for many months hence.

And now it was breeding season for the mares, their first foal heat having passed, and a good six weeks having been accomplished for their recovery from the birthing. Prentis had purchased one new maiden mare to join them, and his mind was often focused on which mare was ready to welcome Apollo. In between times, the stallion was taken out to run frequently, helping the horse to vent his frustrations, for the air was often filled with the scent of mares awaiting his attention.

In the middle of this busyness, they celebrated Jack's second birthday with a quiet gathering, just the two of them, along with Mary Beth and also Mark Wallock. Their goal had been to get Mary Beth out of the house and to include Mark in their family life, as they often had included Tom. The party was pleasant for all, the conversation good. Mary Beth seemed much encouraged by time with others. Mark appeared less lonely when he departed. All had engaged in some well-needed laughter and lightheartedness, and Jack had a wonderful time being the center of attention from four adults he knew and loved.

Shortly after that, having once ventured out safely, Mary Beth began to come over to knit and sew on

Wednesday afternoons again, though she still avoided the crowd at church. Socks were now needed, for the conditions in the trenches were dire. As they knit, their conversations centered on Joseph. By talking, Mary Beth worked through her grief over losing him so soon, just as she had realized the depth of her love. Avery mostly listened, allowing Mary Beth to talk through her loss as her heart led.

Into all of this springtime activity, war news periodically intruded. They had no idea where Tom was. It had been a while since a letter had arrived, so they knew he was incredibly busy wherever he was located. Charles's family had heard from him. They had written to tell Prentis that all was well. So, at least one of the men they had sent off was still in good shape.

As if on cue, exactly when they were feeling the lack of it, a letter arrived from Tom. Such a relief! It had taken only slightly more than two weeks to arrive—an astonishing feat from the other side of the Atlantic!

March 31, 1918

Dearest friends,

I've been constantly at work with the men—over a million have arrived here in France. But I knew I needed to write, lest you worry. Hope you all are well. I can imagine what you're up to with spring upon you. Calving and foaling, weather changing, gardening. How I miss you and home!

Yet, I'm glad I came! Daily the Lord affirms that I'm right where He wants me to be. Four of our battle-ready divisions have been put into combat under French and British command to get them some experience. They've been assigned to relatively quiet sections along the line, but the trenches are more horrific than I ever imagined, relatively quiet or not! No Man's Land is a Book of Revelation beast of nightmares and horror. The men are lonely and sick, haunted by the specter of the dead before their very eyes daily where bodies lie to rot, bringing a sense of hopeless inevitability concerning their own looming deaths. The comfort of Christ and of a friend to listen is powerful in this situation. I help them draw near to God.

So many diseases – trench foot from the constant wetness and the inability to ever get their feet dry, trench fever, typhus, dysentery, and plain old diarrhea. There are vaccinations, but the conditions seem to override everything, producing sick men mad with the horror of it. Then there's shellshock from the constant bombardment and poison gas arriving at unexpected moments—the horrific nature of modern warfare.

I'm glad I came. This is where I belong. It's much like the ministry I did with Mary at the Pacific Garden Mission before I lost her, but far more violent in every way.

Well, Pastor Moody calls for me. We ready our troops to push forward very soon. I must end. Thank you for praying for us. God bless you both! How I miss you! I think of the three of you and pray for you daily. I'm glad you're on the mend, Avery. Praise God that you are well!

In Christ, your friend,
Tom

After reading the letter out loud, Prentis folded it neatly and placed it back in the envelope. Somberly, he studied Avery's face and then he reached for her hand, bowed his head, and prayed for Tom. It was far worse than she had imagined too. How could their boys bear it?

A bare two weeks later at the end of April, another letter arrived, this one in an even hastier hand than any of Tom's previous letters. Clearly, he had written in a rush. The envelope could barely be deciphered.

April 16, 1918

Dearest friends,

I'm writing on Jack's second birthday and missing your family all the more. Word reached me today of Joe Pitzer's death. I was shocked to hear it! How I grieve for the Pitzer family, for all of you, and for poor Mary Beth! Hold her close during this time—I'm certain you already are.

Now we're experiencing outbreaks of that flu all over France as one group of men after another arrives from our American army bases. Soldiers from Camp Funston went on to other camps before shipping here, and it appears they spread the influenza far and wide. There's really no way to stop it with so much movement from one continent to another. The incredible transportation system the military has in place for bringing an army of millions to the other side of the ocean has a flaw after all—the spread of contagious disease! Once men arrive carrying the disease they head for the trenches, where disease is already rampant due to the crowded conditions.

Pray for our troops! This flu takes them down fast! About one of every five or ten

men is going down with the illness so far,
along with doctors and nurses. I pray it
doesn't get worse.
    May the Lord watch over us all!
    Tom

Avery had read this time, and when she looked up from the letter, Prentis appeared stricken, his head shaking slowly from side to side.

"I hadn't even considered that possibility."

"Neither had I," she responded. "It's an entirely unique situation. When did any army ever transport millions of men to the other side of the ocean so rapidly?"

"It's only been done in small batches. Never those numbers."

"When those millions hit the wall of German resistance," she said, "the generals assure us the war will be over. It seems like a worthy result."

"But, we may end up losing more people to the flu than to the war itself?"

"I hope not, and I pray it won't be so. Only God knows."

***

Prentis went into town to retrieve as many newspapers as possible. Thankfully, he'd gone before the rain started, because now it poured down, making a muddy slog of all the roads in and out. Water drip-dropped off the rim of his Stetson, and he pulled his coat tighter over the secreted bundle of newspapers. Now in late May, the wheat was tall and green and in need of moisture, so as he crossed the muddy barnyard and stepped into the back porch to remove his boots and clean up, he took great satisfaction in the rainfall.

Soon their wheat would begin to turn golden, and then harvest would loom on the horizon. The foals and the calves were all growing fast, and Prentis would put Rex in with the cows to breed in June. By then he should know if all his mares were in foal again.

His alfalfa also benefited from the rain. It protected them from the rising feed costs caused by the war. Other farmers weren't so fortunate, especially the dairy farmers who were struggling to find fodder for their cattle, since so many resources were now being shipped over to wartime Europe. As he ticked down his list, all was tallied as well on the farm. A sense of wellbeing filled him, and he couldn't help but smile.

Avery peeked around the kitchen door. Seeing him there, she opened wide, holding her arms out to receive the many newspapers he pulled from the shielding cover of his coat.

"You look happy," she said. "Is it merely this hefty pile of newspapers?"

"Nope. My farming plan is right on track, including this rain right as we need it."

"That's a good reason to be happy. Did you bring back any local news?"

"Heard more about that oil well up the road."

"What did you hear?" She leaned against the doorframe, crossing her ankles.

"Just as we suspected, they're taking that derrick down. Transporting everything north of town. With those materials, they'll continue up there. The test was better up north, and they don't want to continue at the McKee's. They're going to abandon it."

"That's too bad for the McKee's."

"It is, but everything has ground to a halt pretty much everywhere, other than north of town. Not enough casing for the pipe. Costs too much right now, due to the war. Until the war ends, the big companies aren't buying any more leases in this section. No one is investing in the project right now either."

296

"So, it's all over?" she said.

"No, they can resume right where they left off after this war. Casings can be manufactured then. All they need is investors and a change in manufacturing."

"Well, that's something to consider then. I'd like to profit from it."

"So would I." He smiled at her. "Successful money ventures are always welcome."

"Come on in here." She turned back toward the kitchen. "I've got us a late breakfast ready."

"Is that buckwheat pancakes I smell?"

"It is."

"Thanks be to God! All the way home, I was hoping you had that in mind."

After making short work of the pancakes, fried eggs, and potatoes, they lingered at the table, nursing their coffee as the two of them pored over the pile of newspapers. He enjoyed this celebratory late morning of tranquility, and clearly Avery did too. She kept smiling at him. Jack played peacefully on the living room floor with his blocks and handmade cars.

"I'm reading about conservation of food products for the war effort, but each item they've listed here is typical farm practice." Avery peered up at him. "They seem to think we don't know how to avoid wastefulness. Farm wives in Oklahoma don't waste—at least not any I know."

He met her eyes and nodded. He didn't know of any wasteful farmers or their wives. Again, he perused the paper, his eye caught by new information. "Listen to this. *The Wichita Eagle and Beacon* says there are U-boats in American waters."

"How would they know?"

"American boats exploding when they hit the mines laid off the Delaware capes."

"That would do it," she said. "I feel sorry for the poor people whose boats hit the mines!"

"More loss of life," he said. "Apparently, the U-boats also cut the submerged telegraph cables that connect New York with Nova Scotia."

"Just think of all that going on underwater without anyone knowing. That sounds like a complicated repair."

"Especially if there are U-boats waiting to blow you up." He smirked, fixing his eyes on hers over the top of the paper before returning to the article. "The U-boats stopped several schooners off Virginia. Took the crews aboard as prisoners and then sank the ships."

"Off Virginia! Those are American shores! They're here. That's ominous."

"Our navy will soon catch on to their strategies, and that will be the end of that. But the sooner we get our boys into the fight the better."

"My word!" Avery said. "How we've all changed our opinions on that, haven't we?"

"Been forced to change by their aggression."

"Sadly, that's the truth of it. If we have enough healthy fighting men—should that flu ravage our numbers—I hope and pray it will be over soon."

"Yes, we all do." He took a swig of coffee. She topped him off. "These next registrations should build up our military for the push, whenever it comes. The first registration is on June 5 and the next on August 21. Both will include recent twenty-one-year-olds. The third registration will be on September 12—every single man between the ages of eighteen and forty-five."

"That's a broad group! I hope none see action."

"I agree. That's for certain. Hundreds of thousands of our men cross the Atlantic every month. They're trying to get our combat force to two million, maybe even three by November. *That* should end this war. Our troops are pushing into Europe now and making great progress. I hope Tom writes soon with more news."

"So do I. It would be good to know he's well."

Something caught Prentis's eye on the next newspaper. He took a long, hard look and then laid aside his current choice for the other paper. He knew Avery would want to hear this news.

"Sweetheart," he said, "listen to this."

She looked up at him.

"You remember that referendum we had on women's suffrage here in Oklahoma?"

"Of course, I do."

"Well, there's going to be an amendment on our ballot in the fall."

"For women's suffrage? Praise God! It's about time!"

"Here's a list of all the states that have already approved the vote for women, at least in their own states. It includes Wyoming, Colorado, Utah, Idaho, Washington, California, Arizona, Kansas, Oregon, Montana, Nevada, North Dakota, and New York. Other states are considering it."

"That sounds like momentum, especially when added to President Wilson's support."

"I agree," he said.

"You *are* going to vote in favor of the amendment, aren't you, Prentis? We depend on you men, since we women can't vote."

He chuckled. "Wouldn't dream of missing the opportunity. You've got more common sense than most men I know. And all of my respect."

"But, the reason men get to vote has nothing to do with common sense or respect. You can vote merely because you're male."

"I'll give you that," he said.

"Whereas, I can't vote merely because I'm female."

"That's true. Now, if common sense *were* part of it—"

"Not many of us would be voting, male *or* female."

"I think you're right." He laughed, amused by her clever way of defusing her argument.

"You're a mighty fine husband."

"I give it my best shot."

She laughed. "You hit the mark. You don't act as though you have superior wisdom or common sense, merely because you're male, as some of the opponents to suffrage do."

"That's because I know that I don't. Since my wife is a suffragette, that's pretty clear to me." He looked up to catch her grinning at him. "The women of this country have displayed an abundance of patriotism, common sense, hard work, and wisdom during this war. However, you have an inalienable right to vote as citizens of these United States, whether you possess those qualities or not."

"Well said, husband."

"Just have to pray and see what the good Lord does."

Smiling, both of them lifted their coffee cups toward one another, followed by a long swig and a refill for both. Chuckling, Prentis couldn't keep his eyes off her, recovered, blooming, and ready to argue politics and suffrage, if necessary. Her attention had returned to her stack of papers. Tilting back in his chair, her watched her focus on the tightly spaced newsprint.

"Congress has extended The Espionage Act of last year and broadened it to cover more offenses. It's now called The Sedition Act." She paused for a long while and then glanced at him over the top of the paper. "What are you grinning about?"

"You," he said. "You're feisty again."

"I don't know if that's good or bad."

"Oh, it's good!"

"Now, stop your flirting and listen to this." She gave him a coy smile. "I think I've just encountered the longest sentence I've ever read. I'll spare you the entire thing, but let me jump into the middle, so you get the gist." With eyes twinkling, she looked at him. "Are you ready?"

"Let me have it." He chuckled, expecting this to be entertaining.

"Here it comes. 'Whoever, when the United States is at war, shall willfully cause or attempt to cause, or incite or attempt to incite, insubordination, disloyalty, mutiny, or refusal of duty, in the military or naval forces of the United States, or shall willfully obstruct or attempt to obstruct the recruiting or enlistment service of the United States, and whoever, when the United States is at war, shall willfully utter, print, write, or publish any disloyal, profane, scurrilous, or abusive language about the form of government of the United States, or the Constitution of the United States, or the military or naval forces of the United States, or the flag of the United States, or the uniform of the Army or Navy of the United States, or any language intended to bring the form of government of the United States, or the Constitution of the United States, or the military of naval forces of the United States, or the flag of the United States, or the uniform of the Army or Navy of the United States into contempt, scorn, contumely, or disrepute, or shall willfully utter, print, write, or publish any language intended to incite, provoke, or encourage resistance to the United States, or to promote the cause of its enemies, or shall willfully display the flag of any foreign enemy.'"

She glanced up from the paper. "That's not the end of the sentence. It goes on and on and on. Let me skim down to find the penalty. Here it is—all in the same sentence. All of those listed acts and more 'shall be punished by a fine of not more than $10,000 or imprisonment for not more than twenty years, or both.'"

He laughed out loud. "I think Congress is concerned about our patriotism."

"I agree. But we can't even criticize the uniform? And then certain kinds of speech are prohibited. Wouldn't that go against our freedom of speech?"

"Seems to me it would." He chuckled. "You planning on breaking the law, Avery?"

"I may already be breaking the law by criticizing the law itself. But, I have no plans to cross them on this. They seem to be deadly serious."

"If you do, that's a heap of money for a fine." Prentis sipped his coffee.

Shaking her head, she perused the paper again.

"Look here," she said, raising a paper with large font emblazoned across the top. "*The Oklahoma City Times* says, 'Hun Line Pierced One Mile. Pershing's Soldiers Buck the Line as in Football Game, and Race Jokingly Through Town Laid Waste by Guns.' There's even a map." She passed the paper to him. "Well, that tells us what Tom's been up to."

"It certainly does. Though I don't think he'd be joking about it. Let's see what else it says." Prentis read through the extensive news of the battle, feeling relieved that the troops had regained the city and won a major victory. "Listen to this, Avery. 'The Americans fought as though they were veterans, and there was no hesitation when the officers sprang forward and shouted, "Come on, boys!" Several officers describing the scene agreed that the outstanding feature in their minds was the wonderful morale of the men and their absolute confidence in themselves.'"

"That sounds almost too good to be true," Avery said.

"The correspondent says he interviewed the men directly. See no reason he'd lie. Either we won the battle, or we didn't."

"That's true. The report of that victory makes me feel vastly relieved."

Avery rose and stepped toward the front screen door, standing quietly as she watched the rain falling softly outside. He recognized the wistful tilt to her head and body posture.

302

He returned to the paper, but he agreed. It was a relief.

Twenty-four

THE SOUND OF JACK screaming jolted Avery right out of her chair. Knitting needles and yarn flew off her lap and onto the floor. Her heart pounded as she dashed through the kitchen toward the back door.

Prentis threw wide the door, and his expression chilled her to the bone. His face had gone white, and Jack was covered in blood from wounds on his shoulder and forearms.

"Take Jack!"

As she did, he grabbed his loaded rifle off the rack above the back door.

"Stay in the house." He spun round and pulled the door closed, yanking it hard against the frame. She heard him whistle a short blast for Sam outside.

Holding Jack close, Avery hurried into the kitchen and pumped fresh water to cleanse his wounds. The scratch marks again—they were deep this time, and his neck looked as if it had been nicked or cut. How could this be? The rooster was dead and eaten. Something else was afoot. Was there a rabid wild animal on the prowl? Had a crazed coyote entered the barnyard? Prentis had told her about the odd behavior of the coyotes on his winter hike. For a moment, she considered rounding up the chickens, but Prentis had told her to stay inside.

Wrapping Jack's arm in a moist cloth, she held him tight and hurried toward the bedroom window overlooking the barnyard, hoping to discover something. Just in time, she spotted Prentis in the field, his rifle over his shoulder. Sam trotted beside him, both heading down the curve that led into the canyon. There was something in Prentis's other hand, a long implement of some type. Then they were out of sight.

Fear clutched her chest.

Looking into Jack's eyes, she saw the same terror. She needed to be calm for his sake.

"Come on, little man. Let's bandage up your wounds."

"Momma fix."

"Yes, Momma will do the best she can to fix you up. What happened?"

"Sam bite."

"What! Sam bit you?"

Jack nodded, and Avery felt sick to her stomach.

Had it been Sam all along? She remembered his growls at Jack's baby clumsiness, his difficulty adjusting to their attention being on the baby, and the fact that there had always been Sam and a growl whenever Jack was injured. They had thought the dog was protecting Jack from the rooster. She had to sit down. Collapsing into a chair, she wrapped her arms about her boy.

What if Jack had been killed by their own dog?

The possibility was more than she could take.

But then, in bits and pieces, the truth dawned on her.

"Lord!" she cried softly. "You kept him safe when we didn't even know. You watched over him. Help Prentis do what he has to do."

The sharp crack of the rifle sounded from the canyon. Then she bawled, holding Jack tight.

***

Hours passed without her husband's return. Quietly, Avery took care of Jack, fed him some lunch, and tucked him in for his afternoon nap. Sending up sentence prayers of thanks and requests of strength for Prentis, she awaited his arrival. Finally, she heard him at the back door.

Grief-stricken and horrified—that was the only way to describe his expression as he reloaded the rifle and placed it back on the rack.

When he turned toward her again, he stared at her with terror-stricken eyes, stark against his ashen face. There were no words, so she simply opened wide her arms, and he walked into them. She held him tight. He grappled with the same horror she felt about Jack being in danger while they were totally unaware, the same dismay that they hadn't recognized the threat was Sam.

But, he'd also been forced to put down his childhood friend and faithful companion, their watchdog, and the best cattle dog in those parts. The loss of Sam would impact every portion of his life. After a long while, he spoke, his face pressed into her hair.

"Sam growled, and I turned 'round just in time. Saw him lunge for Jack's throat."

Her heart about stopped. Wincing at the thought, she squeezed her eyes tight.

"But Jack threw up his arms to block him." Prentis's voice cracked. "It was like a reflex."

Giving him time to recover and continue, Avery kept her arms about him.

306

"Then I realized it had been happening since those first scratches on his arms. He'd done it so often that it had become his defensive posture whenever Sam growled." He paused again.

She didn't move.

"What if . . ." His voice broke down. She felt him swallow hard.

"God protected him," she whispered.

Prentis nodded. "He certainly did. But why didn't I . . . ?" Again, his voice cracked.

"Neither of us recognized what was going on. The rooster seemed the logical culprit. The chickens were always about when it happened. God watched over him. He filled in the gap. We can't be everywhere and see everything. I think we'll have to remind ourselves of that truth many times throughout Jack's life."

He nodded again. She felt the motion but kept her head against his chest.

"We can't keep him safe," he said, "even when we're on duty. How can we live with that?"

A moan exhaled from Avery at those words. "You're right. We'll simply have to trust God to cover where we're lacking."

"That's what it always comes down to, isn't it?"

***

The following week, the clatter of horses' hooves and the barking of a familiar canine sounded from the barnyard. Avery peeked out the living room window and was surprised to see three of her brothers on horseback. Abe, Gene, and Howard had brought the family watchdog that the boys had simply named "Dog" so long ago.

After lowering the hound to the ground, Abe reached inside his jacket then handed Prentis a puppy he had tucked against him. Avery smiled as Prentis set the small dog down beside Jack, who squeezed him and then took off running with toddling steps, the whelp in playful pursuit. Eventually, both got all tangled up, tripping over one another and ending up in the dust. Everyone laughed, Jack with complete abandon as he rolled around with the small pup.

Avery enjoyed watching this unfold. But Prentis had caught sight of her. He motioned for her to join them. As soon as she stepped out the door, Dog trotted over to greet her. Avery gave the familiar animal a pat and a good scratch, greeting her warmly. Then she examined the young canine, thanking God that both Prentis and Jack could train a new cow-dog for their farm.

"We're riding to Tom's to bring his cows over for breeding," Prentis said. "When that's accomplished in a few weeks, we'll herd them back to their home field. Got to keep my grass and alfalfa use in balance, so I can't keep the cows here all summer. Seemed like the best strategy, since we don't have Sam to herd Rex over there. I need my own dog for herding a bull. Not that I don't trust Dog." He glanced at the boys. "But I prefer my own herd animal."

The boys all nodded their agreement, clearly understanding entirely.

Prentis looked at her again. "If it's all right with you, Dog's staying for a while, so I can begin training this puppy by her example. Howard's staying too, to help with that."

"When was all this decided?" Avery said.

They all looked at one another.

"Just this morning, sis," Howard said.

Prentis wore a sheepish expression. "I ran into the boys in town. When I came back, I got busy. Forgot to mention it. Sorry."

"Of course, it's fine. I just wondered if you'd all learned to read minds."

They all laughed.

"I'll get something started for supper right now," she said, "since you'll all be hungry later."

"That always gives a man something to look forward to." Prentis grinned at the boys. "I've told you this before, boys, and I'll tell you again—"

"Marry a woman exactly like our sister," all three boys chimed in, then they all laughed together.

That exchange always amused Avery. She smiled at Prentis. After returning her smile, he plunked Jack safely between Abe's strong arms, where he would ride. He stepped inside the barn and eventually returned with Ulysses saddled and ready to go. Then Prentis grabbed up the puppy to ride in front of him.

As they headed out, Avery heard Abe's command to Dog, then watched Prentis quietly repeat that same command to the puppy, directing its attention to Dog, so it could watch what happened. Training had begun.

When they returned later, Tom's cows were herded into the pasture with Rex. Howard brought Jack in to her, so they could all unsaddle and groom their horses. Jack chattered away about the puppy and the cows. It had been an exciting day for him.

Trying to decipher his baby talk, it appeared to Avery that the puppy had been named Kaiser Wilhelm. Later, when they all trooped in to eat, she asked about it. They told her it was because everyone wanted to tell the human Kaiser Wilhelm where to go and what to do, and that was exactly what this puppy had to learn. Then they all laughed heartily.

She merely shook her head. It was already decided.

***

During the final days of May, the United States troops had their first significant victory. American troops recaptured the French village of Cantigny from the Germans. That engagement occurred during The Second

Red Cross War Fund effort on the home front. The push for contributions started in Oklahoma during the first week of June. Prentis rode into town to donate and to return with any available newspapers, old or new. Simultaneous to the Red Cross drive, one million young men newly turned twenty-one registered in the second round of the draft. Now that millions of Americans were already in Europe, the nation pressed toward total involvement.

The numbers were tallied for the 1918 Red Cross drive. According to *The Enid Events* from June 6, nearly $170,000,000 had been received nationwide. The paper also gave details of an offensive move against German storm troopers. That was the first full engagement for the US Marines, who launched the attack under the command of the French Corps, after undergoing training by British, Scottish, Canadian, and Australian officers. Their training had required six weeks minimum, on top of what they'd already received at the camps in America before they had deployed.

Once it was done, off they went. While approximately fifty-five thousand Marines served with the American Expeditionary Force, most of the navy's responsibilities involved continuing to patrol for U-boats, to sweep for enemy mines, and to escort troop and cargo ships across the Atlantic.

Though General Pershing still worked toward the deployment of his own independent field army and didn't feel they were ready yet, the need was pressing—the Germans were headed toward Paris. Therefore, troops of more seasoned American men who had enlisted early and had been trained during the previous years now fought under French command. Reports came back that every day, ten thousand more of those American soldiers headed into battle.

Prentis and Avery knew they would soon be receiving news of war casualties.

Still, General Pershing maintained his resolve. The American Expeditionary Force wasn't ready yet. He had to answer for the lives of those newly drafted young men, and he intended to deploy them under his command, hoping to end the war with that large focused assault.

That was a serious batch of news. Avery felt exhausted merely hearing Prentis dissect the latest information, reading portions out loud to her and condensing others. The idea of ten thousand more American men going into battle every single day was devastating. She thought of all the local boys and wondered where they were. The last thing she had heard was that most were still in training camps in America, but one had been sent on ahead to Europe—Bliss Markland. She worried about Bliss, along with Charles and Tom.

Then Prentis spread wide a newspaper.

"This is *The Wichita Eagle and Beacon* from June 3," he said. "I want you to look this over."

Avery rose from her knitting and stood beside him. "What's this?"

Prentis studied what looked like a map of America. Jack climbed up on a chair to look.

Prentis smiled at her, his eyes twinkling. "Jack has taken to reading the papers with us."

"Read papers." Jack nodded.

Pleased, they gazed at one another over his head. Prentis tousled his hair affectionately.

Scrutinizing the map, Avery leaned in closer. Her hand flew to her mouth.

"Oh, my!" She grinned at Prentis. "On Saturday, there's going to be a solar eclipse!"

He chuckled softly. "I thought your teacher's brain would enjoy this."

Exuberant, she examined the paper. "This shows us where the path of the eclipse will cross our country at the precise time for each location." With her fingertip, she traced the arc across America. "We're right in the path. This is so exciting! We'll see the eclipse sometime between five twenty-seven and six thirty on Saturday."

"'Clipse?" Jack said.

"Yes, Jack, the moon will hide the sun. That's an eclipse." His little forehead wrinkled as he tried to understand. She smiled at him, before looking up at Prentis. "Around six p.m., it looks like we'll be in total darkness."

"They say it's a once in a lifetime event."

"I'm thrilled you brought this paper home, Prentis."

"Figured your scientific mind would want more information."

"I do, indeed."

"I searched for this copy deliberately," he said. "Heard about it in the general store. They were sold out, but I found a copy in the saloon."

Startled, she looked up. "You stepped into the saloon?"

"Briefly," he stated slowly, fixing his eyes on hers and raising an eyebrow. "Just to grab the paper. Hoped you wouldn't mind."

"In the name of science, a man might do anything. But, I never thought I'd hear of you going inside a saloon."

He shrugged. "Figured you'd think the scientific discovery was worth it."

"In this case, I do. I know you hate hard drink as much as I do."

"Though I may be a little more tolerant toward those who drink."

"You're too kind half the time, Prentis. You know how angry alcohol makes me. I think I need to learn some forbearance."

312

"I'd say you're fine just the way you are."

After that statement, he kissed her full on the lips. Then he winked at her, causing her to burst out laughing. The joy of this unique scientific event and his thoughtfulness filled her heart.

***

Avery awakened before dawn. Today was the day! June 8 had finally arrived. They had an entire day to get through, for the eclipse wouldn't occur until after supper. She anticipated the experience so much that she hadn't been able to stay asleep. Slowly she adjusted her position, rolling ever-so-carefully to face the middle of the bed, lest she wake Prentis.

His wide-open eyes stared back at her.

She had to cover her mouth to keep from giggling out loud—Jack slept right around the corner. Her shoulders shook with laughter as a slow grin spread across his face.

"Didn't expect that, did you?" he whispered.

She uncovered her face. "No, I didn't. You startled me."

"You were either tossing or turning or lying stiff as a board all night. Knew you were excited, but it's a wonder you got any sleep at all."

Pressing both her hands to her mouth, she whispered. "This is far too exciting!"

"The woman in this bed with me is much more exciting than an eclipse."

One long muscular arm untangled itself from the sheets, and then it wrapped around her, pulling her up snug against him. Softly he kissed her on the forehead, then down her nose and onto her lips before planting a tender peck of a kiss on her chin. When he caressed her neck with gentle lips, she melted into him. They had perfected the art of silent lovemaking since Jack had been born. One day, he'd have his own room, but for now they were quite adept at enjoying the pleasure of marital intimacy without waking the baby.

Afterward, they lay wrapped up together. Avery felt entirely content.

"I think I'll just stay here in this bed with you all day," Prentis whispered.

Apparently, he felt the same. She whispered back, "Unfortunately, a certain two-year-old will awaken with the sun."

That caused him to sigh with contentment, a satisfied smile on his face, before he nestled his head in under her chin, kissed her collarbone, and then lay in silent tranquility. They must have dozed off, because Avery was surprised to see the sun shining brightly when Jack's voice called, popping wide her eyes.

Eclipse day!

She remembered all over again, unwound herself from the covers and Prentis, climbed out of bed, resettled her nightgown, and peeked her head around the corner. Awaiting her appearance, Jack stood in his crib, bursting into laughter and clapping his hands when he saw her face. Laughing in response, she grabbed him up, and they rejoined Prentis in bed. He had scooted up under the covers, pulling snug their bedspread, and he held out his hands for their boy.

"Da Da!" Jack cried out, diving into his arms.

"How are you today, son?"

"Good day!"

"Yes, it is. Your momma's excited about the eclipse." Prentis winked at her over Jack's head.

"'Clipse today?"

Avery could barely contain her excitement. "Yes, Jack! Yes, it is!"

With that beginning, it didn't surprise her that the day took forever. The clock seemed to move at a snail's pace all morning as she looked forward to the afternoon. Then

314

she'd track each half-hour increment across the newspaper map, marking the time as it crossed the country.

***

It being a Saturday, Prentis rode over to check on Tom's place, a weekly task. Then he returned to work with Kaiser, teaching him more about sitting, staying, coming, and moving cattle. They used a solitary old cow in the corral for their purposes, and he held Jack on the saddle in front of him. First Prentis instructed Dog, who carried out his quiet command. Then, using a long leash to guide the younger dog and accustom him to the whistles and calls, he gave the same quiet instruction to Kaiser. Jack usually rewarded the puppy with tight squeezes and rolls through the grass, but today he rode.

Avery came out to watch.

"Look at what he can do," Prentis called. "He's accomplished a lot since the boys left."

He gave a few simple commands, and Kaiser obeyed, which delighted them all. Everyone praised him, and the young dog about wagged himself right off his feet in response. Clearly Kaiser had inherited excellent cow dog genes from his dam. Even Dog appeared pleased.

"Went over to Tom's," Prentis told her.

"Is everything all right?"

"Yep. His wheat's starting to ripen too. Seems a bit ahead of mine. Might be harvesting by the end of this month. His cows are doing just fine over here. I'm glad we herded them over. They'll go back to his farm soon." Pulling over to the rail, he lifted Jack and passed him to her. "How you doin' in that house, trying to keep your excitement in check?"

"Well, we've got a few pies to eat now, and the house is spotless."

315

Throwing his head back, he laughed. "Figured you'd put your energy to good use. Looks like it'll be a scorcher. After he wakes from his nap, let's go down to the creek."

She smiled. "That sounds delightful. It's time for dinner now, if you two are ready."

"Always ready when it's time for your good cooking."

"You're the easiest man to cook for on the planet, Prentis."

"That's only because you're the best cook."

She grinned up at him. "Come on in. I'll take Jack."

After a hot, delicious meal and not one, but two pieces of strawberry-rhubarb pie, Prentis headed out to check on the livestock, leaving Avery to put Jack down for his nap. Later, she stepped onto their shady front porch. Prentis spotted her from the corrals where he was examining the mares. Avery scanned the heavens, shading her eyes as she gazed at the sun, as if willing the show to begin early.

It made him chuckle. How he loved her!

Turning, she caught sight of him, left the porch, and joined him. She stepped up onto the bottom rail, hooked her elbows on the top rail, and leaned against it to watch him. He remembered her doing the same at the livery in Kingman the year he'd begun to court her. He'd waited for seven years for the opportunity to win her. Then, one day, there she was, right in line with his desires, exactly as he was prepared to begin his pursuit.

That day he'd been mucking out manure in the livery, stood to straighten his back, peered out into the bright morning, and spotted her there, balanced on the rail. After her father's purchase in the livery office, he had obtained permission to begin. Would she accept him? Well, she had, and here she was, the best part of his life all bound up in one beautiful, energetic, and intelligent package. After beginning young manhood with so many challenges—heading the family and tending to the home farm starting when he was barely fifteen—he'd been

316

blessed more than he'd ever dreamed could occur in this lifetime. God was good!

"What's that twinkle in your eye?" she said.

"I was thinking how you stood on the corral rail at our livery exactly like that, right before I started trying to persuade you to be my wife."

"Yes, I recall that I did. I'm so glad you came after me."

"Best decision I ever made."

Avery's beautiful smile beamed at him. He returned her smile and then got back to the business at hand.

"It would appear that every one of these mares is in foal," he told her.

"Well, glory be!"

"Even the maiden mare you named."

"Priscilla's name is Greek, like the other names you chose for your horses, but she was a woman of God. I hope you don't mind that at least one of these horses isn't named after a pagan deity or a mythological Greek."

"Don't mind at all. If all goes well, we'll have six foals in the spring."

Shading her eyes, she tipped her head back and studied the sun again. Prentis figured it was around two o'clock, based on its position. He watched her face as she made her calculations. Then she looked back into his eyes.

"You've done that several times today," he said.

"I want to see every minute of this."

"Your excitement is endearing."

"Why, thank you!" She laughed. "The map says totality varies from two minutes up in Washington to less than a minute and a half by the time we see it here. We won't dare blink. It's out over the Pacific Ocean somewhere right now."

"Takes less than three hours to sweep all the way across these United States, if I recall."

"Yes, it does. It's astonishing! And we're seeing it backward of the east-west movement of the sun. The state of Washington sees the eclipse before we do, even though we'll still be seeing the sun move westward across our skies. I've been puzzling over that for days, wondering what that would look like in the heavens."

Prentis could only shrug. Her scientific mind had raised a fascinating question, one he couldn't answer either. Anticipating the later show, both stood looking up at the sky.

***

When Jack awoke from his nap, Avery was packing a picnic basket to carry down to the creek. They would eat and enjoy the coolness near the water before the eclipse began.

"Just a minute, Jack!" she called. "Momma's packing our picnic."

"Picnic?" his little voice called back.

"Yes, we're going to eat outside."

She heard him plunk down onto his bottom as he sang a quiet song in his room. That made her smile.

Prentis stepped in and washed up on the back porch as she continued her busy packing of their foodstuffs. As he passed through the kitchen, he kissed her on the nape of the neck. Smiling, she turned her head, and they exchanged a peck of a kiss. Then he headed toward the bedroom, joining Jack in his song, which morphed into *Jesus Loves Me.* That pleased her immensely. Perfect contentment filled her. She thanked God for her family and all He'd done to keep them all alive that past year.

"We'll stop at the outhouse on the way to the creek, unless you want to use the chamber pot," Prentis told Jack as he carried him in.

"Outhouse," he said. "Big boy."

"You *are* a big boy, Jack!" Avery said.

318

She tucked the Wichita paper on top of everything in the basket and closed the lid. Prentis grasped the handle, and she grabbed the quilt they would sit on in the pasture. Out the back door they went, making their requisite stop at the outhouse.

After Jack had finished, Avery carefully tucked his pants into the tops of his little boots, doubly securing them with shoelaces she had brought for the purpose. Due to the chiggers, they didn't usually let him traipse around in tall grass. She had worn long ladies' drawers today for protection, and she paused to make sure hers were tightly secured at the ankles.

Prentis had to deal with that every day, which was why he preferred to wear long union suits. As far as Avery was concerned, chigger bites were one of the worst forms of torture, the welts excruciating. The itching agony must be avoided. After everything was checked and readied, they stepped through the gate and headed across the grass, sticking to the well-worn areas where the livestock had trodden the grass flat. That was the safest route.

Jack ran ahead, giggling with delight and chasing both Dog and Kaiser. Prentis reached for her hand, lacing his fingers through hers, another reason to smile. The land sloped toward the creek bottom, and they gradually circled around, coming down the incline until the cliff along the northwest edge of their property was on their right. The scrub oak and red cedars stood thick along the cliff bank, but on the outside edge of the creek, Prentis had kept the brush cut back to allow the animals access to drinking water.

"Makes me happy watching Jack play with those two dogs," Prentis said.

Avery nodded. "It puts my mind at ease. I'm glad his confrontations with Sam didn't cause him to fear an animal so important to our livelihood and the safety of our farm."

"That's how I feel."

"Thank God that's behind us!"

"One of life's most frightening experiences, so I have to agree."

Their eyes met, and he pulled her close, so they could lean against one another.

"Between this war, your surgery, people we love in harm's way, Pitzer's death, the flu, and Sam," Prentis said quietly, "I don't know if I can take much more of this."

"The Lord has it all in hand." She glanced at him. "I have to keep reminding myself of that, or it all overwhelms me too."

"We've definitely kept the good Lord busy," he said.

The dogs had splashed into the creek, and Jack had plopped onto the ground, attempting to tug off his boots without unlacing them. The day was quite warm, and the heavy scent of the thriving alfalfa on this corner of the property lent an ambience of summertime.

She looked up at Prentis. "Should we let him wade?"

"We may as well." Squatting down, he unlaced Jack's boots. "The dogs will get him wet, because they're already in."

Avery stepped around and lowered herself to Jack's level too, carefully keeping her skirts tucked about her legs, lest the chiggers find an entry point.

"Jack," she said, "look into Momma's eyes."

As Prentis freed Jack's feet from the confines of his socks, he looked up at her. His little toes wiggled free, but he kept his eyes fixed on hers.

"You must only get your feet wet." She grasped his ankle. "Keep the water below this bone." She rubbed the tibia and fibula on either side where they protruded. "You must not go in any deeper than these bones at your ankle."

"Nankle?"

320

"Yes, these bones here," she said, patting the bones. She touched his leg above the ankle. "This part up here, you must keep dry. Do you understand Momma?"

"Yep," he said.

Turning, he stepped right into the creek, sinking up to his knees.

Immediately, Prentis grabbed him up and stood him on the bank. Avery studied his wet denim overalls, soaked far above the mid-calf where Prentis had rolled them.

"Well, those instructions were pointless," she said as an aside to Prentis.

"I was chuckling to myself as I listened. No little boy can stay dry in a creek."

"I know my brothers couldn't, but I thought that surely my son could, if he was adequately instructed."

"Oh, your instructions were good, Avery." Prentis laughed. "Nevertheless, he's still a boy."

"Let's just strip the overalls off, so they can dry in the sun. Do you think it's too scandalous to allow him to play in his union suit?"

Prentis snorted. "I was going to suggest we strip him bare. So, the union suit seems tame compared to my idea."

"Let him swim naked?" She was horrified. "Oh, Prentis!"

"Well, that definitely brought out the prim schoolmarm in you."

"I couldn't help myself. My goodness!"

Prentis looked about the sheltered canyon. "Not a soul but the two of us can see him here."

"But what kind of moral example would we be setting for him?"

"Well, when we were all kids, your brothers, Fred, and I used to strip naked to swim in the creek near my parents' farm. Kept our clothes dry, and once our bodies dried, we could slip them back on. Doesn't appear to have harmed my morality."

Avery laughed. "I never imagined. By the time you all reappeared, you were suitably dry and clad in your regular attire. You're right. It doesn't seem to have harmed your morality, though you *did* step into a saloon recently, so maybe we'll need to wait and see."

Now he laughed with her.

"Since you're his daddy," she said, "I'm going to defer to your decision."

Prentis studied her face. Then he scooped up Jack, holding him close as he slowly turned to survey the landscape. "Look, son. No one can see us here. We're tucked into a canyon. There's brush and trees all around us. Do you see?"

Jack nodded. "No peoples."

"Yes, no people. Since no one can see us here, we're on our own farm, and we know that no one is coming to look for us, I'm going to let you play in only your union suit."

Quickly, Avery looked up at him. His eyes met hers. One of his eyebrows was raised, and he twinkled those bright blue eyes right at her. Then she smiled wide at him, warmed to the core that he had deferred to her preference when given the choice.

"Let's strip off your shirt and your overalls," Prentis continued.

Jack wiggled out of his clothing. Chortling, he stepped right into the water, nearly getting knocked off his feet by Kaiser's enthusiasm. It wasn't long before he landed, plop, right on his bottom. He was one wet boy. Prentis's decision had been wise.

Avery stepped over to a shady spot a short distance from the water. She spread the quilt wide and settled herself comfortably on the ground, so she could watch her men, grown and small. Supervising Jack, Prentis sat on the creek's edge, his blue jeans and union suit rolled to mid-calf and his bare feet in the water.

That small moment would be one she'd never forget. All was well. Her family was thriving. A moment of peace and tranquility during a time of war and hardship had been granted. Her heart overflowed with gratitude to God.

Eventually, Jack tired of the water, and then Prentis played with him, making roads for his cars and farm plots for his wooden farm animals. Avery had squeezed the toys into the picnic basket in case they were needed. When Jack was dry, they dressed him.

Spreading out the contents of their meal, she served supper. They ate right from the bowls and baskets of food—chicken, fried potato strips, green beans, and cookies. Both Prentis and Jack thanked her, causing her to smile. Then she rinsed the dishes in the creek. Later, she'd use hot water and lots of soap, but for now, it made her eventual clean-up much easier.

Throughout their time by the creek, Avery glanced frequently at the heavens.

Now she settled onto the blanket to focus on the sky. Gradually, she detected a difference in the sunlight. It seemed to dim, and an odd refraction caused sparkles of sunlight to glint off objects. A fly buzzed about, distracting her from the sky. Brushing it away, she glanced down at her skirt. Shadows of the tree leaves speckled the skirt. Within each shadow was a small crescent shape. Wherever shadows fell, the eclipse reflected all around them on the ground.

"Look, Prentis! The eclipse is beginning." She pointed. "See the shadows. They're beautiful!"

He studied the ground. "Well, I'll be. That's strange indeed."

High cumulus clouds now drifted across the sky, blocking the entire sun from view momentarily. As the clouds drifted eastward, at each glimpse of the sun, they saw its darkened form diminishing even more, now only half showing. The sun's light grew increasingly dim.

Shading their eyes, they turned their faces upward.

"Wait!" she said, turning to dig in the picnic basket. "I just remembered that I made smoked glass, so we could view this safely."

Using small pieces of glass from Prentis's work area, Avery had held them over a smoking candlewick. Once the glass was darkened by the smoke, she had smudged away a place for them to grip the glass, so they didn't blacken everything when the soot clung to their hands.

"Look through the glass," she said. "If you're not using the glass, don't look too long. It's still the sun, so I know we should look away frequently."

When she averted her eyes, the burned shadow of the eclipsed sun floated across her field of vision. She studied the shapes shadowed on the ground yet again. Bit by bit, more of the sun was blocked. Beside her, Prentis was doing the same thing. Jack merely looked confused, glancing upward, studying the shapes on the ground where they pointed, and then looking around.

"Getting dark," he said. "Bedtime?"

"No, son," she said. "The moon is blocking the sun. The sun is hiding behind the moon."

"Moon?" Jack looked about the sky for the familiar moon, grew more puzzled, and then returned to driving his cars through his dirt roadways.

Avery tousled his hair, smiled at Prentis who had been watching that exchange, and then focused again on the display. Both of them peered through the smoked glass. It worked well, revealing the sun in the same way that the clouds had given a partially covered glimpse. The sparkles and refractions grew with intensity as all around them the light faded even more.

Darkness now surrounded them. The crickets began their chirring, and the frogs began their song. The mosquitoes appeared. Of course, Avery thought, slapping and waving them away.

The moon now blocked the sun entirely, a perfect fit, God's unique handiwork. Around the blackened shadow blazed a corona of light.

"Look!" Prentis said, pointing. "The red."

Streamers of red flickered out from the corona, but only on one side. Avery peered hard at the timepiece pinned at her waist. It was exactly 6:15 p.m., just as she had calculated when studying the map in the *Wichita Beacon*. It was amazing that scientists could compute this entire event with such precision.

For more than a full minute, they gazed at the eclipsed sun and the stars twinkling along the far edges of the sky, away from the glowing corona. And then, ever-so gradually, the light began to shift, growing brighter with each passing minute. Through all the stages previously witnessed, the process reversed, and before they knew it, the entirely unique experience had ended.

"How glorious!" she said. "I'm so glad the Lord blessed us with this experience."

"Definitely once in a lifetime!" Prentis said. "I'll never forget it."

Twenty-five

THE WHEAT HARVEST WAS now upon them. Prentis would have been tempted to despair over the profit The Lever Act prevented them from making, but Congress had passed an increase in the price originally approved for wheat. Their wheat was in high demand in Europe, and prices needed to remain stable, so as not to bankrupt those who needed the grain. The entire western world needed food. That was understood. But, Congress also understood the plight of the American farmer, and so they had raised the price per bushel to $2.40.

Knowing he'd at least get a decent price put heart into a man. That was a guarantee this year, if he got his wheat in. It would bring him close to the same profit he'd gotten last year.

Prentis chuckled as he recalled Avery's initial enthusiasm about this governmental involvement, mostly because it curtailed alcohol consumption. However, most people talked about the money they would *not* be making, due to the price already being set. None of them had dreamed that it might protect them financially. It was like an insurance policy going into this harvest. Last year they had signed up for the draft during harvest. This year they would be protected from financial loss. To gain some benefit from the behind-the-scenes wrangling of government was like a salve, softening just a little the horrific losses they'd suffered.

Joe Pitzer would have enjoyed this, had he lived.

Prentis stepped into the back porch, saw Avery in the kitchen, and began scrubbing up.

"Avery," he called. "Remember when we discussed The Lever Food and Fuel Act last year? We sold our wheat for higher than the price they ended up setting."

She turned from the countertop, wiping her hands on her apron. "Yes, as I recall it was then labeled 'An Act to Provide Further for the National Security and Defense by Encouraging the Production, Conserving the Supply, and Controlling the Distribution of Food Products and Fuel.' Am I correct?"

"Yes!" He chuckled. "Of course, you would remember that."

"Well, at least we know my schoolteacher's brain still works." She laughed with him. "What about The Lever Act?"

"I'm going to take the positive view, rather than complaining about what we might have earned had the market been free. That long-winded name of an act is going to guarantee almost the same price I got last year. I won't have a loss."

"That's true! I told you it was a good bill."

"Yes, but I believe you were focused more on curtailing whiskey production."

"Indeed, I was," she said. "Less grain spent on the production of strong spirits resulted in more grain to help feed the world and to care for our troops."

"We could discuss how much grain is in a glass of beer compared to a shot of whiskey."

"We could." She paused, putting her hand on her hip and cocking one eyebrow. "But, I'll grant you that they're about the same."

"And I'll grant *you* that lower whiskey consumption is a good thing, and it does save grain."

"That's one argument averted." She smiled.

"Always a blessing." He stepped up into the kitchen and kissed her on the lips.

She gazed up at him with her shining black eyes. "With a guaranteed price, we won't lose any money if we get our wheat in."

"It's like a gift from God, Avery. The president's guarantee of grain prices stands until May 1919." He chuckled softly. "But, I doubt we can squeeze in one more harvest before then."

"We can always pray."

***

The harvest was successful. After all the snow they received right before springtime and the growing season, they had high yields. Everyone from their country church pooled their efforts to reap Tom's wheat and then Prentis's. He sold his wheat and Tom's immediately, as required by the US Food Administration, taking in the newly mandated $2.40 per bushel. Thank God for Congress! He had never imagined that he'd ever have that sentiment toward their lawmakers.

He tucked Tom's earnings into Tom's account at the Citizens Bank of Wakita. The total for Prentis's wheat went into his joint account with Avery, a nice take for both farms of about $2,500 each. Thanks to the wet spring, it was even more than they had gained the previous year when they sold their wheat before the government set prices. And it was much more than they usually received during peacetime but was neither exorbitant nor greedy. He was content.

Prentis stopped by the general store to purchase a dress he'd seen Avery admiring every time they came into town. She mostly ordered from the *Sears* catalog now, but he loved bringing her unexpected surprises from their farming gains. When he presented the dress, she threw her arms around him. Then she held the dress up to her body and danced around the room.

Laughing, he watched her. "It's nice to see you happy and dancing again!"

She grabbed up Jack and danced him across the room, where she leaned in to kiss Prentis. That caused Jack to giggle, so she paused to blow on the soft baby folds under his two-year-old chin, making him laugh out loud.

The Shadows Come

A successful harvest was always a joyful time, especially during a time of war. Prentis tucked away the newspapers he'd also purchased, hiding them in the back porch, leaving all the bad news until tomorrow's breakfast table. The headlines told of a major victory, but many American deaths. Tonight, he decided they needed to simply enjoy the harvest.

***

The following morning over coffee, hash browns, and scrambled eggs, he brought forward the newspapers to peruse as they worked their way through the coffeepot, commenting to one another on this or that detail as they came across it. Prentis had the *Wakita Herald* spread wide with all the local news. The first detail he noticed was that fifteen more boys from their county had left for Fort Oglethorpe in Georgia to begin their military training.

"More boys heading off to war," he told her. "Fifteen this time. All headed for Georgia."

"Oh, no! More of them!"

"Looks like it. But here's some good news."

He paused. She met his eyes.

"The Wakita Food Administrator, Mr. H.T. Smith, says merchants are permitted to sell twenty-five pounds of sugar for your summer canning."

"Is that twenty-five pounds total?" she said. "Or is that twenty-five pounds per customer?"

"Doesn't say."

Avery sighed. "Of course not."

"We'd both better head to the dentist." Prentis looked up again.

"Why would we do that?" Her eyes stayed fixed on a different paper.

"Our dentist is leaving in August for military service."

She looked up at him. "Where is he going?"

"Camp Fremont in Colorado for his training."

"He's our only dentist!"

"Guess the city fathers had better look for another."

"Rural communities are being ransacked," she muttered.

The war continued to touch and indeed to dig ever deeper into their community. But, of course, the main impact of the war occurred mostly on the other side of the globe. As they had harvested and hauled in their grain to feed the people of Europe and their own fighting men, they discovered that the Battle of Belleau Woods had played out on the other side of the ocean. It had been a victory for American forces, but over ten thousand men had been killed, wounded, or were missing in action—the largest list of casualties for America to date.

As the sweltering summer continued hot and muggy in Oklahoma, weeks of fighting were read about over their breakfast table. America's manpower had now fully entered the fray. Each day Prentis and Avery prayed for their friends and family at every meal, begging God for a swift end to the war and for protection for those they loved.

***

Jack slept, and Avery studied. Digging into the ramifications of Greek culture as it affected the interpretation of the passage that she examined in 1 Corinthians, she was lost in the text.

A shout sounded. The back door banged open with a crash.

Startled, Avery jumped, pulling her mind and her eyes away from the theological text. Why was the light so dim? No wonder she was having such difficulty seeing the tiny words in her concordance. Had she studied all afternoon? Was it evening already?

"Avery!" Prentis yelled. "Grab the baby!"

Bursting in, Prentis stared at her in consternation.

"I've been calling you. There's a tornado headed our way!"

"What?" She couldn't understand. He seemed to be speaking an unknown language.

"A tornado, Sweetheart!" He grabbed her by the elbow, lifting her to her feet.

She began to straighten her papers. But, with a strong hand, he turned her away from the desk and aimed her toward the door. Her eyes lingered on the work spread all over the desk.

"There's no time!" he said. "It's right outside."

Stepping away from her, Prentis threw wide the bedroom door. Jack startled and screamed in terror. Prentis hurtled toward the crib, grabbed him, rushed back into the living room, and seized Avery's hand, tugging her after him.

"Sweetheart, let's go!"

As she was spun away, she caught a glimpse out their bedroom window. Ominous gunmetal-gray clouds hung low. Fierce winds peppered their farmyard with dirt, straw, and chaff. The serpentine coil of a tornado flung debris high into the sky immediately southwest of their barn. The roar of powerful winds finally reached her ears, bringing her back from the first century world she'd been examining. Her mind snapped into action.

Hurrying after Prentis, she no longer weighed him down with her incomprehension. How had she not noticed the weather? She was a farm wife. It was it her job.

As if sensing that she was now on the move, Prentis let go of her hand and cradled Jack as they descended into the dark cellar. The boy was afraid of the spiders down there, and quite frankly, Avery didn't like them either. But it came with the territory. Thankfully, she had recently swept under the stairs as she reorganized her shelves for canned goods.

Stooping, Prentis bent in under the stairway, sliding his body and Jack's onto the dirt floor and against the cellar wall. Avery followed. Once there, she laced her fingers through his and looked at him. Turning toward her, he met her eyes.

"I'm sorry," she said. "I was buried in my studies. I couldn't understand what you wanted."

"You did have a faraway look in your eyes." His face softened, and his lips curved upward. "I've seen it before, so I knew I had to get you moving. Sorry for yelling. Needed to get you down here in time. Still, I'm glad to see you studying again."

Returning his gentle smile, she nodded.

Jack continued to wail. Over the baby's head, Prentis gave her a pointed look.

"Lord Jesus," she prayed, keeping her eyes on his. "Save us from the storm. Keep us safe. Protect our home, our goods, and our animals. Calm our baby. We ask this in Your name."

"Amen," Prentis said.

"'Men,'" Jack whispered, sniffling.

Praying together had calmed their son. Clasping hands in the greenish dusk, together they reassured him as he nestled between them on their laps, all huddled together. Trying to maintain parental calm, they attempted to keep their voices pleasant as the violent storm whistled over their home, hail pounded, and trees thrashed. Between the cacophony of noise and her focus on Jack, Avery couldn't tell what had been hit or missed. They'd find out when it was all over.

Soon all was silent, and Prentis extracted himself from their cramped position.

"You two, stay put. Let me check to see if we're all clear." He disappeared up the stairs.

"Dad bye-bye?"

Noting this sudden change in what Jack called his father, Avery filed it away to mention later. The terror of a tornado seemed to have bumped their son up to a more mature rendering.

"Dad will be right back. He'll let us know if the tornado has passed."

"'Nado?"

"Yes, a storm called a tornado just blew through."

Avery listened to Prentis's footfalls throughout the house as he checked in all directions. Finally, he called from the top of the stairs. "All's clear, but there sure is a mess."

That short statement didn't adequately prepare Avery. The farmyard was filled with wet debris—boards, shingles, tree branches, tumbleweeds, newspaper. Part of her peach tree had been ripped away from the trunk. Her laundry was missing from their clothesline, though two of Prentis's shirts and a pair of her drawers were plastered against their house's siding. Their garden had been pulverized and flattened by the hail that came with the whirlwind. A portion of the barn's roof was ripped away—the corner that had faced the storm. It left a gaping hole. The pile of straw from the harvest was gone, simply vanished. Their livestock were all missing.

When they stepped outside, Dog and Kaiser crawled out from under the henhouse, both covered in mud. The dogs proceeded to shake themselves dry. As she turned away from the splattering mud, Avery noticed that their bedroom window was broken out.

"'Nado bad," Jack said.

"Yes, son." Prentis lifted him from Avery's arms. "This tornado was bad. Let's go see if we can find our animals."

Terror struck at her heart. "Have they simply vanished?"

"I hope not." He stared back at her. "That would be a huge loss. I threw wide all the gates, so the livestock could run to safety. The tornado itself blocked the way to their usual hiding place down by the creek. It came snaking down right over there." He pointed. "Soon as I find Ulysses, I'll go searching. Pray I find them. God, help us."

She nodded in agreement. "My chickens?"

"They were already mostly in the coop. I slammed the door on them, but if any weren't inside, we'll have to find them too. That is, if they're still with us." He raised an eyebrow at her, his meaning clear. They tried not to frighten the baby. The chickens were his friends.

Taking Jack, Prentis headed toward the mess.

Avery stepped into their bedroom to put on her work pants. But first, she had to mop up the water and clear away the broken glass. When she slipped on the pants, she was glad she'd made them when she and Prentis were newly married. They had plenty of work to do. Thankfully, their loss wasn't tragic. They still had each other. They still had a home and a barn.

"Lord of the universe, thank You for all You've given and for all You've taken away. Blessed be Your name. Thank you for sparing our lives, our home, and everything but a corner of roof. Help us to find our animals and to be thankful and content with whatever remains."

***

Though Prentis had given the animals complete access to the wider world and total freedom to run off their farm, he discovered all their livestock, except Apollo, in the far southeast corner of their property, huddled against the fence as far away as they could get from the tornado while still remaining within the property lines. After passing Jack to Avery, he saddled Ulysses to go in search of his prize stallion. More than an hour later, he was greatly relieved to find his horse two miles away, just off the road two sections over, leaning into a barbwire fence as he attempted to get at another farmer's mares. The mares appeared cooperative.

Thankfully, that fence had prevented Apollo from acting, thus protecting Prentis's entire horse-breeding operation from potential contamination by mares who might bear disease. Not all ranchers maintained his exacting standards of cleanliness. It also preserved Apollo's good seed for Prentis's profit alone. For both of those reasons, Prentis was glad the fence had held.

He slipped the harness over Apollo's head and knotted the reins over the saddle horn, turning Ulysses's head toward home and bringing the stallion along with them.

"Let's giddup, you two!" He clicked his tongue against his cheek.

Off they went, both horses skittish from the tornado. These storms always unsettled his animals, making them jumpy and nervous. As they trotted into the farmyard, he saw that Avery still struggled, attempting to restore some semblance of order and to find all their laundry.

***

After the storm, Avery could only continue to search for their laundry and to wait. For weeks, neighbors returned Prentis's union suits, Jack's diapers, and her knickers, whenever they turned up. It embarrassed Avery, but at least they received back most of their undergarments.

A third of the chickens were never seen again, so she set a couple of the hens on nests full of eggs to replenish their flock. Hoping for at least some produce, she reseeded the destroyed garden. Slowly, the root crops came back, bits of leaf reappearing. Prentis hauled back wagonloads of straw from Tom's, splitting the straw pile for use in both barns. He also remained Dad.

They were thankful that, once again, they had avoided a direct hit. Other than the broken window and the barn roof, their house and goods were mostly intact. Gradually, day after day they worked on repairs. Meanwhile, the papers informed them of an

334

entirely different occurrence, far removed from farm life. It felt entirely incongruous that both occurred simultaneously.

One thousand men from the 33rd Division of the American Expeditionary Force fought The Battle of Hamel with the Australian Corps, under the command of Lieutenant General Sir John Monash. The Allied forces in that battle combined artillery, armor, infantry, and air support. The paper called it "combined arms," and speculated that it might be the blueprint for subsequent Allied attacks. Therefore, Prentis and Avery realized they'd need to become familiar with that new method of fighting.

The war and the news didn't stop, not even for their closest tornado scare yet. The Battle of Hamel raged in faraway Europe as they repaired fences and windows, calmed their animals, and accepted pieces of their missing laundry from neighbors, knowing full well that people they loved and cherished had to be involved now that the purpose for those millions of American troops was being realized.

The Germans had positioned themselves to launch an aggressive new offensive on the Western Front, all their troops having made it over from the Eastern Front, now that Russia wasn't a threat. But then, the Allied troops under General Pershing hit them hard, catching the Germans by surprise before they were ready. At last, the general had engaged his troops.

Wherever they read of Pershing, Tom would be in the trenches with the men. Meanwhile, among the millions, Charles would be fighting. Those facts they knew at the very least, giving fervency to their prayers, each of them pleading with God together at meals, as they went to bed, and alone as they worked. Their own boys were now involved, giving the news a heightened intensity.

Thus, the Second Battle of Marne began in mid-July with a fight at Chateau-Thierry. Throughout July, bolstered by Pershing's fresh American troops—*their* troops, the Allies carried out a series of sustained attacks, pushing the Germans back east toward their homeland.

In the middle of all the fighting, word arrived via the newspapers that the Bolsheviks had murdered the entire Russian royal family. Tsar Nicholas II, his wife Alexandra—who was the granddaughter of Queen Victoria—and all of their five children were no more. That senseless slaughter of an entire family sickened Avery to the core.

The newspapers kept them informed. Surprising the nation, off the coast of Cape Cod, Massachusetts, a German U-boat sank four barges and a tugboat and then fired on the town for nearly an hour before it was forced to dive by the attack of two navy planes. That was the first attack by a foreign power's artillery on US soil since the Mexican-American War in the 1840s.

The military had stepped up its use of aircraft to patrol and to police the waterways where great ships transported to Europe fighting men, support staff comprised of men and women, American-manufactured supplies, and American-grown crops. Now the number of planes was increased, and the patrol widened to include even more of the American coasts.

Those events and policies were discussed over their breakfast coffee throughout July. Prentis and Avery praised the navy's efforts and the skillful work of the airplane pilots.

Aircraft surveillance forced the U-boats to dive, thus rendering them blind and mostly immobile, having no way to surface to use their periscopes or to view their surroundings from the decks of their submarines. If they didn't dive, the enemy U-boats risked warships being sent to the scene. So far in 1918, no convoy supported by an air patrol had lost a ship, and they hoped it would stay that way.

Throughout the entire year, the U-boats had been increasingly forced to operate at night or far out of range of the targets they sought. Indeed, news filtered in of German U-boats actually sunk in northern waters, causing them to wonder what American military secret was behind the successful attempt to curtail the work of the U-boats.

***

At the end of July, Prentis brought a letter from Tom into the house. They hadn't heard from him since April, and it was certainly a relief to see his handwriting on the outside of the envelope. Knowing how happy Avery would be to see the letter,

Prentis decided to give her the pleasure of reading it, so they could enjoy it together.

When he walked in the back door, all was quiet, and he realized it was Jack's naptime, something he skipped on some days and seemed to need on others. This was one such day.

Avery stuck her head around the kitchen doorway with her finger pressed to her lips. He stepped in to find her buried in theological books, scribbling away in her bound journal with a pile of Bibles of different translations opened in a stack, one on top of another, all heaped on her thick concordance. In other words, she was back at her favorite work again.

He smiled widely, then whispered, "Thanks be to God, Avery! This time we're not interrupted by a tornado. Now I can say what I wanted to say when I first saw you bent over your books. You're sharpening that theological brain of yours again. I'm glad you're back at it."

Returning his smile, she welcomed his offered kiss. "I'm having so much fun in here during his naps. It's wonderful, Prentis!"

"We have a letter from Tom." Prentis watched Avery's eyebrows shoot up and a smile spread wide on her face. "Let's go outside. I want you to read it to me."

Nodding, she followed him out the front door, which he closed quietly behind them. The windows on that side of the house were opened slightly, so they'd hear Jack when he awakened. He handed her the letter and sprawled out on the front porch in the shade, surveying with satisfaction the horses grazing and the harvested wheat fields shorn of their golden stalks.

Avery opened the letter with care, spread it out on her lap, and checked the date.

"By the date, he must have written this right before our boys engaged in battle."

Glancing up, she looked into his eyes. Holding still as stone and barely breathing, Prentis awaited whatever she spoke from that letter. He flicked his eyes toward the letter, and she began.

July 18, 2018
Dearest friends,

We're between Fontenoy and Chateau-Thierry, and we're soon heading into a big battle. I'm grabbing a minute to write, because I know how very long it has been. When we add our manpower, we hope our forces will bring an end to the fight today. General Pershing is finally ready to use our men at full force.

"That's what I thought," she said. "They hadn't gone in yet." She continued reading.

I hope to write again on the other side, but there's no guarantee I'll be able to find the time. The men in combat will be in need of pastoral care, and now that the flu seems to have subsided a bit, I have the time I need to help those who are actually in the fight. I'm glad the Lord brought me here. This is exactly where I'm supposed to be.

We were moving our troops, and I saw a soldier sketching as we passed. Being a pastor, I decided to stop and inquire. Professionally, we pastors are allowed to be nosey, but I know you both know that.

Here, Avery paused, chuckling. "How like him to add that!"
"That's what I was just thinking." Prentis smiled. "Read on."

This soldier reminded me of a young man I knew in Chicago, but he didn't turn out to be my friend now grown to adulthood. Rather, this man's name was Horace Pippin, and if he ever becomes famous as an artist, I want you to remember that I said he surely would be. The man is gifted! Mr. Pippin is with the 369th Infantry Regiment, which arrived in December from New York City. In March they were trained by the

French and integrated into the French 161st Division.

They're known here as the Harlem Hellfighters. A hundred men from the regiment were awarded the highest honor of the French Croix de Guerre. When he told me his regiment, I already knew of their history and their fame and congratulated him and all of the men with him. They're a regiment of Negro[1] soldiers, and their regiment has a mix of white and Negro officers, unusual in our time and place. I count it a blessing that these brave and patriotic men can serve our country here in France!

Their Colonel is a good man—respects his troops and lobbies for their fair treatment and additional support from New Yorkers at home. Man, oh man, can they fight! I felt honored to have met them and to have seen Mr. Pippin's artistry. I pray to God that he and his friends survive the war and that some of his sketches make it home. Keep an eye out for these men in the news.

Well, too fast my time is up. Duty calls. I'm sending all my love to you three. I pray the Lord showers every blessing upon you, and I hope to see you soon.

With love,
Tom

Avery looked up at him. "It's so strange to think that he finished that letter and then headed out into an awful battle. And then, we read about it later in the news."

---

[1] *Negro*: This was the proper and respectful term used for African-Americans in the 1910s. "Professor Booker T. Washington, being politely interrogated ... as to whether negroes ought to be called 'negroes' or 'members of the colored race' has replied that it has long been his own practice to write and speak of members of his race as negroes, and when using the term 'negro' as a race designation to employ the capital 'N' [*Harper's Weekly*, June 2, 1906]."

"That's what I was just thinking. Have no way of knowing if he's all right until we hear from him again. Hope he writes soon."

"I do, too. How like Tom to have stopped to see if that soldier was a young friend from so long ago, now grown to adulthood and fighting in this war."

Prentis nodded, considering how sorely he missed his friend. "Of course, being aware that soldiers of African descent are paid less than whites and often have no officers of color, he would be pleased to see that those injustices are being righted in some way for those men."

"The citizens of New York who donate are trying to make up for those wrongs."

"Yes, they are. Much needs to change in America."

***

In August, Prentis began plowing both farms, a hot and tedious job. Every morning Avery asked if he might want to break down and purchase a tractor. He always laughed and told her that at twenty-seven, he was still young and strong enough to plow his own fields. He wasn't an old man yet. He preferred to see what he was doing, watching the dirt turn over with his own eyes, rather than constantly looking over his shoulder at a plow dragged by a tractor to see what he was accomplishing. He wanted to know the plowing was done right.

As Prentis worked, he often took Jack out with him to play. Just as Howard used to do when he was small, Jack chased around the horned toads and little rabbits that were disturbed by the plow. Both of them drank out of the old Civil War canteens used by Prentis's grandfathers who had fought for the North.

While they were in the field, Avery relished the solitude in the house, and she continued her theological study with great joy. About midway through the afternoon, she usually saddled up Daisy or Mabel to check on her men, bringing Jack home if he was too hot or tired.

Today, she had all the more reason, for another letter had arrived from overseas, and it wasn't addressed in Tom's writing. Once she spotted them, she headed that way, handing down the next canteen, full of fresh, cold well water. Prentis let Jack drink first. Once the toddler had slaked his thirst, he handed their son up to Avery, so she could give the boy a hug and a kiss. Then, Prentis drank as much as he could hold from the canteen.

"Mom-Mom, looka I find!" Jack fished something from the front pocket of his overalls.

Out wriggled a tiny horned toad about three-quarters of an inch across, a little soft and flattened from being in a toddler's pocket. Avery was glad she had six brothers and that she had been a one-room schoolhouse teacher, because horned toads were a fairly familiar sight.

"Well, look at him, Jack!" She lifted up the little toad and seated him on her outstretched palm, where he jumped about. "He's a little one, isn't he?"

"Yep. Little." He seized his prize and returned him to the pocket.

Avery made a mental note to check pockets thoroughly before washing clothes. Mabel shifted under their weight, her tail flicking hard to the side, attempting to scatter the biting flies. Avery brushed at them, then looking down at Prentis, she pulled the envelope from her pocket.

"Prentis, this letter came from Europe. I think you'd better open it."

With one hand, Prentis shaded his eyes from the sun, fixing them on her. Then he slowly trickled water onto his head before reseating his Stetson and reaching for the letter.

"Let's see what you've got there." He tore it open and exhaled in a puff. "It's from my cousin Charles. It's not official. Thank God he's still alive somewhere!" He glanced at her.

Quickly, he shaded his eyes and began to read aloud, "Sunday night, August 1. The Germans started at twelve o'clock." Prentis stopped speaking, scanned down a bit, then looked up at her. "He writes what he's just lived through in battle, all the details. This is difficult to read."

"You read the account silently, and then hand it to me. It's probably best not to read this out loud, lest someone hear something he need not hear."

"I agree," he said to her.

Jack was busy with the horned toad and appeared not to realize they were talking about him.

Breathlessly, Avery watched the horror of battle play out upon her husband's face. What was written there was surely horrific, given Prentis's tortured expression. When he finished, he met her eyes, handed her the letter, and walked away, heading toward the creek and taking the hitched team of Ulysses and Hector with him. It looked as if plowing was done for the day. Jack ran and jumped over the furrows as he followed his father across the field.

Avery pulled the letter in close, under the shade of her big hat, and focused on the writing. From the date, the letter had probably been written after the big battle Tom had mentioned. Charles had ended schooling at eighth grade, as did most boys who were involved in farming and other trades, so Avery quelled her inner schoolmarm and the temptation to edit.

```
Sunday night, Aug. 1  - -

The Germans started at 12 o'clock and just
rained down gas and shrapnel on us for 48 hours.
It was awful! Some of us were on a hill. The
other boys ran off and left me alone. I lay in
a little hole and waited. Tho't every minute I'd
be killed, but am still alive. The French said
it was the heaviest shell fire the Germans ever
put over. The Germans thought all they would have
to would be come across the Marne and go on to
Paris, but they met their matches. We mowed them
down like grass.  The Marne River was thick with
boats and dead Germans. We would capture them by
the hundreds. Some bunches we marched back had
300 in them. There were majors, colonels, and
everything else among them.

Two of us boys were in a little thicket all
alone. A German shot the other boy within three
feet of me. I picked him up and carried him a
quarter of a mile and they turned machine guns
```

on me and I had to drop him to save my own life; ran by them and they were only 50 feet from me. God surely was with me or I would have been killed. For at least eight miles the dead Germans were lying thick.

God! It was awful! I know the Germans lost 10 men to our one. They made a drive on a 60 mile front and we captured 30,100 men and 600 cannon, and I believe the number of dead was greater than the prisoners. Just a little way from us, the Germans were killed about four deep. The boys buried them in a space of about 5 acres. After the battle was over we boys were a sight - - dirty, lousy, muddy. Our clothes were all torn off. All I had was one shirt and a pair of pants with the seat torn out, but today I am all dressed up; new clothes through and through.

Tell father I saw 103 head of fine horses tied to a picket fence, dead, killed by gas and shrapnel. That gas turns one's money black as coal. I had on my mask for ten hours. The explosion of the big shells in the river even killed the fish and the river fairly stinks.

We were decorated with the Croix de Guerre for holding the Germans and for something else, I don't know what, and also for being the first to cross the river. We crossed the morning of July 22 and marched up the road in daylight. The airplanes dropped bombs on us and would even come down and turn their machine guns on us. We entered a village and they gave orders to, "Fix bayonets" and we went and took the town.

I was up on top of a hill and I could see down the river. At the zero hour the Germans started their attack. All of a sudden, the whole front

343

broke out in a blaze and shells began to fall as thick as hailstones. It sure scared me for awhile. I just laid there in a little hole waiting for my time to come. Some of the shells hit within three feet of me. That was the night of July 14. Some of the boys thought that the world was coming to an end and when Boche broke out. The west was on fire, a 60 mile front. Village after village was shelled to the ground, but the old Kaiser's Prussian Guards are about finished. He will find out who he has to deal with.

After the battle a lieutenant and I were looking at the tags on some of the killed. One fellow looked like Pearl and I thought I'd look and be sure. It was Fairchild and I was much shocked. I looked again and it was Charles W Fairchild.

There is no trench fighting in this part of the battle. It is open warfare, fighting in the woods or any place we find the Germans.

Charles

Speechless, Avery understood why Prentis had merely walked away. It was too much. He now had to make a trip to Kingman to relay the news to his Uncle Grant, Charles's father, and to see if the Fairchilds knew about their son. This account had to be the same battle Tom headed toward when he last wrote. Clearly, Charles had gone into combat a few days before Tom.

Avery returned the letter to the envelope and tucked it back safely into her pocket, feeling as if it contained treasure. An eyewitness account of one of the bloodiest battles of the Great War had been entrusted into their care. She knew Prentis would want to take it to the *Wakita Herald* to be printed, so all could understand the horrors of war. It had to be shared.

344

This was why they scrimped and planted to the fences and conserved every little bit of extra flour and sugar. This was why Mary Beth met with her and other women gathered all over the country to knit socks and hats and mittens. This was why they donated as much as they were able to the Red Cross and why they prayed day and night for those they loved who were off at war.

Twenty-six

NOW THAT THEIR TROOPS were engaged, everyone pored over the newspapers and gathered after church to compare stories of what they had heard or read. Their boys were now over there, and everyone was worried. They tried to trust God, and trust God they did, but the daily uncertainty wore on them all. Prayers were uttered day and night as they went about their work.

No additional letters arrived from either Charles or Tom, though several Wakita boys had written, and their friends and parents had shared the accounts through the *Wakita Herald*—no sickness and no combat for the other boys yet. Reports were received from Alden Loomis at Camp Dewey in Illinois, Percy Harp in France, their neighbor across the road—Will Hern in Georgia, and Oliver Hott in New York City. They were scattered far and wide.

Having completed that walk in the snow with Oliver, Prentis read his letter with interest. Before shipping out, Oliver had seen the Statue of Liberty and had taken a ship that passed right under the Brooklyn Bridge. He wrote that it was two-hundred feet high and about one-hundred-fifty feet wide. Oliver also praised the

Red Cross and all they did to take care of the soldiers. Clearly, their donations were accomplishing good for their men.

From France, Percy Harp wrote, "We are all well, healthy, and having lots to eat and are enjoying the sights of a very beautiful country. That is the best I can say. France truly is a beautiful country, but give me old Oklahoma for mine, and there's a little town in that old state that sounds good to me, Wakita, and its dear people; and after this is over and us boys return home that's going to be my home."

Their boys were homesick, and everyone missed them as well.

Will Hern reported that one hundred soldiers from the front lines in Europe had been brought back to the hospital where he served in Georgia. The report from those returning soldiers was that the war wouldn't last long. The entire community hoped and prayed that would be true.

So far, they had lost only Joseph, and that was one man too many. However, now the newspapers began reporting mortality numbers, and as expected, the numbers were high. Guesses of the total number killed so far in this conflict were between seven and eight million military personnel on all sides, with civilian casualties coming in at perhaps half that. But the war was not over. For America, the bloodiest part had only begun.

Reverend Wallock left the Methodist Episcopal Church open for community prayer, so that if any of the townspeople simply needed a silent place to gather and to pray with others, it could easily be found. Prentis informed Avery that the last time he went into town, he had seen several buggies and horses outside the church, so the reverend's decision was one that the community appreciated and desired. He had stopped in to talk briefly with Mark and to pray together with him for a few minutes.

"I always appreciate how Mark can squeeze a good bit of praying into one or two minutes," he told Avery. "He matches the Lord's own prayer for brevity every time he prays with me, though I know he goes longer in the pulpit."

Avery smiled, glad that Mark understood her husband as Tom had before him.

***

Prentis carried on. For farmers, the struggle was often a quiet and lonely one pondered over solitary work. His troubled thoughts were his companions, day in and day out.

The alfalfa produced abundantly, and the soil lay ready for sowing. Before he sowed the wheat at the equinox, he used early September for repairing implements put to hard use during the summer months, readying the equipment for sowing, and fattening his and Tom's remaining steers for the market. He surveyed his fields, assessing their condition.

Alongside their mothers, the newly weaned seven-month-old steers and heifers grew fat—though the heifers weren't destined for the market. Next year these heifers would be bred and these steers sold. Last year's steers would soon be over a thousand pounds, the previous year's steers having been sold in Wichita. The cows were all bearing calves again, and the horses were all in foal. Rex and Apollo had done a fine job, and now both ate placidly in their pens.

All the animals seemed to have recovered from the shock of the tornado. Animal husbandry required Prentis's constant diligence, and so he took great care during all seasons.

Yet, as he worked, gnawing anxiety over his best friend and his cousin in particular chewed him up inside. He wondered where they were and what they were doing, but there was really nothing he could do but trust them into God's hands, as he had done with Avery this past year. It required constant yielding, a repeated giving over of loved ones to God. For all he knew, they could both be gone already.

On September 4, Prentis and Avery celebrated their fourth anniversary, trying to act as if nothing troubled them, focusing on one another and the great blessing of marriage. Avery prepared a special meal, and Jack joined them on that Wednesday night. Afterward, he was tucked away in bed.

Then, in the darkness, the two of them sat quietly on the front porch, staring up at the stars after two days of solid cloud cover. Those days had been spent within the house or the barn as northern Oklahoma had been drenched with two inches of rain, right before the wheat planting. Prentis regarded the rain's timing as a gift from God.

The Shadows Come

On the porch, they held hands, and each leaned hard against the shoulder of the other. But, of course, they talked of Tom, Charles, Joseph, the other boys, and the war.

There was no escaping it.

***

Meanwhile, in Wakita, musical harmographs—phonographs and talking machines for those with city electricity—went on sale at $75, $100, or $125, depending on the customer's preference. The stockholders of the American Petroleum Company met and decided to wait before making further decisions about the two northern oil wells. Mr. Guthrie received a shipment of oats that he put on sale for twenty-five cents a bushel. The lumber yard ran an ad in the *Wakita Herald* to remind them all that they were still in business. P.F. Wright & Son advertised delivery of produce and merchandise right to your door, complete with stamp books to earn future savings. And the Biby girls had a run-in with their pony when the creature got spooked, turned over the buggy, and threw them out onto the ground, breaking the arm of one.

In middle America, the mundane and daily continued unabated. Simultaneously, their minds were elsewhere—on the fighting fields of Europe.

On September 12, 1918, the final round of the draft registration was held. In order to prepare for whatever might befall them in Europe, the military now cast the net wide. All men between the ages of eighteen and forty-five had to register. Once more the registration was held at the local school, and once more the citizens of Wakita all turned out.

When the official number was tallied for the entire country, the government notified them that nationwide approximately twenty-four million men had registered in this final round, roughly 23 percent of the US population. If this war continued and these men eventually had to go due to the horrific massacre in Europe, all of them wondered what would become of the earth.

All of these events were attended to, but the citizens of northern Oklahoma and the nation sensed and felt the faraway events, as if they all had one ear cocked toward a faraway sound that they needed to hear, yet dreaded hearing at the same time.

In mid-September news of a resurgence of the flu and simultaneously of a great battle in northeastern France at Saint-Mihiel reached them. The American Expeditionary Force, over one hundred thousand men from the French Army, and the US Army Air Service engaged the Germans in combat together—more than half a million men all under the command of General Pershing.

The main goal was to push the Germans eastward and out of France. Charles would certainly be out among the fighting men, right in the middle of the battle. And now that the American Expeditionary Force was engaged, anywhere General Pershing was named, Tom would be there as well, alongside the men as one of their pastors.

The generals hoped the American boys could break through the German lines to capture the fortified city of Metz. This offensive action caught the Germans as they were disorganized and attempting to retreat. Therefore, the attack was highly effective. The French and British generals' esteem for the American army was splashed all over the papers.

The disarray of the German Army and the total surprise with which they had been caught gave the Allies a superior advantage. Unfortunately, the attack was so successful that American and French soldiers got ahead of their supply lines and fell short of food and artillery, which had been left behind on the muddy roads in the rush. That caused the battle to drag on for days. As a result, the Germans had time to dig in, and Metz was not captured.

Their American soldiers were now thoroughly acquainted with death and war. It haunted them in the camps, with their numbers still being decimated by the flu and other diseases. And now, they were experienced in the horrors of battle itself. The exploding sound of rounds leaving the muzzles of the German guns could be heard, followed by a faint whistling sound that grew increasingly louder and nearer until the shell hit, and then the explosion reverberated. Those constant sounds of war left the soldiers continually aware that they could be struck at any moment.

The Shadows Come

Prentis thought of Charles's comments—that the German guns made them feel as if the world were going to end. He described those guns as setting the whole world on fire. The sounds and sights of combat had impacted his cousin's emotions. It sounded downright terrifying. Whatever the outcome, they would each surely return as different men altogether.

With the Germans ensconced in Metz, the Allied generals now turned toward the rugged terrain of the Argonne Forest, a stretch of hills and valleys covered with dense forest along the Meuse River. That area in the northeast corner of France bordered Belgium, Luxembourg, and Germany. Saint-Mihiel, the spot where the American Expeditionary Force under General Pershing had earlier made their fighting debut, was situated on that river.

Here on the Western Front—a front five-hundred fifty miles long—the entire force of the Allies with their millions of fresh American fighting men pushed hard against the invading German military, trying to compel them to retreat step by step back into Germany.

In that battle, General Pershing commanded the US First Army, which had been established on August 10, 1918, as a field army when enough American men had arrived in France at last. That army was now a branch of the American Expeditionary Forces, one of three field armies fighting alongside the Allies. From all they had read in the papers, it seemed this might be the battle that would decide the war. They hoped and prayed it was so. But it wouldn't be over quickly, and it would require all the mettle left in the Allied forces.

While war raged in Europe and their troops engaged in the much-anticipated battle to push the Germans back toward their homeland, the mundane and the local moved forward in Oklahoma, as if none of those earth-shattering events occurred on the other side of the ocean.

Prentis got the wheat sown at the equinox on both his farm and Tom's. Life carried on as usual when fall began in Oklahoma. Avery's dad came down to discuss getting last year's steers to market. All of Europe and their troops needed to eat, so they might need to sell them light, but Prentis preferred that the steers weigh at least twelve hundred pounds.

They decided on a Tuesday when they would jointly move their stock up to the sale barn in Anthony, foregoing another trip to Wichita. Prentis had purchased corn to fatten his steers over these final few weeks. Most of the men of Wakita performed the same tasks at this time of year.

Meanwhile, the women set about canning everything they hadn't yet preserved from their summer gardens and fruit trees. With the sugar that Mr. H.T. Smith—the Food Administrator for Wakita—had permitted merchants to sell, Avery busied herself with applesauce. Earlier, she had completed the peach and apricot preserves, as well as jam made from both fruits. After their losses from the tornado and hailstorm, she didn't have as much as last year. She also made Prentis plenty of cookies and as many pies as the man could hold. Life felt somewhat normal.

But, constantly, they prayed.

***

By the end of September, the Allies had reversed every single victory the German offensive had gained in eastern France and western Belgium since the war began. Alongside the Brits and the French, the full might of the American military had been hurled at the Western Front in the Argonne Forest. Together, they drove the Germans back to their last line of defense—the Hindenburg Line, a German defensive position constructed during the winter of 1916–1917 snaking all the way across northwestern Europe.

Then chaos broke out among the German high command.

General Erich von Ludendorff had been responsible for the successful German spring offensive. But, after the many Allied victories, on September 29, 1918, he demanded that Germany seek an immediate armistice based on the terms President Wilson had spelled out in his Fourteen Points address back in January. And so, feeling usurped by his own army's leadership, German Chancellor Georg von Hertling resigned.

As a result, on October 1, Kaiser Wilhelm appointed his second cousin, Prince Max von Baden, to assume that position.

The Shadows Come

The Kaiser had no intention of admitting defeat or of asking for an armistice until his German troops had regained at least some ground on the battlefield. He wanted some leverage to negotiate with the Allies. The Kaiser wouldn't change his mind.

But then on October 3, General Paul von Hindenburg, now lacking the fighting prowess of his fellow general, Erich von Ludendorff, informed the new Chancellor Max von Baden that, though the German army still stood firm, the fighting needed to stop "to spare the German people and their allies unnecessary sacrifices." He insisted that "every day of delay costs thousands of brave soldiers their lives." Other German advisors agreed, causing even more chaos among their high command.

Meanwhile the battle continued, and more lives were lost.

But now, at this most decisive of moments, with troops fully engaged in warfare along the Western Front, the flu—now called the *Spanish Flu*—became deadly. With all the troop movements from home to Europe and back, as well as new units brought forward to support the troops in battle, including General Pershing's forces on the Western Front, flu casualties surged.

Since late summer, there had been only brief reports of short-lived outbreaks here and there. But now, sick men and women arriving from various locations infected others who were traveling out. Those people became sick on the way over or when they arrived, thus spreading the contagion into new locations. Alarming rates of sickness now interfered with the military's induction and training, as if the earlier flu had somehow fortified itself, remaking itself into a more virulent and deadly opponent.

Though the military had 30 percent of the physicians in the entire country now in its service, as well as a network of hospitals readied for this very moment of crisis, they were prepared for the typical injuries and sicknesses of wartime and couldn't do much for those stricken with the flu. Medical staff could only relieve the pain of flu sufferers, make sure the patients rested, and provide a diet that helped them to feel better. They could only hope and pray that their patients didn't then develop pneumonia on top of the influenza. The staff tried to make more space between patients, and they even hung sheets between each bed, hoping to prevent the spread of the illness, but it continued unabated.

This or that doctor would demand that troop movements cease in and out of different camps until the flu was more in hand, but marching orders for war took precedent. And so, the movement of troops continued unabated, regardless of what occurred in the sick wards. No one seemed to understand the connection, except the doctors who were working with the sick. Sometimes those very doctors succumbed to the illness themselves.

As a result, between twenty and forty percent of US Army and Navy personnel on both sides of the world were taken ill with influenza and pneumonia, more than one million before they ever arrived in Europe. So much sickness among personnel also diverted resources needed urgently for combat support over to the transportation and care of the sick and the disposal of the bodies of those who died from the flu.

And thus, Grant County heard of further loss.

On October 1, John and Mary Zeman of Medford had received a telegram informing them that their son Joseph—who had been perfectly healthy the previous week when he had written to family members in Nebraska—was now sick with pneumonia after having the flu. Joe was a member of the 19th Battalion at Camp Greenleaf in Georgia.

October 3—the day Von Hindenburg appealed to the German Chancellor and the Kaiser for peace—the Zemans had received another telegram informing them that Joseph was gone. He was only twenty-three years old. His body would be shipped as soon as the army was able.

The day after that, the man who had newly been appointed the new German Chancellor—Prince Max von Baden—listened to his generals and sent a telegram to President Wilson in the wee hours of October 4, requesting an armistice between Germany and the Allied powers.

On October 5, the Allies broke through the last remnants of the Hindenburg Line, guaranteeing victory over the Germans, who continued to retreat before them.

The Austro-Hungarian Empire of central Europe had existed for over six hundred years. On October 6, part of it broke away, and a provisional government announced the state of Yugoslavia.

The following day, Poland, which had been a part of the Russian Empire, proclaimed itself to be an independent state. On October 8, more than eight thousand Germans were taken prisoner by the British as they advanced toward Cambrai and Le Cateau.

As the countries that comprised the Central Powers crumbled, that request for an armistice still sat unanswered on President Wilson's desk.

The entire world held its breath.

Meanwhile, the flu's vicious effects went global.

The Zemans especially felt it as they awaited their son's body coming by rail. People had been advised to stay home, and morticians were behind in their work, because of the amount of sickness and the number of deaths occurring at Camp Greenleaf and in nearby Chattanooga. Other Wakita boys were there, and so the townspeople prayed fervently.

A report published on Oct. 11, 1918, estimated that nearly three thousand cases of the flu existed at the posts near Chattanooga, and seven thousand cases flared up within the city and the surrounding area. Because of the crush of sickness and the fact that the hospitals were all full, local residents attended to their own family members and neighbors, turning their homes into small hospitals, caring for several people at a time.

Almost overnight, the flu exploded across the world.

At the rate that sickness and death were working their way through the military camps, officials feared the epidemic would burst out into the general population. Cities near military camps cancelled all public events until the flu could be brought under control. People were told to stay at home, so as to not contract the deadly infection.

On that same day, John and Mary Zeman met Joe's coffin at the railroad station and transported his body home to Medford for his funeral. Friends and family gathered, in spite of the public warnings, but attendance was low because the flu was now spreading in Grant County.

Also, on October 11, 1918, the schools in Wakita closed, for there were now cases in both the country and in town. The high school had seventy-six students and the grade school many more. There was no use putting the children at risk. The local picture show and the churches also shut their doors and so did many businesses.

This flu was nothing to mess around with, so Avery and Prentis gladly stayed home with Jack, hoping to avoid exposure as the flu came to visit their rural world.

On October 14, hard on the heels of Joseph Zeman's arrival for burial, a telegram arrived for Wakitans Joseph and Katarina Kovarik Cink, informing them that their son Joe, Jr. had died at the same camp. With no word of his sickness, their first notification was that he was gone.

Joseph, Jr. was also only twenty-three, and he had served in the Motor Transportation Corps at Camp Greenleaf, also in Oglethorpe, George. His primary job had been to transport doctors and patients with his motorcycle. Of course, that had exposed him to the flu.

Meanwhile in Europe, the Central Powers continued to disintegrate. Along a sixty-mile section of the Western Front, the Germans engaged in a general retreat. French and American armies continued their unstoppable advance, the German army fleeing before them. Along the Belgian coast and in the northern parts of France, Germans abandoned their positions as the British and the Belgians pushed them out. King Albert returned to Belgium.

Anticipation of an armistice grew. This awful war looked to be at its end.

Then, on October 16, Samuel and Sarah Cranmer received the dreaded telegram that their son Ray had died of the flu at age thirty-one, miles away at Ft. Dodge, Iowa, where he had served in Company 12-3, Battalion 163 of the Depot Brigade. A quarantine had been imposed when cases there had numbered over fifteen hundred, but the death rate was low in camp. Unfortunately, Ray Cranmer was one who didn't make it. On that very day, the *Wakita Herald* announced that all public gatherings were forbidden until citizens were notified otherwise.

So, when young Joseph Cink's body finally arrived by rail, the family had a small funeral with little attendance at their family plot up in Pleasant Hill Cemetery in Harper County, Kansas, the county of Prentis's birth. But everyone was quarantined. Prentis had been acquainted with the family all his life and deeply regretted the ban that kept everyone but family away.

Meanwhile, Avery read in the pile of newspapers passed to her by Mary Beth, suffragists held mass meetings in Tulsa. It was Suffrage Week in Oklahoma City in preparation for the upcoming vote. But the restrictions brought on by the flu were also in force there. Nevertheless, the suffragettes persisted.

The ratification of the suffrage amendment and the assault on Oklahoma by the deadly flu occurred exactly as the dreadful war neared its end. A state of constant awareness of those facts agitated Avery day and night. She didn't always succeed in turning her anxiety into prayer.

So far, all the flu cases around Wakita had been mild, and no one had died. In addition to suffrage, there was much to pray for as the battle still raged along the Western Front, the flu moved and spread in their own neighborhood, and the death toll in the military and connected cities continued to rise dramatically.

When Ray Cranmer's body arrived, everything was still closed down. A small crowd gathered at the Wakita cemetery on the overcast day, and since it was right up the road, Prentis attended, standing on the cemetery's far edge as the young man was laid to rest. After the burial, he offered what words of comfort he could to Ray's grieving parents, but as a father, he didn't know what kind of consolation mere words could give.

When he returned home, Avery assured him that if Jack had been lost under similar circumstances, merely seeing a friendly face at a funeral few people could attend would make a big difference to the parents. Prentis wasn't so sure. This flu seemed like more than they could bear on top of a war that had nearly destroyed them.

On October 20, the *Wakita Herald* printed a letter from one of their young men who was not sick. It was a great encouragement to read that Clarence Swayze at Camp Sherman in Ohio was doing well, other than a case of homesickness. Yet, with the battle being fought at full force, there was still no word from Tom and nothing further from Charles either.

Meanwhile, President Wilson had sent a note back to Chancellor von Baden on October 14, and now another on

October 23, stating clearly that the Allies would not negotiate with a dictatorship set up by a military coup of the German Supreme Command. He would not confer with the current generals or imperial leaders in place. Wilson said he would only negotiate with a democratic Germany, for von Baden had declared he had already begun to establish a parliamentary democracy on the day after he requested the armistice.

The leaders of Britain and France wholeheartedly supported President Wilson in this decision. None of them trusted the German generals, and neither did they believe that von Baden would establish a democracy.

Upon receipt of Wilson's second note, the man who had started all of this—General Erich von Ludendorff—became infuriated. His resolve returned. Demonstrating who was really in control in Germany, the general announced that the president's note should be rejected.

The war resumed in full force. The world had come so close! And now, hope for peace was shattered.

Nevertheless, the Allies fought onward. Although they were embattled by the flu and the resulting loss of manpower and reinforcement issues, they were resolved. Troops continued to prosecute the war at full force with every healthy man they could keep on the line.

In southern Europe, the Allies crossed the Piave River to combine forces with seven Italian armies to route the Austrians out of Italy. British, French, and American divisions fought alongside the Italians, attacking what remained of the Austro-Hungarian armies. In that battle, the Austro-Hungarian army was badly beaten with over thirty thousand soldiers killed and over four hundred thousand men taken prisoner. The Allies were victorious on all fronts.

Behind Allied lines on the Western Front, American stretcher bearers, triage areas, horse-drawn ambulances, field hospitals, and evacuation hospitals attended to round-the-clock injuries of all varieties. The medical staff turned around slight injuries and shellshock, so men could be back on the line within three days, fighting alongside their fellow soldiers. Severe injuries were removed from the front, through the field hospitals, and on to the evacuation hospitals. All were portable as the line constantly crept toward Germany, driving before it the fighting German army. American doctors and nurses in the field worked themselves to exhaustion, attempting to give Allied soldiers the best care ever seen during any war in the history of mankind.

Unfortunately, the flu had spread out from the training camps onto the battlefields, hampering the war effort, though the Allies continued to prevail against the Germans, pushing them ever backward toward their homeland. This invasion of the flu onto the battlefield touched the citizens of Wakita, for one of their own was a member of the medical detachment, bravely wading into the Meuse-Argonne battlefield in France to tend the injured and the sick alike. Bliss Markland fell ill with the flu while performing battlefield medical care.

And thus, Wakita didn't leave October behind without further loss. On October 27, 1918, Emory and Lottie Markland received a telegram informing them of their son Bliss's death of pneumonia at Evacuation Hospital #21, somewhere in France. He didn't make it home.

As the Marklands awaited news of when Bliss's body might arrive from overseas, the war began to wind down on all fronts, one Central Power after another disintegrating as their casualties mounted. The Czechs declared their independence from Austria on October 29, which was followed shortly by Slovakia declaring theirs from Hungary. A new country called Czechoslovakia was birthed in that part of a rapidly changing Europe. Two days later, Turkey quit the war, signing an armistice with the Allies.

On November 1, after pausing briefly to regroup and resupply their heavily hit encampments and medical hospitals, the Allies continued the fight eastward, attacking all German positions along the Meuse River near southern Belgium. Meanwhile, the Belgians and the British pushed the effort from the other side, from within northwestern Belgium.

The German Navy mutinied on November 3 at Kiel and Wilhelmshaven, as sailors refused to put to sea and engage in a final battle with the British Navy. Revolution and uprising that appeared to be suspiciously Bolshevik in nature erupted in Munich, Stuttgart, and Berlin. The entire world watched to see if all of Germany would erupt into revolution, as Russia had done. This made the armistice and its arrangement ever more urgent.

Germany's only remaining ally, Austria-Hungary, signed an armistice with Italy, leaving Germany alone in the battle. On November 5, an election day that saw President Wilson's Democratic Party lose control of the Senate, just as they approached what looked like the end of the war, the president informed the Germans that they could now begin discussing the armistice based on his Fourteen Points, as they had requested back on October 4. But, the Germans now had to secure that armistice through the Supreme Allied Commander.

The Kaiser forced General Ludendorff to resign. And finally, on November 7, German General Paul von Hindenburg contacted Supreme Allied Commander Marshal Ferdinand Jean Marie Foch to open armistice negotiations. Meanwhile, the Allies fought on, pressing the German Army eastward, out of France and Belgium, and back into their own homeland.

However, there would be no peace until an agreement had been made and signed. But now, at last, the president and the German leadership were talking.

Though the Democratic party had lost control of the Senate and the war continued, the consolation of November 5, 1918, was that the men of Oklahoma had voted 106,909 to 81,481 to ratify the universal women's suffrage amendment, granting women the right to vote in their state and becoming the twenty-first state to do so. In Oklahoma, the vote for women was now law. Avery hoped and prayed that the US Congress and the president would work to bring about universal suffrage for all women in America.

Those prayers were whispered alongside her fervent prayers for peace and safety for loved ones. However, as peace was discussed, they all teetered on a strange precipice of unabated war.

Twenty-seven

THOUGH THE BATTLE CONTINUED to be hotly contested and men continued to lose their lives, it seemed the war was working toward its end. The family of Bliss Markland learned that it was impossible to predict when their son's body would be shipped home to Wakita. Eventually, they hoped for his final resting place to be the Wakita Cemetery. But for now, the war must be won.

Then the care of the living still in Europe and the recovery of the cities and countryside destroyed by shells, trenches, booby traps, and poisons that the German army had left behind had to be dealt with first. War was a messy business, and even more so, the end of a war.

Every morning, Prentis rode to town to bring home the papers. They had to see this war all the way to its end before they could draw a deep breath. They dissected everything, as they had when the flu had become interwoven with the final battles. Every day they dug hastily through the mail, hoping for letters from Tom and from Charles.

So far, none had been received.

As the final days of The Great War—a war they hoped would end all wars—ticked down, they prayed fervently and continually

361

for those they loved, hoping Tom, Charles, and all those remaining would make it through these final days and not be lost in the last minutes. They were vastly relieved when they received a letter from Uncle Grant, informing them that Charles was still alive and fighting onward.

While the fighting continued, six representatives of the German government met in Compiegne, France, on November 8, 1918, to receive the terms of the armistice, exactly as had been spelled out in President Wilson's Fourteen Points address.

The Germans must evacuate all occupied territories and surrender every one of their weapons, including submarines and battleships. The Allies would occupy all German lands west of the Rhine River, and the naval blockade would continue indefinitely.

Of course, the following day, the Kaiser's imperial government came to an end, and he abdicated when a new provisional government was proclaimed. Friedrich Ebert would now head the new German republic. In the night, Kaiser Wilhelm fled to Holland to seek refuge, for his generals had informed him that given the volatile situation in Germany, they wouldn't be able to offer him adequate protection.

At last, at 5:10 a.m. on November 11, 1918, the Germans signed the armistice in a railway car at Compiegne, France. The battle would end at 11:00 a.m., the eleventh hour of the eleventh day of the eleventh month. However, fighting continued along the Western Front until precisely that time with two thousand more killed that very day, right up until the moment the war ended.

Avery could only shake her head. Deep sadness overwhelmed her. Hatred had been so strong that even though the war was effectively over, men had still been so enraged by the actions of the other side that they had continued to shoot and to kill for nearly six more hours over an entirely lost cause.

Now that the Armistice had been signed, and the flu epidemic was beginning to subside within the military at least, they knew exactly how bad the carnage from the flu had been. Avery still couldn't fathom the fact that all over the globe, between twenty and forty percent of US army and navy personnel had been taken ill with the influenza and pneumonia.

War casualties due to other causes than the flu were still unaccounted. Though the war itself had proven to be the vehicle for the flu, it seemed, according to the doctors researching what had happened, that more had died from influenza than from being in battle, exactly as they had feared. The mobilization of people for war had destroyed the health of the world and decimated the population, particularly their generation.

An assassination of a European head of state had prompted this. All the empires of the world had then rattled their sabers, desiring to use the stockpile of arms they had on hand. That hubris had driven them all to war. Had it been worth it? To Avery, it seemed a deplorable waste of human life, demonstrating utter contempt for humanity at large.

And yet, she knew God was with them in spite of the foolish decisions of their world leaders. That Christ had come to die for them, a mass of sinners willing to fight and kill and hold enmity toward their neighbors, never ceased to amaze her.

***

The week of Thanksgiving, a familiar vehicle pulled into the barnyard. Prentis and Avery both stepped onto the front porch. At the wheel was Mark Wallock, manning his first automobile. They smiled in anticipation of a visit, noticing that he'd brought a guest.

Suddenly, Prentis leapt off the porch and hurried in long strides toward the passenger side as the car door opened. Surprised by his actions, Avery lingered on the porch, uncertain of the visitor's identity. With both hands, Prentis pumped the man's hand. Speaking words that Avery couldn't make out, he leaned toward the visitor, who nodded. At that nod, Prentis's head bowed.

Avery listened for Jack—still asleep—and then she slowly descended the steps, hesitant for some reason and entirely unsure why. Something about the man's face in profile was familiar.

As she stepped closer, Prentis turned toward her. "Mr. McKinney, this is my wife, Avery."

Confused, Avery put her hand to her mouth, rather than shaking his hand. Who was he?

Prentis reached for her other hand, gently drawing her near, and then he spoke softly, "Avery, this is Tom's father. I recognized him from the photograph in Tom's house."

"Tom's father? But, why—" A sob of comprehension cut off her voice.

Mr. McKinney nodded, his lips pressed together, his forehead creased in sympathy.

"Yes," Prentis told her gently, "Tom is gone."

Tears burst forth. Avery couldn't contain them. Spinning away from Mr. McKinney, she was captured in Prentis's arms, his eyes overflowing as well. He held her tightly while she cried out her grief, unable to understand yet another loss of such huge significance.

Why, God? Why? Not our dearest friend!

Once she could compose herself, having no idea how much time had passed, she straightened and turned toward Tom's father.

"We're grieved to lose your son, Mr. McKinney. He was our best friend and a superb pastor. Tom made an enormous difference in our lives."

"That's good to hear. The boy was called by God to serve, and serve he did."

"Yes, he did," she said. "Please, come in."

"Thank you, Avery. I wish I had the time, but I need to go to Tom's home and gather his things, so I can prepare everything to travel back with me by rail. I can't stay from home long. We've had a double heartache, and I'm needed back as soon as possible."

Prentis glanced at her, then back to Mr. McKinney. "We're sorry to hear it, sir."

"So many losses overwhelmed Tom's mother. Tom's wife Mary and the newborn baby had already been lost, and now Tom himself. She could make no sense of it. Her heart was broken, and her health spiraled downward as she wrestled with God over it.

She simply couldn't accept it. The doctor thinks she suffered a heart attack. We buried her last week. The Lord gave me a wonderful wife and son, and now the Lord hath taken away."

"Blessed be the name of the Lord," they uttered softly together.

Tears flowed again, running down Avery's cheeks.

Wordlessly, Prentis handed her his handkerchief.

"We don't always understand the whys, especially in this war," Mark said, standing behind Avery. "The acts of sinful men create new and horrific ways to kill one another. Millions have died. It's a wonder God would love Adam's race so much that He sent His own Son to die for us. And yet, He did."

They all murmured their agreement.

"We seek to discover the whys," Mr. McKinney said, "and yet we don't always receive that knowledge this side of heaven. The lesson is to trust God, even when we don't know the whys. We don't need to know. We only need to know and trust Him."

All of them agreed, nodding together.

"That's a lifetime lesson," Avery said.

"Yes," Mr. McKinney agreed. "The Lord has promised to work all of this together for our good, even if we can't comprehend why. It's a matter of trust."

"I can see where Tom learned his strong faith," Prentis said.

"He was as much my teacher as I was his," Mr. McKinney replied.

"He taught me much too."

They all nodded.

Avery wiped her eyes. "We knew from Tom's last letter that the AEF had gone into war with all their might, and that they were pushing across France toward Germany, so we reckoned Tom simply hadn't found time to write. We continued to pray for him daily."

"Where did he die?" Prentis said. "And where is he buried?"

"That last bloody battle, the Meuse-Argonne offensive, caught Tom early. Of course, he was with the men, right at the front of the action. They headed out on September 26 and made great progress, fighting until the very end. General Pershing himself wrote on October 1. He told us of Tom's brave death as he bent over a wounded man, shielding him from the bullets as the man lay dying in great distress and in need of a pastor. He praised Tom's efforts with the troops there. Even then, General Pershing expected that battle to bring the war to an end, and he was right. It took time, but now they've achieved victory."

"Thanks be to God," Avery said softly.

Tom's father nodded.

"So, he's buried in France?" Prentis said.

"He is."

"That's fitting."

"I agree, young man. It is fitting. He fell where he served so bravely. I'm honored to have his body lying right there, though his mother couldn't bear it." He sighed.

"How can we help you, Mr. McKinney?" Prentis asked. "I know Tom wrote you about all the arrangements we discussed before he left. Since you must go back today, I can sell his remaining livestock and send you the funds."

Mr. McKinney hooked his arm over Prentis's shoulder. "Thank you, P.J. Let's go see what needs to be done at Tom's farm. We can talk about all of that as we go."

Prentis turned toward Avery, a question on his face.

"I'll stay here with Jack," she said, "and make you all a quick, early supper. Go on ahead. I'll have it ready when you return, so you can head back to Wakita, Mr. McKinney."

The men thanked her, and then off they went.

Standing on their lawn with her arms wrapped about herself, she watched the three men talking in Mark's automobile as they loaded up and then rolled by. It was almost as if Tom was with them in spirit. Had he lived, he would have enjoyed being with that group.

Maybe the Father allowed the dearly departed to look on at such times, perhaps along with the heroes of the faith in that great cloud of witnesses mentioned in Hebrews 11 and 12. Undoubtedly, that passage was figurative, rather than literal, giving an eternal perspective of all the faithful believers who had gone on before them. However, on this sad day, Avery felt great relief in musing over the idea of Tom hovering near, even though she knew their dear friend was now with the Lord Himself.

The Shadows Come

As she turned toward the house, Avery recalled the last verse of the song that had given so much comfort throughout all these trials. She would simply have to rest in this.

Whenever I am tempted, whenever clouds arise,
When songs give place to sighing, when hope within me dies,
I draw the closer to Him, from care He sets me free;
His eye is on the sparrow, and I know He watches me;
His eye is on the sparrow, and I know He watches me.
I sing because I'm happy, I sing because I'm free,
For His eye is on the sparrow, and I know He watches me.

MELINDA VIERGEVER INMAN

End Notes

This novel is based on a true story and on real people, my own great-grandparents, Prentis and Avery Pinkerton. Their son Jack grew to manhood, and far down the road from these events, he became my grandfather. These notes are provided for the curious student of history.

Chapter 13, *"Red Cross Mission, Vision, and Fundamental Principles."* Accessed July 13, 2017, http://www.redcross.org/about-us/who-we-are/mission-and-values.

Chapter 15, *His Eye is on the Sparrow*, Civilla D. Martin, 1905, in public domain. Verses used at various locations in the novel.

Chapter 16, *Journal of the American Medical Association, Volume 74, 1920*, was consulted, but never quoted, http://bit.ly/2tt4Xci.

Chapter 19, For information about this historic livestock exchange in Wichita, consult this source:

http://www.historicpreservationalliance.com/WichitaHPA/Livestock_Exchange.html

Chapter 22, Regarding the 1918 influenza epidemic, its beginning, and the effect on Camp Funston, these sources were consulted for information, but were never directly quoted:

Death from 1918 pandemic influenza during the First World War: a perspective from personal and anecdotal evidence, Peter C Wevera and Leo van Bergen, https://www.ncbi.nlm.nih.gov/pmc/articles/PMC4181817/.

1918 Influenza: the Mother of All Pandemics, Jeffery K. Taubenberger and David M. Morens, https://www.ncbi.nlm.nih.gov/pmc/articles/PMC3291398/.

History.net, http://www.historynet.com/1918-spanish-influenza-outbreak-the-enemy-within.htm

The U.S. Military and the Influenza Pandemic of 1918–1919, Carol R. Byerly, PhD: https://www.ncbi.nlm.nih.gov/pmc/articles/PMC2862337/.

Chapter 23, pg. 277-278. Quoted from The Sedition Act of 1918. Sixty-Fifth Congress, Session II, Chs. 74, 75. 1918, pg. 553. Approved May 16, 1918.

Chapter 23, pg. 278-279 quote: *The Oklahoma City Times*, Late Street Edition, Volume XXX No. 48, Oklahoma City, Wednesday, May 29, 1918. Price two cents.

Chapter 23, pg. 279 quote: *The Oklahoma City Times*, Late Street Edition, Volume XXX No. 48, Oklahoma City, Wednesday, May 29, 1918. Price two cents.

Chapter 24, pg. 287. Solar eclipse map with dates and times from *The Wichita Eagle and Beacon*, June 3, 1918. The source of this map was an article by Kelly Burley for KOSU, *How Did Oklahomans*

The Shadows Come

Experience the Solar Eclipse 99 years Ago?, August 18, 2017: http://kosu.org/post/how-did-oklahomans-experience-solar-eclipse-99-years-ago. Yet another source: http://www.thegazette.com/subject/news/archive/time-machine/time-machine-the-total-solar-eclipse-of-1918-20170819.

Chapter 25, pg. 316. The words expressed by Professor Booker T. Washington regarding the preferred use of the term "Negro" when referring to a person of African descent at that time came from an interview in *Harper's Weekly,* June 2, 1906, and was quoted from http://www.etymonline.com. Tom, of course, would use the term preferred by African Americans of that time period.

Page 319-210. This is an original and authentic family letter from the front by Charles Pinkerton, received by Prentis Pinkerton, 1918.

Chapter 26, pg. 321. This excerpt was quoted from: *Wakita, the First 100,* a collection of newspaper stories, advertisements, and bits and pieces from the *Wakita Herald*. Printed March 1993 by The Dougherty Press, Inc., 324 West Oak, Enid, Oklahoma, 73701. Many local events and bits of news were gleaned here, but this is the only direct quotation.

Chapter 26, pg. 328. *This Day in History.* 1918 Germany telegraphs President Wilson seeking armistice https://www.history.com/this-day-in-history/germany-telegraphs-president-wilson-seeking-armistice.

Page 330. *The US Military and the Influenza Pandemic of 1918-1919*, US National Library of Medicine, National Institutes of Health. Find the report here: https://www.ncbi.nlm.nih.gov/pmc/articles/PMC2862337/.

Page 331. Local History Column: October 1918, *Chattanooga paralyzed by Spanish flu epidemic*. Sam D. Elliot. April 16, 2017.

Page 333. *Women's Suffrage in Oklahoma, 1890-1918*. Thesis by Mattie Louise Ivy, pg. 54-55, Oklahoma College for Women for

MELINDA VIERGEVER INMAN

Bachelor of Arts, 1957, Oklahoma State University for Master of Arts, 1971, referred to for local information, but not quoted: https://shareok.org/bitstream/handle/11244/23429/Thesis-1971-I95w.pdf?sequence=1&isAllowed=y.

Page 337. Oklahoma Historical Society. *Suffrage Amendment*. Bill Corbett. https://www.okhistory.org/publications/enc/entry.php?entry=SU002

Chapter 27, pg. 339. *The US Military and the Influenza Pandemic of 1918-1919*, US National Library of Medicine, National Institutes of Health. Find the report here: https://www.ncbi.nlm.nih.gov/pmc/articles/PMC2862337/.

Author Note:

I hope you enjoyed this story. It was a pleasure and a privilege to portray more of the events of my great-grandparents' early life and my grandfather Jack's youngest years. I have incorporated true events, including real conversations and family stories passed down through time. But I've also included fictious persons and occasions and stories, weaving together a tale set in Wakita, Oklahoma, the home of my earliest years.

This is a novel; therefore, most conversations are fictitious, but they're written in the cadence of speech my loved ones used daily, including each one's favorite phrases and ways of stating things, carefully replicating them and bringing these dear ones to life.

**Please take the time to write a review.
Visit the site where you purchased your copy
and let future readers know your honest opinion
of this novel.**

**If you enjoyed this story and want to read more
of my work, I would be honored. To find my
fiction, please visit my Amazon Author's Page at
the link below:**

https://www.amazon.com/-/e/B00GFYI0RU

The Shadows Come

MELINDA VIERGEVER INMAN

Made in the USA
Middletown, DE
09 December 2019